HIS TEMPORARY FIANCÉE

NADIA LEE

1

JOSH

You're the most like me.

Mom's sickening whisper swirls in my head. I run, my heart pumping wildly with denial and fear. The wildfire casts an eerie orange glow around the nighttime forest. The acrid smell of burning wood stings my nose. I look in every direction, quickly scanning the area for the log cabin where Mom took my older brother. If he hadn't fought so hard, she would've grabbed me and my twin brother Bryce, too. I have to do my part. Save Ares. And to prove to everyone, *especially her,* that I'm nothing like her.

Ares, I'm coming!

In a small clearing ahead stands a dilapidated cabin. The door sits skewed, not fitting the frame correctly. The big hinges are covered with thick rust. I can see Ares tied to a chair through the broken window. He's slumped, his head hanging limply.

Drugged. Mom loves to drug people. She gave us tainted cookies. She probably fed more of them to Ares to make him malleable.

I dash forward, ready to pull him out. I might be younger and smaller, but I can help.

Suddenly, arms wrap around me from behind, trapping me. I twist around. "Let go!"

"My love, stop. For your own good." Mom's voice is soft and sweet, her breath brushing over my ear like a feather.

A chill spreads over me, fear keeping me immobile.

"Who do you think you are? A savior?" Amusement brightens her tone. "You aren't like Bryce. He's too obedient to know what's good for him. But you? *You're* special."

"N-n-no." I barely manage to push the word out.

She gives a thoughtful hum, still holding me tightly from behind. I twist and kick, but can't get her to let go.

My eyes dart to the cabin. The fire's too close, the flames licking at the cabin walls greedily. Ares is going to burn to death.

Urgency hammers in my heart. I double my efforts to struggle out of her hold, but she's like one of those huge snakes.

"He's going to die!" I scream. "We have to save him!"

"If he dies, he dies. That's just his fate."

Her bland reaction makes my stomach clench. "What's *wrong* with you? Let me *go!*"

"No. I'm not letting you throw away your life like that. You know why?" She sighs softly. "Because you're *special.*"

My skin crawls. I don't want to hear her praise. *No, no, no. Don't say it, don't say it.* I try to voice the words, but my throat is too tight.

"Ares is too much like your father. Too rigid, acting like the world's weight rests on his shoulders. Bryce is too much of a good boy. Overly sentimental. Soft-hearted. But you? You're nothing like them." She tightens her arms, pulling me even closer. I can hardly breathe. "You and I, Josh. We aren't afraid of doing what must be done. We'll go the distance. Together. I recognized your potential when you were just a baby. And I plan to hone you until you can fully realize your promise. You're most like me—the best of my children, the one I'm *most* proud of." She spins me around, holding my face between her strong, hot palms and forcing me to look into her glowing blue eyes.

A deafening crash jolts me out of my daze as the cabin wall in the back collapses. "*Ares, no!*"

The scream tears from my throat. She cocks an eyebrow as she glances at the fire...slightly distracted. I shove away with a burst of strength and lunge forward. "Ares!" The roof starts to sag. Heat sears my skin, my mouth dry. Tears burn my eyes.

Then the entire structure caves in with a thunderous boom, creating a burst of flame and heat spreading all over the area.

"You can't run from your destiny, Joshua Huxley. *You are my son!* Zoe Dunkel's son! My blood flows in your veins, thicker than any of your brothers'!"

No, no, no—

I spin around, clenching my hand around her neck to stop the flow of her words. I shove her down, and I'm on her. I raise my fist. Her icy blue gaze slides to it, to the Japanese sashimi knife in my grip. A corner of her mouth tilts with satisfaction, and the air in my lungs freezes. Terror knots my throat at the realization that I'm only focused on my fury, reacting *just like Mom—*

Suddenly, my vision dims.

I blink. Pitch darkness. No fire. Just cold air cooling the clammy coat of sweat on my body. I drop my head into my hands, pressing the heels into my eyes. They come away wet.

A breath shudders out of my lungs. *Shit.* Another nightmare. It's the one I have the most frequently. Me trying to save Ares. Mom stopping me. Me trying to kill her—

My head throbs. The dream is mostly just wishful thinking on my part. I never got a chance to save Ares. I never knew where Mom took him after she kidnapped him. My mind fills in the blanks in the dream, so I can try to play the hero...and fail.

I might not have been in the burning forest, but what Mom said was real. *You're just like me, Josh. You always do whatever necessary to get what you want. I'm the most proud of you.* She told me that so many times when I was growing up. Her blue eyes glowed with pride—and she surreptitiously rewarded me with an extra chocolate chip cookie whenever I brought home a perfect one hundred on a test. Or did well in athletics. Except now I understand she wasn't proud of my accomplishments.

She just loved the fact that every time she looked at me, she saw the core of herself reflected. The triumph in her eyes when I raised the knife in the dream says everything. She rejoiced every time I single-mindedly focused on whatever I needed to do, including that one time when I punched an older kid who kept picking on Bryce after I told him to back off. Dad said that violence wasn't the answer...but Mom secretly gave me an extra chocolate bar.

She said Ares was too rigid, Bryce too soft-hearted. I'd rather be rigid with a soft heart than somebody like her—a complete sociopath who thinks nothing of drugging and kidnapping her own children. *She left Ares to die in a fire.* Thankfully he survived, mostly intact. She claimed she didn't mean for it to happen, but I don't believe her.

I don't believe anything she says. My mother—Zoe Dunkel—is a fucking selfish liar.

Decades-old loathing churns in my heart, along with fear—that maybe she's right. That deep inside, where it really counts, I *am* like her.

I flex and unflex my hand. I can still feel the smooth handle of the sashimi knife, the perfectly balanced steel. When I was fifteen, my stepmother Akiko used a hand-forged knife to slice open a bluefin tuna. It glided through the thick, resistant flesh like it was cutting through water. While she marveled at how wonderfully crafted the knife was, I was wondering how well it would slice something that wasn't tuna.

When I learned Mom was secretly interfering in my dating life, I almost used it on her. Fueled by teenage hormones and impulses, eliminating her and the emotional turmoil her existence represents seemed like the perfect solution. If Ares hadn't happened to send me a text at the precise moment I stood across from the hotel she was staying at, the knife clenched in my hand, I might've taken a step I could never undo.

Shaking off the old memories, I put on shorts and head to my basement gym. It has no windows, just walls covered with spotless mirrors and black rubber matting on the floor. A heavy bag hangs from the center of the ceiling. The fluorescent lights make me look unnaturally pasty—like I'm anemic or something.

I stare at my face. It looks exactly like Bryce's. The same slightly slanted dark eyebrows. The straight, high-bridged nose. The chiseled cheekbones from our mother, and our father's strong jawline. I step closer to the mirror. Just where does Mom see herself in me? Is it the eyes? The gray of our eyes came from the Huxley side of the family. *But she never thought Bryce was like her.*

There must be something in mine that says I harbor darkness like her. Swallowing, I look away from the reflection.

On the bag, at about shoulder height, is a photo of Mom and me from my toddler years. She smiles straight at the camera—that soulless smile that never reaches her eyes unless she's hurt somebody.

My eyes are on the smile as I tape my hands and do a few warm-up stretches. Then I go at the bag, taking out all my rage and fear on the rough canvas. My breathing sounds loud in my ears as punches and kicks make the bag jerk on its chain. Mom's smile doesn't change. Still soulless, still eerie.

Fuck you, fuck you, fuck you.

I pummel the bag until I start to get sloppy from the exertion. Rivulets of sweat pour down my face and body, my hair stuck to my skull.

Finally, I stop, stretching again, harder this time, while my muscles are warm. I towel the sweat off the floor, then run my fingers along Mom's face, trace the smile I loathe.

"One of these days," I whisper, "I'm going to show you I'm nothing like you."

Her smiling face seems to mock me. *A laudable goal, sweetie. But are you capable of it?*

I lock the door behind me and take a cold shower. Still, my gut burns uncomfortably. The images from my nightmare keep flashing in my head, pushing away the peace I need to function during the day.

I put on a robe and head to the meditation room. A stone path cuts the space from the door to the seating area in the center, floored with tatami mats flown in from Japan. A rock garden occupies the rest of the space, with windows on two sides to let in the sun. The pale gravel is raked like a river surrounding the center. A few bigger rocks add variety, some arranged like mountain ranges and some like cliffs. I purposely created this in my home because I once found a modicum of calm at the rock garden in Ryoanji with my late Japanese grandmother.

I sit *seiza* on the mats, butt resting on my heels, then heat some water in the small cast-iron pot, whisk up some matcha and serve it to myself. The soft, grassy scent of the tea helps with focus. I try to empty my mind and concentrate my attention on the frothy tea, its intense flavor spreading on my tongue, and the air filling and leaving my lungs. With each breath, the tension in my shoulders begins to ease a little. Still, a remnant of the fear lingers. And violent urges from the nightmare continue to nip at me.

I take the final sip of tea and exhale. Frustration bubbles that the gym workout and meditation failed to settle my mind.

I bite back a curse, get up and get ready for work. It's necessary to select my mask with deliberation—to contain my urges and show only a civilized veneer to the world.

The careful styling of my dark hair. A crisp white shirt. Silver cuff links in the shape of wolf's heads with ruby eyes. A muted burgundy tie with a Novotny knot. A navy three-piece suit by Lorenzo Cifonelli. Hand-stitched shoes, laced straight and polished to a mirrorlike perfection.

Now I no longer look like a potential monster, but a successful lawyer. The kind of civilized person who upholds the law.

I run my hand over the silver cane hanging in my walk-in closet, from the knob in the shape of the wolf's head to the long, slim body. My fingertips linger over the *Pietas et unitas* etched on the side in fancy filigree. It's a reminder of who I am and how I should live my life. To protect my family against my mother and her schemes. Perhaps from myself, if I really am anything like her.

It's not quite eight by the time I arrive at Huxley & Webber, the family's law firm and legacy. The floor is half full with over-caffeinated lawyers, ready to destroy the opposing counsel one argument at a time. The firm thrives on ambition. Those who can't feed off it don't last for long.

"You're late," Bryce says as I step out of the elevator. My twin's already got a cup of coffee in hand—probably his second. He's addicted to caffeine, and coffee is his vice because nobody in the States can brew green tea to his taste. He got spoiled by our grandmother's tea, but then, she was a master of the Japanese tea ceremony.

I've never told him I can make tea the way she could. If he knew, he'd be over at my place every morning. But I need my meditation time to center myself before starting each day. I can't afford to slip and show my dark side to anybody, especially anybody in my family. And most especially not to Bryce, who even our own mother said was the good boy.

I stare into his eyes. *What's the difference between us?* We're identical twins. Raised by the same parents, influenced by the same relatives. Went to the same college and law school, even shared an off-campus apartment for years before returning to L.A. to start our careers at Huxley & Webber.

"Not giving you my coffee, no matter how much you give me that longing look," Bryce says, pulling his cup protectively toward him.

Thankfully, he doesn't realize the real reason I've been staring. "Don't want your coffee. I'm late because I had some things to do." *It took longer than usual to settle myself this morning.*

His eyes glint. "Uh-huh. Was she your soul mate?"

I snort, but don't want to tell him about my messy nightmare. I never told the entirety to my past therapists, either. "No."

"Use your heart, Josh, use your heart," Bryce intones, like he's Yoda imparting some ancient wisdom. "Your dick can't feel for you."

"It feels plenty," I shoot back before heading to my office. My brothers know about my sex life—and my policy of not sleeping with the same woman twice. It isn't an official policy, but my brothers have assumed since I never repeat with the same woman. I claimed I'd know if someone was my soul mate once I became intimate with her. My family expects me to be normal—as normal as I can be, given who my mother is—and that includes acting like a typical guy and being seen with women.

Despite my reputation, I actually don't sleep with all of them. But perception is more important than reality. And being regarded as a player is far better than living a monk's life. Like Ares did until he met his wife, which caused the family enormous worry.

To avoid any concern, I try to select women pretty enough, with sufficient brainpower to hold a conversation for the duration of a dinner. But in the last two years or so, the percentage of women who make it from hello to dinner has decreased significantly. And from dinner to the bedroom? Hardly any now.

Perhaps I'm scraping the bottom of the barrel. But I feel guilty about approaching nice women, the kind you build a home and hearth with, as old-fashioned as that sounds. What if I hurt them the way Mom hurt the family?

I enter my office and flip the light switch. It's economically arranged—a huge desk and a wheeled chair with superb ergonomic design. A couple of filing cabinets and bookshelves bursting with reference material I keep close for easy access. Two chairs for visitors—functional, but not exactly comfortable. It's to discourage any overly long conversations, which is for their own good.

My specialty is entertainment and intellectual property law, and many of my clients tend to be needy, insecure types who seek validation from everyone around them. It's my pleasure to help them with legal matters, but guiding them through emotional upheavals? They need a date with Jack Daniel's—much more effective and economical than talking to a high-priced lawyer.

I start my laptop and pull up a contract to review for Ted Lasker's company. Everything from the big-shot movie producer is "super urgent." It's gotten so ridiculous that the firm and I decided to charge him extra, but he doesn't care as long as everything he sends ends up at the top of my priority list.

A couple of quiet knocks; the door opens, and Ailee Klein steps in. Standing at about five-six, she's a bundle of sweet energy. As usual, my assistant is in a pretty dress—today it's creamy beige with cosmos prints that flatter her curvaceous figure. Long, curly platinum hair frames her face. She has adorably soft cheeks that remind me of the sweet Fuji apples from Aomori I used to enjoy in Japan.

Klein's violet eyes crinkle. I zero in on the generous lines of her lips, which I could stare at literally forever. They're always soft, and usually curved into a sunny smile—like now—that never fails to brighten my mood.

And suddenly the ugly tension that's been lingering since the nightmare dissipates.

"Good morning, Josh," she says cheerfully. I smile back because it's impossible not to when dealing with her.

"Morning, Klein." I always try to use her last name. Don't want to mess up and call her by the nickname I shouldn't use.

"Here's your coffee." She places an iced latte—what I prefer in the morning—next to my laptop. "And your flowers." She puts a vase full of pink echinaceas on my desk, next to the mini-clock. The office transforms from an efficient workplace to something more welcoming and soothing.

She hands me an expense report with receipts for flowers for the month, neatly organized chronologically. I told her it wasn't necessary for purchases under fifty bucks. Each associate gets an annual use-it-or-lose-it budget for office décor and improvements, and the expenses for the flowers come out of that sum. But she said it didn't feel right for her to spend my money without giving me all the receipts. More proof that I made the right decision three years ago.

I wasn't sure about her in the beginning. Although I was inheriting her from another lawyer at the firm, she had only two months of relevant experience. I was going to decline without an interview, except her previous boss said he felt bad about her situation. He was quitting due to health issues, and she'd rejected a good offer to come to Huxley & Webber.

When she stopped by my office for a quick interview, I had plenty of pointed questions ready to go, determined to prove she really wasn't the right fit for the position. But she greeted me with that sunny smile...and every nerve in my body relaxed, like it was basking in a kind of honeyed warmth. I couldn't think of a single reason to say no.

She turned out to be an excellent assistant. Hardworking and quick to learn new skills. I secretly think she's more amazing than Bryce's assistant Amélie, although he would disagree to his dying breath.

"You have two appointments, one with Georgia Noir at ten," she says, naming a writer whose work is about to be turned into a Netflix show, "and the other with Ted Lasker at two." *Lasker*. Probably has another "super-urgent" matter. "I sent a bouquet of white lilies to Sandra Dunn to express condolences on your behalf. Apparently, she's heartbroken over losing Angel and can't make it to the four o'clock to discuss the details of her new contract."

I nod. Sandra is an up-and-coming starlet, and was obsessed with her angelfish. She won't be any good for at least a month.

"She invited you to Angel's wake next week, but I declined for you, citing family obligations you couldn't back out of."

"Thank you," I say sincerely.

She nods. "Oh, and Coco wants to know when she can see you again."

"Who?"

"Um. The model you had dinner with five weeks ago?"

Doesn't ring a bell, but I nod because otherwise Klein will list everything I supposedly did with this model. Well, her source would be Coco, and who knows what this Coco might've said. Given that I can't recall her name, it's likely we didn't get past the dinner stage. I have dinner with at least one different woman per week to maintain appearances. If I tried to remember all of them, I'd have no room for more important things.

"She said you weren't responding to her texts."

Probably because I blocked her. It's my policy to block the numbers of all failed dates to avoid clinginess, even though many of them try to cling anyway.

"She's wondering if you blocked her by mistake," Klein adds.

"Can't believe I blocked her, eh?"

"She's beautiful."

"She's certainly trying to make an impression." Most get the hint that I'm not interested after a few unanswered texts, especially if we didn't move past the dinner stage.

From the way Klein merely smiles, either my ironic tone went over her head or she doesn't want to presume anything.

"Lose her number and don't waste any more energy on her," I say.

"I think that's all for the day." Klein folds her hands in front of her with an extra-bright smile that doesn't quite reach her eyes. Most people would assume she's merely waiting for further instructions, but I know her habits. This is her nervous pose, which she seems to strike every morning. Not sure why. By now she should know I value her work, and she's indispensable. The quarterly feedback I provide is stellar. And

I've made sure she's properly rewarded with an annual performance bonus and raises.

I haven't done anything to make her doubt her abilities or place at the firm. But maybe I should directly address the subject and put her mind at ease. "Listen, Klein, about—" Something glinting on her left hand breaks my train of thought. "What's that?"

"What?" She looks down. A lovely shade of pink colors her cheeks, and I can't tear my eyes from her as an odd tingling sensation spreads in my chest. "Oh, this?" She lifts her hand so I can see better. "It's just a ring." Her tone is shy, almost embarrassed.

Just a ring? "It's on your fourth finger." My voice is terse, like there's something gravely wrong with its placement. I squint at it. "Just a band—"

Klein turns the piece, flushing slightly. "Sorry. It's a little loose."

"A lot loose," I say slowly like she just told me there's a piece of dogshit in my coffee. Other than the size, the ring isn't too bad. A huge marquise-cut diamond sits in the center, with three small, round diamonds sparkling on each side. There's even some engraving outside of the rose-gold band. "What does it say?"

"*Forever and ever.* There's *Love you* inside." Her cheeks turn redder, making her look like a pretty young woman in love. "I need to get it resized. But we just got engaged yesterday."

Engaged. The word hits me like the rock that cracked Goliath's forehead. I stare at her for a moment, searching for something to say. Thankfully, I manage to swallow *Are you leaving me?* which was the first thing that popped into my head. Blurting it out would be awkward and embarrassing.

Why think that anyway, though? An engagement isn't a resignation. She'll still be around. *But when did she get engaged?* She's so low key about her private life. I didn't even know she had a boyfriend. She only asks for time off once a year, on her best friend's birthday. She even worked late last Valentine's Day.

But then... Well, I supposed a girl as pretty and sweet as Klein would have a boyfriend. If I think she's lovely, so would others, unless they're just blind. Obviously, her boyfriend has eyes.

I look at her again, note the softness of her mouth, then hate it that some asshole kissed her, tasted her. I don't have to meet him to know he isn't worthy of her.

"Congratulations." I try for a casual tone of voice. "Anybody I know?" *Please don't let it be one of my clients.* They might be rich and famous, but most of them aren't marriage material. I'd have to ask Bryce to take her on as his client to handle the inevitable divorce.

"Um. No. I think you'd like him, though. He's a dentist, but he's really into movies and things." She flashes a small but blindingly white smile. Jesus, did he hit on her while cleaning her teeth?

The notion seems wrong. I'd be creeped out if my dentist tried to flirt with me while I was lying in the chair with my mouth wide open. Never mind he's fifty-two and Grandma's good friend.

"Anything else, boss?" she says softly when I continue to stare.

"No. That'll be all. Thanks."

2

AILEE

MY HEART IS STILL HAMMERING and the warmth in my cheeks is slow to dissipate. I close the door to Josh's office behind me and sit at my desk, exhaling softly and willing my pulse to ease up and my body to cool.

Sometimes I wonder if it's his exceptional good looks that make my belly flutter, but they don't explain everything. When I'm standing next to his identical twin Bryce, I feel nothing but friendliness. The only way I can explain the phenomenon is that Josh has some kind of unique pheromone that makes my body sing.

Or maybe it's because of the way he immediately trusted me and helped me out when I was harassed by a collection agency for an old medical bill I'd already paid off. They called me multiple times, then went after my parents. And of course my always-supportive folks told me to just hand over the money and stop embarrassing them—because obviously *I* must've screwed up.

Still, I refused to pay twice, and they escalated to harass me at my work number. Josh overheard the call and asked me for an explanation. I told him the story, unable to meet his eyes. I felt awkward and had no expectation that he'd care—after all, my parents didn't, and at that time, I'd been working for him for only a few months. But he merely nodded and drafted a terse letter on the Huxley & Webber stationery for me to mail, and the jerks never bothered me again.

I still can't find the words to describe how I felt. The only thing I remember is that my hands shook a little, and my eyes stung with unshed tears of gratitude. My heart might've started to warm toward him for giving me the gift of his trust.

My hyperawareness is too bad, though. It's futile to feel anything for my boss, no matter how much my belly flutters around him. He's a playboy who seems absolutely unable to settle down. One beautiful woman after another hangs from his arm—and undoubtedly shares his bed. They don't last, though. A month is the max, then he cuts them out of his life completely.

When they can't get through to him on his cell phone, they reach out to me at Huxley & Webber. Although he pretends he knows who I'm talking about, more often than not, he doesn't. Whenever I bring one up, a hint of impatient confusion almost always flashes in his deep gray eyes.

I must be a secret masochist, because I Google all those women to see how they stack up. Every single one is worthy of his attention. Those chiseled cheeks. The pouty mouths glistening with expertly applied lip gloss. The perfect hair and toned bodies I might be able to achieve if I gave up food for the next decade, and legs that look like they should be measured in furlongs. Priceless haute couture gowns and sky-high heels that make my feet cramp in sympathy.

Even if I could measure up, he's likely going to end up as Katt's man. She's set her sights on him, and my fraternal twin sister has never failed to get a man she wanted. She's gorgeous, with a bone structure that could make Venus weep with envy. And she has a superpower to make her golden hair lie sleek and straight, whereas mine rebels constantly into unmanageable curls.

She was on all the prominent fashion magazine covers before she hit seventeen, and everyone says the baby blue of her eyes is of angelic purity. She's more comfortable in formfitting couture dresses and stilettos than a T-shirt, shorts and bare feet, which is my wardrobe of choice when I'm not working. At twenty-four, she's about to launch a second career as an actress. I'm sure she'll reach levels of success I can't even imagine, just like she has with modeling.

She often mentions that she's waiting for Josh to have his fill before settling down with her. Otherwise, he might "become restless," which is "the last thing" she wants. Apparently, she knew he was the man for her when she first hired him to review and negotiate her modeling agency agreement. I had no idea he was her lawyer back then, since my family never involved me in anything related to her career.

But even if she hadn't told me all that stuff, I could tell there was something between them because even when he's out with other women, he's still seen with my sister, their photos gracing her Instagram. I'm not sure when he'll get tired of dating around, but once that happens, he won't just be my boss. He'll be my brother-in-law.

Not just out of my league, but forbidden forever.

The idea sends a sharp pang through my chest, but I maintain a serene smile. As Mom often told me, I need to know my place, although I still haven't figured out exactly where that is. Doubt Mom has, either, but she's satisfied as long as I'm out of Katt's way.

It's best if I'm by his side as a *valued assistant.* He makes sure to rate me highly on my quarterly and annual evals, enabling me to get the best bonus and pay raise I'm eligible for. Not going to ruin that by acting like a teenager in throes of her first crush. I call him *boss* to remind myself of the only thing he can ever be to me.

It makes more sense for me to aim for a man who's in my league. *Chad is great,* I tell myself, looking at the diamond ring. He's reliable... nice...has a good sense of humor. He's also attractive enough, and competent in bed. And being with him is making me more diligent about flossing, so that's, you know...also great. Healthy gums are *always* a bonus.

Even my bestie Max seems okay with him. Well, she did text me, *You sure?* after I shared the news last night, but she probably wanted to make sure I wouldn't regret my decision. She thinks I should aim as high as possible. Except I don't want to break something by overextending myself.

Exhale. Expel all the heavy thoughts.

I start working. Josh expects me to handle everything on his calendar, including some of his personal agenda. It's nothing egregious —just reminders about his relatives' birthdays and poker nights with his brothers so that he doesn't forget, no matter how busy he is. He's devoted to his family, and would do anything for them. Everyone in the legal trade knows the Huxleys are exceptionally tight, and you simply do not mess with them if you don't want to antagonize the entire gang.

"Morning! Here are the supplies you requested," comes a cheery voice. "Thanks for your patience. They finally made the delivery this morning."

I look up from my monitor and smile into the friendly green eyes of Kenna, the office admin. She's one of my favorite people at the firm. As usual, the lithe blonde is in a cute sleeveless top and slacks. I don't think I've ever seen her in a dress or a skirt. She places a thick stack of legal pads, a box of pens and some sticky pads on my desk.

"Thanks, Kenna."

"Oh, no problem." She starts to leave, then stops with a gasp. "Is that...?" She blinks, gesturing at my ring.

"Yeah. Chad proposed."

"*Seriously?* Lemme see!"

My cheeks warm as I extend my hand so she can study the hardware.

Her eyes sparkle. "Oh wow, that's amazing. Love the cut. It's so *you*. How romantic! Congratulations."

"Thank you. It couldn't have happened without you." Kenna referred me to Chad after my dentist retired last year.

"Oh, pssht." She waves me off with a big grin. "I'm just happy for you. I *am* getting invited to the wedding, right?"

"Of course! You'll be the one of the first once we finalize all the details."

"Awesome. Again, congrats. I want to hear all the deets, but I gotta get this stuff to Jeremiah." She gestures at the huge stack of papers.

I nod and wave her bye. Jeremiah Huxley is not someone you keep waiting. A name partner and Josh's aunt, she sort of scares me. And that fear is almost universally shared at the firm.

My phone buzzes with a message.

–Chad: Sorry, babe, but I can't meet your parents this Saturday after all. My father got hospitalized with chest pain, and we aren't sure what's going to happen to him.

My heart drops.

–Me: I'm so sorry. Do you need me there with you? I can ask for time off.

–Chad: No, it's okay. Charlotte is so far.

Chad's parents moved to North Carolina after his father quit practicing dentistry in SoCal. I unfortunately haven't had a chance to meet them, and Chad never got to meet my family before popping the question yesterday.

His proposal was actually kind of shocking. I was wondering if the relationship made sense for both of us. My feelings for him were growing rather slowly, and I wasn't sure if he was really into me because he's so busy—especially on weekends, with seminars and further studies for his profession.

But I couldn't say no. After all, he is probably the best I can get, and Max always says the best way to get over a crush is to find a new man. Chad promised to propose again, more properly, after getting my father's blessing.

I had to laugh. Dad will probably have nothing to say except, "Thank God we can offload her onto someone gainfully employed." Well, he'll say it more diplomatically—*I hope*—but that'll be the message. His biggest worry is that nobody will want me. It's incomprehensible to both my parents that Katt is kicking ass and taking names, while I'm more or less "just getting by." My salary looks like a joke compared to Katt's millions, even though I earn enough to meet my needs and then some.

We're sisters, after all. Twins even, albeit fraternal. With the same set of parents. There must be some kind of failing on my part stopping me from being the kind of success Katt is.

They believe that my job at Huxley & Webber makes me a disaster. In their worldview, unless I'm making millions a year, I'm losing at life. They did their best to make me move into the condo Katt bought so I could be less of a loser, but I know the real motive. A rival model bought a house for her younger brother, and my parents thought Katt should do something similar to boost her image. Katt didn't really want to give me the condo, so it's under her name—I was just supposed to live there, rent-free, even though it's way too far from the office. They acted like I told them I snort coke on weekends when I declined. Even if it's rent-free, I can't drive three hours each way on commute. That'd be six hours of my life, *poof*, gone every day.

No more updates from Chad. Guess he's already on his way to Charlotte if he isn't there already. My phone buzzes again.

–Mom: Katt got a callback from the movie Ted Lasker's producing!

–Me: Wow. That's huge!

It *is* huge. Ted Lasker is one of the most successful movie producers of all time. He's turned countless newbies into major stars. I'm happy for Katt for getting the opportunity.

–Mom: We're going to Peking Town for dinner tonight. You should come and celebrate Katt's big milestone.

–Me: Peking Town?

–Mom: Yes. Can't you make it?

I sigh with a slight resignation because Mom's probably genuinely confused. I push down the feeling. It won't do any good to be upset.

–Me: Seafood allergy.

–Mom: But Peking Town is Katt's favorite. And it's just one meal. Don't make things difficult. Besides, not eating much won't hurt. Might even help. Free immunotherapy, you know?

The words sting. Mom's never hidden her disappointment that I'm nothing like Katt. She believes if I were more like my twin, I'd be doing so much better at life, making significant monetary contributions to the family, so everyone could enjoy greater abundance. After all, it was Katt who single-handedly saved us from financial ruin when she was discovered by a modeling agency. Mom told me if I were just thinner and taller, I could've been a successful model like Katt because we're twins. We could've helped each other's careers, too, by sharing opportunities and pulling each other to the top. Katt had to struggle alone—and harder—because of my shortcomings.

The muscle under my right eye starts twitching.

–Mom: It's at seven. Don't be late. Bring a gift for Katt.

–Me: Okay.

—Mom: Wear something pretty. A cute dress maybe, but nothing too slutty.

I try not to sigh too loudly.

—Me: I'll head over right after work.

—Mom: Good. Say hello to Josh for me. Can't wait to welcome him into the family.

She can share that sentiment with him directly. I'm not going to bother him with messages about how my family can't wait for him to become my brother-in-law. Just too cringey.

I put down my phone and close my eyes for a moment. Purposely, I imagine some beautiful scenery. A crystal-blue ocean. The rhythmic sound of waves. Briny air. The image is everything I need to settle my emotions. I exhale, releasing negativity with the breath. Within a few moments, I'm much calmer.

"It is what it is," I tell myself. "Know your place, Ailee." Then I put on a smile, turn to my laptop and continue with my day. I have a great boss who values me and a fiancé who loves me. What more could I want?

Barry, an associate from Georgia who looks like he could've had a more successful career as a bouncer than a lawyer, comes over to grab Josh for lunch. "Wanna join us?" he says with a wink.

I shake my head. "Thanks, but I brought a sandwich."

"What? Beaten by a *sandwich*? You just broke my heart." He puts a hand over his chest dramatically.

Snorting, Josh smacks his back. "Let's go." He turns to me. "Don't take this idiot seriously."

"I won't." I smile. Barry got married recently, but rumor has it he's still a player. He even organized Ares's bachelor party, which was a bit ridiculous because the party took place *after* the wedding. Apparently, the timing wasn't important. What mattered was that Barry got to party with strippers.

Wonder if his wife knows...or cares? Despite his player rep, Barry's one of the most capable lawyers at the firm, so maybe his wife married him for his career prospects and money. Hard to say, since I've never met her. But Katt might be wiser than Barry's wife because she's willing to wait until Josh's done playing around.

Pushing away thoughts of my sister and Josh's future together, I nibble on my PB&J and browse a couple of clothing sites. I need to schedule a trip to meet Chad's parents—hopefully his father recovers soon—and can't decide if I should buy something new or pick something out of my closet. I want to make a good impression on his family, even though they live in North Carolina. I'm hoping we could spend warm, loving Thanksgiving and Christmas together. I've always longed for holidays where I fit in and not get judged because I want to have another helping of stuffing—

"Still at your desk?"

I jerk my head up at Barry's voice. He's standing at my desk with my boss. "You're back already?" I glance at the clock. "Wow. Already one fifteen."

Josh hands me a box bearing the Bobbi's Sweet Things logo. "Here. I just happened to walk by on the way back to the office."

"On the way? We took a detour that—"

Josh buries an elbow deep into Barry's side, which produces a thin, choking sound. "Don't you have a meeting at one thirty? Better get going."

"Fine," Barry wheezes, and blows me a kiss before disappearing.

Josh turns to me. "They didn't have the nama-cream cupcake flavor I wanted, so I picked up the last strawberry." He scratches the tip of his nose.

I beam. "Strawberry's my favorite."

"I know."

Sweetness spreads through me. "Thanks, boss."

"My pleasure." He starts to smile, then his eyes fall on my ring and his eyebrows pull together. "When's the wedding, by the way?"

"I'm not sure yet. Chad and I haven't set a date, since... Well, there's just a lot to consider. His family's in North Carolina, mine's here, stuff like that." I shrug.

He purses his lips. "You should take plenty of time to rethink your decision."

"Rethink?" I frown. Josh isn't the type to pick the wrong word.

"Better safe than sorry. Marriage is a serious matter. The kind that requires a lawyer beforehand and maybe after."

Oh... I smile. "Appreciate you watching out for me, but I'm not important enough to need a lawyer for my marriage."

The grooves between his eyebrows deepen. "Like I said. Take your time and really think it through. *Chad* isn't going anywhere."

"Thanks, boss." I widen my smile. "But Chad's perfect for me."

3

JOSH

At two sharp, I steeple my fingers and watch as Ted Lasker settles his imposing frame into a seat on the other side of my desk. He still has a full head of hair—dark too, although the color might be from a bottle. He has twinkling eyes that look blue-gray under the light and the square jaw he gave to all seven of his sons. They were born to seven different women, one of them being my aunt Jeremiah.

He's in a sapphire short-sleeve, button-down shirt and light beige slacks. His assistant Joey Martin takes Ted's sunglasses and places them in a case with reverence reserved for the Holy Grail. His orange hair is cut short and spiked, showing every square inch of an enormous forehead. I told him if he'd comb his hair down a little, he might look better. At least it'd provide some coverage for his ridiculous forehead, but he refused, saying Ted likes his hair up.

If Ted told him to lick his own balls, he might do just that.

"What's wrong with the options contract now? You didn't have any problem before," I say when Ted's finally comfortable enough in the chair not designed to be comfortable.

"I didn't, but now it seems the author has designs on me."

"Who could blame her, sir?" Joey lays it on thick.

I keep my expression perfectly professional. Ted thinks everyone wants him, man or woman, old or young. And Joey feeds Ted's delusions because he's the ultimate sycophant. "Well…" I say, "if she's bothering you, you need to call the police. I can't add a clause telling her to stay away to the options contract."

Ted's eyes widen with horror. "Oh, I wouldn't want to do *that*. Her story's just the thing I'm looking for, for my next project. *Baby for the Asshole*."

"*Baby for the Billionaire Boss*, sir," Joey says quickly.

Ted waves a hand. "Whatever, something like that. Point is, the main character reminds me of *me*, if I ever got crazy enough to go into finance." He laughs.

"You'd be great at it, although thank God you didn't because Hollywood would've lost its brightest star," Joey says.

Why don't you lick his toes, too? I keep the thought to myself because Joey might just do it. "Then what is it you'd like me to do?"

"Add a clause to the contract that says I reduce her payment by fifty percent if I sleep with her."

I'm so glad I'm not having my post-lunch coffee right now.

"She has the hots for me," Ted says, by way of explanation.

"Understandably," Joey puts in.

Ted smiles. "And honestly, for a chance to sleep with me? She should just give me the book for free. But at the same time, you know, I'm not a total bastard. She's probably poor. I don't even think she has a private jet."

"Most people don't," I point out.

Ted says, "I think fifty percent is more than fair. Half-half. Am I right?"

"Absolutely," Joey says, nodding furiously.

"Although she could get difficult. If so…" Ted shakes his head. "I guess she'll just have to miss out." His tone says that would be a tragedy rivaling *Romeo and Juliet*.

"I don't think it would be wise to put that in the contract," I say, since I'm a lawyer dealing with reality, not delusion.

"Why not?" Ted looks genuinely confused. Joey's expression snaps from woeful loss to nuclear glare in an instant.

"Because it sounds uncomfortably close to prostitution."

"Hey, it's not prostitution if she likes it."

Joey leans forward, forehead glinting. "And really, what young woman *wouldn't* pay to be with someone like—"

"Just pay the money." I maintain my professional demeanor. "It isn't that much, and it'll be better for you down the road. Less chance of things getting muddled. She could—"

A piercing scream outside cuts me off.

"Who the hell do you think you are? You aren't even that cute!" comes a loud female voice outside my office.

Klein says something in even, measured words, which I can't make out through the door.

"I don't care if he's in a meeting! I deserve to see him!" Miss Shrill screeches.

Banging and things falling. The door to my office burst opens, and a tall, lithe blonde struts in, her hips moving with exaggerated swings. Her dress is so tight that everything is outlined, including her nipples. Definitely no underwear.

Behind her, a stapler and desk phone lie on the floor. She must've knocked them over on purpose. Klein rushes in, her cheeks flushed and mouth tight. I stand up. "Excuse me for a moment." The blonde's eyes light up as my strides eat the distance between us, then her jaw drops when I go past her and stop in front of Klein. "Are you okay?"

"Yes," she says. "Sorry, I couldn't keep her—"

"It's all right." I pick up the stapler and the phone and place them on the desk. "Give me a moment with her."

Klein's eyebrows pull together. She nods, then turns her cellphone to show building security on the screen. "Just in case."

A corner of my mouth quirks up. Despite the absurd situation it's difficult to remain upset for long when I'm in Klein's presence. "Good. Call them up here." Then I turn around to face the intruder.

Before I can speak, Ted squints. "Nelly?"

"You know her?" I say, although I'd bet my left ball the blonde's name isn't Nelly. Other than Joey, Ted *never* remembers names. The only exceptions are the seven women who bore him sons, and he named each child after the mother so he could associate the mom-and-son pairings correctly.

"Ted!" she screams, fluttering her lashes as she folds both hands over her impressive double-E chest. "You didn't tell me you'd be here! You know I've been looking for you, too."

Ted shrugs. "Why would I tell you? You aren't that special."

The corners of Joey's mouth twitch, his eyes gleaming maliciously. He loves it when Ted arrogantly exerts his power. Probably it makes *him* feel special. "Should I call 911 and report her for stalking?" he asks.

"I'm not stalking him! Although I do want to talk about this new movie. I can play an excellent femme fatale. No," she says dramatically, probably already starting to audition in the moment, "I'm here to deal with *him*." She points a long, lacquered nail in my direction, and her volume rises again. "*How* could you ignore my calls?"

"I'm sorry, who are you?" She looks vaguely familiar, but it's probably the lip filler. So many women these days look like they stuck their mouths into a beehive.

She turns red. "Don't be an asshole. We had the hottest connection of my life in April!"

I stare at her, studying her features more closely. Her forehead isn't moving—Botox. Her cheeks seem overly textured and red underneath the concealer. Probably had some work done on them recently. But she doesn't ring a bell. Not even close. Although I don't always remember the numerous women I've had dinner with, I do remember those I've slept with. Given her propensity to shriek, I'm pretty sure I didn't have dinner with her, much less actual sex. My penis has standards.

I look toward Klein, who's watching the scene with an avid, unblinking gaze. *Awkward.* She's aware of my dating habits—thanks to certain persistent women who refuse to give up—but it's one thing to know, another to witness. I want to pause the scene and explain, but that'd just be weird.

"Guess it wasn't that hot for me." My muttered response is still loud enough for everyone to hear.

"Really?" Ted gives the blonde a once-over. "Joey, make a note of that."

"What? Why?" the woman says, finally realizing that getting on Ted's radar like this might not be the best way to advance her career.

"I can't cast a woman who leaves a dick cold and shriveled. This man is in his prime!" He gives me a meaningful look.

I rub the spot between my eyebrows. My dick doesn't shrivel, thank you very much—except pointing that out is going to become even more awkward and might even encourage Ted.

He continues, "A true measure of a woman is her ability to make a guy get hard."

"Exactly," Joey adds with too much enthusiasm.

"Are you kidding? Men *love* me!" Nelly—or whoever she is— gestures from her shoulders to her hips, displaying her assets. "This isn't something you can get just anywhere."

"I've seen better," Ted says with a shrug.

The woman seethes. "This is all your fault, Josh! You heartless asshole! You stood me up and humiliated me!" She screeches a string of curses that would make a rap star blush. People around the office crane their necks to watch the drama.

Great.

She bellows a battle cry, then lunges at me, her talons extended toward my face. I step left to avoid the attack. She moves surprisingly well for a woman in heels.

Thankfully, security comes in and grabs her arms. "You crazy asshole!" she yells again. "You're going to be sorry when I'm famous!"

Ted turns to Joey. "They didn't sleep together. If she screamed like this in bed, he'd remember." Then, to her: "You have a nasty voice. A doc could IV Viagra into a guy and he'd stay wilted like month-old broccoli in the back of a fridge."

"Ted, *don't*! Give me a *chance*!" She shrieks and struggles as security drags her away. "I can make it worth your while!"

"Sorry, Sally. Too old." Ted stands. "Well, that was exciting, but I gotta get going. I feel like I have an appointment."

"You do, with Warren from Starlight," Joey says.

"Right." Ted turns to me. "Anyway, just see if you can add that thing about the fifty percent off. I didn't get rich by giving my stuff away for free."

He starts walking out, then says, "Oh hello, Preston."

"Hello, Ted."

I wince at Dad's voice. That cool, even tone means he's furious.

He appears in the doorway, dressed in a bespoke three-piece suit somewhere between midnight blue and navy. His tie is a muted wine color and knotted impeccably into a classic Windsor. As a senior partner, he exudes the confidence and authority many at the firm would love to emulate.

He gives me an unreadable look. "Joshua. To my office."

4

JOSH

As soon as Dad issues the order, he turns and heads toward the elevator. His office is on the floor above. Klein looks at me, eyes wide.

"Boss, I'm so sorry! If I'd just stopped her…" she says in a small voice, biting her lip.

"Ah, don't worry. Nothing I can't handle." She shouldn't worry about it. It's the blonde's fault for barging in the way she did.

"You aren't in trouble, are you?"

I have to smile. "Why? Worried about me?"

"A little." She squirms. "But maybe he won't be too upset because it's never happened before." She sighs. "I'm sorry. I should've called security sooner."

"Not your fault. You did what you could. Who could've predicted she'd be so…out there?" I shrug and give Klein a reassuring smile before going up to face Dad.

Dad has one of the nicest corner offices at Huxley & Webber—a perk he's earned through his brilliance in the legal field. He has the kind of career and admiration I'd love to have.

One of these days, I'll have an office like this, too. After all, it's the family legacy I was bred to take on, and I plan to embrace it—and prove to myself I'm nothing like my mother.

He looks up from his throne-like seat behind the massive mahogany desk as I shut the door behind me. He steeples his fingers. "Have a seat." He gestures with a raised eyebrow at a plush armchair.

I sit, keeping myself relaxed. Dad has wide-set gray eyes, straight eyebrows and an even straighter mouth. He has a booming voice to match the girth of his chest, but he keeps his tone modulated. He says that only people who've lost the argument raise their voices. Despite that, he has a way of commanding attention when he speaks.

One heartbeat. Two... Three... I wait, not willing to start. Dad's upset about something, and I'd rather have him tell me plainly, rather than me trying to guess.

"Just what was *that*?" he says finally. "That mindless screaming. Everyone on the floor must have heard it. Hell, even I heard it from here. I actually thought there was a damn murder."

Irritation surges at the unfair reprimand. It's never happened before, and it isn't my fault that the woman has the intelligence and honor of a banana republic bureaucrat caught siphoning public funds. But getting into the nitty-gritty won't make him feel any more generous toward me right now. "A minor incident. Sorry. She won't be back. I'll make sure to let security know."

The end of Dad's left eyebrow twitches. "A minor incident? She made quite a spectacle."

"If you're worried about Ted's reaction, he won't mind." My tone is a tad defensive, despite my effort to stay calm and even. "He thrives on drama."

"I'm not worried about him. I'm worried that she did it *here*. At the office. It's disruptive and unprofessional."

My mouth tightens. I have no defense for that, as infuriating as the situation is. "I apologize. It won't happen again."

"Won't it? I know you find Ted and his lifestyle *aspirational*."

The statement stuns me into silence for moment. Finally, I gather myself. "I don't—"

He cocks an eyebrow. "Really? Because you're seen with a different woman every week. At the rate you're going, you'll have dated more women than him."

His assertion stings. "Oh, come on."

"And you show as much discernment as he does. Or dogs noticing a bitch in heat."

"That's unfair."

"You think so? What's unfair is my having to worry about one of them showing up pregnant." He points a finger in the general direction outside, his eyes flashing with fury and concern.

"That won't happen. I got a vasectomy."

"Look how that worked out for Ted Lasker! Seven kids! Ha!"

"From a highly reputable doctor," I add tightly. *And Ted's was performed over thirty years ago.*

"Good. That way you won't produce heirs for the family. But that doesn't mean I'm fine with you bringing your personal baggage to the office."

"I didn't bring her. And I've already said it won't happen again. Twice."

"It should *never* have happened. You've spent your entire adult life unable to stick with anybody for more than a month. The frustrating thing is, you didn't stay with any of them because they were never right for you. You're a smart boy. You've been purposely selecting women you know are unsuitable, wining and dining them a few times, and then breaking up with them." Dad gives me a long, steady stare. "What are you afraid of?"

The question sucks the breath out of my lungs. "What?" My response is barely audible, then I manage a fake laugh to hide the tremor starting in my heart.

Dad picks his words with care. "Do you think you'll end up with somebody like Zoe? Because I initially fell head over heels in love with her?"

It takes all my effort to ignore the need to look away. His incisive questioning hurts, especially since I look up to him so much. "This isn't about your past with Mom," I manage hoarsely. "I'm just having some fun before settling down."

"You're thirty. Not exactly a hormone-driven college kid."

"Still young."

He gazes at me for a moment. "*Pietas et unitas.* What do you think the family motto means?"

"Loyalty and unity," I say promptly, relieved he's switched to a subject I'm more comfortable with. "That's how we treat family. I've never deviated from that."

"Yes, but that isn't all. It also means you need to be somebody worthy of our family's loyalty and unshakable trust. Do you believe how you're behaving in your personal life is worthy or even honorable? You think your personal life has no impact, but look how it's bled into your professional life—and the family's legal legacy."

Dad isn't cruel or harsh. But the matter-of-fact way he speaks...the sympathy mingled with pity in his eyes cuts me deeply.

He continues, "Only you can look inside your own heart. So how you present yourself to the world matters. You aren't acting like a true Huxley, Josh. Take some time to reflect. If you believe you're on the wrong path, correct course before it's too late. And don't let my mistake with your mother affect you. I'd hate to see you throw away a chance at happiness and fulfillment out of fear. She isn't worth it. Don't forget— you're my son. A Huxley."

What about the Dunkel blood in my veins? I'm at least half Dunkel. The words get stuck in my throat like scalding iron marbles.

"You can return to work," he says, switching to partner mode. "If what happened with that woman happens again, it will affect your future at the firm."

Nodding woodenly, I stand, then walk out. My feet move mechanically, carrying me to my office.

Dad probably hasn't had this kind of talk with Ares or Bryce. After all, they haven't done anything like me.

You aren't acting like a true Huxley.

Then am I acting like a Dunkel?

I shudder. Cold sweat coats my skin, creating a clammy film. The need to pound on something is almost overwhelming, but I'm at work. A familiar restlessness churns in my belly, the same as after one of my nightmares. I clench my teeth and curl my fists.

Settle the fuck down. Dad's just worried and disappointed.

Still, I can feel the sticky whispers in my ear—the sugary breath that tickled as Mom spoke to me. *You're the most like me. I'm most proud of you.*

I walk past Klein's desk. She jumps to her feet and follows me into the office, closing the door. "Are you all right?"

I spin around and give her a long stare. Her violet eyes meet mine, shining softly with warm care. Would a girl as nice as Klein look at me like this if I were as horrible as Mom?

But what if she just...can't tell? It isn't like Mom walked around sounding like a sociopath. I know how to look and sound sane. What if I'm good enough to fool Klein? Mom totally hoodwinked Dad—and the rest of the family—for so long. She made them think she was worthy of being a Huxley, of deserving everything the family motto conferred.

It occurs to me that I've been acting like an idiot. All I wanted was to project normalcy, a regular guy unencumbered by an ugly childhood event, to make sure my family wouldn't worry. Instead, I've caused them concern, and actually embarrassed them by having that horrible woman barging into Huxley & Webber.

"You look like the world just ended," Klein says when I don't respond. "You're so pale."

"I'm fine," I say automatically, my tone too smooth, my smile too practiced. It's my default response to everything, to ensure people don't probe too deeply.

"Oh. Sorry." She clears her throat. "Didn't mean to be nosy." Disappointment fleets across her expressive face.

Suddenly, I feel like an asshole. Klein is great—and quick, too. She knows I'm dismissing her concern. The old fear sits in my belly like cold, concealed fat, ugly and nauseating. I run a rough hand over my face. "Actually...no. I'm not, really. I..." The weight of the nightmare from the morning and what Dad said presses me down. I plop down on a chair and bury my face in my palms.

"Want to talk about it?" she says softly.

I can't unload everything, but maybe she can help with—

"Am I a user?" I lower my hands and look up at her. "Like, with women?"

Her eyes widen. "Who told you that? No! I think you just like women and can't settle. But that's no crime. Plenty of men play the field." She shrugs. "Maybe you just haven't met the right person yet."

Except Dad thought I was afraid—that I'm not living my life like a true Huxley. And if I'm not a true Huxley, I can only be a Dunkel—my mother's son.

"Uh. I didn't say that to make you feel worse," Klein says, peering at me with even greater concern in her eyes. "Do you want to head home early? You don't have any more appointments today."

I shake my head. I'm not giving anybody the power to disrupt my day. "No. I can handle the rest of today's agenda."

The corners of her mouth turn down. She bites her lower lip. "Do you, um, need a hug?"

I force a wan smile. I must look really awful for her to offer a pity hug. I should probably decline, but the bright glimmer in her eyes is nearly irresistible. If some of her light can touch me, my darkness inside might not feel so grim. I swallow the urge to say yes. "It's okay. But thanks for the offer. What would I do without you?"

"Still be awesome," she says, her voice full of earnest conviction.

The vise around my chest eases, and in a moment or two I can breathe without feeling like I'm about to suffocate.

"You really are perfect," I say, looking up at her. The afternoon light pouring in from the windows illuminates her from behind, creating a halo and making her glow like an angel.

My angel.

I freeze. Where did *that* come from? Klein's too good to be dragged into my messy life. *Plus she's engaged,* I remind myself, feeling like I just downed a shot of acid.

I let out an awkward cough. "I mean, you know, a perfect assistant."

She blushes. "Sure, boss." And then rolls her eyes cutely.

5

AILEE

Peking Town is a popular Chinese restaurant not too far from the office. I can't eat anything there due to my seafood allergy, which apparently is quite rare; most people are either allergic to fish *or* shellfish. However, I've been there a few times because Katt loves their lobster fried rice and dumplings.

It done in a gorgeous red-and-gold décor—shockingly colorful and decadently luxurious at the same time. I adore the golden dragons glittering on the walls and the stunning calligraphy, even though I can't read the characters. The only negative about the place is that parking is inconvenient—even by Los Angeles standards. I walk as quickly as possible without running because I don't want to be sweaty for dinner or ruin the bouquet of tiger lilies I bought for Katt.

My watch says I'm fifteen minutes late. But I don't regret staying behind and making a list of all the women Josh has dated in the last twelve months and handing it to security for extra scrutiny. Seeing his shell-shocked expression after speaking with his father made me want to do something concrete to help him.

"Petra Klein. Party of four," I tell the hostess breathlessly. She's a lanky Asian in a fashionably tight-fitting blue dress.

She checks her tablet and smiles. "This way."

I follow her inside. All the tables are round, with lazy Susans in the center. Every single one is occupied, which isn't surprising. The delicious aromas of food fill my senses. My belly rumbles, and I swallow a sigh, wishing there was a cure for my allergy. Man, I miss Chinese food. But eating any might literally be the death of me.

When Katt and I turned fifteen, the family went to a local Chinese place to celebrate, and I had a reaction after taking a bite of shrimp fried rice. Terror seized me as my body swelled and it became increasingly difficult to pull air into my chest. Everything was a blur—and somebody must've called 911. While I was dazed and out of it, I vaguely overheard Mom lament that she and Dad could've driven me to the hospital because an ambulance ride was so expensive. We didn't have health insurance, and she worried that the bill would make things worse for the family's already tight finances.

"Why does she have to be allergic to something like Chinese food? How are we going to pay for all this?" she added with a sigh full of exasperation and worry. Guilt crushed me, even though I didn't mean for any of it to happen. Why did I have to develop an allergy to something I used to enjoy? Why did I have to hurt my family this way?

At least I didn't have to stay at the hospital overnight. Even if the doctor had insisted, I wouldn't have wanted to burden my parents more than I already had. They always agonized over every expense until Katt hit it big. Then—everything changed. No more pinching pennies. Mom and Dad could be as extravagant as they wanted. Katt always beams proudly for being able to give back to our parents. I applaud from the sidelines because, well...that's all I'm capable of.

My stomach growls again, and I put a hand over it. I can wait until I get home to have dinner. A nice piece of leftover lasagna is waiting in the fridge.

Even before the hostess gestures, I find the table. It's impossible to miss Katt's golden hair or the gorgeous magenta Versace minidress, which is her favorite. Or Mom's bright red lipstick. She didn't used to wear vivid tones until Katt started making money. Now she's like a peacock, a blue-and-purple Dior dress draped over her like it was made to order. The bleached hair is twisted into a knot at the nape, and a pair of huge sapphire earrings dangle from her earlobes. Two enormous diamond rings glint on her hands—gifts from Dad on her birthday and Mother's Day. Her violet eyes smile at Katt, her entire face charming and sweet. I've seen photos of her when she was younger, and she probably broke a lot of boys' hearts growing up.

Dad occupies a chair next to Mom, his tall frame neatly folded—Katt probably got her height from him, while I failed to get any of the height fairy magic. He's trim. *Another genetic lottery I missed out on*—everyone on his side of the family is as slim as cigarettes except me. Dark eyebrows and deep-set pale blue eyes with lines fanning out from their corners give him a friendly, all-American appearance. He's in a white polo shirt, pale khakis and shiny leather shoes, and the tip of his straight nose glows red. Must've played a round of golf with his well-heeled friends before coming over.

The table's already laden with food—lobster fried rice seemingly being the main course. Lots of shellfish dishes swimming in glossy sauces and an egg drop soup. Mom and Dad each have a small mound of seafood before them. Katt only has some fried rice and a couple of shrimps on her plate.

"Hi," I say. "Sorry I'm late. Something came up at the last minute."

"*Finally* you're here." Mom's gaze rakes me up and down, cataloging everything from my hair to my outfit to see if I'm Instagrammably fashionable.

I resist the urge to shift my weight and just smile. I know exactly what she's going to say.

"Honey, you really have to do something about your hair. Why is it always so messy? And that beige is terribly dull. Makes you look like a lump of mud. You need something brighter. Maybe violet or vermilion. You know, *feminine*. And pretty."

Last time I wore a vibrant red-purple dress, she told me I looked like a two-legged highlighter. I'm sure Mom didn't say the same to Katt in her magenta dress today. "I'll see what my stylist recommends," I say vaguely, keeping the smile on my face.

"Better do it soon. You're wasting your youth away. If you made some real effort, you could do better than being somebody's coffee fetcher," Mom says, another not-so-subtle reminder that I should audition for movie roles before I'm too old. She's convinced if I can just try to make myself prettier, I'll make a fortune in the entertainment business like Katt.

Mom doesn't care that I don't want to be in Hollywood, and I certainly don't want to rely on my looks to earn a living. I can't imagine crying over a pimple or agonizing over an extra scoop of ice cream the way Katt does. Besides, looks fade, and fame is fickle. No matter what, I'm just not celebrity material, even if we *were* twins born from the same womb at the same time. I'd rather depend on my brain for my career. "My coffee fetching is appreciated by my boss, so I think I'm okay."

Mom's mouth purses in disapproval, but I ignore her and hand the tiger lilies to Katt. I used to give her accessories and things, but stopped when I discovered my gifts in the trash can in her room. At least flowers are meant to be tossed when they wilt. "Congrats, sis."

"Thanks." She takes the vivid orange blossoms, then promptly puts them on an empty chair next to her before posing with her elbow on the table. No need to turn to know that somebody's discreetly taking a photo of her to post on social media.

I park my butt in the only empty chair left, between her and Mom, and serve myself oolong tea out of the blue-and-white porcelain pot. If my mouth is full, people won't try to talk to me.

"You should've gotten her something innocent and pretty. Like white camellias. That's the kind of role she's auditioning for," Mom says, her voice full of reproach. At least she doesn't call them unlucky.

"Sorry. Didn't realize." Katt was hush-hush about the role when I asked at our last family dinner. I didn't probe since it was none of my business. Ted Lasker is an eccentric man, and he might've had people sign NDAs.

"You should pay more attention to Katt's career. Something might inspire you," Dad says. As if I spent more time studying her career, I'd become like her—a star with fame and fortune, the latter being the more important.

I merely smile and knock back the lukewarm tea to douse the searing sensation creeping up from the pit of my belly. The uncomfortable burn is probably from the guilt and sad realization over not being good enough to make my parents proud.

"Try some lobster in black bean sauce. It's very good," Mom says to Katt, as she gestures at a pile of heavenly smelling food.

Twisting to ensure she looks good from every angle, Katt smiles at Mom. They're the perfect picture of mother-daughter harmony. I wish I could disappear into the ground, knowing someone is snapping photos of us and feeling like I don't belong in the pictures. Maybe my twin likes this restaurant because the entire dining area is open—no privacy walls or partitions. It's great place to be seen.

"Thanks, but I already had a bite," Katt says. "Can't eat too much. It'll make me bloated." She always complains that Chinese food makes her gain water weight the next day, but she never fails to pick it for most of her outings. Guess even a dedicated model like her can't stay away from "bad" food.

"She can always indulge after she gets the role," Dad says. He's probably calculating all the money it'll add to the family coffers.

I pour more tea to fill my empty stomach. Since Katt needs to stay lean, maybe dinner won't last too long. Mom and Dad are always worried about making dieting more difficult for her.

Mom turns to me. "Oh, by the way! I found the perfect man for you. His name is *Neville*."

My stomach sinks. Mom's definition of "perfect" is usually somebody with money. The rest is "negotiable." Ever since I started working at Huxley & Webber, she's been determined to pair me up with a man who meets her approval. "Well, Mom—"

"Look," she cuts me off. "He's a real estate developer. Recently divorced and looking for the right girl to spoil. I think you'll approve."

"But—"

Mom shows me a photo from her phone. The guy's gotta be in his fifties at least, with graying hair receding like a tide and a doughy complexion that would make a beluga whale proud.

This is her idea of a "perfect guy"? She wants somebody like Josh for Katt, but this for me? Hurt and anger at Mom's blatant favoritism dig their talons deep into my heart, but I press my lips together. She's on a roll, which means nothing's going to penetrate right now.

"He won't even need a baby from you, so you don't have to go through labor and ruin your body more than it already is. And he's fabulously rich. What do you think?" She sounds entirely too pleased with herself.

She isn't going to listen to anything I say, so I just show her the back of my left hand.

"What's that?" Katt's eyes narrow.

"I got engaged."

Mom's jaw slackens. "*Engaged?*"

"You have a boyfriend?" Dad's tone says, *That's news to me,* with a hint of displeasure.

"Yes. I mentioned him on Father's Day, I think?" I'd bet my big toes that he doesn't remember. He was too entranced with a new golf club Katt bought him. But it was a very handsome club. Limited edition. Autographed by some pro golfer Dad loves. "But I guess he's a fiancé now."

"Let me see that ring," Mom demands, leaning over. I extend my hand. She grabs and pulls it toward her. "How many carats?"

"Not sure." I shrug.

"You should know things like that." She tuts. "They're important. The bigger the rock, the more he loves you."

I pull my lips in. "I'll, um, make sure to find out."

Katt studies the ring. "Eh. It's not bad, just tiny."

Dad's expression stays taut as he leans over to glance at the ring, then looks at the stones on Mom's hands. Mine's smaller than Mom's for sure. His mouth relaxes a little. "Less than eight carats," he announces with authority.

"It's the sentiment that counts," I say, but I don't think anybody hears me.

"This barely passes for a ring. Why is the band loose?" Mom's eyes light up. "Wait—are you finally dieting like I told you to?"

I cough awkwardly. She's going to be disappointed. "No. There was a mix-up at the jeweler. We're going to get it resized, so it fits properly."

Mom visibly deflates.

"So who is this man? Shouldn't he have spoken to me first? Gotten my blessing?" Dad demands. "Neville and I already met. And I told him he was welcome to you if he wanted."

"You haven't met him," I say, ignoring Dad's statements about

Neville. "He was going to talk to you, but then got carried away in the moment. And I said yes because he's right for me."

"Right *how*? Is he rich?" Mom asks.

I swallow a sigh. Money never came up. It's so weird and awkward to ask anyway, like asking a guy you just met about his favorite sex position. "Well... He seems to be doing pretty well for himself. He drives a brand-new Lexus and has a swanky condo with the right zip code, so... I guess...?"

Mom looks at me like she's raised a hopelessly challenged child.

"Didn't you check?" Dad frowns. "Things like that are important. You need to make sure the man you marry can support you properly. It would be awkward if you had to rely on others." Translation: *You shouldn't think about mooching off Katt.*

"I *do* have a job. One that pays well."

Katt scoffs. "A pittance. Besides, it isn't a stable career. Josh can replace you any time with somebody better qualified. You didn't even go to college."

"Community college isn't bad," I say quietly.

"Still..." My sister shrugs.

I don't bother to point out she didn't go either, since it'll only escalate into a battle, with three of them ganging up on me. She barely finished high school, as her modeling career kept her too busy for something as plebian as going to school.

"Does it matter? With Josh wrapped around your fingers, surely he'll give her some slack," Mom tells Katt.

"I've been working for him for three years." It's like I'm talking to an empty room—nobody's looking at me.

"There are plenty of younger and prettier assistants," Dad says finally, swallowing a prawn.

It's very difficult to grind your teeth while smiling. "Assistants actually have to be able to perform."

Mom snorts. "How hard can grabbing coffee be? And doesn't AI do everything else? Once they figure out a way to get computers to brew coffee, you won't have a job."

"Please." Katt places a hand over Mom's arm. "Let's not be so judgmental. Besides, it's better that she works for Josh. I can trust her to keep an eye on him, if you know what I mean. Even if he means to stay faithful, there might be other women trying to seduce him."

The dismissively stated truth lances my heart. I hold my breath for a moment to contain the pang. I've been working so hard to get over my unrequited crush on Josh, and every time I think I'm making progress, something happens to show that I'm not. Still, I *will* get over it. It's for my own good—my own mental and emotional health.

But first, I have to stop Katt and Mom. Otherwise, they'll continue and plan out the entire wedding between her and Josh, and I'm not ready to smile through it yet. "Anyway, when are you going to know for sure about the role?" I change the subject to something the family can't resist.

Katt immediately perks up. "Hopefully in the next month or two."

"That's amazing." *Go on. Keep talking about yourself.*

"Maybe Katt can get you on as an extra. Help you break into the business," Mom says, leaning forward.

"If Ted Lasker needs somebody who can grind her teeth and smile at the same time..." I say, doing exactly that.

Mom laughs, oblivious. "That's just someone with a freak talent, not an *actress*."

"Yeah. Wonder what that would make the person's mother?" I say sweetly.

"Probably somebody just as freaky, but sometimes kids never end up the way you want." Mom looks at Katt indulgently. Dad nods before grabbing more fried rice.

I just refill my empty teacup. I should be used to this more. Katt's prettier and more successful. More confident too, and acts cute and spoiled around them like a little puppy princess. I'm the opposite. Not pretty enough, not tall enough, not thin enough. Not very bright, either. Too stiff, too awkward. And when I speak my mind, I apparently sound like a bitch, so I'd better think twice before saying anything.

I study my family. They're chatting and laughing, glowing like the happiest family in the world. I might as well be an outsider.

Maybe the problem is me. I don't fit in, like a glob of wasabi in a taco.

It's okay, I tell myself. Soon, I'm going to have my own family, where

I won't be wasabi. I'll be cheese. Or guacamole. Chad doesn't make me feel excluded. I feel okay around him.

"Excuse me," comes a hesitant voice. A visibly pregnant brunette in a wine-colored empire dress stops next to Katt with a slight smile. Her cheeks are flushed, and she bites her lower lip. "You're Katt Klein, right?"

"Yes." My sister's expression couldn't be more gracious. She believes in maintaining an angelic public persona.

"Oh *wow*! I'm *really* sorry to interrupt. I kept thinking and debating, but I just couldn't resist. Is it okay if I ask you to sign this for me?" The woman pushes out all the words in a breathless rush, then pulls a pastel-pink onesie and permanent marker out of a glossy white paper bag. "You're my *favorite* model."

Katt beams. Nothing makes her happier than people's adoration. "Of course. What's your name?"

"Autumn." The woman is absolutely crimson with shy joy.

My parents nod with approval. "We hope your baby will be as wonderful as our Katt," Mom says.

"Oh, is this a family dinner?" The woman grows even more flustered. "Oh my God, I'm so sorry."

"It's all right. We love meeting Katt's fans," Dad says with a broad grin.

My sister autographs the onesie with a flourish. "Here you go. Want to take a picture too?"

Autumn looks about to faint. I shift to catch her, just in case. Can't have a pregnant lady landing on her butt on the hard floor.

"*Can* I?" she squeals.

"Of course." Katt turns to me. "Could you do it for us?"

"Sure." I take Autumn's phone and take the photo. The woman's smiling so widely she looks like a crocodile. Katt made her night, if not her year. My chest tightens. Katt and I weren't like this before. We used to be close, sleeping under the same blanket and whispering our secrets and dreams until Mom came in to tell us to shut up and go to sleep.

But somewhere along the way, after her debut as a model, things changed. And now... Well. Here we are.

"Thank you," Autumn says to me as she takes her phone, then

pauses. "What an interesting ring." She looks up and gives me an odd look, her eyes darting at Katt and my parents briefly.

I frown a little, unsure why she's showing a low-grade hostility toward me.

"She just got engaged," Katt says.

"Engaged?" Autumn stares at my ring with unblinking intensity that makes me want to lower the hand. Except somehow that feels like a defeat. "When?" Her tone is oddly sharp—maybe even a little rude.

"Last night," I clarify, although her nosiness combined with suspicion is starting to irritate me. Why is it that even strangers treat me with disrespect? Do I have SUCKER written across my forehead or something?

"How odd. I recently lost a ring that looks *just* like that one. It was a first-anniversary gift from my husband." Her lips purse, her eyes still on *my* ring.

I stiffen. Is she accusing *me* of stealing *her* ring?

My parents and sister shoot me probing looks. *Are they kidding?*

Resentment starts welling. Why are they siding with a total stranger? This woman hasn't provided any evidence. But my family's subtle support seems to embolden her as she continues to stare down at me like she's a cop interrogating a suspect.

Continuing to sit puts me at disadvantage—she's doing everything possible to loom and physically intimidate me without actually touching. I stand, my right hand on the table. "Are you calling me a thief?"

"Maybe you should produce this fiancé of yours. Why would you have a dinner with your family without him? Shouldn't you be celebrating your engagement?" Autumn says.

I point at Katt. "This dinner isn't about me. But even if it weren't, he's in Charlotte, checking up on his ailing—"

"Hey, honey, what's taking so long? Didn't you already get the autograph for the baby?" A trim man in a button-down shirt and slacks rushes over and wraps an arm around Autumn protectively, keeping his back to me. But there's no way I'd fail to recognize that soft male voice.

Shock and outrage sucker-punch me. "*Chad?*"

6

JOSH

"You okay?" Ares asks as I methodically chow down on chow mein. Peking Town has the best noodles in the city, and carbs never fail to make me feel better.

I feign nonchalance. "Yeah. Dad had a 'chat' with me, but considering the situation, it wasn't as bad as I thought." *He thinks I might be fucking up my life and not living like a true Huxley. Where do you think I failed?* But I swallow the question along with the noodles. My suspicion is that he wants me to pull my head out of my ass and find someone I can imagine my future with, the kind of woman who would be worthy of belonging to the family. Except who could be the one? He might be right that I've purposely avoided suitable women, but—

Want a hug?

Klein's voice keeps ringing in my head. The offer felt like an escape into sanctuary, but she's totally off-limits. The firm doesn't have a rule against interoffice dating, but it's definitely frowned upon because of so many ways things could go wrong. And she always calls me "boss," like she can't imagine me as anything else. The soft gesture in the office was her pitying me because I probably looked like absolute shit after the talk with Dad. I should know better than to confuse the charming blush on her cheeks and the bright smile she gifts me every morning with something more intimate.

"What the hell was that about with Sarah?" Bryce scowls as he picks up a lobster chunk with a set of ivory chopsticks.

"Who?" I ask. He handles divorce, so he tends to get a fair number of highly emotionally clients who sometimes lose control in public.

"Sarah Norwal. The banshee in your office today. I thought my clients were bad, but..." Bryce squints at me. "You didn't know who she was?"

"Not really. Besides, Ted called her Nelly, then Sally."

"That's Ted." Ares shakes his head. "But shouldn't *you* remember her name? I mean, you slept with the woman."

I scowl. "I doubt that. She left no impression. At all."

Bryce swallows his lobster. "Then how did you check if she was the one? Don't you need to use your dick radar?"

"I think it's more like a probe," Ares says.

I sigh. "Sometimes my brain can tell without having to go that far."

"Hopefully this won't impact your performance eval," Ares says. He knows my tendency to downplay things to avoid worrying him and Bryce.

"I just got a warning not to have a repeat performance." I don't want to get into the details. "How's Fiona, by the way?" I change the topic before my brothers can probe too deeply. They're great at cross-examination. I can handle one, but when they tag-team? Yeah, not putting myself through that. "Still suffering from morning sickness?" It's been about three months since she found out she's pregnant. Bryce is crazy about her and the coming baby.

He shudders. "The only thing she wants to do is sleep and sleep some more. She avoids eating as much as possible. Apparently, the smell of food makes her nauseated. She can tolerate about a cup of dry cornflakes a day, but anything more than that..."

"Makes sense. It's your child, after all," I say.

"Hey now! I was an *angel*," Bryce protests, and throws a wadded paper napkin.

"At least she isn't craving celery sticks topped with key lime pie, like

Queen's friend," Ares says. His wife's name is Lareina, but he adoringly calls her Queen.

Bryce gags a little. "That's disgusting."

"Could be worse. Canned tuna and broccoli," I say. "That's what Jeremiah ate when she was pregnant."

"Ugh." Bryce shudders. "I guess I should count my blessings that Fiona doesn't want to eat bowls of boiled brussels sprouts."

Even though he acts like Fiona's food choices are the end of the world, if she told him that's what she wanted, he'd get it for her like a hopeless simp. It's fascinating how love has changed him. Just a few months ago, he swore he hated her.

I didn't trust her, either. I even put a bug and a tracker on her. Bryce was furious when he found out.

I study my twin. Has Dad ever said that *he* didn't act like a true Huxley? Or are things different with him because he's living his life the right way? We even put our poker nights on hold because Bryce can't bear to stay away from Fiona more than he has to, and we can't host it at his place since the smell of food would bother her too much.

So instead, we're meeting for dinner. That way Bryce can eat without triggering her morning sickness.

Ares's expression grows serious. "Mom hasn't tried to reach Fiona since the pregnancy, right?"

"No. If she had, Fiona would've told me." The muscles in Bryce's jaw flex.

Apprehension slithers down my spine. It isn't like Mom to be so quiet.

She isn't known for patience or subtle finesse. But then, she never had to suffer the consequences of her actions because her mob boss father Vincent shielded her.

Perhaps his actions created her belief that she'd be able to push her brother Harvey aside and take over the mob when her father passed away. When Vincent wanted to extend his criminal empire from Nesovia to the States, she decided seducing and marrying Dad in a whirlwind romance was the way to go. Huxley & Webber doesn't take on clients associated with organized crime, but she thought that once the Huxleys became the Dunkels' in-laws, the firm would be willing to help them plant their criminal roots here. When Dad discovered the truth and attempted to divorce her, she somehow decided that drugging and kidnapping us would change his mind.

Unfortunately, she never went to jail for that. Vincent offered up a low-level goon to rot in prison instead, and promised to keep her away from us kids until we all had turned thirty. There were other concessions, such as a smooth divorce, with Dad getting almost everything he wanted, but stopping her from getting to us as long as possible was the main one.

Except Mom never planned to honor the spirit of the promise. When I was fifteen, I caught my first serious girlfriend Jessica trying to slip something into my drink at a party. I flipped out; she burst into tears and confessed everything.

Mom had been supplying Jessica with party drugs. All she had to do was tell Mom what she wanted to know about my life, nothing complicated or bad. But then it escalated to having to hand over photos and stories, the kind of slices of life Mom couldn't get a hold of easily. Then the drugs in my drink because Mom wanted to see me without my noticing.

My mind went white, then red with rage. Uncontrollable tremors ran through me, and—swearing I'd kill Mom—I went home and grabbed Akiko's sashimi knife. Although I didn't go through with the impulsive plot, I did dump Jessica.

The only person I told about the incident was Grandma Catalina, although I didn't mention my fury-induced plan to murder Mom. Grandma said she'd deal with it. But I've never had a serious long-term girlfriend afterward. I kept an eye on Bryce's girlfriends as well—I didn't trust them to not sell him out either, even if Grandma *was* "dealing with it."

After all, the family thought they'd taken care of Mom, but it didn't really work. I felt the need to do something about it without sharing what happened and freaking out my brothers. Ares was already so damaged he couldn't even date, and Bryce only coped by getting a golden retriever that loved him unconditionally.

"I thought Mom would make a move by now. She tried to drug you to create a baby," Ares remarks.

My mouth twists in distaste. She hasn't changed her MO. Actually, that MO runs in the family. Harvey tried to drug Ares before, ostensibly to hire him. The Dunkels don't seem to realize drugging a Huxley isn't the most effective means of convincing us to do their bidding.

"Yeah, but maybe she gave up after I let Harvey have our sonograms," Bryce says.

My jaw drops. "You gave that son of a bitch sonograms of your baby? Why?"

"It was a figurative flipping of the bird. Mom wanted to use our baby to earn brownie points from Vincent."

That man's apparently become sentimental with age and ill health. Too bad he hasn't keeled over. For some reason, assholes seem to live forever. Probably not even Satan wants Vincent in hell.

Bryce continues, "I'm thrilled that my wife's pregnant, and I'm pretty sure it happened when Mom drugged me. But that doesn't mean I forgive her." His jaw hardens. "I'll never forgive her."

Ares pats his shoulder. Bryce carries guilt from the kidnapping— that Ares got caught trying to help him escape. I carry it, too, but do my best not to show it too much because it bothers Ares. He did it so we'd be spared some trauma, not live with the weight of self-blame.

"She won't stay down for long," Bryce says. "Harvey warned me that she isn't just fighting to take over the mob. She's also fighting for her life. Vincent might not be so forgiving if she had anything to do with their younger brother's death."

"I wouldn't put any stock in what a snake like Harvey says. He's probably mixed in enough fiction and exaggeration to manipulate us. He'd do anything to take over from Vincent," I say.

"Regardless, Mom's a ticking time bomb. And she won't tick forever." Ares turns to me, his eyes concerned. "I'm worried she's going to shift her focus to you."

I shrug. "Let her. I'd love a chance to tell her what I really think about her." For some reason, she hasn't tried to mess with me since her failure with Jessica, at least not that I've noticed. No notes, no calls, nothing.

You're just like me.

Fuck you, Mom. If I'm really like you, I hope I get to end you.

Bryce gives me a narrow, penetrating look, then scowls. "Don't try to be a hero. She's been patient, but when she's pushed too far, she pushes back. She hit me when she got frustrated at my lack of cooperation."

"She *hit* you?" Ares looks incredulous.

"When? Where?" Bryce never said, and I never noticed.

"A while ago in the parking garage." When we continue to stare, Bryce adds, "It was before I found out Fiona was pregnant."

Typical. Mom always claims she loves us, but ultimately it's just about her own selfish needs.

"I swear to God, when I see her—" Suddenly the fine hair on the back of my neck bristles. I stiffen, scanning the restaurant, and spot Klein walking behind the hostess.

The tension drains from my shoulders, but the prickling sensation lingers.

She's holding tiger lilies. What are they for? Is she here to meet with her fiancé and her family? Giving a little gift to commemorate their engagement is so her, but the idea sits badly in my belly.

And what is she doing here in the first place? She shouldn't even be in this restaurant. She's allergic to seafood, and Chinese cuisine is known to use a lot of seafood and seafood-derived ingredients. When I take Klein out to lunch to discuss her performance and quarterly metric goals, I always select restaurants where she can eat safely. Shouldn't her fiancé show at least that much consideration?

Maybe not. He couldn't even get the ring sized right. Careless son of a bitch.

She sits at a table occupied by a party of three. I recognize the blonde there—some model I reviewed a couple of contracts for when she was younger and fresher, before Klein started working for me. I try to recall her name. Kiara? Karina? Whatever. She made an impression because she spent more time trying to come on to me than listening to my explanations about the legal terms. Her mother, present at the meeting, beamed like she couldn't be more thrilled her barely legal child was acting like a cheap ho.

Some months ago, I ran into her at a social event. She acted excited to see me, and I smiled to avoid any awkwardness. Since that encounter,

I've seen her at several places, a little too often to be mere coincidence. I just ignore her, since she's too dumb to be working for Mom or Harvey. She's harmless, just annoying. Like a buzzing fly.

Does Klein know them? If so, how? She's nothing like those weirdos.

"What are you looking at?" Ares asks.

"Klein's here," I say without taking my eyes off her. She's so pretty with the flowers. The overhead lights hit the ring on her finger just right, making it glint. She adjusts the band position. I can't help thinking it again: *What kind of loser proposes with a ring that doesn't fit?*

Maybe that explains the tight set of her mouth. I'd be pissed if somebody gave me a shitty gift like that. Her smile is so pasted on, it looks painful. But her dinner companions don't seem to notice as they speak. Karina, or whatever her name is, takes the tiger lilies from Klein and puts them aside like some sort of spam. How rude.

"Didn't you say she's allergic to seafood?" Bryce squints at the table. "Huh. That really is her."

"Yeah." I grind my teeth when the people at the table look at her ring. Is she trying to show off her new relationship status? She must really love the asshole who couldn't get her ring size right. Maybe it's a metaphor—his dick's too small to fill her.

No. Don't think about her naked with another guy. Actually, why am I thinking about Klein being naked at all? She's a nice girl. Deserves a nice, normal guy with no baggage and no hang-ups. Somebody as sweet as her, not a man who might be genetically patterned like a sociopathic mafia princess.

But part of me wants to argue. What if I'm like Mom in everything *except* marriage?

Yeah, bet Mom thought she'd be great at it until she decided to kidnap her own kids.

"Stop staring at her like that. You look like you're starving. The food's on your plate, not between her boobs," Bryce says.

"I'm not staring at her breasts." My tone is testy. I wouldn't disrespect her like that.

"Fine." Bryce rolls his eyes. "You were staring at her lips."

I frown harder. "No, I was looking at her *smile.*"

A corner of Ares's mouth quirks. "She sure has a nice couple of smiles."

I shake my head, ignoring my brothers' teasing. How can they not notice the tension pouring out of her? Her shoulders are taut, and the smile is stiff. The poor girl hasn't touched anything on the table except some tea. What kind of shitty people invite you to a place where you can't eat, then proceed to feast in front of you?

Thankfully, Karina isn't a client anymore. I quit representing her after those awkward come-ons. And I wouldn't want Klein to have to deal with a woman that unpleasant.

Someone walks right into my sight. My heart stops, then starts racing, adrenaline spreading with each beat.

Harvey.

His dark brown hair is slicked back from his face, complete with soulless, hooded amber eyes and a mouth that always bears a fake smile. He tries to give off an air of civility by wearing dark suits. But tailored clothing can't hide the air of danger about him or the cruel savagery he's been known to unleash.

A sleek woman on his arm says something with a grin. Her hand rests on his chest, as though she's soothing a wild, unpredictable animal. The man is just as capable of the kind of unhinged violence as Mom. After all, they're siblings.

"*Harvey,*" I mutter.

"What?" Ares swivels, his body immediately coiling tight.

"Where?" Bryce turns, then stiffens. "What the hell is he doing here?"

"I'm going to murder that son of a bitch," Ares says. He's still bitter about Harvey drugging him. You can never be careful enough with the Dunkel family.

Harvey keeps on walking, smile bright. He sees us, points with his index, middle and ring fingers, then waves like a beauty pageant contestant about to walk off the stage. Then he jerks his chin at Klein's table.

I glance over, wondering what the hell he's been looking at. My gut tightens when I spot a strange woman hovering there.

I don't like it that Harvey specifically brought my attention there—

he doesn't do anything just for the hell of it. Why is Klein on his radar? And who's the pregnant woman, anyway?

Suddenly a man inserts himself between the woman and Klein, then spins around to face her with all the aggression of a rabid dog. I almost do a double take; it's a familiar face that I used to take great pleasure in punching, but there's no way I can ever forget the beady eyes and the smarmy smirk on his thin lips. Chad Buell, one of the greatest dickheads I ever had the misfortune of knowing.

I jump to my feet.

7

———

AILEE

"Wʜᴀᴛ ᴀʀᴇ ʏᴏᴜ ᴅᴏɪɴɢ ʜᴇʀᴇ? Aren't you supposed to be in Charlotte to see your father?" I demand, trying to control my emotions. My mind wants to jump to the most obvious explanation, but I take a deep breath. I'm not going to assume anything until I hear his explanation.

"I have no idea what you're talking about," Chad says. Despite his blustery and accusatory tone, his eyes are wide and pleading. *Please shut up.*

Except I'm not going to shut up. For God's sake, he just proposed to me last night! Got on his knees and told me he loved me, couldn't think of a better future than one that we shared together.

"Honey, do you know this woman?" Autumn says, her eyes on Chad.

My mind turns blank. Guess that's what happens when your head can't process what's going on. "I'm his—"

"She's a patient."

"A patient?" Autumn's eyes narrow, her hands clutching Chad like she's protecting her precious man from me. "Why is she wearing the anniversary gift you gave me, then?"

"Yes, why am I?" This ought to be good.

Chad maintains eye contact with Autumn, doing everything he can

53

to avoid looking at me. "I'm not sure. I found it in my office some time ago—you probably left it there when you came by, and I meant to bring it back and give it to you. Guess she took it during our last appointment. She must have seen it on my desk."

Katt raises both eyebrows. Dad chokes on his tea, and Mom clucks her tongue.

Blood shoots straight into my head as humiliation wells. "Are you calling me a *thief*?"

"No." Chad finally turns back to me. "I'm giving my wife a possible explanation as to why you might be in possession of her ring."

"*Wife*?" I screech.

He puts on a let's-all-be-reasonable expression, then attempts to spread his arms and fails, since his wife is still clinging to him. "Look, I don't want to make things more difficult. I know you're obsessed with me, but all I've ever done is clean your teeth—"

"Yeah, with your *tongue*." I fantasize about drilling his teeth without any anesthesia.

Chad flinches, his face turning white. Calculations flash in his eyes as he struggles for something to say that will salvage the situation.

"Oh my God, are you a home-wrecker?" Mom says with a hand over her chest. If she were wearing a necklace, she'd be clutching it.

Dad pats her back. His judgmental eyes accuse me of destroying a man's family. Katt merely presses her lips together, and but there's a hint of gleeful *schadenfreude* in her gaze.

Tears start to fall down my cheeks. I feel terribly alone. It's obvious that Chad is a shitty human being and a cheater, but *this*? "Shouldn't you at least have some faith in me and ask me for my side of the story before ganging up on me? He's a stranger to you!" My voice rises at the end despite myself.

My parents look at me like that thought has never crossed their minds. My chest feels weighted down by a giant boulder.

"What's going on, Klein?"

I close my eyes, then wipe the tears off my face as more of them fall. *Great.* Just *great.* Now even my *boss* can witness this embarrassing scene. There's no way I'm attending Katt's and his wedding. I wish an alien ship would just suck me up into it. Being kidnapped and experimented upon would be preferable to this.

"Hey, Josh!" Katt says with a wide grin. My parents wave as well, all smiles and warm welcome.

Josh ignores them. As I finally raise my eyes to his, the weight of his gaze intensifies the suffocating feeling knotting in my chest.

"She stole that ring," my sister says when I stay quiet, trying to find some dignified explanation for the situation. She points at the ring I showed him just this morning. "Apparently she's obsessed with her dentist."

"The man is *married*," Mom says in a scandalized voice.

"With a pregnant wife," Dad adds in case Josh is blind and missed Autumn's very noticeable bump.

I can barely breathe through the ball of resentment and misery lodged in my throat. Chad won't have to come up with anything to defend himself with because my family is doing all the dirty work. Their accusations pierce me, making my heart bleed. I brace myself for Josh's judgment. What else could he say after what my family told him?

"Interesting." Josh glances at the horrible ring I'd love to take off and throw in Chad's face, except that feels like admitting that Autumn and the rest are correct—the jewelry doesn't belong to me and I'm a weirdo who's harbors an unhealthy obsession with her dentist.

I press my lips and firm my chin. The tears finally come under control. Guess I'll get to maintain at least that much dignity.

"But Klein didn't steal anything," Josh states.

What? I jerk my face up at him, my jaw slack.

"But it's the same ring as the one he gave his wife," Katt insists before Autumn can say anything. The latter shoots my sister a grateful look, as bitterness surges within me again.

"Guess you just earned yourself a fan for life," I mutter. "Better yet, maybe *Autumn* can be your sister."

Autumn glares at me, while Katt snorts.

Josh lifts my hand, his thumb and forefinger toying with the diamond. "Actually, *I* gave her this ring."

I blink slowly, unsure if I heard correctly. Katt gasps, and my parents look at him wide-eyed. Even Chad opens and closes his mouth a few times. "Um. About that. Er..." he begins finally.

"Hey, Chad. Long time no see. How's your nose?" Josh's smile doesn't reach his eyes.

Wait...Josh and Chad know *each other...?*

"It's fine," Chad grinds out.

"Your plastic surgeon must be pretty good at his job, unlike you."

Chad turns crimson. "Stay out of this." He puffs his chest, although the move is counterproductive since it only accentuates the fact that he's shorter than Josh. And thinner too. Chad got his body from running and swimming mostly. Josh is built like he could rip Chad in half and throw both pieces to the North Pole.

Katt steps in between the two men radiating enough testosterone-laden hostility to start World War III. "You don't have to lie to protect Ailee, Josh."

I almost nod—for once, she's correct.

She adds, "I'd never ask you to sacrifice your integrity, not even to protect my family."

"Your family?" he says blankly.

"Yeah. Ailee's my twin sister. Fraternal, of course. And you know my mom, and that's my dad."

Josh gives her a funny look. "Huh. Would've never guessed you and Klein were twins."

I press my lips together, ignoring the small pang in my gut. Nobody realizes we're even sisters, so it shouldn't bother me that he didn't, either. We're just too different in appearance and temperament.

Then his gaze cools. "But what makes you think you're in a position to ask me anything?"

Katt turns white. "Josh—"

He puts his arm around my shoulders. His body heat envelops me, chasing away the chill. I shouldn't let him hold me like this, but I can't bring myself to pull away. Suddenly my family's betrayal doesn't seem so painful.

"It's absurd." Mom lets out a shaky laugh. "She said the ring was an engagement ring." The subtext is clear: *Why would a man like* you *want a girl like* her?

Thanks, Mom. I bite my lip, feeling small.

Josh's eyebrows pinch tightly, forming deep lines between them. "Yes, it is." He shoots my parents an even look. "Because I proposed to her." He turns to me with the most saccharine look in his eyes. "Didn't you tell them, honey?"

8

JOSH

The whole table falls silent. **Klein** looks at me like I've just lost my mind. But I'm not letting a bunch of donkey-butt lickers bully her, especially not on Chad Buell's behalf. I've met a lot of trust fund babies—hell, I *am* one—but he's the worst. Entitled, spineless and prone to cheating to get what he wants.

He and I belonged to a kickboxing team in high school, and he once tried to punt my balls in a bout that he wasn't going to win otherwise. He said, "Sorry," when his foot missed—because he was that foolishly uncoordinated—but his eyes gleamed with disappointment.

So I punched him in the face. It was fun to listen to his high-pitched, gurgling scream. And satisfying as hell to hear his knees hit the ground. Not my fault his nose was so fragile. He dropped out afterward and joined the golf team. Heard he wasn't very good at that, either— probably couldn't hit a ball that small. I didn't realize he'd became a dentist.

I resist the temptation to strike him in the mouth, just because it touched Klein's. Actually, he slept with her. *Disgusting.* That poor girl's going to need a whole-body bleach. He's probably more diseased than a wild dog covered in fleas, and far less redeemable. The bastard couldn't even buy a ring for Klein. What kind of asshole not only cheats but gives his wife's ring to another girl?

Now I want to break his balls. Don't even feel guilty about it, since he already managed to procreate. God have mercy on his wife.

Karina finally jumps to her feet. "*What?*"

"You heard me. Klein and I are engaged." Why is she so upset?

"You don't have to go that far. Or...wait. Is this because you fucked my sister once? Oh my God, don't worry about it! I won't hold it against you." Karina's voice says every man makes mistakes, and she's magnanimous enough to let it go.

Except I didn't make a mistake, and I couldn't care less what she thinks. To be honest, I have no clue why she's acting like she has some sort of proprietary claim on me. It's more than a little creepy, especially coming from a woman who's virtually a stranger.

"This has nothing to do with you, her relationship to you or what you imagine might have happened between me and Klein." My tone is arctic, the kind I reserve for assholes who try to mess with my clients.

"But..." Chad begins, his eyes skittering everywhere as he searches for something to say. He undoubtedly wants his ring back, but isn't sure how to get it. His brain isn't big enough to come up with something slick to say and calculate how much he may have to pay out in alimony at the same time. He was always slightly below average, barely climbing up to "average" if he cheated. "But that can't be right. The ring's engraved. *Love you* on the inside and *Forever and ever* outside."

"Exactly." Karina's sharp nod irritates the hell out of me. This doesn't concern her. She isn't smart enough to speak for Chad, either. "Besides, the rock's too small," she says to me. "You'd do better than that, even if it was just for Ailee."

Klein isn't "just Ailee," but Karina's right that I'd never buy a ring this shitty. I pretend to consider for a moment. "The rock looks pretty on her finger, so I didn't think the size would matter so much. But maybe I shouldn't have given her a family heirloom for the engagement. It might be better suited for the actual wedding or when we have our first baby."

"A family heirloom?" Karina spins toward Klein. "*You really got engaged to Josh?*"

I wince at the shrill tone. *My ears.*

"Is this true?" Karina's mother demands, her face red and her eyes blazing. "Did you steal Katt's man?"

Klein shrinks back at the feral way the older woman glares at her. Her mom looks like she might jump over the table to claw her.

Not on my watch. I step forward, placing myself in front of Klein like a shield. "Who's Katt?" I ask, bristling with annoyance that the woman's acting like I belong to a someone I've never heard of.

Karina looks at me like I just gut-punched her. Klein stares at me, then her sister, then back at me, confusion clouding her pretty face. It dawns on me. *Ohhh... Katt. That's it.*

"Me!" Karina—or *Katt*—slaps a hand over her impressive bosom, which is heaving right now, drawing all the male attention to it. "We've been together for months now."

I raise an eyebrow. "I have no idea what you're talking about, and I don't think you do, either."

"We texted—"

"Never received one from you."

"—and have been to a lot of the same events—"

"I had my own dates, none of whom were you."

"—and we had so many deep conversations."

"Nothing comes to mind."

"Josh!"

"Yes, that's my name. So what?" My eyes sweep over the table. "Guess you didn't order anything Klein could eat, given her seafood allergy. I'll take her someplace where she can enjoy her food. Didn't realize my fiancée would be dining with people so inconsiderate and crude. Otherwise, I wouldn't have let her ditch me for *her family* tonight."

Katt's shaking so hard, she looks like she's about to have a stroke. Actually, seeing how unnaturally red she is, she might've already had one. Her parents are too busy fussing over her and arguing what to do about a child as unruly and evil as Klein. The pregnant woman is speechless. Chad continues to stare at the ring like a dog staring at a steak getting away. But he knows better than to act. Aside from the potential for another rhinoplasty, he's aware that my family owns one of the most aggressive law firms in the country.

Klein looks down, her cheeks scarlet and her teeth digging into her lower lip.

I cup her chin and swipe my thumb over the mouth. "Don't let the opinions of people who don't matter get to you."

She blinks up at me, her mouth parted. Her sweet breath feathers over my skin. A tingling sensation spreads all the way to the top of my skull.

I pick up her purse, then squeeze her shoulders and turn her around. She stiffens at the sight of Ares and Bryce, who just witnessed the scene. They give me knowing grins, then smile at her. Klein's muscles grow tense under my palms, and I give my brothers a warning look. Unlike them, she's sensitive.

"Hey, sister-in-law," Ares says with a laugh.

I nod inwardly with approval.

"What?" Klein croaks.

Bryce winks. "Be gentle with Josh. His heart's more delicate than you think."

9

JOSH

Klein takes my arm and pulls me out of the restaurant. My brothers wave goodbye with little smirks, most likely amused that I'm letting my tiny assistant drag me around. My heart is beating a bit wrong—too funny, too unsteady—but I know I'm doing the right thing.

It didn't take long to figure out the relationship dynamics at Klein's table. Her family... They were absolutely horrific. And I've seen my share of ugly things families do to each other.

Klein's family wasn't even fighting for money or power. At least I could understand that. They were putting her down just because they could—and because they enjoyed cutting her to pieces. Their eyes were practically glowing.

As soon as we're out on the street, Klein starts swiveling her head. What's she looking for? If I were her, it'd be a murder weapon to use on Chad.

"What do you need?" I ask, ready to give her my Huxley cane if she wants something to beat Chad up with. I'll even volunteer to hold him down so she can focus.

"A quiet café..."

A little disappointing, but Klein is a pacifist.

Her phone buzzes in her purse; she glances at the screen before dropping it back into the bag. "Or maybe a Starbucks?"

I point to a little mom-and-pop doughnut and coffee shop tucked between an independent bookstore and a narrow alley. "How about that one?"

"That works."

Klein's hand remains on my arm. *Does she know what she's doing?* She's always been careful to maintain a professional distance. Harder to do now, of course, since I announced in front of everyone that we're engaged. If Bryce is smart, he'll give Chad's pregnant wife his card. It looked like she could use his expertise.

I don't say anything because the feel of her hand on me is as sweet as a slice of heaven. Not sure why Klein has such an impact on me. It wasn't like this when we first met, but over the years, her unique influence on my mood has grown. My family arouses feelings of duty and loyalty, my clients...obligation. But Klein's touch makes me want to wrap myself around her and bask in that special warmth that makes me feel good to the core.

So I let myself indulge with a bone-deep appreciation that elicits a sigh. This won't last forever. We need to go back to keeping things proper between us soon, although with an appropriate exit plan, so Klein doesn't end up getting embarrassed because of me. My heart rebels, but I clamp down on it. I know better than anybody why it's necessary.

Ultimately, I don't trust myself. Mom said she loved Dad—and us—but betrayed everyone to get what she wanted. And Harvey apparently said that Mom even killed their younger brother because he was in the way.

What if—someday—I do the same? Hurt everyone I vowed my loyalty to, to achieve my goal and not feel any guilt about it? What if I become blind in the pursuit of my own goals and forsake my loved ones?

Although I'd like to believe I'm not a sociopath, part of me is deathly afraid of turning out to be like her. There have been dark urges and thoughts over the years.

When the Dunkels are out of the picture and Mom's not around to trigger me... Only then might I be able to relax—*possibly*. When I'm completely sure of myself, I might be worthy of a good girl like Klein.

So ask her to wait for you.

For how long? There's no deadline to this. She could wait forever.

We step inside the charming little café. Some upbeat Taylor Swift fills the quaint space. The pleasantly cool air smells like sugar, butter and flour. Perfect. Just the thing Klein needs. She's gotta be suffering from low blood sugar by now. The strawberry cupcake was hours ago, and I know she didn't touch anything at Peking Town.

She lets go of me as she peers at the glass display. I eye her hand wistfully, wishing it was still on me—but the moment is broken and isn't coming back.

Turning my attention to the cheery cashier, I order a couple of chocolate-glazed doughnuts and a cappuccino. Klein gets a decaf latte. Her phone buzzes again. While she's busy checking it, I pay for everything, since that's the least I can do. After the cashier places everything on a tray, we move into a relatively empty seating area. Most people are having dinner, not munching on over-sugared fried dough.

"Here." I push the plate of doughnuts toward her.

"How about you, boss?"

Her calling me boss is like a needle prickling the pad of my thumb—irritating and stinging. It's a constant reminder of where she's placed me in her world. At the same time, I should be grateful she doesn't want to cross any lines. It keeps her safe. "Ate at the restaurant. I got these for you. Chocolate's your favorite." Just like the strawberry cupcake. The latter's my favorite too, but Bobbi's Sweet Things only had one left earlier today, so I had the raspberry cupcake, my backup choice.

Klein gives me a wan smile. "Thank you. You're always so thoughtful."

The smile soon disappears as she bites into the doughnut. Is it not very good?

"I don't even know where to begin..." She sighs. "I'm sorry you had to get involved. And your brothers for having to see the scene. You must be thinking I'm an idiot to fall for a guy like that." Her entire body collapses like a broken accordion.

I put a finger under her chin and lift it up. "Hey. Chin raised and back straight. Don't beat yourself up. You just got fooled. He's the bad guy for being dishonest."

The corners of her lips twitch, but she doesn't smile. "Yeah...but I should've known it was too good to be true."

What does that mean? The only thing too good to be true was a maggot-eating invertebrate like Chad getting her to agree to marry him. "Don't let him win by dragging you down, Klein. I got your back."

The downturned tips of her mouth begin to lift. She polishes off the first doughnut, then begins to lick the melted chocolate on her fingers. The motion is small and economical, nothing like the disgusting, giraffe-like displays my exes have tried. And I can't look away, absolutely mesmerized by the innocent act.

The air becomes thick. My dick starts to stir.

Shit.

I tug at my tie, feeling suffocated. Shifting my weight, I glide the plate closer toward her, hoping she doesn't notice anything.

"I hope what happened tonight doesn't mess up your future plans," Klein says.

"Future plans? You mean my dinner with my brothers? Because it really wasn't that big of a deal."

"No, you know... Your wedding." She clears her throat. She can't quite meet my eyes as she uses a finger to dab up the crumbs on the plate. "You should marry the one you love. And I should, too."

The words hit me like a series of well-executed punches. It sounds like she's saying she could never love me. Well, I already knew I wasn't her type, but hearing it from the source cuts deep. "I don't have any plans for a wedding." My voice is a lot terser than I intend.

Her shocked eyes collide with mine. "Still?"

"What do you mean, 'still'? I've never had any." The kind of women who buzz around me aren't the type who'd last, not when they find out what I'm really like. Actually, that isn't precisely correct. To be honest, I don't even know what I'm really like. I try to avoid giving in to my impulses and instincts as much as possible when I'm around people.

I keep things light. Simple. Make sure nobody takes me too seriously, except for work. I also make sure to not care too much about other people, except my family. That way I'll never be in a situation where I'll have to make a difficult choice and learn something about myself I never wanted to discover.

There's a part of me that wonders what might've happened if Ares hadn't called me when I glared at the hotel she was staying at, the knife clenched in my hand. I managed to conceal the fact that I took Dad's car out, but I wouldn't have been able to hide stabbing my own my mother.

Klein's phone buzzes yet again.

I frown. "Is it important?"

She shakes her head. "No. Just...some spam. Anyway, I guess...she'll be disappointed."

"Who?"

"Katt, of course." Klein gives me a puzzled look.

I cock my head, still not getting it. "Why will she be disappointed?" And why does Klein care anyway? Katt was a complete bitch to her.

"Because she was planning on marrying you, and I just ruined it for her."

I close my eyes briefly and wait for Klein to elaborate. Why would Katt—and her family, apparently—have ever thought that? She acted like a tramp when she was my client years ago. Has she harbored some weird obsession since then? I shudder. That's creepy, a lot like Mom's unhealthy obsession with me and my brothers.

Klein fidgets a little and clears her throat. "I didn't mean to make things awkward by hiding my relationship with Katt or anything. She doesn't like it much if I let people know we're related. I'm sort of... embarrassing."

What the fuck? What's embarrassing is Katt and those shitty parents, not Klein.

She continues, "It's just best if I stay away from her personal life. It bothers her when it looks like I might have an opinion about something related to her life, or—worse—like I might've interfered. I mean, she's doing way better than me anyway. So when she told me about her and your marriage plan, I just smiled and nodded."

"Okay." I hold up a hand. "But *why* would you think I'd marry your sister? It's not like she can unilaterally just decide to marry me."

She shoots me a look that says, *Are you kidding?* "Boss...you've been seeing her for seven months, while she's waiting for you to...get things out of your system. Nobody lasts that long in your dating life." She shrugs helplessly.

"*Seven months?* I didn't even know her name!"

"But..." Klein taps her phone a few times and flips it toward me to show what's on the screen. "Look."

I glance at the Instagram account—which belongs to "Katt"—and scowl. It has tons of photos, most of them too perfect to be mere snapshots, although she tried very hard to make them seem that way. Many of them are of me and her, except I don't remember being this close to her. When I go to any sort of social gatherings, I stick to my network, people who have been vetted not to have any connection to the Dunkels. When I go clubbing and hook up with someone, I make sure to pick women who are so transparent Mom would never consider using them against me.

"These photos are fake," I say.

Klein's eyes turn as round as mini saucers. Guess it's never crossed her mind that her sister might be a liar. "They are?"

"I was never around her like this. Besides..." I squint at one where I have my arm around Katt's waist and a shit-eating grin on my face. "It's AI. I certainly never put my arm around her."

"AI?"

"Yeah. Look at the fingers." I point to the corner. "They're a bit too long and awkward."

Klein takes her phone and stares. "Oh wow. You're right."

"So you don't have to feel guilty toward your sister. You haven't ruined anything, Klein. You could never ruin anything."

She lowers her phone and gives me a soft, shy smile. "Thank you. I think that's one of the nicest things anybody's ever said to me."

I shrug. "Just being honest."

"Well, honesty deserves gratitude, too. Also, thanks for coming to the rescue, boss. I'll find a graceful way to get us out of the situation soon. Count on it."

Her reassurance should cheer me up. After all, isn't this what I want?

To protect her from the humiliation of being deceived by Chad and the judging eyes of her shitty parents? I knew I had to come up with a plan to undo my lie about proposing to her—even reminded myself of all the reasons I'm not right for her.

But I can't feel anything positive about her eagerness to be free of me.

10

AILEE

By the time I get home, my phone is about to explode with notifications from my parents and Katt. They kept texting when Josh bought me doughnuts and coffee. Ignoring them didn't seem to help. The longer I stay silent, the more determined they become.

Now a new text arrives every minute. I ignore them, since nothing good will come of it. I don't want to upset myself anymore, especially when I'm still reeling from what happened.

I can't figure out why Josh jumped in like that. He's a lawyer—a great one—not a sucker. He has to know lying like that in public would create problems for him. He even gave Katt a verbal smackdown, then said he didn't know her.

Surprisingly enough, I believe him. I even believe him over the photos on her Instagram account. The fact that I trust him so easily is a bit surprising. After all, I just got burned by Chad. You'd think it'd be a long while before I'd believe any man again. About anything.

Josh offered to buy me dinner, but I declined since I didn't want to take up more of his time, especially when he'd already eaten and probably wanted to go back to his brothers. They're tight, unlike me and Katt. I envy the bond he has with them—it would be nice to have people unconditionally on my side. The only time my family's on Team Ailee is when it can benefit Team Katt.

Letting out a breath and expelling the messy emotions from the evening, I toe off my shoes and toss my bra into the laundry basket. I microwave the leftover lasagna and grab a flavored tea from the fridge. Although the doughnuts were fabulous, they aren't a substitute for real food.

About the time I place the reheated lasagna on the table, the door opens and Max walks in. She vibrates with the boundless energy born of late-afternoon cappuccino. Her copper-red hair lies sleek—unlike mine—and her makeup is flawless, the mascara and eyeliner still looking fresh. Even the emerald sheath dress she put on yesterday morning before going to the office is wrinkle-free and pristine. Her green eyes are wide as she comes straight for me.

Before I can say, "Hey," my best friend lets out a piercing scream of excitement and outrage and hugs me.

"You're going to turn me deaf," I say, wincing.

Finally, she calms down enough to pull back and articulate. "Holy *shit*, roomie! What the *hell*? The fucking asshole is *married*, and you're actually engaged to your hot-as-hell *boss*?" The glint in her eyes ping-pongs between rage and admiration.

I blink. "What? How did you know? Did Katt harass you, too?"

Max snorts. "She wishes!" Unlike most people, Max isn't impressed with Katt's fortune or fame. Probably because she was our next-door neighbor and grew up with us since we were five. "It's all over the internet."

"Wait, wait, wait. What is? Start from the beginning." I take a bite of lasagna.

"Everything that happened to you today since you got to the restaurant. By the way, Katt's a bitch for having you go to Peking Town. I think somebody filmed it when they saw her talking with the fan girl, you know, the one who turned out to be your *dentist fiancé's pregnant wife*? And then they couldn't stop themselves and posted the whole thing live on Instagram, and it went viral. It's like Jerry Springer, but more modern and upscale, without the moron audience."

I wince and swallow the lasagna. *Great.* "Was I recognizable in the video?"

"Totally. And of course so was Katt."

I exhale shakily. This just feels...surreal. I'm not the kind of person who stars in a viral video. Actually...was I even the star? Whoever put it up probably wanted to focus on Katt. "Oh, I see," I say, although my tone's more like *shit.* "And Mom was checking me out to see if I looked good when I arrived."

"Girlfriend, you looked amazing. And your boss? That man's ass is *chef's kiss.*" Max makes a kissing noise and does the fingers.

Totally, but I'm not sharing my thoughts on that with her. It'd only encourage her. "Were you staring at his ass the entire time?"

"No. But the person who filmed it moved their phone around until they could get his ass, too. Priorities. Anyway, that *jerk!* I *knew* something was off about him! He was just too slick for a dentist!"

"You didn't think he was too bad last night," I point out.

She crosses her arms. "No. I texted to ask if you were sure, then told you not to do anything hasty, like eloping, until we could talk today. I swear, my boss is the least helpful person in the world!" She shakes her head.

I nod in sympathy, since she couldn't even come home last night. The man works her hard. If the pay and perks weren't so fabulous, she would've quit a long time ago.

She continues, "I've been trying to tell you this. When I went into that monkey-butt-face's office for a cleaning two weeks ago—"

"You mean to check and see what he was like," I correct her dryly.

"—he fondled my gums with his finger with this *look* on his face. You know, the look guys get when they're watching porn and jerking off."

"I'm afraid I don't have your depth of experience. But how could you tell? Wasn't he was wearing a mask?"

"Yeah, but his eyes—they were creepy. Looked like he was getting a hard-on from it. And trust me, I recognize hard-on eyes when I see 'em."

"Ew. How come you didn't tell me?"

"I *tried*, but you got distracted because he kept texting you that evening. You were annoyed, and it sounded like you were going to dump him, so I didn't want to pile on when you were already acting really bummed about it. If he was on the way out anyway, why add insult to injury?" Max clears her throat awkwardly, then purses her lips. "I totally freaked out when you texted that you got engaged!"

I sigh. "I should've paid more attention to you."

"I'm just glad you're done with him!" Her eyes flash with renewed annoyance. "Scumbag. I should've punched his face when he told me that a gum massage is complimentary to all new patients. Ugh! With that smarmy smirk!" She executes a pretty decent left hook, making me laugh.

My phone vibrates on the table again. Another text from Mom. I try not to sigh, but it's impossible.

"What's that? Better not be that asshole trying to get you back."

"It's just Mom, wanting to know when I'm coming back to apologize to Katt."

"For what?"

"Stealing her fiancé." I shovel more food into my mouth.

Max's jaw slackens. "She was engaged to Chad, too?"

"No! Josh. Well, he hasn't proposed, but Katt called dibs on him, I guess? I mean, they were seen together all the time, at least on Instagram. Except he told me Katt faked those photos."

"*Loooooord*." Max's voice is full of an eye roll. "That girl's about as genuine as Corinthian leather. And I don't want to say this, because I know you care about your mom...but she *sucks*. I'll probably never forgive her for calling you a home-wrecker."

I sigh. "Yeah. That's why I've been ignoring their texts. I don't want to see them until they get a chance to calm down."

"I get to be your maid of honor when you marry Josh, right?"

"You'll be my maid of honor no matter what, but I'm not marrying him."

"Why not?" She narrows her eyes. "Wait—some kind of disease?"

"What? No! He's fine! It's just... He didn't really mean it, Max. It was a pity engagement, something he said to save my dignity. It'd be weird for me to act like it was real. Plus, he's almost never seen with the same woman twice, and I'm ninety-nine percent sure he's blacklisted *all* his exes. Lucky for me, he likes me and I do a good job for him, so I'm safe for the moment. But if I want to *stay* safe, I need to get the hint and do the right thing and end the 'engagement' before he gets restless. I'll *die* if he starts looking at me like I'm pathetic."

"Oh, come on. Give yourself some credit. What's wrong with you?"

"Have you seen the women he dates?" I shake my head. "Trust me. It's best I stay in my lane."

"Change your damn lane. Carpool! Problem solved."

"Ha! Easy for you to say. You're gorgeous."

"So are you." Her phone pings, and she looks at the screen and lets out a frustrated breath. "Ugh. I gotta pack."

"For what?"

She closes her eyes wearily. "My boss wants me to accompany him to London. *Now*. It's a good thing I have a passport."

"Don't let him work you too hard." Her boss can be more melodramatic than a husky that's been left at home. The man lives to work.

She blows air out through slack lips. "I'll try, but no guarantees." She pulls out a suitcase from her closet and curses. "Hey, mind if I borrow your suitcase? One of the wheels broke on mine and I forgot to replace it."

"Yeah, sure. Go ahead." I gesture for her to raid my closet.

"Thanks, girl."

While she gets busy packing, I put the plate in the dishwasher and take the trash out. Tomorrow's pickup day, and I don't want to rush in the morning.

On the way out, I run into a new neighbor. I haven't learned much about her, except that her company sent her here from Vegas at the beginning of the month. A large black duffel bag is slung over a shoulder, and she's in a dark gray tank top, black sports bra and yoga pants. A thin sheen of sweat still glistens on her flawless skin and clings to her dark hair. She must've expended quite a bit of energy in the gym, but her steps are extra light, deep satisfaction etched in every line on her stunning face. Her blue eyes light up when she sees me.

"Taking out the trash?"

"Yeah. How was the workout?"

"Fabulous. You can never get strong enough." Her eyes drop to the ring on my finger. "Nice. But...an heirloom?"

"What?"

"I saw the video. So you're engaged to that tall guy. He looks like a fighter."

I flush. "Uh. Yeah. He's my boss, actually. And the ring is...a bit complicated."

"I suppose so." She smiles, the corners of her eyes crinkling. "Well, regardless, congratulations. One of these days, you should tell me all about it."

"There isn't much to tell."

"Nonsense. When a woman gets engaged in a viral video, there's plenty of gossip. I'll even bring over some chocolate chip cookies to bribe you after my business trip. They're to die for. Everyone says so, including my kids. Even my younger brother."

"I'd love to try your cookies, but don't blame me if you're disappointed by the lack of juicy details."

She laughs. "Never."

"If you're sure." I grin. Good night, Zoe."

EARLY THE NEXT MORNING, my apartment complex goes up in flames.

11

——————

JOSH

THE MOMENT I step into the elevator in the Huxley & Webber lobby, I run into Dad. It's early enough that the car's empty except for us two.

A bit unusual. One of the perks of being a senior partner is that you don't have to come in at the crack of dawn. Aunt Jeremiah likes to come in early, but she's single and addicted to work. Dad prefers to have a light breakfast with his wife before coming over, unless there's a crisis that can't wait.

"Why are you here so early? Some emergency too urgent to allow coffee with Akiko?"

"She couldn't fall asleep last night. Then as soon as the sun was up, she pushed me out the door." Dad sounds like a grouchy bear.

Akiko can be a little out there—being born to a Zaibatsu family that controls a fabulously wealthy and powerful multinational conglomerate in Japan makes her a bit out of touch at times. But she's one of the nicest people I know. And she was brave to marry a single father with three trauma-impacted boys.

"What did you do?" I raise an eyebrow, unable to imagine how he could've upset her that much. She's too even-tempered. You'd have to cover yourself in dogshit and roll around on her freshly waxed floors before she *might* raise her voice.

"*Me?*" Dad bristles. "I'm not the one who announced an engagement to his assistant in a ridiculous video that went rival! A *family heirloom?*" If words had legs, his would be kicking my ass. "Akiko wanted to know which ring you were talking about because she swears she hasn't given you anything. And I know it certainly wasn't from your grandmother or aunt. And Jeremiah isn't sentimental enough, anyway." His eyes narrow with suspicion. "It isn't from Zoe, is it?"

I recoil. "Hell no!"

The car stops on my floor and the doors open. He puts a restraining hand on my chest, hits the *Close* button and gives me an unreadable look. "My office."

Oh, joy. Two office chats with Dad in less than twenty-four hours. *This will go well.*

We go up another floor and walk down to his office. He takes his seat and gestures for me to sit down.

I park my ass and face him, propping an ankle on my knee and trying to stay relaxed. It's obvious that being the spokesperson for the Fogeys—the elders of the family—has been delegated to him. Grandma doesn't believe in interfering unless she thinks Dad isn't handling us correctly. What little maternal potential Aunt Jeremiah might've had she used up on her son, who, despite having excelled at Harvard Law, refuses to join Huxley & Webber in a blatant show of rebellion against the Fogeys. And Akiko feels uncomfortable lecturing us, keenly aware that she's our stepmom.

Dad will likely complain about the heirloom lie, and then he'll want to question my relationship with Klein. The Fogeys rarely deviate from their desires and preferences. They'd like all of us boys to be settled, successful and happy. They want proof that all the expensive therapy they got for us was enough to repair all the damage Mom's kidnapping did. They even forced a relationship on Ares to see if he was healed. Bryce, fortunately, got married before they could get involved.

But me? I'm the black sheep. The one who's still "out there." Their needs might appear selfish on the surface, but they're only doing it because they care—and they desperately want to be sure they were able to fix us.

"Tell me honestly. Why are you suddenly engaged?" Dad asks finally. "This isn't like you."

"Oh? What *is* like me?"

He blinks. "I'm...not sure, actually."

The response cuts. He would never say that about Ares or Bryce.

"Are you going to dump her within a month?" he asks, his eyebrows snapping together.

"No!"

"She's a nice girl, Josh. So don't embarrass her. That'd be disappointing."

"I won't." My voice is firm.

"Good. I expect you to stick with her for at least six months and listen to your heart rather than your head when you deal with her as your fiancée. Otherwise, there will be both familial and professional consequences."

My gut clenches. Does he mean the family will shun me as being unworthy of the Huxley name, and the firm will withhold my path to partnership? It's a little unusual for him to be vague, but then, he might want me to suffer in suspense. Or to just keep his options open. "Fine." It comes out curtly, but I don't care.

"By the way, Akiko wants to meet her. Tonight."

"Jesus, that's less than eight hours' notice. Klein might have plans."

Dad gives me his I-thought-so nod a little too easily. Guess meeting Klein tonight was really Grandma's idea; otherwise he'd argue. You'd think retirement would have mellowed her out, but she's gotten more impatient, like she's keenly aware of how little time she has left now.

"This Friday at seven, then," Dad says.

"I'll ask, no guarantees."

"Try." His tone says, *Make it happen.*

"I'll *ask.*" I'm not subjecting Klein to anything she doesn't want to do. "Just so you know, Klein's allergic to seafood. And small portions."

I like Akiko, but she serves food portions so miniscule they would barely satisfy a two-year-old. My brothers and I always feel like we're starving at the family dinners. It's so bad that Ares grabs a Big Mac and Bryce scarfs down half a pizza before heading over. I usually get a couple of beef-and-cheese tacos from Manny's.

Dad snorts. "I'll let Akiko know."

I make an exaggerated motion to check the time. "Well, gotta go. Those contracts aren't going to review themselves." I get up and go to my office.

The pink flowers Klein placed on my desk yesterday make a cheery greeting. I start my laptop, pull the largest blossom to my nose and inhale. The baby-soft petals tickle, the scent soft and sweet, just like the woman who brought them in.

How am I going to ask her to stay engaged to me for six months?

Based on the conversation yesterday, she doesn't seem to believe that there's any future between us. Not only that, she wants to marry somebody she loves—and I'm ninety-nine percent certain that isn't me. It doesn't seem fair to ask her to waste half a year of her life just so I can avoid Dad's consequences.

But a selfish part of me wants to. I can't bear to be seen as unworthy of the family motto—or of carrying on the legal legacy. Without those, I'm just...lost. Might as well be a fucking Dunkel.

I shove my hand into my hair and flex my fingers, huffing out a frustrated breath. The slight pain on my scalp doesn't help me focus any better.

A knock at the door, and I put the flower back into the vase. My heart skips a beat with anticipation at the idea of facing Klein, even though I still don't know what I'll offer to convince her to stay with me for six months.

The door opens, and Barry sticks his head in. Something inside me deflates.

"Hey, heard you got engaged," he says.

I sigh. "The video?"

"Of course! Everybody's seen it, unless they live in a cave somewhere."

I make a bland noise in my throat. He isn't here to congratulate me.

"We gotta have a bachelor party," he says.

I knew it. "That'd be a little premature. We haven't even set a wedding date."

"So? We can have one now...and then another one later, if you want."

"You mean *you* want to have another one later."

"Hey, practice makes perfect. Have I ever failed anyone at the firm? It's going to be amazing. And you should thank your lucky stars—I have this *great* idea for your party."

"What about Bryce?"

Barry makes a face. "I was actually going to use it for Bryce's party. But he says he can't until his wife gives birth, so you're the lucky winner."

"Let me guess." I tap my chin with mock seriousness. "Instead of ten strippers, I get twenty."

Barry's eyebrows go up. "That's not a bad idea. You're learning."

I roll my eyes, although I can't help my mouth twitching.

He just laughs. "Anyway, congrats! I'll let you know!"

"No party until the wedding date's set—!" But the door shuts, and knowing Barry, he'd just ignore me even if he heard.

I read an email from Ted, which happens to be at the top of my inbox. He's insisting on getting fifty percent off on the option if he and the writer happen to sleep together, especially since he's convinced he can sleep with her before the contract's executed. I swear to God, the man's mind has one track, nothing else. I almost wish his vasectomy would fail again and he'd get hit with another seven children, all under the age of one. That would keep him occupied. When he's distracted, he makes a great client because he basically does what I tell him without arguing. The real problem is Joey. He flatters and encourages Ted in every ridiculous folly, clapping and cheering like some kind of demented one-man fan club.

I send a quick email shooting down the idea and advising Ted to just lower the sum if he doesn't want to pay what the author asked for. That's part of a proper negotiation, not trying to put a clause accepting monetary compensation for sex into the contract. Besides, the author lives in Vermont. She's not going to fly out to California for Ted, no matter how nice his dick might look in a pic.

I drop my forehead in my palm. Good God, I hope he hasn't sent one to her. That would really mess things up—*for me*. Why can't I have normal clients? I picked entertainment and intellectual property law because I love movies and music. But if I'd known practicing it would bring in so many weirdo clients, I would've done something more like corporate tax, or mergers and restructuring, like Ares.

I roll my shoulders and check the time. Klein is late.

That's odd. She's always been on time in the three years she's worked here. I check my phone for messages—*nothing*. No email either.

Is she okay? Did she get into an accident on the way? Is Chad harassing her to get his ring back?

Suddenly my phone buzzes with a text.

–Unknown: Your assistant doesn't seem to be doing very well. But don't worry, I'm watching out for her. And you're welcome. One of these days, I'd love to meet you in person. Have a civilized conversation. Talk about things that would benefit both of us.

What the...? Who is this? Not Mom or Harvey, because they would've made sure I knew it was them, especially when they're acting like they're doing me a favor by taking care of Klein.

But then who?

Vincent? But it's not his MO. He likes to make a statement, the kind you don't forget. A low-key, unsigned note just isn't his style.

I open the attached photo to see if it provides any clues. The shot's grainy and slightly out of focus with a dark night sky—obviously taken from far away with a phone, not a camera with a decent lens. Weird. Mom or Harvey would definitely would've used a pro. Same for Vincent.

A lot of people in the frame, but I spot Klein with ease. It's impossible to miss the platinum curls. She's in nothing but a T-shirt and shorts, her arms wrapped around herself. In front of her is a burning building. Firefighters bustle around, water spewing from multiple hoses aimed at the fire.

I narrow my eyes. When was this taken?

I'm watching out for her.

It's something Mom or Harvey might say, but nothing else adds up to it being one of them. When did this happen? Anxiety spreads through me like acid. Surely this can't be from today...

But Klein is late—

My phone vibrates in my hand.

–Klein: Hi, boss. I'm so sorry for the short notice, but I don't think I can come in today. Amélie can probably cover for me for one day. I think

I should be able to come back tomorrow, but I'll let you know for sure by noon.

My mouth dries. She isn't providing any details, but the photo can't be ignored. Mom didn't just drug me and my brothers. She also left Ares to burn in a forest fire. If Lareina hadn't found him back then and rescued him, he would've died.

Don't jump to conclusions. Klein could've caught something. Or maybe she just overslept. Things happen.

–Me: That's fine. What's wrong?

–Klein: My apartment building burned down.

I stare at the phone. My hands start to tremble. I clench them into fists, swallow the ball of panic suddenly swelling in my throat. Klein doesn't need me to lose control. She needs me to be cool-headed and fix the problem.

I call her immediately.

"Hello?" Her voice is shaky and slightly hoarse, like she's been smoking a pack a day for the past year, or spent the night screaming at a concert. My money's on smoke inhalation. When Ares was rescued from the wildfire and finally regained consciousness, he sounded awful from breathing in too much smoke.

"You sound terrible."

"It's nothing. Don't worry about me. I'm fine, really." Suddenly she has a fit of coughing. It goes on for at least a minute.

"Where are you?" I ask, after she finally regains control. "Did you go to a hospital? Are you injured?"

"Oh no, that wasn't necessary. It's just a minor burn."

I lean forward. *"A minor burn?* Where?" I hate that she keeps downplaying what happened. Reminds me too much of Ares, who always acts like his experience in the cabin and fire was no big deal. It was a big fucking deal—big enough that it made him unable to form any sort of relationship with a woman because he couldn't bear being touched without feeling suffocated, until he met Lareina. He never shared what happened, but Mom must've abused him in ways I can't even imagine.

You're the most like me.

The words slither in my mind like vipers. I grind my teeth.

"On my arm," Klein says with a soft sigh.

I get an instant visual of a long, ugly burn scar covering most of her arm. I shudder, my belly twisting into a torturous knot. Ares had some burn injuries. They were nasty, red and oozing as blisters formed over seared flesh. Took a while for them to heal, and the scars remain.

"But it really isn't too bad," Klein rasps.

"Right." *I don't believe you.* "You really don't sound good."

"It's just the shock. I don't think I inhaled much smoke. I managed to get out pretty quickly." She lets out a wheezing sound.

The muscles in my jaw tighten. "Klein, go to the hospital."

"But there are so many people more seriously injured than I am. Mrs. Choi didn't get out until an hour after I did."

Good God, Klein isn't listening. She isn't going go because she doesn't think she merits getting checked out, not when others might need to be prioritized. Probably because her family is horrible. The kind of people who asked her to join them at a restaurant where she couldn't eat and then sided with total strangers. They've done a number on her self-esteem—to the point she doesn't think her injuries are worth being looked at.

"Send me your location," I say as I gather my fob and start to head out of the office.

"What? Why?"

"Because you need somebody to make sure you're all right. Don't do anything, and don't go anywhere. Wait for me."

"But what about your morning appointments?"

If I could, I'd reach into the phone and shake some sense into her. "Who cares? Amélie can cancel them."

She gasps. "But you can't just *cancel* them. Ryder Reed is coming to see you!"

He's one of the hottest stars in Hollywood, and one of my best clients because he loves to consult me on all sorts of things—and unlike Ted, he actually listens to good advice. "So? He can reschedule."

"But—"

"Klein, don't argue. It's nonnegotiable."

12

AILEE

"Hello, Ailee. Here."

I lift my head from the phone and see Zoe holding out a bottle of water. "Oh, thank you!" I take a long, grateful swallow. "You're a lifesaver." My throat feels so much better already. It's been parched—I haven't had a drop since leaving the building. The morning air is slightly cool, the acrid scent of burned concrete and belongings lingering like a miasma. Who would've guessed a building this tall could go up in flames so quickly? It's almost like somebody doused the whole structure with gallons of gasoline.

The fire also consumed a couple of smaller buildings near the apartment, but the firefighters managed to get it under control and kill it.

"You look a bit dazed," Zoe says before sipping her own water and pulling the lapels of her bathrobe tighter against the morning chill. She tilts her jaw at my phone. "Is everything okay?"

"Yeah. I just texted my roommate, then called the office to let them know I'm not coming in today." I look down at myself. I'm in mismatched shoes—one coral flip-flop and one black sandal—and an old white T-shirt and boxer shorts with red and pink hearts, no bra. I cross my arms across my chest and try not to worry too much about work.

Josh ended the call so abruptly, like he's really upset. He has certain habits he sticks to—starts his laptop and reviews a doc or two, then has me lay out his day and update him on any changes while he sips the iced latte I bring from the break room.

Or maybe he's upset that I was so late *to call him.* I should've been at work an hour ago. But I was in absolute shock, having witnessed the entire twelve-story building go up in flames. Now I know why people remain frozen when they're faced with a certain unimaginable danger. Your brain just gives up on you, like it's too overwhelmed to process.

The sprinkler system apparently failed. The smoke alarms didn't work either. The elevator quit operating—for good reason, since it probably wasn't safe. If Zoe hadn't banged on my door when she did, I might've been stuck on the fourth floor until the fire trucks arrived to get people out. Then I would've really been hurt, enough that I might not have been able to call work at all. Zoe said she couldn't sleep and was reading some romance novel when she smelled the smoke and grabbed me. Now I feel like I owe her a lifetime's worth of romance novels.

The EMT didn't even check us out, since Zoe and I were among the first group of people to evacuate. But my throat feels scratchy from being near the burning fire and not having had anything to drink for hours.

"Do you have a place to stay?" Zoe asks, her eyes shifting to the husk of the building.

"I guess... I'll figure something out. You?"

"My company's arranging for a hotel until I can find a new place."

"That's nice," I murmur. I should probably find somewhere to crash. My parents' place is out of the question—they're still furious about what happened yesterday evening. Mom's final text read: *You're such a disgrace. Always wanting what isn't yours, rather than working to get what you can.*

It's like, what does that even mean? I've never wanted what wasn't mine, and I've worked hard for everything I have. The day I turned eighteen was the day my parents asked me to move out and make my own way in the world. And I did, by getting an associate's degree while waiting tables, and then a full-time job as soon I was able.

"If you need anything, let me know," Zoe says kindly.

"Of course. Thanks, Zoe. I don't know what I would've done without you."

She waves it away. "Just being neighborly. Anyway, I have to get going. I'll talk to you later."

I wave her goodbye and sigh, then scan the surroundings. A lot of people are still milling around, dazed because of what they've lost. There are exhausted firefighters covered in soot, buzzing cops and EMTs. Ambulances for the elderly and those who inhaled too much smoke while trapped inside. A few local reporters breathlessly speak to their cameras while keeping the charred, still-smoldering structure in the background.

I open the news app on my phone. Articles and videos about the apartment fire are already trending locally. At least nobody died, thank God. No known cause for the fire yet. I sigh. At least my car's safe in a lot several blocks away. I couldn't find a spot any closer, so maybe the universe was watching out for me.

The problem is that I don't have the fob. I only grabbed my phone before rushing down the stairs with Zoe. My laptop's gone, too.

I place a couple of fingers on my forehead. *Shit.* There were a couple half-finished memos for Josh on the hard drive, which I hadn't had a chance to back up.

Okay, I've got some time before he arrives. And my first order of business is to make a to-do list on my phone: find a cheap motel or somewhere like that to stay at. File an insurance claim—hopefully they'll be quick to reimburse, but I have no idea how that's going to go. I've never had to get money out of a renter's insurance policy before. Usually it just flows from me to them.

I need to figure out what's going to happen with my security deposit. Hopefully the property management company returns it as soon as possible—Max and I will need it for our next rental.

But the very first thing is to go shopping and at least replace my clothes and shoes and all the basics. I don't even have a toothbrush right now. I also have to call the banks and see about getting my credit cards and ATM card reissued. Or will that mess up my Apple Pay account? Maybe I should find a local branch for my bank and withdraw some cash. That way I'll be able to get by until the new cards arrive—

The more I think about it, the more overwhelming everything seems. The only good thing is that I haven't lost anything that can't be replaced. All my personal photos are stored in the cloud. My high school year book is toast, but it isn't going to break my heart. Hopefully Max didn't lose anything irreplaceable, either.

My stomach growls. *I probably should get something to eat.* The leftover lasagna last night was smaller than I thought.

A golden Lexus rushes into the compound, way too fast and with lots of tire screeching. I scowl. *What's* Chad *doing here?*

The sedan stops several feet behind a fire truck. The door swings open, and Chad steps out. He's in a suit with a neatly knotted tie, the picture of success. So apparently his wife *didn't* murder him last night. He's even wearing an irritatingly smug smile. What I wouldn't give to strip that arrogant smirk off his face, especially since I'm standing here in an old T-shirt and boxers. And mismatched sandals. My hair's likely a mess, too, after our sudden, before-sunrise evacuation.

He stares at the burned husk of the building. "Holy shit, that's fucking karma," he says, then covers his mouth with a fist as he cackles.

Oh my God. His lack of humanity makes me want to squirm in shame —why did I ever say yes to his proposal? I need to learn to be a better judge of people. "What are you doing here, Chad?"

His eyes swing in my direction. He parts his mouth, then points at me and laughs. "What the hell? What's up with the hair?"

"Didn't really have the time to worry about it when the apartment caught fire," I say dryly. "Kinda like how you didn't have the mental capacity to keep up with your lies when I ran into your pregnant wife."

The mocking chuckle dies. "That was all your fault. You weren't supposed to be at the restaurant. You said you don't eat Chinese food!"

"So. Are you telling me you took your wife to Peking Town because you thought you wouldn't run into me?"

"Well, that and a good meal, obviously. I'm not stupid."

I give him a slow clap. "Wow. Not mentally challenged, just morally challenged. And a liar, to boot."

He sniffs. "I didn't *lie*. I just omitted a few facts."

"Uh-huh. That's still lying."

"Well, do you blame me? Didn't you see what Autumn looks like?" Disgust twists his mouth.

What's wrong with his wife? The biggest mistake that poor woman made was probably marrying him.

My bewilderment seems to piss him off. "She's like a freakin' *cow* now! It isn't much fun trying to have sex with somebody that big. Hard to get it up."

What the...? My jaw drops.

"Which is why I went for you."

"You think your wife, whose belly is swollen with *your* baby, is disgusting? For real?" My voice grows shrill with anger and humiliation for me and his poor wife. We both really deserve better.

"No!" he protests, although his tone says, *Yes.* Maybe he realizes that he made himself sound like an asshole when I laid it out like that. "I just wanted to be nice. It was a service to humanity—actually to you. You don't have self-esteem, no self-worth. For you, being with someone like me is a dream come true. A boost to your self-respect. I could tell you only tried to distance yourself from me because you wanted to force me to make some commitment. Anyway, the sense of accomplishment from being with someone like me will linger and improve your future prospects, even after I quietly dump you when my wife delivers the baby and snaps back into shape."

The *gall!* I've run into some self-absorbed clients at work, but Chad takes the gold medal in the Narcissism Olympics. "I should murder you just for saying that," I say between clenched teeth.

"Ah, you don't mean that. You're a good girl." He says "good girl" like it means "doormat." He extends his arms as though to place them on my shoulders, and I recoil. He frowns, but doesn't try to touch me again. "Look, you need to give me the ring back. And apologize to my wife."

"Me?" I point to myself. "Apologize to your wife? For what? For being deceived by her dickhead husband who lied to me that he was single?"

Chad doesn't have the grace to blush. But then, if he knew what shame was, he wouldn't have done what he did. "For creating unnecessary emotional distress. Just tell her you stole the ring when you saw it in my office because it looked too pretty to resist. And hey, I'll let you stay at my downtown condo for free for a week because I like you and"—he gestures—"your place burned down. But you can't let Autumn know."

He stops and gives me a soulful look that's as fake as a fifty-dollar Gucci bag on a shady website. My blood pressure shoots up so high, my vision turns red.

Sadly, he seems oblivious. He folds his arms over his chest. "I still have feelings for you, Ailee. I'm not a complete asshole."

"Of course not." I lay the sarcasm on thick. "Just a cheating, lying dickface."

"It's going to be awkward if I have to call the police for the theft."

"I'd love to see you try because I'm not giving back an *heirloom* from my fiancé," I say with a faux-sweet smile.

Chad scoffs. "Don't be ridiculous. There's no way Josh proposed for real. When did he have the chance? I proposed two nights ago, and you said yes. And even if you hadn't, you're a C-minus lay. Why would he want to be tied to you for life?"

My hands shake with the urge to strangle this asshole to death. I'd love to come up with a killer retort, but—frustratingly—I have nothing. Chad's right about one thing—the engagement isn't real. Josh only said what he did yesterday because he felt sorry for me.

Chad seems to understand that instinctively. He smirks. "You know what? If you can convince that insufferable asshole to stay with you for at least three months, you can keep the ring. I'll even throw in an apology. But otherwise, you're going to return the ring to my wife and tell her you took it. If you grovel, I'll even convince her to not involve the police. Help you out, because I'm sure a criminal conviction would mean no more job at the law firm."

His sanctimonious tone goads me until I feel like I'm about to spontaneously combust. "Fine," I snap before I can stop myself.

He starts laughing. "You're going to lose so bad. I can't wait to see you beg for mercy. Not even your hot tamale sister could lock Josh into a committed relationship. He'll dump *you* before the sun's down tomorrow. Then you'll learn where you rank."

I bite my lip. Although Katt made up her dating history with Josh, he's dated plenty of gorgeous women without settling down with any of them. He could snap his fingers and have models falling at his feet.

There's a sudden, small *thwack*. Chad grabs the back of his head. "Ow!"

"Oops, I missed," comes Josh's voice. He tosses a small pebble in the air and catches it.

I cover my eyes with a hand, wishing for a sinkhole to appear right under my feet. *Just how much of Chad's crap did my boss hear?*

Chad spins around, his fists raised aggressively, like he's ready to pounce. "I'm going to fuck you up!"

13

———

JOSH

"Sorry," I say. "I was aiming for a bee."

Chad blanches, jumps like he just stepped on a thumbtack. "Holy shit, *where*?"

"Right behind you."

"Fuck!" Chad slaps the back of his skull, then hops around without checking to see if I'm telling the truth.

Klein stares at him like he's lost his mind. I just let him make an idiot of himself. That's what he deserves for saying all that shit to her. I didn't hear the entire exchange, but what I did hear was enough make me fantasize about breaking his nose again.

What gave him the nerve to come and harass Klein? Can he not smell the acrid smoke in the air? Or see the remnants of the building behind her?

My heart was hammering as I drove here. It's still beating fast, even though I can see with my own eyes that Klein's standing on her own two feet, no blood, nothing broken. The scene reminds me of my nightmares, where I can't save Ares in the burning cabin.

If Chad possessed even a tiny bit of decency, he'd show some sympathy, even if he had just cause to be upset with her. But obviously the finer emotions are beyond a two-faced asshole like him. Even if she said she was in love with him for some reason, I'd never let her be with a guy like him. He doesn't deserve her.

"That bee must really like you. It's going right for your neck," I call out.

Screaming, he covers his neck then hops into his car and drives away like Satan's coming for his soul—assuming he has one. *Loser.*

Klein blinks as the Lexus swerves along the road. "What's wrong with him?"

"He's highly allergic to bees. We used to call him Chadaphylactic back in the day."

She frowns. "But...there aren't any bees around."

"But there are some flies buzzing back and forth. I saw, and decided to use them. Hope he likes being tricked as much as he likes tricking others," I say, narrowing my eyes with petty vindictiveness and satisfaction.

Klein laughs. The sound is as beautifully soft and direct as a lover's caress, and something hot and volatile knots in my belly. I realize abruptly that I've never heard her laugh. She smiles a lot, but doesn't laugh.

I want to hear her let loose again. Then kiss her happy, relaxed mouth. My head says that's a bad idea, but the rest of me thinks it's fucking fantastic.

"*That*'s karma for sure," she says. "How do you know him so well? He isn't your dentist, too, is he?"

I shudder. "No. I wouldn't trust him with my worst enemy, much less my teeth. We went to the same high school. Met on the boxing team."

"Ah... And that's when you broke his nose," she says, finally putting it together. She was probably too overwhelmed yesterday.

"Uh-huh." I study her, from head to toe then back up. She doesn't sound too bad. Was it just the phone making her sound weird earlier? No soot on her. Her curls are gloriously untamed and frame her face like a cloud of spun silver.

The T-shirt is worn, but looks surprisingly nice and comfy on her. The boxers are cute with heart prints. Her shoes don't match, and my heart aches in sympathy. She must've been in such a panic. I'm surprised she didn't fall during the evacuation and scrape her knees.

Klein flushes under my scrutiny and crosses her arms tighter, self-conscious. "I'm fine. I swear."

"The burn?"

"Like I said earlier, nothing serious." She shows me a Band-Aid on her wrist.

Okay. If that's all the treatment the EMT gave her, then she really wasn't that badly hurt.

"I probably sounded bad earlier because my throat was so dry," she says.

Relief crashes over me. As the worry for her recedes, I start to notice other things. The freshly scrubbed face with bright violet eyes and a soft, rosy mouth, the lips full and pillowy. The long, pretty legs—I've never seen so much of them before, because at work she either wears skirts that end an inch above her knees or slacks. The softness of her breasts presses against the shirt. I can see the outline of her nipples, and suddenly *my* throat is parched.

She isn't wearing a bra.

My blood heats, draining from my head to my dick. *For God's sake, control yourself.* She just had a major crisis. Plus, it isn't like I've never been around a braless woman. My dates have shown up in clingy dresses with necklines so plunging, they couldn't wear anything underneath, and I felt nothing but mild interest. But with Klein, it's irresistibly erotic. Her breasts are just big enough to fill my hands, and I can already imagine how they'd feel.

The tips of my ears grow hot, and I bite back a curse. She doesn't need me to act like an immature teenager right now. "Is there anything I can do? Anything you need?"

"Um... I guess I need a ride."

"Is your car damaged?"

"No. But the fob's..." She makes a *poof* motion. "I only grabbed my phone before leaving."

"Good, although you shouldn't have wasted time to grab it, either. The only thing that mattered was you getting out safely."

"It was right next to me, on the nightstand."

I take her to my Rolls and open the passenger door. She climbs in with softly murmured thanks and settles down. I shut the door and get behind the wheel. "Where to?" I start the engine.

She worries her lower lip with her teeth, making the pink flesh glisten. She doesn't even know what that's doing to me, which makes it even hotter. My cock's most definitely perked up, and I shift to hide my reaction.

"Well, uh…" Awkward embarrassment fleets through her eyes as she looks at me. "I guess I should find a…a hotel or something."

She doesn't have anywhere to go. "Why don't you stay with me?" I say as I maneuver the car into traffic.

Her eyes nearly bug out. "With *you?*"

She doesn't have to make it sound like I'm a cannibal or something. "Yeah, with me. Not sure if you noticed, but that video from yesterday evening went viral."

"Yeah, I heard. My best friend freaked out."

I wait a beat, but she doesn't continue. Huh. She has no intention of revealing what her best friend said or what she herself thinks about it. I'm dying to know what's going on in her head—everything rolling around in her mind when she thinks about the video and what happened. But most importantly, I want to hear her thoughts about me.

She always smiles at me with such sweetness, does little things that make my day brighter and my mood lighter—but then pulls away and draws a line of professional distance that says, "Thou shalt not cross." She doesn't seem to do that with anyone else in the office. But then, she doesn't gift them with the same brilliant, warm smile she has for me. Or do anything special for them. *What gives?*

When I don't say anything in response, she clears her throat. Her fingers nervously intertwine. "Sorry I got you tangled up in my mess. I'm sure having everyone know you're 'engaged' to me isn't something you wanted. I'm sorry—"

"Stop saying *sorry*." Sorry isn't what I want her to feel. Hot, happy, thrilled, aroused, excited, relieved—but not sorry. "It isn't your mess, and you didn't get me to do anything."

"But if you hadn't tried to help me—"

"No one put a gun to my head. I did it because I wanted to."

"But you felt sorry for me, didn't you?"

I stop the car at the red light, then glare at her. "Who put that nonsense into your head? Say I felt sorry for you again, and I'll show you how I *really* feel by kissing you until you shut up."

Her eyes widen, her mouth parting. Rose colors her cheeks, but can't tell if it's from shock or horror. Her violet gaze is like a deep pool, impossible to read. She even stops fidgeting with her fingers. Her little tongue darts out to lick her lips, and I feel the motion like she's stroking *my* damn tongue. *Fuck me.*

"Uh…" She clears her throat. "You didn't have to… I mean… You're my boss."

The reminder is like a bucket of cold water, but it doesn't do much to settle me down. I run a hand over my face and let out a rough breath.

"That wasn't appropriate," I say, before Klein feels scandalized enough to contact HR. "But look. I don't claim to be engaged to everyone I feel sorry for. I did it because—" Suddenly the words get stuck in my throat.

I sense her turning toward me. "Because…?"

My head says I shouldn't, but my gut says fuck it. *Listen to your heart, rather than your oversized head,* an inner voice that sounds awfully like Dad advises.

I turn to look at her squarely. She's staring at me, her eyes wide and guileless. Her breasts rise and fall gently, and the leather interior of the Rolls feels too full of her female sweetness.

She raises her eyebrows, urging me to finish. The car behind us honks as the light turns green.

"Because…" I swallow. *The hell with it.* "Because I like you."

14

AILEE

My brain freezes. Four very simple words, but they don't compute.

I open my mouth, feeling like I should say something. But nothing suitable comes to mind. *Oh my God, you like me, you really like me!* seems immature. Grabbing his hair and kissing him is out of the question—he's driving. And even if he weren't, he brought the idea up a few moments ago but then immediately said that it wouldn't be *appropriate*.

Should I tell him I've been crushing on him since forever? But what if he means he likes me as a capable assistant rather than as a woman? We've been working together for three years, and he's never done anything to hint that he felt any sort of attraction. Not to mention, he's been seen with one stunning woman after another. Unlike me, they'd look like Aphrodite even in mismatched footwear.

Chad's cruel words stir—no self-esteem, no self-respect. I don't think I'm that bad. I shouldn't give him any power over me, but the scars he left are too fresh to ignore. And even though I should be happy that Josh said he likes me, I keep second-guessing it. Chad said he liked me, and later that he *loved* me. Not that Josh is a jerk like my ex-fiancé, but an instinctive need to be extra cautious remains.

"What?" Josh finally prompts me when I continue to stare and keep opening and closing my mouth.

Oh, shit. Now I really have to come up with something. "I don't know what to say," I blurt out.

Something flickers in his eyes. *Disappointment?* But it's gone in an instant. "You aren't obligated to say anything," he says calmly. "You didn't have to do anything unless you want to. We aren't here as boss and assistant."

"We...aren't?"

"No. We're here as an engaged couple."

I make a small strangled sound at how serious he sounds, although a gleam in his eye hints at playful teasing. An urge to remind him that our "engagement" was an impulse on his part because he wanted to protect me swells, but I shut up in case I inadvertently say something that upsets him and makes him kiss me. Not that I'd be against that. But I'm not ready. I probably taste like burned apartment or something. And I *know* my hair smells bad. I should at least brush my teeth and shower. Beat my hair into some kind of submission before I let his fingers tangle into my curls and—

Oh my God, stop thinking about it like kissing is inevitable! But the image won't leave my head, and I can't quit staring at his mouth, fantasizing how it would feel on mine. It's really beautiful—sensual and firm... Would he move his hands over me? Stroke me, trace my body—

I squirm a little, swallowing a groan. I'm getting wet just from the thought of his mouth and hands on me. I inhale and imagine a tranquil sea. *Just paste on a friendly smile and pretend everything's fine.*

"My family saw the video," he says.

I gasp, whatever little peace I managed to achieve vanishing. "Prescott and Jeremiah too?" I squeak. The two people I'm most worried about.

"Probably the whole firm. Barry stopped by. Offered to organize a bachelor party."

"Ack." I bury my face in my hands. "Crap. What do I tell Kenna?"

"Kenna? Kenna Miller?"

"Yeah. I told her about my engagement to Chad yesterday. She's the one who referred me to Chad when my dentist retired."

Josh's eyes narrow, his lips pursing. Hopefully it doesn't mean she's in trouble. He doesn't seem to like her very much for some reason, and she tries to avoid interacting with him.

"She was being nice," I add.

"Mmm. I'm sure." He doesn't sound convinced. "Tell her you traded up. By the way, Akiko wants to meet you. Host a family dinner and invite you over."

I shake my head. No way am I meeting Prescott's wife! "Shouldn't we just tell them the truth?"

"Do you want to?"

"I mean…" I hesitate. We should come clean, not deceive his family. But at the same time, Chad's cruel taunt—and the stupid bet—comes back to me. Should I pretend the bet never happened? Or is it going to be a problem? I glance down at the ring, then pull it off and turn it in my hands, considering. He really wants it back. If I give it to him now and be done with it, he might just go away permanently—

"Jesus, you're still wearing that ugly thing?" Josh takes my hand and plucks the ring out of my fingers as the driver's-side window lowers. Then he throws it out into the traffic.

"Oh my God! *No!*"

"Yes." He raises the window.

"That's a *real diamond*!" I raise my voice without meaning to, panicking. How much is it going to cost to replace it? No matter how much I hate Chad's guts, it wouldn't be right to keep the ring, which technically belongs to his wife. "Can you turn the car around?"

"In this traffic?"

I flop back against the seat and close my eyes. Josh is right. There are way too many cars on the road. Not to mention, how would I look for the ring anyway? It's so small, and I'd be lucky if the L.A. drivers didn't run me over in road rage.

I slap my cheeks a couple of times, panicking.

"What's the problem? Tell me," he says.

"I was going to return it to Autumn!"

He looks at me like I've lost my mind. "And apologize?"

Oh, God. He overheard the bet. "Of course not. I didn't do anything wrong, but neither did she."

"I doubt she wants it back. I wouldn't if I were her. I'd be too busy hiring the nastiest divorce lawyer I could afford," he says. "And if Chad bothers you again, tell him to go fuck himself."

The muscles in Josh's jaw twitch as his eyebrows snap together. His grip on the steering wheel tightens until the knuckles turn white. Probably he's remembering how I said "fine" to Chad's ridiculous bet. I shouldn't have involved him so deeply.

I flame with embarrassment. "I'm sor—" I stop short, in case Josh really was serious about kissing me. "I messed up."

"No, you didn't. Anybody would've done the same." He considers for a moment. "But don't worry. We can stay engaged."

I straighten in shock. "Really? You don't mind?"

"Nope. I was actually about to propose the same thing, except for six months."

My shoulders sag with relief. Whew, I'm glad he's being so accommodating, although part of me harbors guilt that he's doing this to salvage my pride—*again.* "Great. I'm happy—and grateful—to hear that. You don't even have to stay for all six months, just three. And then you can dump me. That way, it'll all be neatly tied up."

"That's ridiculous." He scoffs. "*You'll* dump *me.* Nobody's going to believe it, otherwise."

Uh... *What?* My brain freezes again. He must be confused—nobody will believe *I* dumped *him.* "Normally whoever who has less to offer clings to the one with...more going on."

"That's right." His eyes slide toward me for a second before returning to the road. "Normally."

"Are you—" I stop and recalibrate. *You know what? I can just pretend he considers me that amazing.* Cinderella got to feel like a million bucks until midnight. Why shouldn't I do the same?

"Am I what?"

"Nothing." I clear my throat, then realize six months is a long time. He brought up kissing me earlier. Does he think I might want something more? Everything a couple does when a relationship *isn't* fake? "I won't get in your way at all," I say.

"How do you propose to do that?" Amusement softens his voice.

"Um... Like not expecting you to do things that, um, I can do myself?" I say awkwardly.

He frowns. "I'm not following."

I cringe inwardly. This is awkward as hell, but I want to clarify everything before we head into this. "You have, um, personal needs, and I'll let you do whatever's...necessary. Just—*please*—do it discreetly. It'll be embarrassing if everything becomes public, you know? At the same time, I can totally take care of my, um, issues if they ever present themselves because I have, ah, my own ways." Shit, I'm babbling. I press my lips together.

His jaw flexes and the lines between his eyebrows deepen. *What part of that annoyed him?* I don't think I'm being unreasonable by asking him to be careful. I mean, it's for both our reputations. Plus Prescott seems pretty strict, and I don't suppose he'd be okay with his son "cheating."

"Do you know what my family motto is?"

"The Huxleys have a motto?" I chew on my lip, feeling like a kid who slept through class and missed a very important lesson. "Up or out?" It's a phrase the lawyers at Huxley & Webber seem to use a lot.

He frowns. "That's the firm's unofficial policy. No, it's *pietas et unitas*. Loyalty and unity."

"Wow. That's cool," I say quickly. "Better than 'up or out.'" Should've known that wasn't the family motto, since it can't really be applied to families. But then, I haven't had coffee. And didn't get much sleep last night.

"So obviously cheating doesn't fit into the way we Huxleys are expected to live our lives," Josh says.

"Yeah, no, of course not. But it's not really cheating if we agree it's okay ahead of time. We just have to be discreet, so nobody else knows."

"No. Nothing stays secret forever." The car stops at a red light, and he turns and gives me his full attention. Thoughts I can't read cross his face, and something volatile burns in his eyes as they trace mine. My mouth dries. "If you ever let another guy touch you while we're together, I'll personally rip his legs off and shove them both up his ass. Then I'll fuck you until you remember you're mine. Just because the engagement is fake doesn't mean we fool around with other people."

His eyes narrow to brilliant slits I can't look away from. Every word out of his gorgeous mouth is totally wrong, but so freakin' hot. My cheeks are warm enough to feel feverish. I squirm to ease the ache between my legs, wishing my boxers weren't so thin. I'd better not leave a wet spot on his leather seat.

When I don't say anything, his eyes darken. Then I realize maybe he mistook my suggestion to mean that *I* would like to cheat on him. "I wasn't saying I'd do it with other guys. I have, ah, tools. And plenty of batteries. Thanks to Amazon subscribe and save, I get fifteen percent off on Energizers."

Josh stares at me like I've sprouted flowers from the top of my head, then his gaze drops to my crotch briefly before rising to meet my eyes. "Are you telling me that you managed to save a vibrator or two when you evacuated?"

My face heats instantly. *Shoot.* I totally forgot about the fire incinerating everything. "No. Of course not," I say hastily. *Does he think I'm wearing a toy right now?* Still, the point I was trying to make seems important. "But you need a variety. Don't like to sleep with the same woman twice—"

"I don't need a variety. And a Huxley does not cheat. Period."

"Right." I nod quickly at his hard tone. That's his we-aren't-continuing-this-discussion voice. He's never directed it at me, but I can see why people shut up when he uses it on them. It has the power to make you sit up and nod. Besides, I'm starting to realize how odd I'll sound if I insist that he go to other women when he says he won't. And it's kind of thrilling that he wants to be true to me, even if temporarily.

"Good. Glad we could come to an agreement on this point." The light changes and he resumes driving.

My heart continues to beat rapidly. After stealing a glance to make sure he's focused on the road, I pinch my inner thigh and almost hiss in pain. Okay, not dreaming. But this is just surreal.

What's happened to me since yesterday evening *doesn't happen to somebody like me.* Well...I guess cheating could happen, but everything else, including my panty-meltingly hot boss claiming to be my fiancé, my apartment burning down, and being taken to his place to move in—

and us being fake-engaged for six months? And he wants me to dump him after it's over because that's supposedly more believable…

He doesn't even want to look at another woman for six months. I gaze at the late morning sky. The sun has to have risen in the west. Or some really potent talisman must've burned up in the fire. Or maybe I've been kidnapped by aliens, like I hoped for in Peking Town, and they're doing some kind of mind experiment on me.

15

JOSH

Klein finally stops talking and becomes quiet. Telling her I'd violate another guy's rectum with his legs and fuck her probably wasn't the best way to encourage conversation. Normally I would have just laughed it off, but imagining her with another guy made my blood boil until I wanted to strangle the imaginary man, and I couldn't stop myself from saying it. Something about declaring her as my fiancée seems to have destroyed all my filters. There's a searing feeling of awareness in my gut that has to be an unholy mix of jealousy and possessiveness.

We arrive. I hit a few buttons on my phone screen, and the main gates open. They're solid wood laid over heavy metal frames. It would take a tank to break through.

Discreet cameras are everywhere, recording and backing up to the cloud. This ensures no one from the Dunkels will be able to get inside unobserved. They can claim to be civilized and honorable all they want, but the fact that Mom broke the spirit of the agreement and messed with my girlfriend way back when speaks volumes about that side of the family.

There's no lawn, since grass is so demanding of water, but there are various rocks to create a landscape, a larger, rambling version of the famous rock gardens in Japan. To add interest and color, common jasmine plants grow in abundance, emitting a sweet, soothing fragrance.

"Very interesting," Klein murmurs as she takes in the landscaping. "You'd think gravel would be boring."

"Not *just* gravel. A rock garden," I correct her with a laugh, then point out some long, wavy lines raked into the tiny stones. "See those? They represent a river."

"Oh..." Her eyes grow wide. "How do you get the rocks to stay put in the wind and so on?" She frowns as a few birds hop around on the "river" and one of them makes a small mess. "Or birds." She squints. "Are those sparrows?"

"Yes. As for keeping the lines intact, you really can't. You have to re-rake every so often. I have my gardener do most of it, but I take care of that section over there." I gesture to our right, at a sizable patch. "He isn't very creative, so he sticks to the original design, but I change things up, depending on my mood."

"When do you find the time? You're always working unless you have a poker night with your brothers or a dinner date."

I frown a little. My life isn't as dull and rigid as she makes it sound, and the fact that she thinks so is vaguely annoying. "On weekends. It doesn't take that long. And it's very soothing. If you want, I can show you." The offer slips out before I can stop myself. I'm protective of my time in the rock garden. It calms the restlessness inside me, helps orient myself. But unlike the meditation I do in the tea room, which clears my head, it provides a sense of control as I create a vista with my own hands.

But I don't rescind the offer. Something tells me I might enjoy having her with me—that the time might even be extra soothing because of her presence.

"Sure. I'd love that as long as I won't be in the way."

"You won't. You might even inspire me to try something different."

"Cool. In that case..." She smiles, then gets distracted. "And those are...? The leaves are too big to be ivy, and there's fruit hanging, too." Klein points at the dark green vines covering the massive archway that leads to the stone pagoda in the back.

"Passion fruit. I planted them three or four years ago, and they took over. My gardener prunes them aggressively, but the more he prunes them, the faster they seem to grow back."

"Resilient. You can cut me down"—she makes a small fist—"but you can't make me cower!"

A corner of my mouth lifts. "Exactly. And the fruits are delicious once they ripen. I had them on a vacation in Thailand when my brothers and I went. Couldn't find them around here, so I decided to plant the exact same species. I'll let you try some when they're ready next month."

She smiles, her eyes sparkling like they always do when she's about to experience something new. Her excitement is cute and contagious. "I'll look forward to that. Don't think I've ever had them before."

We drive by the pool, which is half indoor and half outdoor. "Feel free to use that whenever you want."

"Thanks. You swim a lot?"

"When I get a chance, or when I'm getting too pasty. It's one thing to work indoors, another to look like a marshmallow."

"I don't think anybody would mistake you for a marshmallow just because you turned pale. More like a great white shark with extra-big teeth of doom."

I laugh, glad she isn't allowing the horrible start of her day to bring her down. Apparently, underneath that sweet and sunny exterior lies an admirable inner fortitude. But it makes sense. If she weren't so strong, she probably would've let her shitty family bring her down a long time ago.

I pull into the garage, which can be converted into a ballroom if I ever lose my sanity and decide to hold a party with hundreds of guests. The space is mostly filled with sparkling cars, all chosen for beauty, power and performance. I don't collect cars like some of my clients, but when something catches my eye, I buy it.

We get out. "Wow," Klein says softly, her cheeks pink. She's so pretty as she takes in my fleet.

"See anything you like?"

"That one's gorgeous." She gestures at a silver Aston Martin convertible as sleek and beautiful as herself.

"Smart choice. You can take it."

"What?" She pulls back like I just tossed her a snake. "No! I have my own car."

"But no fob," I remind her, unsure what her objections are after calling it gorgeous.

"Which the dealer can replace."

"I think you're wounding the pride of British engineering."

She shakes her head with a laugh. "No need for British engineering's pride to be hurt. It's just that my car is very dependable. And, uh, cheaper."

"Sounds about as exciting as property," I mutter, thinking back to a class at Harvard Law that never failed to put me to sleep. "Look, just enjoy the ride until you get a new fob. You'll look totally cool driving around with the top down. The weather's great." And her curls will blow gloriously in the air.

Her eyes dart everywhere as she searches for something to say. "But what if something happens to it?"

"Do you drive recklessly?" I already know the answer. But I want to remind her she's a safe driver, somebody I can trust with one of my prized cars.

"No, but other people do. And my luck hasn't been the greatest in the last twenty-four hours."

Guess finding out all the crap about Chad was shocking. Although it's better that she found out now, before she wasted more time on that unworthy piece of shit. It probably doesn't help her optimism that her apartment burned down, but it's likely somebody else's bad luck rubbing off on her. "Then we'll call the insurance company and have them take care of it. It's no big deal."

Her eyes widen. "But it's an Aston Martin!"

"It could be God's personal chariot, and I'd say the same. Don't worry about it. If I didn't want you to drive it, I'd say so."

"But—"

I place my index finger over her mouth. Her breath, hot and slightly moist, fans the skin. A prickling sensation spreads all over me, and suddenly my pants are too tight again. Her lips are soft and malleable under my finger. It's all I can do to not push it into her mouth, feel the wet heat of her tongue gliding over… "Just say thank you," I order her, my voice a tad rough and low.

Her lashes flutter as she looks at my finger, then my face. Her cheeks flush, and she swallows. "Thank you."

She murmurs the words against my finger. Excitement sparks along my spine, but I rein myself in. I know better than to pounce on her in the garage. It's a luxury garage, but for a first time with Klein? Not worthy.

It feels a bit oddly vulnerable to invite Klein into my home. I don't bring women over. Normally we either go to their place if they insist— or ideally, we hit the hotel because that's convenient and impersonal. Homes are too intimate and prone to unrealistic expectations.

I show Klein my place—from the foyer to the vast living room where my brothers and I hang out, smoking cigars, drinking good Japanese whiskey and playing poker. It's furnished for comfort and lingering conversations, with plush leather couches and armchairs. Contemporary crystal chandeliers from Sweden—a gift from my Japanese uncle—are suspended from the high ceiling. A few postmodern art pieces hang on the walls. I don't know much about them, but they add interest to the space and they've appreciated significantly over the years.

Klein trots over and stares up at them, her eyes bright.

"Enjoy art?" I ask.

"Uh-huh. But I've never seen any originals outside of museums." Her entire being seems focused on the paintings. "These are original, right?"

"Yeah. I got them at auctions in Japan. If you want, we could hit a local one or two."

She pivots fast, her attention really on me now. "Seriously?"

"Of course."

"Oh my God. I'd love to go, just so I can see what it's like. I've only seen them in movies." She beams. "Your home is beautiful."

She runs a hand over the comfy furniture, cherry tables, bookshelves heavy with leather-bound classics. "Have you read them all?" she asks.

I snort. "One day. The only reading I have time for now is work stuff."

She nods. "Make sense, given how many hours you bill." Her eyes twinkle as she turns around and explores the kitchen. Fancy copper and five-ply stainless-steel pots and pans hand-crafted in France hang from the hooks. "Mauviel?" Klein squints at the label, her voice vibrating with excitement.

"Yes."

"Wow. I've only seen them in Williams Sonoma and drooled over them. They're so pretty. Do they feel good when you cook with them?"

I shrug. "I wouldn't know. Never used them."

She spins around, her jaw slack. "No way! But you have this *amazing* kitchen!" She sweeps her arms around, indicating the massive twelve-burner stove, complete with two ovens and a griddle, two stainless-steel refrigerators and every type of appliance you could ask for.

Wonder how she'd react if I tell her there's a fully stocked extra kitchen in the back? The architect said they were all the rage and insisted that I add it, so I did.

"I had to choose between becoming Wolfgang Puck or a great white shark," I say.

She laughs, shaking her head. "Still! Oh my God, just *look* at this kitchen! Damn."

Her eyes shine as she takes in the space. If she starts drooling, I might become a little jealous of my own kitchen. "Well, it's all yours. Take whatever you want from the fridge and pantry," I say with a small grin. "Or order and stock up on whatever you like."

"Thanks. I'll have to think about what to make. It has to be something special, to do justice to this—this incredible..." Words fail her. Damn, she's so adorable.

"I look forward to it."

"You should. I'm a pretty good cook, if I do say so myself. Everyone loves my Thanksgiving turkey and ham."

A sudden smidgen of wistfulness dampens the bright joy in her voice, and I can guess her family probably uses her like an unpaid cook for holidays. She, in her sweetness, has also probably decided they adore her cooking.

I know families can be vicious and nasty, but what kind of people would be cruel to someone like Klein? You might as well kick a puppy. My estimation of her folk drops deeper into negative territory. "Akiko's probably going to take care of the main dishes, but you could do a pie or two, if you like baking."

As intended, Klein shakes off the shadow of her family and brightens. "Sure." She snaps her fingers. "Ooh, I'll make my special eggnog cream pie for Christmas! It's to die for, although it doesn't need baking. I never had a chance to bring it to the office for a holiday potluck because somebody else always called dibs on the desserts."

I grin at her enthusiasm. "Come on. Let me show you the basement." We walk down the staircase. "This is basically just a gym and a boxing room. You can use the gym, but maybe not the boxing stuff unless you know what you're doing. Don't want to sprain a wrist or anything."

She shakes her head in agreement, taking in the state-of-the-art workout equipment. "Don't want that." She doesn't ask to go inside the boxing room, thank God. It'd be awkward explaining why a half-torn photo of my mother is taped to the big bag.

"All the bedrooms are on the second floor," I explain as I lead her back up.

"Which one's yours?"

"Second door to the left. And nothing's off-limits. Not for you, anyway." I realize with a shock that I want her to want to get to know me, not just as a boss, but as a person and a man, even though the fear that she might see the darkness inside runs its icy fingers along my spine.

"I should probably get my own room, right?" Klein asks.

"Sure. You can take any room you want." *You can even take mine.*

"Okay. Thanks. Maybe this one?" She indicates the one across from mine.

I open the double door for her. "Not a bad choice." It's almost a mirror image of my own bedroom, except the en suite bathroom's smaller because it has a cozy reading nook with a massive bay window and a cushy chaise longue.

She cranes her neck to look at the vaulted dome ceiling. I commissioned a mural of white flowers on a whim because they represented innocence, something I wish my brothers and I hadn't lost so soon.

"Wow. That's masterful," Klein breathes as she walks inside, her eyes still on the mural. "I didn't realize you liked white flowers. I'll make sure to bring more."

"Don't change," I say. "What you do at work is already perfect."

She flushes with pleasure, then looks around the rest of the room. The bed is pristine, white sheets threaded with gold and silver, all very chic and discreet. The walk-in closet is empty, as is its center island. I realize she has nothing after the fire. I'll have to correct that soon.

"You can have the interior redone if you want," I tell her.

She looks at me like I'm nuts, then shakes her head. "You've done more than enough already. And this room is so pretty." She opens the blackout curtains and looks out into the garden. This side has a view of the arch that's covered with passion fruit vines. She sighs. "Those flowers are just gorgeous."

I check to make sure everything's acceptable for Klein's stay. The walls are covered with a silky, textured paper, but she might want to have a painting hanging instead. I make a mental note to move the piece in the living room she spent the most time staring at up here.

"I love your home. Thank you for letting me stay."

"It's nothing. Where would my newly homeless fiancée live, if not with me?"

Rose colors her cheeks; her eyes lower. I'm glad I spent the money to make my place appear homey. Otherwise, she might've noticed all the security cameras—although none in the bedrooms—and fingerprint locks on all the doors. They aren't engaged now because I'm home, but if an unauthorized person's inside, they lock every door. If Mom or anyone working for her tries anything, they'll be stuck.

I take Klein to the home office and have her press her thumb on the print reader, then have her enter her own passcode to get inside the house. "Wow. You're really serious about security," she says.

I hesitate for a couple of heartbeats, debating whether to tell her about Mom, but it...just seems too messy. Besides, I'm not planning to bare my soul—that I might be like Zoe Dunkel. "I've had a burglar or two."

"Seriously? But this is such an exclusive area."

"Not exclusive enough, obviously." I can't sleep easy unless I know my home is secure against intrusion. Mom can't even fly a drone over without my knowing about it. And I have guns and the training to use them. All my licenses and permits are up to date.

My phone buzzes. I check the message. *Great.*

"What is it?" Klein asks.

"Gina Rad."

Klein makes a face, her eyes full of sympathy. "She doesn't have an appointment."

"I know, but she's in the office, sobbing because her life will end unless she sees me."

"Let me guess. She's panicking because the contract she signed against your advice just came back to haunt her."

"Exactly." My crappy mood is marginally improved by Klein's understanding.

She waves me away. "You go ahead. I'll be fine."

I hesitate, not wanting to leave her alone. But Gina won't go away until she sees me. She could make a mule seem indecisive by comparison.

Klein shoos me away. "Really. I'll just spend my time exploring your house and resting."

"Call if you need anything," I say, although I'm certain she won't unless the house burns down—or worse.

16

AILEE

As soon as Josh is gone, I inhale deeply. *Oh my God.* I had to hold my breath when he put his finger on my mouth. He only did it to shut me up, but the contact sent a jolt through me. I lie on the sofa and stare at the lights breaking off the crystals. I instinctively tried to flick my tongue over his skin. Thank God my brain suddenly kicked in, because I might've tried to pull the finger into my mouth and suck.

Just thinking about it makes my body heat. Not sure why—it's not like I ever got hot and bothered about sucking a finger. But I wanted to run my tongue over his knuckles, taste the salt on his skin, test how far I could push his control. Then—

I cover my flaming cheeks with my hands. *Come on, Ailee. Stop thinking about sucking Josh.*

My phone rings with a call. Max.

"Hey," I say.

"Oh my God, are you all right? I saw the news! I'm so freaked out!"

"I'm fine. The whole building's toast, but I was able to escape before it got serious. I don't think anything from our unit survived except my phone. Hopefully you didn't have anything valuable in there...?"

"Who cares about *stuff?* I can just replace it. Finally, I'm going to get my money's worth out of the renter's insurance."

I laugh.

"I'm just glad you're okay," she says. "I was so worried. Do you have a place to stay? I mean, other than your *family*." Her voice turns bitter. "Maybe I can ask my cousin if you can stay with her until you sort things?"

"Oh, no. Totally not necessary." Her cousin is great if you like to have her nose in your business all the time. She's worse than a dog that wants to sniff your butt to see what you've been eating. "I'm staying with my boss for now."

A beat of silence. "That hottie?" I can hear the slyness in her voice.

"*Yeeesss...*" I tell her what happened between me and Chad earlier today—and the whole "six months of fake engagement" deal Josh and I settled on.

She lets out an outraged screech. "That *fucker*. I still don't know why God made men stronger. If he got punched in the face once for saying crap like that to a woman, he would never do it again. Just imagine the kind of world we could've lived in. Wholesome and civilized."

"Maintained by punches to the face."

"Hey, sometimes violence *is* the key. Some people just never learn. This is why I hate people. Dogs? They learn fast. Only need positive reinforcement. Anyway, I'm glad your boss rose to the occasion. Hey, does this mean you're going to marry him eventually?"

I sputter. "No! I mean, it's fake. I'm not his type anyway."

"Oh, come on. You don't know what his type is."

"Yeah, I do. Gorgeous models with long legs and big breasts."

"Except he tosses them after sleeping with them once. I'm telling you, you're selling yourself short. Besides, this could be like one of those romance novels."

"Which are fiction," I point out. The only real thing between me and Josh is my rekindled crush on him. I was doing my best to get over it. But now, not only am I single, I'm stuck living with Josh as his fiancée. Even though I tell myself the engagement is fake, my belly's done more flips than a gymnast at the Olympics.

"But that man is hot enough to be in one," Max says.

"True." My body tingles again in memory, and I sigh.

She pounces immediately. "*What happened?* I've never heard you sigh like that over a man!"

"Nothing. Absolutely nothing happened."

"Then why are you sighing like he melted the panties off you?"

"Because I'm tired and haven't had much sleep." It comes out testily, but Max is too perceptive. I don't want to give her a blow-by-blow account of how turned on I was around him, especially not when he was as cool as a cucumber. Nothing indicated he wanted to do anything. Well, he brought up kissing, but it was to make me shut up. What's wrong with me that I'm so down about it?

"Okay, okay! I'll let you get some rest. But if you need anything, let me know. Hopefully this trip won't go on forever. I want to be home right now, so we can give each other support."

"You've done plenty already," I say warmly. "Miss you."

"Miss you more."

We end the call, and I sigh. Now that I mentioned being tired, I realize I'm exhausted. The excitement—and adrenaline—of the morning is starting to wear off. Maybe I should nap a little and figure out the clothing situation. I need new clothes. Actually, I need to see if I have any toiletries. I want to brush my teeth and shower to get the ashy smell off me.

I head to the bathroom and almost faint at the fully stocked vanity. I pick up a brand-new toothbrush and use it, vowing to be extra diligent in taking care of my teeth going forward. I'm not planning to see a dentist anytime soon, not after Chad.

The shower in Josh's home is one of the most luxurious experiences I've ever had. Five showerheads and instant hot water, *oh my God, yes.* The body wash, shampoo and conditioner are in discreet bottles with golden dispenser tops. On each bottle is a fancy, swirly writing stating, *Specially formulated for Joshua Huxley, with meticulous attention in France.* Underneath it is another sentence in French, probably meaning the same thing, since Josh's name is in the middle of it.

After the sinfully long and hot shower, I feel so much better, even though I'm back in my white shirt and boxers. My hair's never going to be tamed, so I give up and let it air-dry. I need some products to manage the curls, and Josh doesn't have any. Gotta go shopping, but the idea of taking the Aston Martin out is both exciting and a bit nerve-racking. I'm a good driver, but that doesn't mean I won't get into an accident. Max got rear-ended by a guy driving with an expired license and no insurance. She was totally screwed because she didn't have full coverage on her Camry.

I check my phone for messages, then frown when I see one from my mother.

–Mom: I saw on the news your place burned down. Are you dead?

The way the question is phrased is so blunt and unfeeling. But then, this is the woman who once called in the middle of the night to ask if I was sleeping because she wanted something and didn't care if she woke me up. I decide not to let her rude text upset me too much. She might genuinely be worried. I didn't even contact her after the fire.

–Mom: Nobody would say, and you didn't text me or your dad or Katt. Apparently two people died in the fire. I just want to know. In case I need to file a claim.

File a claim?

–Me: A CLAIM?

–Mom: Oh. So you're alive.

–Me: You took out life insurance on me?

–Mom: Yes, when you were one. It was only two bucks to start. And we sort of forgot about it until recently. But the payout is decent. A million dollars.

My jaw slackens. Tremors run through me, and I can barely hold the phone. *A million dollars.* I can feel her disappointment through the screen. If only I'd been a little slower leaving the inferno, I could've just died and become useful.

–Mom: I guess it's all right. Maybe next time.

I do a double take.

–Me: Next time?

–Mom: You know what I mean.

–Me: I know what it sounds like. That you're sad I didn't die in the fire.

As soon as I hit send, an overwhelming sense of misery washes over me. I bend over, an arm around my belly. Why is it that I feel so small and pathetic every time I speak to my mom? I'm tempted to ask if she bought the same policy on Katt, too, but I'm too chicken. What if she says no? That she only bought one for me because Katt's better alive than dead?

My thoughts are a mess, my emotions a tangled knot that can't be pulled apart.

—Mom: You're being melodramatic. It was just a figure of speech. And a lack of humor is unbecoming.

—Me: Yes, of course. Sorry I'm being too overly serious instead of dead.

—Mom: I didn't even really yell at you for publicly embarrassing Katt in that video. You know you can't hang on to a man like Josh Huxley anyway. Just help Katt plan her wedding to him and stop embarrassing yourself. Thanks to the video, pretty soon everyone's going to know you got dumped. But if you show up at the wedding, people won't think it was such a bad breakup.

—Me: Has it ever occurred to you that maybe—just MAYBE—he likes me?

—Mom: Are you high from inhaling too much smoke or something?

I shake all over as tears gather in my eyes. Why is my own mom so casually cruel to me? Why does she think I'm so *unworthy*?

Then I recall the way Josh looked at me in the car, his eyes steady and unwavering just before said he liked me. How that made me warm, made my heart race.

—Me: He SAID he likes me.

—Mom: And you believe him? Men say things they don't mean all the time, especially to young women who don't have much going for them. I wouldn't confuse pity with affection.

I put down my phone, too upset to continue the conversation. All the delicious tension and fluttery sensations Josh gave me have disappeared, leaving me cold and empty inside.

Then I force a stiff smile. *Should just let all this roll off me.* It doesn't matter what she says. It shouldn't. As long as I can put on a smile, I'll be fine.

17

JOSH

The sales clerk at Sebastian Jewelry hovers as I look around. A soft Mozart piano sonata floats in the air. I walk along the marble floor and study the selection of diamonds, laid out on dark navy velvet. Nothing really screams *Klein*. She needs something lovely, delicate and sweet. Nothing overly ostentatious but something that makes a statement that she's important.

"Is there anything that catches your eye?" the clerk says. His name tag reads Andrew.

"Well, Andrew, I need something grand and sweet. It needs to show that the woman is significant to me."

He considers for a moment. "I have a few items here. Diamonds are classic, but sometimes you require something that's a bit more unique, if you know what I mean." He shows me an exceptional selection of sapphires. "I personally think diamonds are a bit too common. And unless blue diamonds are super-saturated, sapphires look much more regal. Did you know that the royals used to propose with sapphire rings? They're really so much more romantic."

The cuts and designs are stunning, especially set against platinum bands. I take one with a large, round stone in the center, its color the shade of the Pacific on a calm, sunny day, with diamonds surrounding it like little flames. Small sapphire chips dot the surface of the band, giving it a contemporary but classic feel. As I turn the ring, the stones reflect the lights like tiny midnight stars. It's fit for a princess.

I close my eyes for a moment to imagine it on Klein's finger. It'd complement her creamy complexion, and stand out for all the right reasons. People would admire a woman wearing a ring as stunning as this.

Most importantly, it'll show everyone she's taken. *Stay away, motherfuckers. She's mine.*

God, that's going to be satisfying.

"This one," I say.

"A great choice," Andrew says sincerely.

I scan the area again just in case I missed something. I stop as a tiara snags my attention. It's large enough to be noticed without being obnoxious, the clear stones evenly cut and sparkling like each holds its own inner fire. "That one—all diamonds?"

"Yes, set in fourteen-karat white gold," he says.

"Okay. That one, too." I can just picture Klein with the tiara in her pretty curls, looking bright, beautiful and special. A sweet princess.

"Certainly, sir."

"My accountant will arrange for the payment," I say, texting instructions to the man who manages my large expenditures, then share the information with Andrew. The wire should go out within an hour of confirming the price.

"Of course."

"Once the payments are finalized, deliver both to Josh Huxley at Huxley & Webber." I hand him my card.

"Yes, sir."

I nod and head out. I don't want to be late for my lunch meeting with one of the most well-known socialites in the world. Elizabeth Pryce-King is famous for her charitable work, but also famous for being Hollywood megastar Ryder Reed's only sister. She agreed to see me at the last minute, saying her husband canceled a date because of some work emergency. She sounded a bit forlorn, but not for long.

She picked Éternité for the meal. The contemporary Japanese fusion restaurant has a wait list so long, people joke that you might die before you get to eat there. But she can always get a table because her cousin owns the place.

I head inside and give the hostess Elizabeth's name. She nods and takes me through the airy, open hall space all the way to the back where the private rooms are. She opens one to her left. "Here you are, sir."

I take a step inside. Elizabeth is at the round table, her golden hair cascading down her back. She's a beautiful woman with intelligent gray eyes and soft, delicate features. However, I never felt any attraction to her—something about her didn't speak to me, although we're good friends.

As the head of the Pryce Family Foundation, she's an extremely influential fundraiser for a variety of worthy causes. Unlike many charities, her foundation actually sends most of the money raised to the people she hopes to help, which is why I regularly donate to it.

As usual, she is in a well-fitted dress—this time pink—and gives me a wide grin. "Hey, Josh."

"Hey." I start to take a seat, then notice we aren't alone. Her assistant Tolyan is sitting behind her, looking like an even-more-humorless-than-usual version of the Grim Reaper. The man's from Russia, and he doesn't say much. I actually thought he was either mute or didn't speak English until I heard him brief Elizabeth about some embezzlement scandal at one of the organizations she was planning to partner with. There's a thick solidity to him, the kind that has to do with brutal efficiency and physicality. His dark navy suit isn't custom made, but it's well tailored and fits him perfectly. I'm convinced the man's really there to protect her—it's just that she feels a self-conscious about having "a bodyguard" tagging around with her everywhere.

"I didn't realize Tolyan would be here," I say.

"You can trust him to keep whatever we discuss confidential."

I nod, then order the sea bream drizzled with basil and wasabi sauce. It's served raw, which I like. The server leaves, and we make small talk for a few minutes. Then Elizabeth leans forward.

"Okay, so. Who's this woman? Tell me everything," she says.

"My assistant. Haven't you met her?"

"No. You never introduced us, and I never had a reason to go to your office. I'm not my brother."

"Too bad. You could've been a bigger star than Ryder."

"Ha. Say that to his face—but invite me first because I want to see his reaction." She waggles her well-shaped eyebrows.

I laugh. "If you get a chance to drop by, I'll introduce you to Klein. I think you'll love her. She's very nice."

"Nice," Elizabeth repeats. "So. What's going on? I know you didn't invite me to gossip about your fiancée."

"This is why I like you. You never waste my time."

The door opens, and the server brings out three plates—the sea bream for me, some fancy maguro slices arranged to look like roses for Elizabeth, and basic steamed lobsters with butter sauce—specially done for Tolyan, because that isn't on the menu.

I wait until the server's gone. "I need a favor. You use a special team for running background checks, right? I need an introduction."

She cocks an eyebrow. "Doesn't your family have its own? Or the firm?"

"Yes, but they haven't found anything."

"Who are you trying to look into? A client?"

I shake my head. "Kenna Miller. An employee at Huxley & Webber."

Her background report came back too clean, and I don't like it. I saw her arguing with people who stopped her in the lobby, ostensibly to "collect what she owes them," which first got my attention. So I had her investigated because I don't trust that she's just an innocent blonde with a burn scar on her back, exactly like the girl who saved Ares from the fire, and just *happens* to work at the firm.

Although Kenna turned out not to be Ares's savior, something about the situation still feels wrong. She hasn't worked at the firm for long. And if Ares hadn't found Lareina when he did, Kenna might've taken credit for saving him back then and wormed her way into the family. We would've been more welcoming and kinder to her—and let our guard down.

That's exactly what Mom would want. And she's careful enough to ensure Kenna's background is as clean as possible.

I want to use Elizabeth's team because there's nothing she doesn't know—or can't find out. She's very thorough about vetting those she hires and partners with due to the huge sums of money her foundation handles. If there are any skeletons in Kenna's closet, her team will discover them.

"My team may not find anything either," Elizabeth says.

"I still want to try. If this doesn't pan out, then okay."

"I'll have the team lead text you if he's interested in taking on the project. I can't guarantee anything. They hardly ever accept new clients."

"That's fine. I appreciate it."

"And if they say okay, could you do me a favor?"

"Sure."

"I need you and your fiancée to come to the charity opera a few weeks from now. I can send you the details, but the organizers are having trouble selling tickets. Their PR efforts have been less than stellar. I'm helping because they're trying to get some relief to the latest hurricane victims in Florida and Georgia."

"That's fine," I say even though operas aren't my thing. "I'll let my family know too."

"You're a gem. Your assistant is lucky to have you."

I shake my head. "The lucky one is me."

18

AILEE

THE PHONE BUZZES a few more times, but I ignore it. There's absolutely no need to read Mom's texts—half will be making excuses for herself and half will blame me for not being more understanding. Not a single one will make me feel better.

My belly rumbles. *I should probably eat something.* Some food might improve my mood. At least I won't suffer from low blood sugar.

Josh's kitchen is fully stocked, which for some reason I find surprising. I toast an English muffin and munch on it with cream cheese and strawberry jam.

The discreet white panel next to one of the fridges beeps. I look at it, wondering what's going on. This area probably doesn't get door-to-door salespeople. *Did I trigger the security system?*

The full-color screen shows a couple of women.

"Ailee, we know you're home!" Lareina says cheerily.

"Josh sent us. Can you let us in?" Fiona adds.

I blink. What are Ares's and Bryce's wives doing here?

I hit the open button on the monitor, curious about this visit. Did I forget to do something for them on Josh's behalf? I remind him of all upcoming birthdays and any family-related celebrations, but can't think of anything that's happening at the moment.

The door unlocks, and they come in. Lareina is pretty, with unusual eyes—one blue and one green. A teal-and-purple dress with a loose skirt fits her slim frame, her stilettos silver. Her wavy blonde hair hangs down in a heavy mass, and she has the most beautiful smile.

Fiona, on the other hand, is in a white empire-waist top and stretchy blue pants, maximizing comfort. Azure flip-flops slap the floor as she walks, a pink lacquer adorable on her toes. Her mouth twitches awkwardly, like she wants to smile under her mop of red hair, but can't quite make herself to do so. Not sure why. Does she disapprove of the way Josh and I got "engaged"?

Lareina hugs me before I can say a word. "This is so exciting! I'm getting another sister!"

"Thanks..." It's just a fake engagement, but I don't have the heart to burst her bubble when she's so excited.

"I was screaming when I saw the video. By the way, it didn't do you justice. Bad lighting."

"She's right. The video made you look slightly green, but then, it also made your sister look like Shrek, so..." Fiona says.

I giggle, both at the imagery and the very idea that Katt could ever look like an ogre.

She covers her nose. "Sorry. Something smells a bit *off* in here."

I stiffen with embarrassment. *Is it the soot on my clothes?*

"Not you," she adds hurriedly. "Probably some food or something."

"Just an English muffin," I say, in case she thinks I ate something super gross in Josh's home.

"No, it's *cream cheese*. Ugh." Fiona turns slightly pale. "I've developed this weird aversion to almost everything."

Oh, shoot. I should've realized she might be experiencing nausea sooner. "Is there anything I can do to make you feel better?" I take her and Lareina to sit in the living room so they can be away from the kitchen.

Fiona shakes her head. "Sorry I'm being difficult. Morning sickness is killing me. Anything except cornflakes, and my body's like *nope*. I can't even smell coffee on Bryce without feeling like I'm about to heave. He's eating out for dinner and then brushing his teeth before coming home now." Her shoulders sag. "This isn't what I thought would happen when I got pregnant. I thought I'd be glowing, and he'd bring home all the delish things I was craving."

Lareina pats her shoulder. "It'll pass. It's still early."

"Yeah, I read that as the hormones fluctuate, your condition can change with them," I add in sympathy. "I'm pretty sure the glow doesn't come until the second or third trimester."

"I hope so." Fiona smiles wanly. "Are *you* all right, though? I saw the news about the fire. How awful. Josh said you lost everything."

"More or less. Except for my car, which I can't drive until I get the fob replaced. *Buuut*—the bright side is that I'm healthy and unhurt." I smile to let them know there's no need to worry.

"So you only escaped with what you're wearing?" Lareina gestures at my clothes, moving her hand up and down. "Like, literally?"

I nod. "I got lucky because a neighbor noticed the fire and knocked on my door. Otherwise, it could've been much worse."

"Still, it's horrible. What about things like photos with your family and friends?" Fiona asks.

The sincere warmth touches me. "Everything I want to keep is backed up in the cloud," I say. And there really wasn't much except for some photos with friends. My family and I never took a lot of pictures. And the ones we did take were awkward, with me trying to act like I belonged in the shots while Mom and Dad had their arms around Katt. I keep that to myself, though, since Fiona's family situation is worse than mine. It wasn't long ago that gruesome articles about her criminally abusive brother were all over the place, leaving her no dignity or privacy.

"Do you want to head out and get some clothes and stuff?" Lareina asks. "We'd love to take you shopping, if that's okay."

I almost tear up at the unexpected offer. The idea of having to replace everything has been just...overwhelming. I hate making decisions about what to buy—because it has to be affordable *and* nice, since I have to look the part of a successful lawyer's assistant. If Max were in town, I would've asked her to shop with me. But she won't be back for several days, and I can't continue to wear this shirt and boxers, especially sans bra.

I've never seen Lareina and Fiona dressed badly, so I'm sure they both have a fabulous sense of style. Still, I hesitate. "Okay, but..." I turn to Fiona. "Won't you get tired? I don't want to impose if you'd rather rest at home."

She smiles. "I slept in this morning. And my doctor said it's better to get out and about from time to time. Besides, I want to hear *everything* about your romance with Josh!"

Lareina nods eagerly.

My lips curve, although my brain runs ten thousand miles an hour to figure out what to say—because of course there *isn't* any romance, unless they consider my unrequited love for Josh romantic.

I don't want to disappoint the two or say something that could embarrass Josh, so I just maintain a smile and head out with them.

We get into a sleek black Cullinan. "Nice ride," I say, admiring the beautiful leather interior.

"A pregnancy gift from Bryce." Fiona grins as she starts the engine and pulls away from the mansion. "I told him I didn't need one, but he said *the baby* deserves a car." She rolls her eyes, but the corners of her mouth twitch.

"He's looking for a reason to spoil you." Lareina puts on a small mock pout. "Ares says I'm not allowed to drive until he buys me a tank."

"Why?" I ask, surprised.

"I *almost* totaled the Mercedes he bought me."

"Oh my God!" I gasp. "Are you okay? When was this?"

"Mid-April."

"Is this the car Ares bought you for Valentine's Day, even though Bryce told him to get you a beginner's car?" Fiona asks.

Lareina nods.

"A beginner's car?" I say. "What's that?"

"You know, a sturdy but relatively cheap used car you don't mind damaging a bit while you learn to drive," Fiona says.

"Oh. But why would you need that?" I ask Lareina.

"I'm new to driving," Lareina says. "My aunt and uncle were paranoid I might flee with my trust fund, so they never taught me."

I nod, remembering the scandal. "They were arrested and thrown in jail, right?"

"*Yes.*" Lareina nods with a satisfied gleam in her eye. "Anyway, that's I started to learn so late. But a girl's gotta be able to go to places—"

"In a tank," Fiona says, winking at me.

"The accident totally wasn't my fault! That brick wall just appeared out of nowhere in the dark. And I braked as soon as I saw it. Of course, Ares completely panicked, even though I was fine. Not a strand of my hair was damaged. But he acted like I'd died or something."

"Mercs are well constructed," Fiona says dryly. "But you have to give the man some leeway. He's paranoid about your safety."

I nod in agreement. Ares is always careful about the family's wellbeing. It probably comes from being the eldest. And with Lareina, the woman he's in love with, his protectiveness probably goes overboard.

"Are you siding with him?" Lareina says with mock outrage.

"Yes. Because I don't want you hurt, either," Fiona says.

"Well." Lareina gives her a small smile. "I love you too, you know."

A pang of longing pierces me. Lareina and Fiona interact like close sisters might. I wish I still had that with Katt, but she's too cool for me now.

"So. Should we go for the works, Ailee?" Lareina asks, looking at me.

"Anything's fine," I say. "I'm going to need to replace almost everything. What do you have in mind?"

"Let's hit Jun's boutique. It has everything. Josephine took me there last month, and I loved it," Fiona says, then turns to me. "That's Josephine Blackwood, a personal shopper. She's the best."

"She really is." Lareina sighs. "Sorry we couldn't get her for you, but she's booked solid for the next two months. She has the best eye for color and texture."

"I'm sure you'll be fabulous," I say. "You're a world-renowned artist."

Her eyelashes flutter with a hint of shyness even as pride colors her cheeks. "Well, thanks. I hope you don't regret saying that."

We pull into a parking lot for a boxlike structure. I would've missed it if somebody told me to meet them here because nothing on the building indicates it's a boutique. It actually looks more like a warehouse.

Fiona parks the car. I hesitate, now that we're here. "Do you think I can go in like this?" I gesture at my outfit.

"They won't mind," Lareina says, looping her arm around mine. "You're practically my sister-in-law."

"Well, you know that, um, Josh and I haven't really set a date yet."

Fiona waves a hand. "Close enough."

Lareina nods. "Exactly. An engagement is as good as a marriage with him. I'll bet Akiko started hyperventilating when she saw the video."

"Totally. I asked Bryce why he's been withholding the best family gossip, and he just shrugged and presented me with another box of cornflakes. Like that'd be enough to make up for holding out on me." Fiona rolls her eyes, but the twinkle in them betrays her affection for her husband.

I just smile. Nice of Bryce to keep quiet when he has to know there isn't anything romantic going on between me and Josh. But then, he's always loyal to his brothers—and is especially in sync with his twin in temperament and attitude toward family and the firm.

We walk inside the building. The interior is bright, with stunning chandeliers glittering from the high ceiling. Pale cream walls have recessed nooks with large pots of vibrant plants, most of them lilies and irises.

A tall, slim Asian woman comes around the reception counter, her stilettos clacking against the lightly veined marble floor. She's in a fitted scarlet dress that molds to her lithe frame, a pair of diamond earrings dangling from her ears. Her ebony hair is cut diagonally, the slanted edge razor straight. A diamond choker sparkles on her neck, and her nails are impeccably lacquered in lavender.

She smiles. "Lareina, so good to see you." They hug and exchange air kisses. "You're looking fabulous. Literally glowing," she says to Fiona.

"The power of cornflakes," Fiona jokes as they too hug and air-kiss.

"Ailee, this is Jun. Jun, This is my sister-in-law Ailee."

"Oh, the girl in the..." Jun doesn't finish, diplomatically so. But her dark eyes study me from head to toe, her lips pursing a little. Not judging per se, but not entirely friendly, either. Maybe she used to date Josh before I started working for him...? "Lovely to meet you."

I paste on a polite smile. "The pleasure's mine."

"My poor sister lost everything in a nasty fire, and she needs clothes, shoes, the works," Lareina says.

"Then you're in the right place." Jun's smile grows genuine. "I can make magic happen."

"That's what I was hoping for. A girl needs something to cheer her up."

"Exactly," Fiona adds.

"This way," Jun says. She leads us down a spotless, gleaming marble hall lined with potted palm trees and into a huge, airy room at the end. Cushy seats and a big table laden with stacks of glossy books full of fashionable clothing photos occupy one section of the chamber. Other clerks who are dressed as well as Jun roll out racks and racks of dresses, slacks, skirts and tops. One pushes a gigantic sliding door to my right, unveiling shelves and shelves of shoes, each pair spotlighted and shining in the display.

I don't have to see any price tags to know everything in here costs a kidney. I've seen similarly fancy items in Katt's closet. She slapped my hand away when I tried to touch one, saying if I damaged it, I'd never be able to compensate her for it.

"Nice!" Lareina says, her eyes sparkling as she looks over the offerings.

I paste on a smile, a little overwhelmed and regretting that I agreed to come here instead of TJ Maxx or something. I should've given more thought to the kind of places Lareina and Fiona would shop at. Lareina is a shipping heiress who's even richer than Ares. And although Fiona's family fortunes have fallen, she grew up in old-money luxury.

Will it embarrass Lareina and Fiona if I leave without buying anything? It looks like they're close to Jun, and she's already done the work of bringing everything out for me. Maybe I'll just buy a cheap-looking T-shirt and leave. I don't know if there's a T-shirt on any of these racks, but there has to be something close. Even rich people wear the basics.

Another clerk comes over and places a platter of chocolate truffles in front of us—along with hot tea for Fiona and champagne for Lareina and me.

"I had her bring something you all can eat," Jun says. "The tea doesn't have much scent, and the chocolate's... Well, it's chocolate."

Crap. The chocolate looks really pricey, and I'm pretty sure the place doesn't serve the kind of sparkling wine you can buy on sale at Walmart or something. Now I feel like I *really* have to buy something more expensive than a T-shirt for the snack.

Fiona covers her nose, then breathes in shallowly. Slowly, she lowers her hand. "Oh my God... I don't feel nauseated."

Jun winks. "My sister had the worst morning sickness when she was pregnant with her second kid. This chocolate and tea made all the difference for her."

"You try it first," Fiona says to me. "I can't guarantee I'll be able to control my reaction, just in case it hits me wrong."

I glance at Lareina, wondering if I should wait for her to take a bite first.

However, Lareina looks at me hopefully, then explains after pulling her lips in for a moment, "I still can't eat anything unless somebody tries it first."

I stare at her in surprise. I've heard interviews about her past, but thought she overcame it with Ares and the rest of the family behind her.

She smiles ruefully. "I know. But some things just can't be overcome so easily."

I pop a piece into my mouth. The creamy truffle melts on my tongue quickly, flooding my mouth with an intense chocolate flavor. It goes down my throat smoothly too, leaving a trail of richness behind.

Swallowing a moan, I nod at Lareina and Fiona with a thumbs-up.

Lareina takes a bite, then blinks in pleasant surprise. "It's amazing. You have to try some, even if you end up puking," she says to Fiona.

Fiona inhales to boost her courage. "If you say so." She picks up a truffle and bites into it gingerly, then licks her lips and waits a few moments. A slow smile spreads over her face. "I can eat this." She breathes out slowly. "Oh my *God*. I think this might be the elixir of life."

Jun laughs. "You're welcome." She turns to me. "Ailee, you can pick anything you want. I'll have everything delivered to your address, so you won't have to worry about carrying it home."

Home delivery. Just how much stuff am I expected to buy? And then I also realize I don't even have a wallet on me. "Um. I don't have a credit card or anything. Do you take Apple Pay?"

"Yes, we do, but I didn't think you'd swipe plastic," Jun says with a careless shrug.

"You didn't...?" What *was* she was thinking?

"Some people pay on site, but most get invoiced. I was planning to send Josh a nice, fat bill." Jun's eyes gleam. "Love spending a man's money when he's determined to spoil his woman." She puts her fingers to her chest in a delicate gesture. "It would be wrong of me to impede your fiancé's desire to splurge on you."

My mouth forms a small O. Surprised pleasure that he wants to spoil me wars with the need to stay grounded in reality, lest I overestimate my place in his life. We're only together for six months, after all.

"Don't worry. His accountant already sent a text, telling me you can buy anything you want."

I feel a little faint as Jun speaks. *Josh has been* really *thoughtful.* "But everything looks expensive," I blurt.

Jun laughs. "It better. Come on. Let's get started."

19

AILEE

"THAT PINK WOULD BE perfect for you. Super cute. Lively. Adorable," Lareina says, pointing out a fitted dress that would work for an evening out or the office, if paired with a cardigan or jacket.

It looks great on the rack, but...

Ailee, you know pink makes you look bloated, right? It's the kind of color only Katt can pull off. Mom's voice rings in my head, and I force a smile. "Pink might not be right for me, especially something that pastel."

Fiona shoots me a curious glance.

"I think it makes me look...expansive." I spread my arms to illustrate the point.

Lareina stares at me like I just told her I'd like to jump naked into a compost bin. "What? That shade is *perfect* for you."

"Worried about light colors adding a few pounds?" Fiona asks. "Something like that?"

I nod. "Plus, my mother said the same thing."

Lareina scoffs. "Only if the dress hangs on you like a sack. This is well tailored and fitted. Besides, you can always add a belt—like this one—to draw attention to the cinched waist." She picks out a belt made with dark faux-croc leather. "This particular shade of pink would well with almost anything..." She narrows her eyes, considering. "Except red. Trust the artist."

Fiona nods next to her. "If you don't believe us, just put 'em on and see how you look."

Jun hands me a set of nude lingerie as well. I go into the dressing area, strip out of my clothes and try on the items Lareina selected. Jun must have a magic eye—the underwear molds perfectly to my body and provides great support. The dress is made with a silk that feels ultra luxurious against my bare skin, and the color flatters my complexion without making me look "bloated." The belt somehow completes the outfit, just like Lareina said. One of Jun's assistants sneaks in a pair of cute silver sandals. I slip my feet in them and check my reflection. The dress is as lovely as Lareina promised. My eyes shine, and the smile on my face couldn't be brighter.

When I come out, she nods. "Man, I'm good. You're a babe! Josh won't know what hit him when he sees you in that dress!"

Fiona claps. "You look spectacular!"

I grin. "Thanks. I... I didn't know I could look like this." I rest my hands on my cheeks. "I always went for neutral colors like beige."

"Nothing wrong with beige, but do you actually like it?" Fiona asks, her gaze skeptical. "You look more like a bright color kind of girl."

I bite my lower lip as more of Mom's criticism flows through my mind.

That cobalt blue is terrible for your complexion. Of course it looked great on Katt, but really, you should know better.

The pencil skirts are wrong—make your butt look flat. If you hit the gym more, maybe you could pull it off.

"Not really. But it's the least offensive color."

"Offensive?" Fiona looks around theatrically. "To whom?"

"Um..." *My mom?* I swallow the words before they can come out. "People?"

Lareina shakes her head. "Haters, you mean. They aren't worth your energy. Don't dress to please others. Dress to please yourself. You have the most beautiful platinum hair and violet eyes. I know plenty of people who'd love to have that." She speaks like she doesn't notice or care that my hair is curling wildly. "You'd own any color, but with those eyes you'll look stunning in a deep, vibrant blue."

"Oh yeah. Very hot," Fiona says. "And with your figure, pencil skirts would look amazing. Josh won't be able to tear his eyes away from you if you show up in one at the office." She grins.

"Totally."

With their encouragement, I pick out items in shades and styles I've never dared, thinking I couldn't possibly pull them off. But honestly, I look *great*. Feel beautiful too. Lareina and Fiona's *oohs* and *aaahs* start to drown out Mom's critical voice in my head. The vivid colors send shivers down my spine. The various fits and styles boost my confidence that I really *can* wear anything.

Jun keeps the champagne flowing, and Lareina and I clink our glasses after each successful selection, while Fiona gorges on chocolate.

Soon, an elegantly lined, woven-seagrass basket is full. Jun's people bring out makeup too. After selecting a foundation and concealer, I choose several adventurous shades of eye shadow and lipstick. Might as well go all the way.

"That navy is going to be amazing," Lareina remarks as she sifts through some of the colors in my basket. "With your eyes, you can go pretty wild."

"I'm envious." Fiona sighs. "I love that color so much, but it looks weird on me."

"I think I have enough," I say after we pick out several bras and thongs to add to the already fairly large pile. There are countless shoes —my God, Lareina is obsessed with them. I had to surreptitiously remove several pairs from the approved mound. But I keep some dressier ones, others for work and home. Shoes and accessories that I can mix and match. Just imagining myself in those bright shades and various styles makes me feel like I'm a star, in charge of my life, rather than some unseen extra in somebody else's existence.

Fiona leans to Jun and whispers something in her ear. The latter's eyes slide in my direction, then she smiles.

"What is it?" I ask, a little uncertain about the sly smile.

"Just working out the final logistics. Seriously, I love what we picked out. Josh will think it's money well spent." Fiona's eyes gleam.

"Thank you." I flush.

"Aw, it was fun. I loved it," Lareina says. "And your new dress is so cute!"

"I think so too." My cheeks grow even warmer. The bright sunflower-yellow sundress I put on is really adorable. It has a small kitten embroidered on the chest.

"Me too," Lareina says.

"Besides, I discovered something I can eat other than cornflakes. That should make Bryce happy," Fiona says with a grin.

"Yay!" Jun cheers.

We laugh and head to the counter, and I sign for the items on the invoice. The amount is... Holy *shit*. My heart almost stops.

"What's wrong?" Lareina says.

What's wrong *is I spent more money than I should have.* On the other hand, I've never had this much fun—or felt this beautiful and happy about my purchases.

What the hell. I deserve to pamper myself a little and feel pretty. Besides, if I have to buy clothes, might as well buy ones that make my heart flutter.

"Nothing." I sign—firmly—on the dotted line. I'll just pay these off in installments until my insurance cuts me a check for the damages.

Jun gives me two modestly sized glossy paper bags. "Here you go."

"That's it?" I ask in surprise.

"The rest will be delivered to your fiancé's address tonight or tomorrow, depending on my staff's schedule. But this is for tomorrow —a cute dress, shoes and a change of underwear, plus your makeup," she explains. "The set is professional enough for an office setting."

"Oh. Okay. Thanks!" I smile and take the two bags, which are surprisingly light.

Fiona drives us. Lareina starts singing, slightly off key. She slurs her words a little too, probably tipsy from all the champagne. She's adorable. I join her, because why not? I can't remember the last time I had this much fun with anyone other than Max.

Besides, I really didn't expect today to progress to *this*. I imagined I'd be in a cheap, dingy motel room—alone—filling out insurance claims online, then end the day on a high note by hitting Target for the essentials.

Fiona drives past the gates and stops in front of the main entrance. "Can I come in to use the bathroom? It's urgent."

"Of course." I gesture. "Come on in."

She and Lareina follow me inside. Fiona dashes to the powder room.

"I'm a little thirsty," Lareina says, still slurring. Now she's swaying too. "Mind if I have some orange juice?"

"Not at all." Josh said I could have whatever I wanted. I hope that means it's okay for me to give a glass of orange juice to Lareina.

"You're the best." She winks.

"My pleasure." I smile, then pour her a glass and take a quick sip first before handing it to her.

She gulps it down. "That's *so* good. I almost feel human again. I don't know why I'm so thirsty. I had four champagnes."

"Maybe that's why you're thirsty. Alcohol can make you dehydrated."

She frowns. "How come you're not drunk?"

"I'm totally drunk." I giggle. "It's just that I can pass for being sober. It's a special talent," I blurt out, then bite my lip in embarrassment. Mom told me that it was the most useless talent ever, and I feel a little silly about it all of a sudden. A knot forms under my breastbone.

Lareina's eyes widen with admiration. "I wish I could do that. So unfair." She pouts. "Whenever I get drunk, Ares thinks it's funny."

The tension in my chest eases again.

She waves the half-full glass of OJ. "So you aren't even tipsy?"

"Well, I get drunk. I wouldn't drive right now. It's just that I can speak like I'm not affected."

"Fascinating. By the way, do you think—" She starts to lean forward, then stumbles. "Oops, oh crap!"

She's teetering dangerously in her heels, and I leap toward her to catch her so she doesn't hit the hard marble floor. The glass tilts in her hand; the juice splashes over the rim. I gasp as the icy liquid hits my chest.

Her face crumples. "Oh my God, I am so sorry! You *just* bought that!"

"It's okay. I'm sure it'll come out in the wash. I can just put on something different," I say, then stop as I realize that the bags from Jun's shop only contain clothes and shoes for tomorrow and a change of underwear.

Lareina's expression remains scrunched with worry and embarrassment.

I wave my hand dismissively, then smile at her. "You know what, don't worry about it."

"How can I not worry about it? Now you have nothing to wear." Her tone grows increasingly dejected as she speaks.

"What happened?" Fiona says, walking up.

I turn to her—and swear I notice her eyes light up as she takes in the big stain on my dress. But maybe I imagined it, because whatever I saw is gone just like that. She blinks at the wet stain on my chest with a frown on her pretty face.

"My fault. I got clumsy," Lareina says.

Fiona pats her shoulder. "Don't worry. Ailee can just wear a clean shirt from Josh's closet."

What? "No, no, no, those are the boss's shirts," I say quickly. I'm not at all comfortable with rummaging through his closet.

"The 'boss'?" Fiona blinks. "He's your fiancé! What belongs to him belongs to you."

"Well, yeah, but we aren't married yet," I say feebly. Josh is pretending to save my butt—and dignity. Not only that, I'll have to keep working after the engagement is over, and it'll be awkward if I let myself get too emotionally attached to him and end up all clingy like his exes.

"So? You'll be a Huxley soon," Lareina says, totally on Team Fiona. "*Pietas et unitas.*"

"What does that mean again?" Fiona asks, frowning and tapping her lip theatrically.

"It means 'all his stuff is yours now.'"

"Right. And if he complains, you can dump him. Although if he apologizes, you should take him back so we can still be sisters." Fiona's eyes twinkle.

I shake my head.

She isn't giving up. "I can help you pick the cheapest one. Would that help? You can't really stay in that dress. It's almost see-through now."

I look down. Sure enough, the thin fabric's gone semitransparent. It even shows the outline of my bra.

"It's just a shirt. And you can repay his 'generosity' by making some tasty dinner," Lareina says, exchanging a quick, mischievous look with Fiona.

Fiona loops her arm around mine and nearly drags me up the stairs with strength that shocks me. Maybe it's the magical power of chocolate. Lareina manages the stairs with care behind us.

"Which one is his bedroom?" Fiona says.

I point.

"Awesome." Fiona opens the door with all the confidence of a woman who belongs. If I didn't know better, I'd think *she* was Josh's girlfriend. She walks into the closet. Lareina follows in.

I'm amazed at the "closet." *It's bigger than my old bedroom.* The center island holds watches and cuff links I've seen before. A silver cane with a wolf's head sits in a case.

"His Huxley cane," Fiona explains. "Every Huxley has one. Bryce commissioned one for the baby already." She places a protective hand over her belly.

Lareina looks around. "Wow, this is nice. I think his closet is bigger than Ares's. Didn't know Josh was into fashion so much."

"Bryce's is bigger," Fiona says. "He's a peacock." Her voice is soft with affection. She turns to me. "How come there's no space for your stuff?"

"I just moved in, much sooner than expected due to the fire. So, you know, he probably hasn't had time to rearrange his things," I say, sweating a little and praying I sound believable. I don't like to lie, but I don't want them to dislike me or treat me differently because I'm not his real fiancée. In six months everything will be over, and I'll have to give up the nice relationship I could've had with these women.

"I love the way this shirt feels." Lareina runs her hand down one of the white dress shirts. She checks the label. "One hundred percent silk, handwoven. Must be a gift from Akiko. She always gets the coolest stuff from Japan." Lareina takes the hanger off the rod. "How about this one? The fabric is nice."

"No, no, no." I wave my hand desperately. "I can't possibly. Handwoven silk from Japan sounds more expensive than my kidney."

"Nonsense. I think it's the cheapest item in here," Fiona says.

I stare at her in shock. "Really?"

"Yes. The brothers love material comfort. That includes nice clothes that look and feel amazing. Besides, he won't mind. You're his fiancée and it's just a shirt for a few hours. He has so many shirts already. Besides, don't you know men love women in their shirts?" Fiona leans forward, her eyes sparkling with eagerness.

Part of me says I shouldn't. But maybe I'm more drunk than I thought, because part of me thinks it'd be a great idea to borrow a shirt from Josh, especially if he'll end up loving it.

"I'll send you Akiko's recipe for yakisoba—it's Japanese fried noodles. Make that for Josh and he won't complain about anything," Lareina says, apparently mistaking my hesitation for rejection.

"I've never made Japanese food before." My voice is a bit too squeaky, but really, Japanese cuisine might be beyond me.

"It's super easy. You just need some noodles, pork, cabbage, scallion, onions and the sauce."

"You forgot carrots and bean sprouts," Fiona points out, then turns to me. "It's Bryce's favorite, too."

"Yes. Thank you." Lareina whips out her phone. "Let me place a quick grocery order for you. They'll deliver in an hour. And give me your number so I can forward you the recipe. It's simple, but really delicious. Ares can't get enough, either. If you make a big batch, Josh'll love you forever."

20

JOSH

Gina Rad's whining voice still echoes in my head, and a muscle under my right eye twitches like I'm having some kind of drug reaction. *Who leaves, saying she understands, and then comes back three hours later to revisit the same topic?*

God, I don't bill her enough. I should charge her ten thousand dollars an hour for the migraine she's given me. I head home half an hour earlier than usual because I need the break—and I want to see...

Klein. In my home.

I wait for my gut to react to the idea. Most of the time when I think of people other than my family in my place, I feel like a dog, fur bristling and snarling as it defends its territory. After all, my home is my fortress, where I can feel secure.

But with Klein, it's more like I just found the last piece to complete a puzzle I've been working on all my life.

At the next intersection is a flower shop. I've seen it many times before, but never had a reason to stop by. I start to drive past, then notice a stunning bouquet of pink peonies. Each blossom is huge—and the shade is eye-catching, like Klein's soft, vulnerable lips when I laid my finger on them earlier.

I shift in my seat to ease the tightness, then pull over to the curb. As

I hand over my credit card to the florist, I realize I've never bought flowers for any of my exes. The effort didn't seem necessary, and they never asked. Wining and dining and being seen were enough. But imagining how Klein might react to the flowers sends a spark of excitement through me.

By the time I kill the engine in the garage, my chest is bursting with anticipation. She'll blush. Probably smile, too. Will she place a kiss on my cheek? But such an affectionate gesture might be too much for her to try.

I step inside the house, holding the peonies. Instantly, I'm hit with the mouth-watering aroma of yakisoba, which is one of my absolute favorites. It's such a homey meal with great flavor. But it can't be Akiko stopping by. She rarely does. And even if she did, she wouldn't touch anything in my kitchen, respecting my boundaries.

I move silently toward the kitchen, then come to an abrupt halt. Music plays from the phone on the counter, plugged to a charger. Axelrod's lead singer croons about breaking free, and Klein is swaying to the tune and singing under her breath. The other end of the wooden spatula in her hand glistens with a thick, glazy sauce. She's in one of my dress shirts, her shapely legs sexy below the hem, her bare feet with cute pink toenails shifting as she adds noodles to thin slices of pork belly, onions, cabbage, julienned carrots and beat sprouts in a sauté pan. It's a five-ply pan from the set hand-made in France, which I've never used. Aunt Jeremiah said it was smart to hang them without ever cooking with them because that would ruin the sparkly finish and might even leave scratches on the surface.

But seeing Klein in the kitchen, looking so comfortable and using my things, is beyond gratifying. She just...belongs here. And my favorite silk shirt on her? My head says I should be annoyed. Nobody is allowed to put on my things. If any of my exes had done the same, I would've kicked them out. But my heart is... Well, if it were a cat, it'd purr and stretch, its eyes narrowed into satisfied slits.

The shirt marks Klein as my woman—*mine*. It's more intimate than the ring. The rock shows the world at large that she's taken. But the shirt shows who she belongs to in private—me.

She chopsticks up a couple of noodles for a taste. Her lips purse, making them look soft and kissable. "Perfect." She kills the flame and checks the time. "Awesome. Still got a few minutes," she says to herself.

She puts little jars of sauces into the pantry, then jumps. "*Oh!*" She places a hand over her chest. "You're home early." She actually giggles, and I blink at the sound. It's unusual for her, but lovely.

Her eyes are slightly glazed. *Is she tipsy?* Lareina likely got some quality bubbly for the girls' outing.

"Gina Rad finally left." Klein still has a palm over her chest, pressing my shirt over her breasts. I don't think she notices the silk is fairly thin, and I can make out the shape and color of her areolae and nipples. I'm never washing that shirt.

She winces in sympathy. "Was it as awful as you thought?"

No, your breasts are prettier than I thought. The response pops into my mind, but that isn't the topic of conversation. It takes a moment before my brain remembers we were talking about Gina. "Oh. Yeah, um... worse."

Klein's face scrunches.

"But better now that I'm home with you." I look into her eyes. Surprise and delight flicker in the violet depths, a flush creeping into her cheeks. She's such an open book. How could anybody hurt a woman this sweet and vulnerable?

I hand her the flowers. "Here."

Her teeth flash in a wide smile as she takes the peonies and hugs them carefully to her chest. It's too bad the blossoms are hiding her breasts from view, but I absolutely adore her smile. "They're gorgeous," she says.

"I had to get them for you as soon as I saw them." I run my fingertips along the edges of the velvety petals. "Soft and pretty, like you."

She tilts her head and looks at me. "I don't even know what to say." Her eyes widen. "Oh..."

I wait a beat. "What?"

"It's just...nobody's ever bought me flowers before," she says softly. "You're the first."

Part of me is preening that I'm the first to give her flowers and make her smile with joy. But another part is outraged. What the hell? I always considered Chad to be a piece of shit, but this proves it.

Instead of just gift cards, I should've thought to buy her some pretty blossoms, too, for National Employee Appreciation Day or her birthday.

Klein's eyes are bright, full of a cheery affection that lifts my mood.

Suddenly her light dims a little as she continues to hug the bouquet to her chest. "Uh. I was going to change out of the shirt before you came home."

I frown. "Why?"

"Well, I didn't want you to be unhappy that I took the shirt. Fiona said it's probably the least expensive one in your closet, but still... There was an incident with some spilled juice and I need to launder the dress I bought today."

I can only imagine what Fiona must've told Klein. My sister-in-law lied through her teeth, probably as a small, harmless revenge for my putting a bug in her purse that one time. The shirt is one of the most expensive items I have. Handwoven silk from Japan isn't cheap. Not only that, it's tailored and hand-stitched. Still, I'm not upset because it looks fantastic on Klein. "It's fine. You're my fiancée. You're entitled to wear my shirts." Now I'm wondering if she's wearing panties underneath.

She bites her lip shyly. "Okay. Thanks, boss."

"'Boss'?" I take a step forward. Her eyes widen slightly and she steps back, almost stumbling. I take another step, and her butt hits the edge of the counter. The peonies' sweet fragrance fills the space between us. I pluck the bouquet from her arms and place it on the counter. "You really need to stop calling me that."

"But...you *are* my boss..." She sounds a little bit breathless. Her breasts are rising and falling rapidly. The movements push her nipples against the silk, and all the blood in my head starts to travel downward.

I put my hands on either side of her, caging her and letting her feel my body heat. She leans further back, which presses her breasts even more tautly against the shirt. The view is too damn erotic, especially since she has no clue what she's doing to me. I want to find out how she'll react when she realizes the effect she has on me. I want to push her buttons. See if she'll see me as a man rather than the "boss" she's worked for over the last three years.

"Klein." I say her name like it's that of a goddess. "We're engaged. Don't call me boss again."

"Then what do I call you?" Thoughts fleet over her pretty face, her violet eyes wide. I could stare into them all day long.

"Sweetheart. My love. My liege and master." I quirk a teasing eyebrow. "Sugar cock."

A choked laugh escapes her tightly pressed lips, then she bursts out laughing. *Good.* I love the sound—full of humor and joy. It makes me want to let go and join her.

"I don't think I can do, um, Sugar…" She can't even continue, her face red. "But maybe—"

I run my fingertip over her lips. They're so full, so soft. My dick grows harder. I lean a little closer until I can feel her breath fanning my cheek, and the tips of her breasts brush against my chest. "Or you can just call me Josh."

Her eyelashes flutter. Hesitation lingers in her gaze.

Then something like determination and grit firms her jaw. Her eyes dart left and right, then look straight at me, as though she's ready for one of the most difficult tasks of her life. "Okay. Josh."

She breathes out my name like she's calling for a dream. The single syllable hits me more potently than the best whiskey. She's never used my name before, and my head spins with the unexpectedly intimate and erotic impact.

I stare at her soft mouth. "Say that again," I order her.

Her darkened eyes stare into mine. She licks her lips, her pink tongue darting across them like a skittish rabbit. A heartbeat. She inhales, then her throat works. "Josh."

The second time is even better. My blood heats. "I want to kiss you, Klein." Then I wait a couple of beats, giving her a chance to push me away if it isn't what she wants.

"Okay…Josh."

My control shatters. I dip my head, capturing her mouth. I keep my eyes open, wanting to witness her reaction to our first kiss. Her eyelashes flutter like butterflies, then close. She parts her lips, slips her tongue out to flick it over my mouth. My heart rate skyrockets.

I push my tongue inside her. She tastes like a woman and sweetness, dream and desires. Like...celebration. It feels like I've been racing all my life to reach Klein. She's hot under my mouth, almost feverish. Her hands grip the edge of the counter for balance. I slide mine over until I'm covering them.

Her fingers flex under mine. She deepens the kiss, going up on her toes as she invades my mouth with her tongue, running it along mine. A soft moan tears from her throat, as though she relishes being caged by me, enveloped by my heat and taste.

I plunder her mouth. I can't seem to get enough of her. The shallowing of her breathing makes me want to grind my throbbing dick against her. Or maybe put my thigh between her legs and let her ride me. My head says I should seize the chance. Show her what I can do to her. But the decent part of me steps on the brakes.

Underneath the intoxicating taste of *Ailee* is champagne. She must've drunk some when Lareina and Fiona visited. Fiona can't drink, but Lareina can, and she loves to indulge when she can. Not sure exactly how much Klein had, but I don't want to take advantage if there's a chance she's still tipsy.

When we cross that line—when she's naked and begging me to fill her aching emptiness—she'll be sober. There won't be any alcohol to blame for her lack of inhibition or self-control. It'll be driven only by how good I'm making her feel and how desperately she wants the pleasure only I can give her.

With an almost inhuman effort, I manage to tear my lips from hers. *Fuck.* They're so swollen, rosy and wet. She licks them, as though to savor the remnants of our connection. Disappointment darkens her eyes, and her eyebrows pull together. "What... Why?"

"You're intoxicated, Klein."

"No, I'm not."

"You had drinks with Lareina."

"Yes. But not that much."

She sounds sober, but her eyes have trouble focusing. My lips twitch at how badly she lies. "We'll try again when you haven't had any alcohol."

She pouts. "What if I'm not in the mood next time?"

I laugh, then run a finger along the bridge of her nose. "It'll be my job to make sure you are."

21

AILEE

Josh loves the yakisoba I made. I have no idea what it tastes like, though. It's like chewing on cardboard-box pasta. My entire focus is on the kiss. Even when he says something, I just nod and smile.

Now that I'm in the soft bed in my own room and blinking up at the ceiling in the dark, I have no clue who cleaned up after dinner. I'm still in Josh's dress shirt because he didn't ask for it back. I think he even said I should keep it and wear it as a nightshirt. That it looked great on me. But I'm not one hundred percent certain—my brain quit after the kiss.

I've always known Josh was intense and hot, but I never knew just *how* intense and how he could be, or what it was like to be the receiving end of his focused attention. Up to today, kissing a guy was pleasant enough. Our lips met, the tongues got engaged, and then, if the mood was right and everything was going okay, we'd go further.

I probably should've pushed Josh away when he said he wanted to kiss me. Part of me said it'd be the smart thing to do, but the other part —the one with a curiosity intense enough to end every single life of a whole truckload of cats—wanted to know what it would be like to feel his mouth on mine. I'd seen all those gorgeous women on his arm, but never seen a single photo of him kissing any, even though I'm sure he did. Being the focus of his molten eyes made me unable to turn away because the fire they held heated my core.

Just the mere brush of his lips sent an electric jolt through my spine. For a moment, I thought I might just come, it was *that* potent.

The feel of his tongue in my mouth was so carnally *penetrating*, my knees almost buckled. Every time he ran his tongue over mine, my clit throbbed like he was down there instead. And for the first time in my life, I actually *wanted* to be ravished by a mouth.

My face flames, and I cover my overheated cheeks. Oral sex isn't *awful*, but I've never particularly enjoyed it. It's awkward, for one. Sometimes I lie there and wonder if I smell and taste okay, and then I feel like I should hurry up and climax because the guy's trying and he might be let down if I don't come. Which, ironically, makes it harder to relax and orgasm.

So I never really wanted a man down there...until Josh kissed me.

What the hell, Ailee?!

But every time his tongue stroked against mine, I wanted to feel it on my aching clit. If he didn't want to touch me there with his mouth, he could've just used his fingers. I would've loved that, too. And I would've held his dick, which I could tell was hard even though he didn't do anything overt like pressing it against me. But I wanted him to.

I flip over and press my hips against the mattress. God, I'm so wet. I squeeze my thighs together to ease the pressure, but it's no use. I need Josh.

I whisper his name in the dark. Just saying it brings back the memory, and my body reacts, like his mouth is still fused to mine. My panties are soaked through, and I take them off and discreetly drop them next to the bed.

I slip my hand between my legs and touch the slickness there. The pressure in my clit eases a little, but I can't seem to stimulate it enough. I cup my breast, tease my nipple. I undulate my hips. Increase the tempo of my fingers rubbing the clit.

The orgasm comes and pops, then fizzles like a badly stored soda. I bury my face in the pillow and groan, suddenly feeling ridiculous and out of control. I've never just masturbated to a man before. If I'm in the mood, I might do it to a really spicy romance scene, but...

Hopefully, the memory of what I did tonight doesn't come back to haunt me when I face Josh tomorrow. *It's really because I said his name. Just that alone makes him feel more real—more personal.*

22

JOSH

Bright orange colors the black horizon. Trees tower over the blaze like specters, crackling with the heat. I stare, a chill coursing through my veins.

Ares, no! I'm coming for you.

I start toward the fire. A pair of strong hands grips my shoulders, fingers digging painfully into the muscle. "You aren't going anywhere, Josh." The poisonous voice ripples over me, sending cold apprehension slithering along my spine.

No! I struggle. I have to reach the cabin and save Ares before it's too late. "Let me go! I'm going to save him!" I have to, or I'm going to die. At least part of my soul will shrivel forever.

"Him?" Mom sounds oddly detached. "You mean Ares?" She laughs, and her genuine humor stokes my fury.

"You think it's funny?"

"No. It's just that... He's not there. I wouldn't let my own child burn in a fire. I'm not that cruel."

"I don't believe you." I spit it out. Every word from her mouth is a lie.

"Check for yourself." She presses her cool cheek against mine. I shiver, then turn to glare at her. A cold smirk twists her lips. Her blue eyes glow with glee in a face carved with delicate, elegant lines. But her beauty isn't the type that's warm and inviting. It's the kind that leaves you frozen in fear. She tilts her head toward the fire and pushes me toward it. As we get closer, the fiery heat sears my skin.

The person visible through the narrow door is—

"Klein!" I scream her name, but she doesn't move. My heart stops; panic clenches at my neck. She's tied to the wooden chair, head lolling and curls sticking to her skin. The fire turns her face an eerie shade of orange-red. She's in the same T-shirt and boxers I saw her in this morning.

"Klein!" I call out again. The wind from the flames stirs her hair, but she remains motionless.

I start to rush toward her, but Mom's grip grows stronger, tighter... until my shoulders creak. My struggles only seem to add to her strength. "Damn you, *let go*!"

"I didn't bring you here just to have you run to your girl."

Jesus. I blink, trying to concentrate. Mom lies—and manipulates. She has to know if Klein's truly harmed, she doesn't have any leverage over me. But at the same time, Klein's too still, like a corpse—

My hands begin shaking. "Is she—?" I swallow the next word. I can't continue.

"Dead?" Mom lets out a derisive huff. "Do you want to save her?"

"Of course!"

Mom tsks. "I told you, you're the most like me, but you always resist. You want to be like your father and pretend to be nothing like me. You look at me like I'm the enemy, but I'm not. Do you think your father is a capable man, Josh?" Her fingers dig deeper.

I hide the wince. No way am I letting her witness the pain she's causing me.

"He couldn't save you. Or your brothers. But you...*you* could be different. Embrace your true self. Make me proud, demonstrate to the world what you're capable of."

The flames swell around the cabin. She snaps her fingers, and Kenna emerges from the woods to my left and throws several cans full of gasoline into the cabin. They spill, leaving long, wet lines between me and Klein. Greedy flames immediately consume them, creating walls that are already to Klein's waist. The edge of the fire singes her hair, the pungent smell filling my senses.

No, no, no! I kick Mom in the gut, hard. She grunts, letting go, then laughs. "Good. Now you're acting like a real Dunkel! I always knew it was in you!"

I run toward Klein. Kenna lunges for me; I shove her away. She lands in one of burning pools of gasoline and her clothes catch fire instantly. She starts rolling around, screaming.

The blaze at the door is too strong, and I can't reach Klein at all. For some reason, there seems to be an invisible barrier between us.

"Embrace your true self, Josh. If you want to save her, you have to be like me." Mom's laugh brims with triumph.

I shudder with distaste and nausea, but clench my teeth. "I'll never be like you, you fucking sociopathic bitch!"

That only makes her laugh harder. I take three steps back, then sprint into the wall of fire, ready to incinerate myself if that's what it takes to save Klein.

Hot air burns my lungs. My skin bubbles from the unbearable heat, every square inch throbbing with agony. I grit my teeth.

"Klein, Klein!" I try to call out, but struggle to make any sound. It feels like somebody rubbed sandpaper along the inside of my throat.

Desperate, I stretch my arms, my fingertips just brushing her hair. My foot catches on a short log on the floor. I fall, hitting the ground hard with my elbow and chest. The impact is jarring—

I gasp. Icy air fills my lungs, making me twitch.

I blink in the darkness, my cheek on the cool hardwood floor. Sweat has created a clammy film over my body. The A/C hums softly. My knee aches. Probably hit the floor with it, too, when I fell.

I fumble for the phone on the nightstand and check the time—four thirty-two a.m.

My heart is still racing. I rest my head in my hands, take a few breaths, then scrub my tongue over the edges of my teeth, trying to expel the acrid taste of burned wood in my mouth. It doesn't work— almost as though I really was in a fire trying to save Klein.

I push myself off the floor. Count to ten slowly, willing my heart to settle. But it continues to pound at the same rapid pace. The image of Klein, tied to the chair—

I have to check to make sure she's safe.

Exhaling roughly, I throw on a robe, open the double doors to my bedroom and step into the hall with its faint scent of beeswax. There's no extra heat here. The night-lights glow softly just above the floor as they always do.

Everything's the way it should be. No sign of fire.

The door to Klein's room is closed, a barrier from her like the fire in my dream. There's a sudden urge to smash it down, but I rein myself in. *Don't want to scare her at four thirty-two in the morning.* And I certainly don't want her thinking I'm crazy.

I inhale and exhale, then roll my shoulders. The muscles behind my neck are tight; I stretch them a little, but it doesn't help. I move across the space between our rooms, my bare feet making no sound on the comfortingly cool floor. Very carefully I turn the knob and push.

The door opens silently, the dim light from the hall providing some meager illumination. I wait for my eyes to adjust.

Klein is curled up in bed, the blanket wrapped around her, still as a kitten in sleep. I stare at her, looking for signs of life. Finally, she shifts a bit.

Relief washes over me in a sweet tide. *Of course she's fine.* Why *wouldn't* she be fine? My knees loosen a bit and I let out a soft breath. She's under my roof—and under my protection. Mom wouldn't dare. I won't let her toxic presence touch Klein.

I turn away and start back to my room, then notice something on the floor. I pick it up, then blink. A pair of small panties. The soft cotton drapes over my fingers and palm perfectly. The fabric smells faintly of Klein.

My pulse picks up. Heat rushes through me. I look toward her, and just then she flips over, kicking the tangled sheets. She's still in my shirt. Her fingers stroke her collarbone. "Josh," she murmurs dreamily.

I freeze. *Did she notice me?* But then she shifts again, and I realize she's still asleep.

What kind of dream is she having to whisper my name like a lover?

Is she reliving the flowers? Or what we did in the kitchen after I gave her the flowers? Am I kissing her? Doing more?

I want to know what makes her sigh like that. I want to *make* her sigh, make her beg and scream and quiver with pleasure.

I glance at the panties still in my hand. Did she, thinking of me, take them off because they got too wet for comfort?

My dick grows painfully hard as I imagine her warm, naked body under the sheets—and in my shirt.

She sighs softly, and all my blood drains to my cock. She sounded just like that when she said my name for the first time in the kitchen. I so desperately wanted to say, "The hell with dinner," but she wasn't really sober enough to consent. She barely processed anything while we ate, either. Bet none of my compliments registered. Her yakisoba was better than Akiko's—mainly because she put plenty on my plate and used a generous amount of pork.

Klein shifts. The woman is torturing me, seducing me even in her sleep, as naturally as breathing. I want to kiss her, see if she's receptive, but I should probably do the honorable thing and let her sleep in peace.

You're no prince on a white horse trying to wake Sleeping Beauty with a kiss.

I spin around, pad out silently and close the door behind me. I lean against the wood, the back of my head dropping against it. The air in the hall is too hot, and my groin too tight. My dick is so swollen it's touching my stomach. I make a fist, and realize her panties are in it. The top of my skull prickles with heat. I should give them back, but I simply can't go back in her room.

I'm a man, not a superhero.

Okay, what to do? I start toward the gym, so I can pummel Mom's face on the punching bag. But my dick won't die down. It throbs like if I don't do something about its condition, it might just break.

Biting back a curse, I turn around, enter my room and close the door. The clammy fear from the nightmare is gone, replaced by searing heat. It's not even five in the morning. I should try to squeeze in some extra sleep before heading to work, but it won't work. A different kind of restlessness throbs in my veins.

I glance down at my swollen cock. *Dammit.* I try to focus on a boring and obnoxious court opinion, but it doesn't make a bit of difference. I tighten my hand around Klein's underwear. *Fuuuuuuck.* I bring it to my face. Her scent is strong and tantalizing—catnip to my senses. My dick aches so hard I'm afraid that it's going to detonate if I don't do something about it.

I shed the robe and step into the en suite bathroom, then inside the shower stall. I slap a hand against the cold wall and wrap the other with Klein's underwear around my dick. It twitches. An electric shock sends shivers down my body from head to toe.

Instinct drives me. I move on sheer animal urgency, pumping my hand. I squeeze my eyes shut and bite my lip. My mouth tingles as though she's kissing me. My breathing roughens, and my mind replays the way she whispered my name in the kitchen—and in bed only moments ago.

I imagine her lying beneath me, her beautiful platinum hair spread out like a silver-gold cloud. Her lips are pouty, her eyes glazed. Her porcelain cheeks flush with mounting need as she looks up at me.

My hand tightens around my dick until I can feel the veins pulsing against my palm through the fabric of her panties. The pad of my thumb would rub against her wet clit, hidden between her slick folds, while her soft thighs glide along my legs and loop around my waist, pulling me closer until my cock rests against her quivering flesh. She'd be wet and hot—I grip myself tighter with a sigh.

Klein. My little goddess for me to worship, defile and pleasure. She'd break apart in my arms, her nails leaving trails of red on my back. As she marked me, she'd say my name again and again. *Josh, Josh, Josh.*

"Klein," I groan as I move faster. The knowledge that she might've gotten wet thinking about me sends sparks of excitement down my spine until they gather in my balls. Every muscle in my body tenses. I freeze, clenching my teeth...and erupt.

"*Fuuuuuuck, Klein.*" It's a guttural moan. My vision grows dim as my body locks up in orgasm. Cum splatters against the wall, above chest level, the handle for temperature control and the drain. It soaks her underwear as well.

A few minutes later, my cock is still at half-mast and twitching. The climax was nice, but I want more. I want to bury myself in her sweet depths.

Settle the fuck down.

I turn and head to the walk-in closet, then place the underwear in the bottom drawer of the built-in dresser. Nobody touches that one, not even the housekeeping staff. I feel a little silly for keeping it like a pervy dragon hoarding treasure, but it isn't going anywhere.

I lean against the wall and let my breathing settle. Even after several more minutes, I'm nowhere close to being sleepy. My nerves are simply too wired after imagining Klein lying in my bed, welcoming me into her body and greedily taking what's hers.

I dig the heels of my hands against my eyes, then rub them. No more sleep this morning, but I can't face Klein like this, still too horny and desperate for her. I take a quick, icy shower, then head to the meditation room to have some green tea and try to restore my equilibrium.

I walk along the path, cutting through the stone garden to the tatami mats, then stop short. A thick manila envelope is on the low lacquer table where I keep my tea set and a jar of premium Japanese matcha.

My heart drops, and I run toward it. A sense of violation and rage claws its talons across my chest. Who broke into my house, my heavily secured *home*? Even an hour ago, I felt confident that Klein would be safe under my roof. But if somebody can just walk into the meditation room without anyone noticing—

The nightmare of seeing Klein tied to the chair in the burning cabin returns, and bitterness drips through me. Paying attention to her probably put her on Mom's radar. What the hell have I done? And how do I fix it?

I can't undo the video or the situation we're in. And moving her out will likely only make things worse.

What would a Huxley do?

My mind won't process and spit out the answer. I pick up the envelope by the edges, being sure not to crumple the paper. No address, nothing. Bet there won't be any fingerprints, either.

On the front, a pink sticky-note contains a succinct message: YOUR SECURITY SUCKS.

My hands shake. Who did this? Mom? Harvey?

No signature, no other messages. I frown. This is a little too clean and sterile, except for the taunt. Not Mom or Harvey, then. They're both too arrogant to hide themselves. Even when they don't overtly brag that they are the ones who did it, they'll leave some clues, so you'll eventually discover the truth and marvel at their cleverness.

Then who?

I open the envelope and upend the whole thing. Photos and papers spill out like a waterfall, scattering all over the floor. With a trembling hand, I pick up one of the photos, then still as my blood goes cold.

23

AILEE

I OPEN MY EYES, then stretch my arms. My back feels great, and my legs check out. No weird kink in my neck. So *this* is what it feels to wake up in a really luxurious bed.

I hop up, then realize how uncomfortably wet I am between my legs. Uh-oh. The high-tech mattress not only let me sleep like a baby but have some really vivid dreams as well. All of them starring Josh and the filthy things he could do with his mouth.

But whatever. I grab another shower in Josh's unbelievably decadent bathroom. I doubt I'll ever get used to five showerheads and instant hot water. And the perfect water pressure. I wash away all the inappropriate wetness, so I can be ready for the day. My determination to be professional is going great until I realize I'm covered in his scent, and my cheeks warm. It seems more intimate than I can imagine. Not sure why. It isn't like I've never used a previous boyfriend's soap before. Then I realize none of those were unique—just everyday brands you can find in every big-box store in the country. The ones in Josh's home are specially formulated just for him. I place a hand over my belly, where heat unfurls.

Stop thinking about your boss that way. It's morning time—which means I'm back to being his assistant. I don't want to be one of those obnoxious characters you see on TV who become lazy and inattentive once they start hooking up with the boss. Not that we did anything that could be categorized as *hooking up,* but my mind went there multiple times last night.

Multiple.

I step into the walk-in closet, which is basically empty except for Josh's shirt I slept in and the clothes I got at the boutique with Lareina and Fiona. I put on my new underwear and the pretty blue dress and matching sandals. *Wow.* I stare myself in the mirror. The color deepens my eyes so they're a more vivid violet. The red lipstick creates a fantastic contrast, and doesn't look too much at all. I feel like a million bucks in my new outfit.

Now, where are those panties? It'd be embarrassing if the housekeeping staff found my unwashed undies lying around. Except I can't find them on the floor. Weird. I could have sworn I dropped them by the bed last night.

I rip the sheets and blankets off the bed. Nope. Not there, either. They couldn't have just walked out of the room. I drop to my hands and knees and look under the bed, just in case. Still nothing.

My phone rattles on the table. I jump up and reach for it. Maybe it's my panties texting me to come pick them up.

—Max: Hey, just checking on to see how you're doing. Did you end up doing anything exciting with forced proximity to your hottie boss? Oops, fiancé now.

My lips stretch into a smile.

—Me: No.

—Max: Not even a kiss?

The memory of the kiss crashes into me. How he devoured me, and how it was better than any sex I've ever had. I run my tongue over my prickling mouth. But I know better than to tell her the truth because then she'll want to call and talk about it. And I really have to go to work.

—Me: Stop writing romance novels in your head.

—Max: Boooring! Tell me the man at least hinted he wanted to do things to you.

I dreamed he wanted to do things to me.

—Me: I need to get to work. Ugh.

—Max: Why the ugh?

—Me: Because I can't find my underwear. Maybe it got tangled in the sheets.

Except I already shook the sheets out twice. My panties aren't that staticky.

—Max: Underwear? Like your bra or panties?

—Me: Panties.

—Max: Ooooh!

That "ooooh!" sends the wrong kind of shivers down my back.

—Max: Bet Josh took them.

—Me: What? Why would he sneak into my room in the middle of the night to steal my underwear?

—Max: HE'S A GUY. To sniff? Masturbate with? To make a ribbon out of it and tie it around the base of his cock?

A feverish heat suddenly pulses in my veins. Just imagining him groaning my name while he pleasures himself makes me achy between my legs again. I shift my weight, trying to get a grip on my imagination. I don't have another thong to put on, and I really don't want to be dripping when I face Josh in less than five minutes.

—Me: Are you writing romance or porn in your head?

—Max: Don't be judgmental. This romance stars adults with needs.

I laugh softly.

—Me: I know my limitations. I'm nothing like the women he used to date. I'd have to fast and hit the gym for a year before I'd look like them.

—Max: If he wanted to be with them, he would be. Instead, you're in his home.

Yeah, except this engagement has an expiration date on it. I shake the thought off. It won't change anything to think about it anymore.

—Max: You know what? You've had one too many bad relationships, and he probably has, too. You couldn't even come half the time with your shitty exes. So just ride your hottie and see if his dick's magical and gives you what you need.

—Max: If it doesn't work out, I'll just get you an annual subscription to Silicone Dream's Year of Coming First.

—Me: What's that?

–Max: They send you some of their best toys in a discreet package. I did it last year. A-ma-zing!

–Me: So why did you quit?

–Max: Because some fucker discovered it.

I can practically feel her grinding her teeth. She doesn't refer to many people as "fuckers." But there's no way she could be talking about her boss. Could she?

–Me: Gotta get ready for work. Talk to you later.

One more round of searching, but still no underwear. *Argh.* Where did they go? I want to keep looking, but if I don't hurry up, I'm going to be late for work.

I grab my purse and phone and head downstairs. Josh is already at the counter, sipping tea and reviewing some documents. I slow my pace to take him in. Impeccably shaved, he's in one of his favorite navy three-piece suits. A dark burgundy tie completes the look, perfectly knotted. As usual, not a strand of hair is out of place. He always exudes such an easy confidence and competence. Even at home, where you'd think he'd be at ease, he looks ready to conquer the world.

"Good morning." My voice is slightly breathless. But then, it's difficult to control myself around him, especially after the kiss. It smashed the barrier I'd maintained between us—to keep things professional and clean.

Josh lifts his head, then stares at me for a moment, his eyes slightly narrowed as he studies me from head to toe. I resist the urge to shift, hoping he likes what he sees.

Finally, he smiles, showing straight white teeth. "Morning."

The butterflies in my belly launch. Or maybe they're doing cartwheels. Hard to tell from the sensation in my gut. His eyes are intense as they focus on me.

"Isn't blue your favorite color?"

I nod.

"Looks fantastic on you."

Forget the lousy million. I feel like a *billion* bucks.

"Come here." My feet obey before my mind can process. He picks up a discreet velvet box next to his documents. "Your engagement ring." He pops the lid open.

A large, round blue stone sits in the center of a gorgeous platinum band. Smaller blue stones dot the smooth surface around it. It radiates class and elegant beauty, much like the man himself.

"Sapphires," he explains. "Thought the stones suited you better." He lifts his eyes to meet mine. "Unique, charming, lovely."

When he looks at me like that, I *feel* unique, charming and lovely. Not only that, he makes me believe I deserve to be valued and loved, something I don't often feel. Warm emotions knot in my throat, and I have to swallow before I can speak. "This is the most gorgeous ring I've ever seen. Thank you."

With a satisfied grunt, he plucks the ring from the box, holding it between his thumb and forefinger. He takes my left hand, his upturned palm supporting mine. The touch is innocent, but sends a mini electric shock that I can feel all the way to my curling toes. The pads of his thumb and forefinger caress my ring finger as he pushes the ring along the length. My heart races, as though it's pulsing in my hand where he's touching. Finally, the band settles snugly. The stones sparkle, looking like a choker around my finger, marking me as taken—and as his.

Everything inside me shivers, even as I try to remind myself not to get too crazy because *this isn't real.*

"It's more beautiful than I imagined," I say with a tremulous smile. "Thanks, boss." I use the term deliberately to cool my foolish heart.

He raises an eyebrow. "Say that again."

The intense heat in his eyes chokes the air out of me. "Thanks, boss."

His eyes flick to my finger. I feel it like it was his finger flicking over my core. I clench my thighs.

"I thought we already established that I'm not 'boss.'"

"But—"

His gaze lifts to my mouth. "Call me 'boss' again and I'll kiss you until you remember who I am."

Need flares. Part of me wants to say "boss" again. *What's wrong with me?* I'm the nice girl, the one who toes the line and pleases people so that she can be just a little bit more lovable. "Fiancé," I rasp, my throat tight.

His expression eases, although the intensity of his gaze doesn't lessen.

"Josh," I venture.

He closes his eyes for a moment, as though he's either savoring something or pulling himself together, then opens his eyes. "Time to go to work. Ready?"

I nod.

"We'll drive together until you get your car fob replaced." He extends his arm.

I stare at it, unsure what he wants.

"Your hand." He places it on the crook of his arm. "Don't forget—you're my fiancée before you're my assistant."

I shoot him a sidelong glance, then drop my gaze to the stunning ring. I think about all the effort he's making and the money he's spending. He didn't get more than a kiss. It's obvious what I'm getting out of the fake engagement, but...

"What are you getting out of this?" I blurt out as we pull out of the garage. "The engagement, I mean. You said you liked me, but you didn't seem too upset when I said I was engaged to Chad." My face heats a little.

Josh's eyebrows pinch together. "I didn't want to get in the way of your happiness, but if I'd known you were engaged to *him*, I would've objected. After the incident with the woman barging into my meeting with Ted, I'm on a sort of unofficial probation. Need to be on my best behavior for at least six months to avoid 'professional consequences.' That includes staying engaged after the scene at Peking Town." Then he clears his throat, tugging at his tie knot. "But I also like you. So. You know you're a damn good assistant. Just have that same confidence as my fiancée, too."

24

JOSH

I LEAVE the door to my office open, since I don't have any meetings this morning. Klein brings me my coffee as usual and fills me on the coming day like nothing's happened since our engagement announcement and the fire at her apartment. I admire her resilience. Some women would've fallen apart by now. Like that magenta-haired chick I took out for dinner once who completely lost her sanity when she broke a nail. Granted, it had enough cubic zirconia to power a space station, but really.

Klein walks back to her desk, and I can't help tracking her with my eyes. That dress does incredible things to her ass, the deep blue fabric clinging to her curves in all the right ways. She doesn't normally wear such vivid colors, but it looks amazing on her. I almost forgot to breathe when I saw her this morning. When she said blue was her favorite color, then couldn't tear her eyes off the ring, I wanted to push the dress up and have her brace against the counter with her hands and fill her with my cum, so she isn't just marked as mine on her finger, but in her most intimate location too.

Her going back to calling me "boss" was the only thing that stopped me. She isn't really comfortable with the idea of "us" yet, despite the kiss. I made the right decision to pull back last night, but now I'm even more determined to draw her out of her shell. She's like a little hermit crab, only venturing out when she feels absolutely safe, and retreating at the slightest sign of danger.

Except...she doesn't seem to sense any when she speaks to Kenna, who approaches the desk with a grin as fake as a North Korean hundred-dollar bill.

I flex my hand around a letter opener, wanting to yank the two women apart, but restraint is going to be the better play here. I just figured out what kind of pawn Kenna is; if I take her off the board, another piece will replace her. And the next one might be more difficult to identify.

Klein and Kenna talk animatedly about something. Klein flushes. *What the hell did Kenna say?* She fawns over the ring, her fingers fluttering. It's a damn good ring, but I don't buy her reaction.

My mind goes back to the manila envelope. Just thinking about the contents makes my gut twist. The pink sticky note wasn't signed, but it had to be from Elizabeth's team. I knew she had people whose depth of competence was beyond ours here at the firm, but breaking into my home like that was hitting below the belt. At the same time, they alerted me that my security has flaws. I need to be more vigilant and find another, more capable firm to re-secure my home.

But first things first. I turn my focus to Kenna, lest she mess with Klein, who's in the middle of placing a hand over her chest, her eyes wide. Apparently it's a signature move—the green-eyed blonde did the same thing in one of the photos that was in the envelope.

In that shot, she was staring at a diamond bracelet a man was holding out for her at some fancy restaurant, her entire face lighting up like a kid at Christmas. That part didn't bother me. But her date's face? When I saw it, all the air whooshed out of my lungs.

I didn't need to read the enclosed report to know who the man was. He's a carbon copy of Vincent Dunkel, just younger and scarred. It's gotta be his younger son—the uncle I've never met. Mom thought she'd killed him, but apparently she was wrong.

In the high-res photo, a charming smile curves his mouth, and there's a vicious glint in his eyes that's just like Mom's. But he's far more cunning and threatening because he's been living under the radar all these years. My fingertips are still twitchy from the earlier shock. He didn't come back from the "dead" just for the hell of it. He wants blood —is ready to take his pound of flesh from Mom. I'm not sure how he plans to use me and my family. But if he didn't want to involve us, he wouldn't have planted Kenna at the firm.

Klein laughs at something Kenna says. Does he plan to use Klein too? Is that why Kenna stops by her desk so often?

When Kenna leaves after a few moments, I hit the intercom. "Klein, come to my office."

"Coming." She stands and smooths the dress, so the thin fabric lies neatly over her beautiful body.

As soon as she comes in, I get up and close the door. She tilts her head to look up at me. The pulse in her throat throbs, and I have an impulse to press my lips there and feel her reaction.

"What did you talk about with Kenna?" *Focus.* That woman didn't stop by just to chat and gossip.

"Nothing much. Just hellos. She said some nice things about the ring."

I give her the steady stare I give the opposing counsel who isn't being entirely honest.

"She, um…" Klein swallows. "She apologized for referring Chad to me."

"He's her dentist?" Could be a coincidence, but I lean toward deliberate, especially with anyone connected to a Dunkel.

"Uh-huh. Although she said she'd quit going to him and get a new one."

Did she now? I scoff inwardly. I take a step toward Klein. She takes an unconscious half a step back, until she's almost touching the desk. She looks entirely too exposed, her eyes as wide and vulnerable as a doe's. At any moment, one of the numerous predators in my life could come and tear her apart. The younger Dunkels would do it gladly, if it would somehow help them gain power over each other before Vincent croaks.

I slap my hands on either side of her, like gates coming down to keep the bad guys away from her. Her mouth parts. We're so close I can feel her breath feathering on my cheek. She smells like the specially formulated soap I ordered from France—a combination of subtle lavender, sandalwood and bergamot.

Mine. And I'd do anything to keep her safe.

"Do you trust me, Klein?" I ask.

She nods.

"How far?"

"Very," she whispers.

Good. "Stay away from Kenna as much as possible and don't share *anything* with her. Nothing outside of what's strictly necessary for work." I run the side of my finger down Klein's soft, warm cheek. "Do this for me, okay? I'll never let anything happen to you."

25

———

AILEE

"Breathe. It's just dinner."

I nod. It's easy for Josh to say. It's *his* family.

I still can't believe his stepmom wants to meet me. She must've seen the embarrassing video, so...

What if she disapproves of me? She might think my judgment is too poor, my hair weird, that I'm not pretty enough for her stepson. I've never met her, since she only comes to the firm for occasional lunch dates with her husband, who's on a different floor. But I've heard stories from other people—that she's from a massively wealthy family in Japan, and quite fond of her husband and stepchildren.

My nerves are totally frayed. I continue to pace, my pumps clacking on the marble in the kitchen.

The dress I picked out swirls around my legs. It's a pretty pink one I saved for a special occasion. I spent an hour straightening my hair in the morning, with a subpar result.

I glare at my reflection in the stainless-steel fridge door. "Argh, my hair's already curling."

Do I have time to wash my hair and re-straighten it? I check the clock. Of course not. Josh only stopped at home to "have a snack," which was a little strange, because he could've just grabbed something light at the office. He didn't explain why he was planning to pick up beef-and-cheese tacos. At least he skipped the nachos...? There's no way I could scarf down this "snack" *and* nachos, *and* then go for dinner. Or maybe it's all for him.

Josh walks up from behind and takes my shoulders in his strong hands. He leans down until his chin rests on the curve of my neck. His delicious body heat surrounds me, and I want to sink into it. I'd love to have an excuse—any excuse—not to go if I could do it without offending his family.

His eyes meet mine in the reflection. "Klein, relax. Your curls are absolutely adorable. You'll be fine." His warm breath tickles my ear, sending little shivers along my arms.

"Yeah. I'm sure." Except I don't sound convinced, not even to myself.

Josh shakes his head. "Why don't you just have the tacos I bought for you?"

I tilt my head to face him, then realize we're too close this way. Our lips are only a couple of inches apart. I swallow, then manage a whisper: "Why? Aren't we having dinner with your family?" I wince at how eager I sound for it to be a no. But they could've canceled at the last minute.

"Yeah, and you'll be starving afterward."

His expression—from the wide-set, dark eyes to the cheekbones any model would kill for, to the straight nose and the unsmiling mouth—indicates he's serious.

"Trust me," he says. "Akiko thinks we eat too much, so she serves everyone hummingbird portions. Or maybe she's worried that we might develop diabetes. Or high blood pressure, stroke, sleep apnea, endometrial and colorectal cancers all at the same time. And brain bleeds, too."

I let out an incredulous laugh. "No way."

"Very much *way.* Trust me." He presses a kiss on the top of my head.

The spot tingles. I pull my lips in, my heartbeat picking up at this casual display of affection. In the past few days, I've been reacting uncontrollably to every touch and look from him. It can't be normal to get wet every time he gives me a smile...or winks...or cages me between his arms. I wish he'd come just an inch or two closer, but he never crosses the line. As a matter of fact, he hasn't tried to kiss me, either—although maybe he's waiting for me to call him "boss" again...?

If it were anybody but Josh, I might think he's flirting and trying to gauge my reaction. But this is Josh Huxley, one of the most eligible bachelors in the state, if not the country, and he's dated countless gorgeous women, whom he promptly dumped soon after he slept with them. I recall Coco's furious email that landed in my inbox.

You think you're special now? He hasn't fucked you yet, has he? Once he puts his dick in you, his fascination will end. But you can play hard to get for only so long. I hope he dumps you like a piece of trash that you are. And I hope it goes more viral than the stupid engagement! Fuck you!

Intellectually, I understand that she vomited out all that hatred in a fit of spite and rage. After all, she'd sent me dozens of emails to get me to set her up with some time with Josh. But in my heart, insecurity and fear beat up what little confidence I managed to muster after Josh kissed me and gave me that gorgeous ring. And the saddest thing is that I can hear my own mother's voice spewing the same bile.

I shake off the negativity. I can't dwell on it and still face Josh's family. Although I've met his father, brothers and aunt at work, I've never seen his grandmother, Catalina Huxley, or his stepmom.

Josh sits at the counter and bites into his tacos with gusto. *How can he eat like this and still stay fit?* I know he hits the home gym several times a week, but still...

"I can't eat those tacos. Way too tense," I say.

He grunts mild disapproval, but devours his food like it's his last meal before being exiled into a desert. "Don't say I didn't warn you. Now, tell me what's bothering you. I doubt you seriously believe my family's shallow enough to care about your hair."

I stop in the middle of rearranging my curls so they're less noticeable. Heat floods my face. I hesitate, unsure how to broach the subject. "Well. I'm not even sure they'll actually believe we're engaged. You know, for real. I'm nothing like the women you date."

He gives me a confused look. "The women I date?"

"Well...yeah. They all have stunning bodies and flawless complexions and hair that lies all sleek and tidy—"

"You might note that they aren't with me anymore. And my family doesn't care much about appearances."

"Easy to say when everyone's gorgeous," I mutter.

"And you're part of 'everyone.'"

His rebuttal is too swift, like it's something he's been prepping in his mind all this time, like he was getting ready for a trial. It's difficult to believe the sincerity. Not that I think he's really *lying*, but he's probably only being partially truthful. "And I have no accomplishments," I argue stubbornly, determined to make him see things from my perspective and understand where I'm coming from. "Didn't even get a bachelor's degree." I sigh. Katt might've had a point about my lack of a four-year degree.

"So?"

"Everyone in your family went to Harvard Law."

"Actually, Grandma went to Yale—"

"You're *missing the point.*"

"And you're overthinking this. Will getting a four-year degree make a difference in your career?" He pauses, giving me a long, probing look.

I shrug helplessly. "A lot of assistants at the firm have four-year degrees."

"I'm not talking about them. I'm talking about *you*, and you know perfectly well that the answer is *no*. You're still one of the best assistants at Huxley & Webber. If anybody tries to poach you, I want you to tell me so I can outbid them."

I flush. A few headhunters actually have approached me, but I turned them down, not wanting to leave Josh's side. I didn't realize he valued me that much.

"Now, if you want to switch careers and do something that requires a bachelor's degree, I'll be the first to support and cheer you on."

"Even if I'm not going to be your assistant anymore?"

"Even then. Life is short. You should do what you want, what you find fulfilling. I'll never stand in your way if you pursue that."

The naked earnestness in his tone starts to soothe my anxiety. My lashes flutter as I clench and unclench my hands, trying not to cry because that'd ruin the makeup. My parents always wanted me to do something that would complement Katt's career or something that would make them proud. My happiness wasn't even on their radar.

Josh continues, "As for my family, the most important thing will be your dedication to excellence. Nobody at the firm cares about a diploma —or lack thereof—or your hair, or whatever cosmetic thing you think people judge you on. I only got the degree I did because it's necessary to be a lawyer. Plenty of successful people didn't get a college degree. Look at Steve Jobs. Or Branson. Jay-Z didn't even finish high school. So you can tell anybody who gives you shit about a lack of degree that you're overeducated compared to a couple of billionaires." Josh looks at me. "I wish you can see yourself through my eyes. You're the sun in my life, Klein. Brilliant and flawless."

My heart clenches at this unconditional acceptance. I wish I could see myself through his eyes, too, rather than my parents'—always see the flaws, never the perfection. "Thank you," I manage, my voice choked. "I'll try to see myself the way you do."

He beams with pride. "Good. Whenever you feel uncertain, just ask yourself, 'How would Josh see me?'" He gestures at the takeout bag. "So. How about those tacos?"

I shake my head with a laugh. "Definitely not." I don't want to upset Akiko by not having room to eat her food.

The sight of peonies in the vase on the dining table catches my eyes, and I smile instinctively. Those flowers still look fresh and cheerful. Every time I look at them, my mood brightens.

"Do you mind if we stop by a florist and grab some flowers for Akiko?" I ask.

"We can do that. But she really isn't expecting anything from you."

"I feel like I should. And don't tell me you see me as a person who doesn't bring anything to a dinner she's invited to." I don't want his family to be thrilled to hear about our breakup in six months. It might be vain and shallow, but I hope they'll be disappointed—even if it's just a little.

Josh stops at a florist on the way and hands the owner his card before I even pick out the flowers I want to buy. I select extravagant orange-pink roses and baby's breath. The information card underneath them says each rose has sixty petals. His eyes drop to the writing, then he checks his phone and sends a quick text.

Josh looks at me with mild amusement as we get back on the road.

"What?" I ask.

"Akiko will have to spend some time figuring out how to incorporate your flowers into her ikebana."

"Into her what?"

"Japanese flower arrangement. Well, the *art* of flower arrangement. She loves it."

I look at the flowers, then back at him. "Should I have gotten something more Japanese?" I don't recall anything that looked "Asian" in the store. Besides, do flowers even have nationalities?

"Nah. You're fine." A corner of his mouth quirks up higher.

His parents' home is in one of the most exclusive zip codes in SoCal. All the houses in the area are massive mansions with the top-of-the-line security and gates to keep the occupants safe.

Their place is one of the largest, with a sprawling garden full of beautiful flowers and shrubs. The understated elegance and the sweeping architecture exude the sort of old-money opulence my parents strive to achieve. After being at the firm and meeting people from various walks of life, one thing I've learned is that money doesn't always confer taste or confidence.

Josh drives along the winding approach, then parks to the side on a circular driveway in front of the main entrance. A black Maybach and a black Cullinan are parked neatly next to a flaming-red Lamborghini that takes up three spaces.

"Well, we're learning," Josh murmurs with a slightly satisfied smirk.

"What do you mean? And isn't that your aunt's car?"

"The red Lambo? Yeah, that's Aunt Jeremiah's. She always parks like a dick. She's taking up three spots rather than the usual two because she arrived too early to box us in."

Josh makes a throaty noise full of amusement, then climbs out and opens the door for me while I gather the bouquet. "Thank you," I say.

His hand rests at the small of my back as he escorts me up the steps. The warmth from his touch is reassuring, and I inhale slowly. *You can do this, Ailee.*

The foyer is bigger than my old apartment, with a ceiling so high it seems it should have its own weather. An elegant chandelier lights the space. Silver wolves snarling around a shield glitter on a huge navy tapestry hanging from the ceiling. Underneath the crest reads PIETAS ET UNITAS.

"Loyalty and unity," I murmur.

"Family is everything," he says, like it's something that's been ingrained in him since birth.

We go deeper into the house, through the beautiful hall. Several windows on one side face a garden. The opposite side has nooks with individual spotlights to display earthenware that glows with muted grace. I've never seen anything quite so beautiful before. They're the kinds of things I imagine Akiko gesturing at with blasé confidence, casually mentioning they've been in her family for generations. Each piece of pottery features a minimalist flower arrangement. The second one is simultaneously the least complex and the most interesting—it has one long black branch that stretches upward in slanted twists. Only two flowers bloom next to it—both of them simple and white.

"Is this the ikebana you mentioned before?" I whisper, my hands growing clammy.

"Yes."

I look down at the grand bouquet in my arms. Damn it. Now what?

Why can't you even pick the right kind of flowers, Ailee? I swear I raised you and your sister the same, but you're such a failure, comes Mom's voice in my head. I bite my lower lip, suddenly feeling ridiculous for thinking I could make his family feel disappointed when our engagement ends. Then I remember what Josh said earlier and decide to shake it off, trying to imagine how he'd view the situation. *If he thought I'd selected something inappropriate, he would've said so.* There are no right or wrong flowers. Being considerate isn't something to be mocked.

Josh's chuckle jerks me out of my thoughts. "Don't worry," he says. "She'll find a way to use them."

"You think so? The roses are really...*showy.*"

"Akiko won't keep the same design for long." Josh puts his arm around my shoulder and pulls me in for a quick hug. "Trust me."

My breath catches. When he holds me close and speaks in that steady tone, I feel like he'll keep me safe even if the world burns down around us.

The dining room is even bigger than the foyer. I thought Josh's was large, but this is even more massive, obviously built to entertain a crowd. I spot seven people. Prescott is in a well-fitted three-piece bespoke suit. Actually, every Huxley man seems to favor them. His presence is more imposing than a grouchy bear's, although I'd never admit that. Unlike his sister, he's considered the more solid and staid partner, but no less vicious when it's necessary to win. He doesn't smile often at the firm, and I wonder what he's like here in his home. After all, the family motto is *loyalty and unity*, not *surly and snippy*.

Jeremiah's impossible to miss—that bright red hair and mouth and the black power suit that all scream death to anybody who gets in her way. I've seen large male associates stutter when she gazes at them with an arched eyebrow, the corners of her mouth twisting into a subtle sneer. A half-empty glass of red wine sits in front of her. She looks like *she* owns the place. Wisps of smoke rise from the end of a lit cigar. Her eyes glitter with interest as she looks at me through the tendrils.

I smile, hoping she likes me. It isn't always easy to tell. My interaction with her at the firm has been minimal, just like with Prescott. She's always too busy to stop by and say hello to Josh. When she shows up for the firm's Christmas parties, she's surrounded by her favored associates, such as Barry.

My eyes drift to Bryce and Ares, also in suits, since it's Friday and they probably billed till the last minute. Ares just made junior partner, and he's busier than ever, according to his assistant. Lareina waves with a big smile. She's adorable in a teal sundress. She drops her head on her husband's shoulder with a blush, then whispers something to him. He smiles indulgently, and I blink. I've never seen Ares this relaxed and human before.

Bryce's expression is mildly pinched and lonely. The chair next to him is empty, and he checks his phone for the third time.

"Is everything okay?" I ask.

His expression clears as he turns to me. "Yeah, fine. Fiona can't make it because smell of the food bothers her." He heaves a sigh. "But she wants you to know she misses you and wants to have another girls' day out with you and Lareina."

I nod, relaxing slightly. "That'd be great. Any time."

At the head of the table is a black-haired woman with eyes as sharp as knives. She's knotted her glossy mane into a bun at the base of her head, and her skin is pale and smooth, almost unnaturally wrinkle-free. Her dress is deep blue, which brings out her eyes.

Must be the grandmother. Although she didn't work for long at Huxley & Webber, there are rumors about her there anyway—that Jeremiah got her ball-busting attitude from her mother. Guess it's unavoidable that people will whisper behind your back when you're the matriarch of the Huxleys.

"Catalina Huxley, my dear," she says, introducing herself. Her eyes soften as she takes me in. "Welcome to the family."

"Thank you," I say, relaxing a little more. When she smiles the sharp edges vanish, making her appear approachable.

An Asian woman in a stunning purple-and-ivory kimono with luxurious plum blossom embroidery walks over. She's maybe an inch or two shorter than me, and her eyes go warm when she smiles. Fresh white peonies adorn her updo.

"Welcome!" she says. Her beauty isn't showy—it's the kind that lasts regardless of age. "I'm Akiko. You're Ailee, right?"

"Yes. Nice to meet you." I manage a smile that I hope isn't nervous. "For you." I extend the roses.

Her eyes light up with genuine joy. "How lovely! I've been thinking about experimenting more with Western flowers recently, and these will be just the thing."

She puts the bouquet on a side table and hugs me tightly. "Welcome to our home! I'm so glad Josh brought you. I've been dying to meet the final daughter-in-law. And find out who gave him the 'heirloom'!"

26

———————

JOSH

I DO my best not to roll my eyes as Klein flushes. Of course Akiko wants to know.

Aunt Jeremiah's eyes flash over the rim of her wine glass—she knows who the guilty one is. "Yeah, I'm wondering about that too. That asshole John Cocksucking McKinnon mocked my taste."

I press my lips together, trying not to laugh. He's the opposing counsel in a complex lawsuit she's dealing with. She believes God created him to fuck with her because every good woman gets a devil to battle. She's being polite by merely calling him "cocksucking." I've seen her let go when she decides to be more blunt. "It's a long story, but I misspoke," I lie smoothly as I pull out a chair for Klein.

Aunt Jeremiah's expression flickers with approval. Although she's a modern woman, she appreciates little gestures of chivalry. Says they indicate manner and civilization. But that doesn't mean she'll let the video incident slide. "I don't believe you. You aren't under oath."

"Do you want me to be?"

Her eyes narrow, but she doesn't speak to me again. She knows I'd never do anything to hurt the family. "Show me the proper ring, sweetie," she says, shifting her attention to Klein, whose jaw slackens.

"Did you just call *me* sweetie?"

"Yes. You're my niece-in-law-to-be, and this is a casual family gathering."

"Oh. Wow. Um." Klein licks her lips, obviously unsure how to take that. Although we haven't exchanged vows, the family's accepted her as one of us. She just needs to get used it. "Of course." She extends her hand quickly.

Everyone leans forward to look.

"Very nice," Grandma says. "Now, that's the kind of ring that can be passed down."

"Exactly," Aunt Jeremiah agrees with a sigh of relief.

"You all should know by now that I don't do ugly," I mutter.

She gives me a look. "Except you put that atrocious 'heirloom' on her finger. You're lucky Ailee's too nice to murder you. I almost had a heart attack."

"You mean you had an extra cigar and whiskey," Dad interjects with a light scoff, and Ares and Bryce nod.

She shrugs. "Better than therapy."

"It's lovely." Akiko's eyes sparkle. Dad looks at her, then at the ring, with a thoughtful expression, and I can tell that she's going to get a sapphire ring soon. "Did Josh pick it out himself?"

"Yes," Klein says. "I love it." She turns red with a mixture of pleasure and shyness. It's easy to see she isn't used to being the center of attention. Not sure why, because she's a pretty girl with a gentle heart and even more beautiful soul. She's the only woman I know who glows from within.

She's way too worried about pleasing my family, which isn't necessary. They'll love her the way she is because she's the woman I chose. We trust one another to make the best choices we can.

Still, to alleviate her anxiety, I texted Akiko to ask if she could cut a large, colorful flower from her garden and make it part of her ensemble tonight. Klein visibly relaxed when she saw the enormous peony in my stepmother's hair.

"I love the color. Is sapphire your favorite?" Lareina asks.

"You know, I've never thought much about it," Klein says with a small smile. "I never had a chance to buy anything expensive. But when I saw the ring, my heart screamed *yes*."

"You can trust Josh," Akiko adds. "Every woman needs a few classic pieces. And he has excellent taste."

"But...sapphires and stuff? When will I wear them?" Klein asks with a soft, shy laugh.

Lareina shrugs. "You can wear diamond studs anywhere."

"Charity galas. Auctions," Grandma says. "You might want to put something on to attend Lareina's art shows."

"I'd love to invite you to my next exhibit!" Lareina says with a bright smile. "You don't even have to buy anything. I'll give you a small painting to welcome you into the family!"

Klein's eyes start to glaze over. "Well..." Her voice is slightly shaky. "I've never been to that sort of event."

I frown a little. Didn't her sister ever invite her to fashion shows and other events? Then I recall her family's shitty treatment of her. They probably kept her away because they thought she wasn't worthy. Assholes. *They*'re the ones who don't deserve *her*.

"In that case, you should try one or two. Then if you decide you hate them, you don't have to do it again." Aunt Jeremiah sips her drink.

"Am I expected to socialize for Josh's career and to help the family's image?" Klein asks in a small voice. "It might be better if I..." She presses her lips together.

Frustration pinches my eyebrows together. I want to know the rest of the sentence, but her lips are nearly bloodless from pressure.

Grandma shakes her head. "Family is family. We're not PR reps."

"If you don't want to show yourself in public, that's fine." I squeeze Klein's hand. "We can stay home and chill." I'd love to see her in nothing but my shirt again.

"Look at the time," Akiko says. "You must be starving after work. Shall we start eating?"

Dad nods eagerly. Everyone else except maybe Aunt Jeremiah, who forgets to eat when she's working, undoubtedly had something before coming. I just hope Klein had a big lunch when she went out with Bryce's assistant Amélie today.

Akiko brings out her best pinot grigio and Sangiovese, cold and warm sake and Japanese plum wine. Her stemware and glasses are top of the line—and all the liquors from Japan are served in wide, shallow, gorgeous white porcelain cups.

The first course starts with everyone getting an empty white bowl. My brothers and I exchange looks. *Do we have to* imagine *our food now?* You never know with Akiko.

A ladle of clear soup made with chicken stock is poured. As the steam rises, a tree, its gnarled branches laden with countless delicate pink flowers, slowly appears on the bottom of the bowl.

Klein's eyes widen. "Wow. Is that a cherry blossom tree?" She's absolutely adorable as she stares at the elegantly done art.

"Yes! Isn't it pretty?" Akiko beams. "I just had to get these bowls when I saw them in Tokyo last month. This is my first time using them. Thought it was appropriate to welcome you into the family."

"I...don't even know what to say."

"Oh, just tell me you love my food," Akiko teases.

"I thought you wanted honesty?" I say. Dad gives me a warning look, but Akiko takes it in good humor.

Klein laughs. "I'm sure I'll love everything."

Ares dips his spoon into Lareina's bowl and tastes the soup. "Mmm. Light...delicate..."

"A light soup," Bryce says. "Now *there's* a surprise." He gets the same scowl from Dad.

The next course is two bite-sized slices of duck breast topped with some kind of green glob. Each plate has dark sauce, but instead of drizzling it over the pristine bone china, Akiko wrote a highly stylized kanji character, each unique to the diner. Ares, Bryce and I lean over to read everyone's characters, since we can read Japanese fairly well.

I freeze at the writing on Klein's plate: *Ai*—love. Memory tugs me back to the time when Klein first brought flowers to my office. With the morning sunlight streaming in, illuminating her shy smile, she looked like love personified. I started to call her name but stopped at the first syllable because something inside wanted to follow *Ai* with *chan*, a Japanese suffix to indicate affection and familiarity that I often used with my cousins in Tokyo and Kyoto.

So I started calling her Klein in order to avoid slipping and calling her Ai-chan—sweet love. Even though she wouldn't know what it meant, my brothers would. And most importantly, *I* would.

When I'm worthy of Klein's warmth, I might be able to bring myself to call her Ai-chan.

"What do you think? I think they fit every one of you perfectly." Akiko looks at us.

"What do they all mean?" Grandma asks.

"Mine says autumn because that's when I was born," Akiko says. "Wisdom for you, Catalina, and trust for Prescott. Victory for Jeremiah."

Grandma nods, and Dad places a soft kiss on Akiko's temple. She smiles, glowing like the moon. Aunt Jeremiah preens—nothing makes her happier than winning.

Akiko continues, "Strength for Ares and courage for Lareina."

"Wow. That's so cool." Lareina leans her head on Ares's shoulder with a soft sigh. He kisses the top of her crown.

"Dependable for Bryce."

At that, my twin smiles, and I marvel at how accurately Akiko pinpointed us.

"Love for Ailee because she's such a lovely child."

Klein traces the complex strokes on her plate with her eyes, full of surprise and wonder, probably shocked people would equate love with her. I squeeze her hand. "If you want, I'll show you how to write it when we get home," I whisper.

"And honor for you," Akiko says to me. "Can also mean loyalty."

I freeze and do my best to stay still, lest I squirm. I've never felt like I could be worthy of honor and loyalty, not with Mom insisting since I was a child that I'm just like her—a Dunkel.

"Honor. Loyalty. That's so you." Klein looks up at me. "I love it."

Something's wrong. My heart feels tight, and it's racing too fast. I look into her brilliant violet eyes, Mom's evil words fading away, and feel dazed and mildly shaky, like the earth is shifting under my feet.

"The character is totally you," Bryce says with a grin.

"Thanks." I turn to my stepmom. "Thank you, Akiko."

She beams. "My pleasure. I just wanted to show my appreciation for...well, everyone."

"You can do better than autumn for yourself, though," Aunt

Jeremiah says. "Maybe something like 'home'...? You have a way of bringing people together and making everyone feel welcome."

Akiko flushes with pleasure. "Thank you. I'm just happy to be part of the family and glad to provide a warm, comforting place for everyone."

"Except that the kanji for 'home' is a pig under a roof," says Ares.

Dad levels a stare at him that could melt titanium. "That is *enough* out of you three." He turns to his wife. "You've done a remarkable job, my love," Dad says.

We nod even as most of us laugh. Akiko had the unenviable job of marrying a single dad with three emotionally scarred boys. Although she took care to not to poke at our wounds, she always stood behind us, letting us know she had our backs.

"Is there going to be any sashimi tonight?" Aunt Jeremiah asks. She's fond of Akiko's sashimi, even though there are only ever three slices at the most.

"Not tonight," Akiko says. "Ailee has a seafood allergy, and I didn't want any inadvertent cross-contamination. So not even the soup stock base contains fish." She turns to Klein. "You're perfectly safe."

"Oh." Klein stops, then slides her eyes toward Aunt Jeremiah. A moment later, she starts haltingly, "You didn't really have to... I mean, I usually just eat around the fish, you know... You don't have to inconvenience everyone just for me."

My gut tightens. I know exactly who put that garbage in her head: her cunt-tastic mother and dickless father, who think there's nothing wrong with ordering a family dinner full of seafood, not caring that Klein wouldn't be able to eat anything.

Aunt Jeremiah looks at Klein like she just got slapped. "That would make me a bitch, my dear."

"Exactly," Lareina says.

"You're part of the family," Dad says.

"But I really don't want to be a bother," Klein says, almost too desperate to please. It wrecks me to see her put everyone's needs above her own, even when it might harm her. I would've never guessed until I saw the way they treated her at Peking Town. She's always so sweet and considerate. The hatred for her parents that boils up in me is so fierce that it takes a physical effort not to snarl.

But maybe she and I excel at hiding the damage our parents left behind. Is that why something about her calls to me?

"Good God, child. If we can't make such a small accommodation, what kind of people would that make us? It isn't like we can never have seafood again. You shouldn't feel that your needs are a bother for others, especially not here, not with the family." Grandma says it warmly, but the firmness in her tone says there won't be any debate on this point.

Klein takes a moment to process. I tighten my hand around hers, hoping that what we're saying here sinks in. It's normal to accommodate, to care for, to show genuine affection for one another. I don't want her to feel like she's alone and unwanted, ever again.

"Josh...?" she says faintly, like she doesn't dare believe it.

"You're one of us now." I raise her hand and kiss the center of her palm. "Welcome to the family."

27

AILEE

You're one of us now. Welcome to the family.

I almost burst into tears at Josh's words. I have to bite my lip to contain the sob. Until now, I didn't realize I'd never felt like I had a family. I've never had people become upset on my behalf, or give up their own wants to cater to me.

As dinner progresses, all my anxiety and apprehension vanish. Josh's family isn't judging me or trying to put me down. They genuinely want me to belong—and to *feel* like I belong.

I'm also thinking of the beautiful character Akiko wrote for me: *love*. It's one thing I never felt I deserved, whether from my family or anybody else. I don't know how to put the emotions swelling in my heart into words.

So I do what I can—enjoy myself without wondering if anything has seafood in it. Or how big the bill would be if I had to hit the hospital for my allergy because an EpiPen wouldn't be enough. Or how inconvenienced and annoyed everyone would be if I had a reaction. Everything Akiko serves is perfect—delicious and gorgeously presented. And the plum wine is just chef's kiss. I've never had anything this sweet and delightful before. I don't understand why Josh ate the tacos earlier. I steal a quick glance. He seems to like what he's eating.

"You could open a luxury restaurant," I blurt to Akiko.

Ares and Bryce exchange a discreet look. Akiko laughs with delight. "You think so?"

"I *know* so. This is amazing."

"Thank you. I enjoy cooking, but I also like to experiment. I doubt anybody would be coming to a restaurant that changes its menu and recipes all the time."

"You could make a fortune catering to the dieting types from Hollywood," Jeremiah says before sipping another red wine.

Akiko looks doubtful. "My food is fairly rich. I don't skimp on butter, cream or duck fat."

Jeremiah snorts, and Prescott gives her a dirty look. Catalina turns her attention to me. "So. When is the wedding?"

Oh...crap. I glance at Josh, but he seems at ease as he bites into a thin slice of beef that's been folded into a tiny triangle. It's stuffed with some tasty green onion and cheese mixture. I already finished all three of mine. Now I wish I had something to stuff my mouth with so I could avoid answering.

Thankfully Akiko intervenes, leaning forward eagerly. "Yes! I can finally plan this ceremony!" Then she presses her lips together for a moment. "Ah...if that would be okay...?"

"Uh... I guess." What else can I say when she's looking at me so hopefully? *No?* And the engagement is going to end in six months, so...

I should tell Akiko not to plan anything until we know the date for sure, to avoid wasting her time. That way I'll feel less guilty.

"And we'll actually be invited to this one," Jeremiah adds dryly.

"Precisely." Catalina levels a meaningful look at Ares and Bryce.

I stare at the sad smears of brown sauce on my plate. Josh is still chewing the stuffed beef.

"Do you have any ideas about what you'd like for the wedding?" Catalina asks.

"A white dress?" I venture, staying on the safe side.

"Or black. I saw Grace Huxley's wedding photos, and she looked super chic in black," Lareina says.

My jaw slackens. "A *black* wedding dress? Like at a funeral?"

"It's fashionable in certain high society in Asia," Josh explains. "If you want black, you can wear black."

"Really?" I thought he would want something more traditional.

"It's a once-in-a-lifetime event," he says. "There shouldn't be any regrets. I want you to be happy."

My mouth dries. He seems like he means it—like he can see us together for a long, long time. Longing unfurls in my heart. I wish it *could* be like that.

"White is the default, but I saw a pale champagne wedding gown that was stunning. Lots of sparkly beads and details," Lareina says. "I think you'd be gorgeous in any color, to be honest. You just have to pick one that speaks to your heart."

"And you can decide on the scale of the wedding, too. Big or small. And the reception menu." Akiko's eyes sparkle. "I'd love to see what you select because no matter what, it'll be fabulous."

I look at her in surprise. Most of the time, my preferences aren't that important. Well, at least not with my family. But here, what I want seems like the *most* important. "Maybe something small," I finally manage, since Akiko's waiting for an answer with such eager anticipation. "Probably more economical that way."

Jeremiah gives Josh a stern look. "Surely you can afford a ceremony as grand as she wants it."

I shake my head. "Oh no. I mean—"

"Nobody pinches pennies for their wedding. Assuming, of course, that one actually holds a real ceremony rather than eloping." Jeremiah smiles thinly at Ares and Bryce. Ares got married in Vegas and Bryce had a courthouse ceremony. I heard no Huxley was present at either. "Anyway, I think you should splurge. The family will take care of it."

"Uh, I thought that was the bride's family's responsibility...?" Even as I say that, I cringe a little inwardly. If Akiko calls my mom to talk about the wedding, she'll say that any money spent on me is money wasted.

So embarrassing. I'd rather die first.

"We won't be relying on your parents." Underneath Josh's smooth tone is a mild disapproval. He seems to hold my parents in low esteem.

"Don't let antiquated ideas limit your options, Ailee," Catalina says. "The family will be honored to bring you into the fold properly."

The skin around my eyes grows hot. I blink away any moisture to ensure I don't cry or act too flustered. *My* needs. *My* preferences. They're actually being valued and respected. I realize I've spent much too much energy on suppressing my own desires.

Thankfully, the arrival of dessert stops the flow of the conversation and gives me a little breathing room to gather my shaky emotions. I pour myself more plum wine. This is my second bottle, but they're so tiny, just like the amazing food Akiko has served so far. I'm still hungry, but it's probably because I haven't eaten much today.

The dessert is a miniature—a soft matcha mochi ball stuffed with vanilla ice cream. I bite into it and press my lips together. The ice cream is so buttery and sweet, balancing out the intense matcha flavor.

"This is amazing. I think it's better than the one you made last Christmas," Prescott says. He devours his in two bites.

Akiko brightens. "You think so? I used a heavier cream and a small bit of raw apple honey from Aomori."

He nods, smacking his lips and gazing at his bowl sorrowfully.

"I don't think I've ever had a dinner this delicious. Thank you," I say.

"Oh, it's my pleasure—"

My stomach, oblivious to social niceties, chooses that moment to let out a loud growl. I slap my hands over it—like that will help. If I could, I'd crawl under the table and never come out.

Jeremiah covers her mouth, but a giggle escapes anyway. Josh gives me a look that says, *I told you to have the tacos.* I close my eyes for a moment. He's right, of course.

Akiko gasps. "Oh my goodness! Are you still hungry?"

"I'm so sorry. I haven't eaten much today. I was really nervous about meeting everyone, and I—" I quit talking. *Don't ramble.*

"You should've said something. I always have extra portions in the kitchen if anybody wants more."

Josh, Ares and Bryce's heads jerk in Akiko's direction. Jeremiah's mouth hangs open. The spoon in Catalina's hand falls to the table with a clatter. Prescott stares at his wife like she just told him she found herself a younger man with a bigger penis.

"You liked the stuffed beef, right?" Akiko asks, ignoring the reactions.

I nod. It was my favorite, and I'm surprised she noticed.

She smiles. "Give me a second." She disappears, then soon returns with a plate set with four pieces this time.

"You never told us there was *more*," Josh manages, his voice hoarse.

Akiko purses her lips and shrugs. "Nobody ever asked."

"So if I'd wanted more, I just needed to...?" Hopefully Prescott isn't having a stroke. He doesn't look very good.

"Well, of course! I always make sure everyone has plenty to drink, don't I?"

Bryce covers his face with a hand. "Oh God."

"What?" Akiko says.

"I can't wait to tell Fiona our child will have enough food to fill its belly when we visit," he mutters, which only seems to confuse Akiko more.

"I think we're all having regrets about being too circumspect to spare your feelings." Jeremiah knocks back her red wine like it's whiskey. She probably wishes it *was* whiskey.

"Thanks to Ailee joining the family, we all learned something valuable today," Catalina announces. "If you want something, you should just ask."

Akiko nods, a smile blooming on her bright face. "Very true. The answer will more often than not be a yes."

28

JOSH

"Thank you. And you're the best, Akiko." Klein sounds absolutely sober. No slurring of words, no hesitation in speech. But she also has no balance or dexterity.

She seems totally unaware of the fact that she's pressed against me, with my arm looped around her waist to keep her upright as we move toward the car at the end of the dinner.

Ares, Lareina and Bryce shoot us amused looks. Grandma and Dad nod, while Aunt Jeremiah smirks, her eyes knowing. Akiko beams as usual, her demeanor soft with affection.

I always thought Klein's smile was gorgeous, but the one right now? Stunning with unguarded warmth and happiness. She stumbles a little as she waves at everyone like a newly crowned Miss U.S.A. I tighten my hold, and her cheek rests on the inside of my shoulder. She's so warm and soft, and she smells amazing, like woman, flowers and aromatic plum wine. Although its sweetness and smooth finish make it very drinkable, the plum wine Akiko serves is stronger than it looks, and Klein had one—or maybe two—too many cups.

I manage to get her into the car and start driving home. Five minutes in, she begins to sing. No matter how charitable I want to be, singing isn't her forte. She's slightly off-key, and when she can't seem to recall the lyric, she just makes up some nonsense words to fill in. Still, I can't complain. She sounds deliriously joyful, and her mood is contagious. I love the way her eyes crinkle and the little wagging motions she does with her fingers to the beat.

Smiling despite myself, I join in.

"Hey, you sound good!" she says, eyebrows rising.

"Of course. I used to sing a cappella in college." I say it with a healthy dose of mock arrogance.

"Really? I didn't realize. I thought you did something like…debate or something in college to prep for your legal career. Did Bryce do it, too?"

"Nope. Just me." I wink. "I have many hidden talents."

"I bet, and I'd love to discover them all," she says with a grin.

"We'll have plenty of time." *Plenty of time? It's just six months,* I think. *Then again, we can always extend it.*

She laughs. "Now it's going to sound even better with both of us."

And we sing all the way home. She knows quite a few songs—even if not every word—and I love the way her face glows as the freeway lights flash past.

When we reach the garage and the engine dies, she lets out a soft sigh. "Thank you for the dinner. Your family is wonderful. I loved it." She fumbles with the seatbelt, but has trouble unbuckling. "Huh. Wonder if it's broken."

"Or maybe you're just drunk," I say.

"I am *not* drunk." She makes sure to enunciate every word with precision.

"Of course not."

She purses her mouth, making it look eminently kissable. "Who should we ask?"

"About what?"

"The broken seatbelt! Akiko said if I want something, all I have to do is ask."

I try not to laugh. She's so adorably inebriated. "The God of Cars?"

She nods. "Hey, God of Cars, can you fix the seatbelt?" she says, looking up at the roof of the vehicle.

I reach over and click her seatbelt loose, then rest my elbow on the edge of her seat, my torso still turned toward her. "Ask, and ye shall receive."

Laughing softly, she drops her gaze to my face, her beautiful violet eyes dark in the night as they search mine. Her mouth softens. "Thank you."

"My pleasure." I enjoy catering to her little whimsy. It isn't every day I see her this relaxed with her guard down. My eyes stay on hers. They're so bright, so open. They pull me in deeper, and I want to drown in them, become one with her.

Jesus, get a hold of yourself.

"We should go inside," I say hoarsely before I cross a line I shouldn't.

"Okay. Open sesame!"

Shaking my head, I climb out of the car. She fumbles with the handle, so I open the door and help her out. She's even less steady now, her feet tangling.

"The ground is quite uneven," she declares, pushing her hair out of her face. "Who should I ask about making it better?"

"How about me?"

"You?" She blinks slowly. "Can you make the ground even now?"

"In a manner of speaking."

I put her arm around my neck and pick her up. She gives a soft yelp and clasps her hands to hold on to me. The move pulls her so close that her breasts are crushed against my chest. Heat sears through me, my cock perking up.

Not now. At least not so much that it pokes her.

She gazes up at me, her eyes wide. "I'm too heavy," she whispers.

I tighten my arms, enjoying the solid feel of her as I carry her into the house. "If I wanted to hold cotton balls, I would. I want to hold you."

"What if you hurt your back? I need to lose, like, forty pounds."

"Won't happen, Ai—Ailee Klein." I catch myself before I call her Ai-chan because she feels so lovely and sweet in my arms. "And you don't. You'd turn into a stick."

She nods, taking me seriously. I like how alcohol has mellowed her out, made her more pliable and honest about what she wants. Love it that she changed her mind so quickly about the forty pounds—*as if!*—

without arguing. I want her to see that she's wonderful the way she is. There's nothing she should feel compelled to change about herself.

"Oh, oh, wait!" She looks up as we get to the stairs. "Who do you think I should ask about my missing underwear? God seems a bit...too high on the pay grade."

"The ghost that took them?" I say smoothly, hoping she didn't notice the slight flexing of my fingers.

"They were my favorite. Where did it go with them?"

"To hell?" I quip, feeling like I might just go there myself for lying to her when she's looking at me with such trust.

"No. It's just a pair of panties. Let's not be so mean." She sighs. "I just want them back."

"Maybe you can ask to have another pair delivered. Or better yet, I'll get you some."

She laughs, the pink in her cheeks getting rosier.

"I'm serious."

She stops laughing, but her mouth remains curved. "This is so nice. To be able to ask and be confident that the answer is more likely than not a yes."

I open the door to her room, then place her gently on the bed. Her hair spreads around her like cloud, and she looks like an angel, eyes glazed and mouth pouty. I should pull away and leave, but my palms stay rooted to either side of her pretty, flushed face. I can't tear my gaze from her. My heart beats faster. My mouth dries as the blood boils in my veins. I want so badly to kiss her, to see the violet of her eyes turn dark with desire.

She sighs, her eyes growing slightly droopy. "Coco told me you'll be done with me if we sleep together. Even once. What do you think about that?"

"She's deluded. I don't think I could ever be 'done with you.'"

Klein purses her lips. "I think you're mistaken there."

What? "Why?" I ask, aghast that we went from having Klein accepting that the world is much kinder and accommodating than she expected to *this*.

"'Cuuuuz... You never tried anything. With me." Klein pouts.

My dick is instantly, fully erect. *Prove her wrong. Try something—now.*

No, no. Shut up. She's really drunk. "I kissed you."

"And stopped. Was it...not good?"

I scowl. It was the best kiss I've ever had.

Before I can clarify, she lowers her gaze and continues, "Or was it because you could tell I have trouble with orgasms?"

I go still for a second, then cock an eyebrow. "Uh...I'm sorry?" *Where did* that *come from?*

"No, I mean, I *have* them. But they aren't very good. I usually fake it to spare the guy's ego. And also because I don't want him to keep going because it's frustrating and it makes me want to take charge, but then... That's weird for me, right?"

I stare at her. Sympathy and triumph tug at me from opposite directions. It's criminal that a woman as beautiful and sexy as Klein has never had a great orgasm. But I want to crow that I'm going to make her feel damn good. "You'd better not fake with me. And you can take charge all you want—I won't mind."

"But wouldn't that make me kind of slutty?"

I narrow my eyes. Where's this coming from? Her shitty family, who's done everything to bring her down? Her crappy exes? Either way, it's infuriating. "No. I think it's hot as hell." I place a firm kiss on her forehead.

Her eyelashes flutter as she raises her eyes to meet mine. "Why are you stopping?" she whispers.

"Because, my dear Klein, you are adorably drunk."

"I'm not."

"Yes, you are. If you were sober, you wouldn't have been so open and forthcoming." I kiss the corners of her eyes. The soft vulnerability shining in their depths sends tenderness rippling through me. A need to turn that self-doubt into confidence and make her smile swells up inside. And the words roll from my mouth before I even really know it. "Ask me again when you're sober, and I'll make it so good you won't be able to go a day without tearing my clothes off."

29

———

AILEE

"Ow." I groan against the pillow in the cool darkness, then shift to get comfortable as something hard jabs into my ribs. The movement sets off a bunch of toddlers banging on drums inside my head. Or at least that's how it feels.

So unfair. I didn't even drink that much. The bottles were tiny, and the plum wine was too smooth and sweet to have much alcohol. I open my eyes gingerly, willing the drum beaters to settle down. On the nightstand are a bottle of water and a selection of aspirin, Tylenol and Advil.

Must have been Josh. This act alone makes him God's gift to humanity. Practically groaning with appreciation, I down four aspirins and then take stock. I'm still in my dress from yesterday, and the bra's digging into my chest—so annoying. And the fabric's totally wrinkled, but maybe it'll smooth itself out after a wash.

I massage my throbbing temples and try to recall what happened after Josh and I left the family dinner. We got into his car, and then...

Oh shit. My face grows hot with embarrassment. *The singing.* Josh joined in, but... *Ugh.* I don't have the best voice, but when I'm happy *and* drunk, sometimes I let go.

Note to self: Don't get drunk in front of Josh again. Ever.

And… Oh my God. Did I make him *carry* me? And then I told him about the missing underwear, and he offered to replace it. I press my fingers to my face, wishing it hadn't happened. But nope. I even told him that I've never had a really good orgasm.

Ack!

I swallow a scream and flop back onto the pillows. I got so carried away after hearing Akiko say that if I wanted something, I should ask. It felt so liberating, full of potential. I felt like a lonely child given permission and encouragement to go out and play with the other kids.

But I shouldn't have been so bold with Josh. What's he going to think of me? How am I going to face him?

Ask me when you're sober, and I'll make it so good you won't be able to go a day without tearing my clothes off. I roll over—slowly—and bury my face in the pillows. *Holy shit.*

If he hadn't said that he wouldn't touch me until I was sober, I might've done something I shouldn't have. Like grabbing him and kissing him, with my tongue in his mouth. I want to see if the hot, shivery experience from our earlier kiss was real or a fluke, because that much chemistry has *never* happened for me.

Okay. What happened when you're drunk stays unremembered, I tell myself. *That's the only way you can act unaffected.*

Still, my mind is going wild with things he could make me feel. If he could make me wet and wanton with just a kiss, imagine the things he could do with the rest of his body. He might prove that romance novel sex scenes aren't all fake. Just thinking about it makes me fan myself.

I'm not sure what's wrong with me, but something about him makes me want to let loose. He provides a sense of security I've never felt with another man. His words from last night actually seemed genuine. If I fall, he'll catch me. If I make a mistake, he'll make everything all right again. And throughout it all, he won't judge me. My heart beats so hard, I have to press a hand over my chest.

My phone rattles on the table. *Maybe it's Josh.* I take a deep, steadying breath and peek at the screen.

–Max: I thought I'd be in L.A. by now, but noooo! The fucker is taking me to Tokyo to make me work on some BS project. Can you be my alibi? I'm only going to murder him. Just a little.

—Me: LOL What's "just a little?" You gonna just mur him? Besides, didn't you say you wanted to go to Tokyo? Make it a semi-vacation.

—Max: He'll work me like a dog to "get his money's worth."

—Me: Stay strong. You can do eeeet!!!!

—Max: Thanks, girl. You too. Do everything I'd do. Like riding that hot-as-hell lawyer of yours who charged in like a knight in shining armor. And for our next apartment, I want to consult a feng shui book before we decorate it, in case bad furniture placement gave me this hellhound with rabies for a boss.

I laugh softly. I've already done some dirty things with Josh in my head a few times, but that's about it. I don't have the courage to actually go for it for real, especially if I'm sober. Even though he said to try it when I'm not drunk, I'm terrified I might not measure up somehow to his gorgeous exes, and he'll end up disappointed. Sort of like how my parents felt as I grew older and they realized I'm nothing like Katt.

Still, the impulse to give in to the urge to kiss him is becoming increasingly difficult to resist, especially since he insisted that I call him *Josh*. How can the way I address him decimate our professional distance so easily?

Sighing, I get up—slowly—and shower. I probably smell like lingering alcohol if nothing else. Afterward I brush my teeth, then gargle twice, just to be sure. The mirrors reflect a chalky complexion. I seriously need to tan or something. If I had a little more pigment, I wouldn't look this awful after an evening of mild drinking.

The walk-in closet is now fully stocked with everything I need. I throw on a comfy white T-shirt and teal knee-length skirt, then pad barefoot downstairs to make coffee. The rhythmic sound of a knife hitting a cutting board comes from the kitchen. Josh must be up and making something. Interesting. I thought he didn't cook. As I get closer to the first floor, the smell of coffee drifts up. *Oh my God.* Josh is the man.

I freeze on the bottom step because Josh is—*topless*. I blink a few times just in case I'm still dreaming or seeing things, but he's real.

My hangover instantly vanishes.

Not only is he topless, but a baseball cap is placed backward on his head, giving him a casual, bad-boy charm. He looks younger than his thirty years. And eminently more approachable, without the usual razor-sharp lawyerly aura.

The morning light pouring in through windows show every contour of lean, strong muscle in his long arms and gorgeous chest. Veins stand out on his surprisingly thick forearms, which are covered with a light dusting of hair. The muscles flex as he cuts some green stuff on the cutting board. That's literal forearm porn material right there. And those abs! I've only seen abs like that on fitness magazine covers. Every ridge is perfectly defined, not an ounce of fat anywhere. He even has that V-line on his lower abs... I lick my lips before I can stop myself. At least he hasn't noticed me yet.

A pair of gray sweats hangs low on his narrow hips. He lifts his head. "Good morning," he says cheerfully.

Don't step away from the counter, don't step away from the counter!

But of course he does, to toss whatever he's been chopping into the pan on the stove.

Don't look below the hips...!

Aaaaand my eyes immediately drop. I almost swallow my tongue at the impressive outline.

How would it fit?

Of course my mind immediately goes...there. I mentally smack myself, but my mind won't get off the rated-R track it's on.

Wait, wouldn't it get bigger when he gets hard? So what's the final girth and length?

He checks whatever's frying in the pan, then smiles at me again. His eyes roam over me, and the weight of his gaze is almost physical. My cheeks warm. I resist the urge to squirm and merely smile, hoping it's hiding the fact that I've been mentally measuring him.

"Feeling better?" he asks.

"Yeah. Thanks for the aspirins." I clear my throat. Now I wish I'd put on at least blush so I don't look so pale compared to him. I pour a coffee for me and stir in some sugar. "Didn't realize you like to be topless on weekends." I flush as soon as I blurt it out. That sounds a bit judgmental, which isn't what I meant. I take a very long sip of the coffee to hide my face.

He laughs. "Why? Like what you see?" He flexes his pecs—left, right, left, right.

I stare, absolutely mesmerized. "I thought that was a trick that people posted on social media using AI."

He chuckles. "Just so you know, I go outside to check on the garden on weekends. And to get some sun on my skin. Otherwise I spend way too much time inside." He cuts the gas to the stove. "Hope you like eggs. They're the only food I can make with confidence." He serves, creating generous mounds of fluffy scrambled eggs on a couple of plates.

"I like anything," I say quickly. "I'm surprised you cook."

"I do when I want to feed someone." His eyes crinkle with a soft smile, which feels so intimate.

I pull my lips in and swallow as heat pulses through me.

He sprinkles chopped green bits on the eggs. "Chives from the garden."

"You grow chives?"

"There's an herb garden over there." He tilts his chin toward a side door I didn't notice before. "Picked out some seeds and planted them on a whim. Now they're growing like weeds."

I blink slowly. The image of him squatting down in the dirt and messing around with seeds and fertilizer and all the things that go with gardening is just... It simply doesn't fit his whole killer lawyer vibe. I tried to start a small garden in a box on my balcony, thinking it'd be great to have fresh herbs and save a little money. More than half the stuff I planted died, including the green onions that my nice Asian neighbor said would outlive me.

He puts the plates on the counter, then stretches his arms up for two long-stem glasses hanging upside down from a rack above his head. His muscles stretch across his massive ribcage, the triceps and biceps flexing and sliding. As the stems come free from the rack, he deftly turns them and cups the bowls in his large palms, holding them in front of him.

What would it be like if he held my breasts like that?

My nipples suddenly ache at the thought. I try to shake it off, but the tingling lingers. *Thank* God *I put on a bra.* No need to point my headlights at the man who's just doing his...morning kindness of feeding me eggs.

"I made some agua fresca de maracuyá," Josh says. "Basically, a passion fruit drink. Used some ripe ones from the garden, and here are some more if you want try the fruit itself." He gestures at some half-cut deep purple fruit, then pours a pulpy, yellowish liquid into the stemware and extends a glass to me.

I stare at the drink, his beautiful hand and the bare arm stretched toward me. My gaze travels to his face, the stunning lines that blend to create an absolutely mesmerizing masculinity. His eyes are too warm, too captivating, as he studies me.

Suddenly, it doesn't seem real. Things like this don't happen to somebody like me. I thought this was like Cinderella's ball before the stroke of midnight, but it's still too good to be true.

"By the way, Klein?"

"Yes?" I say, unable to look away from him.

He lowers the glass to the counter and pushes it toward me. "Regardless of what you might've been told or think about yourself, you're a beautiful person who deserves *everything* you desire."

30

AILEE

Two weeks later, my face heats as I scarf down my breakfast. Something's definitely been up with Josh since the dinner at his parents' place. Thankfully, the dealer finally replaced my fob, so I leave the house as soon as I finish eating. It's either that or jump him or do something seriously inappropriate. Hopefully I was subtle. I tried really hard to avoid staring.

You're a beautiful person who deserves everything you desire.

Two weeks since he said it, and I've been going a little crazy because my heart won't quit racing every time it pops into my head—which is every time I see him, whether it's in the office or at home.

If I didn't know better, I might've thought he was trying to...well, court me. A homemade breakfast. The display of his magnificent body. The gray sweatpants and that *outline...*

I fan myself, trying to come up with an alternate explanation. Josh was probably just being comfortable in his house. He's entitled to chill on weekends, including going topless. Right?

Yeah, your exes only did that when they wanted to get lucky, an internal voice reminds me.

But Josh wasn't aiming for any horizontal action.

Because a kitchen's more suitable for vertical *action. Like against a counter. Or bent-over action over a counter. Or the brace-your-hands-against-the-counter-and-stick-your-ass-out...*

Okay, now the voice sounds awfully like Max. I'm definitely muting it.

I tap the steering wheel as I drive to Target. The insurance is taking its sweet time with the claim I filed, and the same thing with the property manager, who likely wants to hold on to our security deposit as long as legally possible. At least Max and I aren't in urgent need of a place. She's still being dragged around the world by her boss, and she texts me from time to time to whine, swearing she's going to quit as soon as she finds a position that pays as well as her current one.

I frown, wondering about the roommate situation when she's finally back in town. Should I continue to share a place with her and pay half the rent? After all, I'm going to need to have to move out in about six months—actually less than that now. Max and I get along great, and I'd hate to leave her high and dry. And having to struggle to find a new roommate when the engagement is over seems...overwhelming.

I park my car in the lot and head inside the huge store. Josh's place has everything I need, so I'm just here to browse the books. This location is one of my favorites because it has a great selection of romance novels. I love reading on my phone and Kindle, but sometimes I just want the heft of a print book in my lap. Plus, the reading nook in my room is so perfect, I have this yen to curl up with a nice special edition and lose myself in the story. That should give me something to occupy my time, instead of drooling over the memories of Josh's abs or thinking about what to do about a new apartment.

One of the nicest things about living with Josh is that I don't have to do any housework. No cleaning, no laundry, no grocery shopping or cooking. I didn't realize until I no longer had to do any chores how much time those things take up. But that also means I have way too much idle time to obsess about him. I still can't get used to wearing his ring. I love how elegant and stunning it is, but it just seems too perfect to be on my finger. It's the opposite of how I felt about Chad's ring—not a bad item, and my hand was good enough for it.

I pick up a book that has a black cover with elaborate gold filigree. Some kind of mafia arranged-marriage romance. Do mafiosos do arranged marriages all the time? Wonder what that'd be like—marrying a man you've never met. Or aren't even sure you'll like. At least in romance novels, you're guaranteed to get a gorgeous guy who knows his way around a woman's body.

"That's a great story," comes a familiar voice. "I read it last week and loved it."

I spin around. "Zoe! How are you?"

"I'm good." She hugs me, then checks me out, as though to make sure I'm really okay. "How about you? Did you find a new apartment after the fire?"

"I'm doing well. I actually moved in with my"—I clear my throat—"fiancé."

"Good for you! Glad it worked out. Is he treating you well?"

I remember our weekend scrambled eggs. And how his muscles go taut over his gorgeous frame as he moves around the kitchen. "Very." My voice is a little hoarse.

"I'm glad. Got time for coffee or something? My machine broke this morning, and I haven't had anything yet. Of course, it had to break on a Saturday, when the office is closed."

I gasp with sympathy. "That's positively criminal." I gesture in the direction of the café across the street. "Let's head over there. I can come back for the book later."

"I don't mind waiting."

"No. Coffee is more important."

"You're the sweetest." She smiles winsomely, her blue eyes crinkling. Still, she refuses to leave without me getting the book first, and I can't say no. There's something oddly maternal about the way she treats me that tugs at my heart.

Upon arriving at the café, Zoe gets a hot cappuccino and I get an iced Americano, hoping it cools me down more before I drive home. "Want some syrup?" she says, gesturing at the sweeteners.

"Sure."

She hands me one, and I pour it into the cup.

"This might sound strange, but I could have sworn you had a *diamond* ring," Zoe says as we sit down and sip our coffee. "I have a nearly photographic memory," she adds. "But now I'm wondering if I'm just imagining things after the fire...?"

"Oh no, you're not." I look down at the sapphire and smile. "It was diamond, but..."

"What happened to the heirloom ring?" She picks up my hand and studies the sapphire ring with keen interest. "I wish my husband had proposed me with something that sentimental. Perhaps then our marriage would've lasted." A wispy regret fleets through her blue eyes.

"Oh. I'm sorry to hear that." My voice softens. "Well...the fact is, that ring was, you know, *technically* an heirloom...but it really wasn't that special, trust me. This one is much better. And it'll become much more sentimental, too." I tilt my hand toward her.

"Very tasteful. I'm sure it will." She nods with approval, then squeezes my hand before letting go. "It suits you perfectly. Your fiancé must have great taste. You should introduce us one of these days." She flashes a charming smile.

"He does, and of course, I'd be happy to. You'll love him. He's fantastic."

Her smile broadens. "I'm sure I will. By the way, have you gotten your deposit back?"

"Not yet. You?"

She shakes her head. "They're taking their time. Probably collecting interest on our money." Her mouth twists cynically.

"I'm sure they'll wait the entire twenty-one days." When she looks at me blankly, I add, "That's the legally mandated deadline."

"Ah." She nods. "I'm in a support group for the fire victims. Are you in it too?"

"No. Didn't know there was one."

"It's on Facebook. I'll invite you, if you want."

"Sure. I'd love that!"

She texts me the group invite, then leans forward. "By the way, did you see the news this morning?"

"A little bit of it. Why?"

"They caught the arsonist."

"Somebody set our building on fire *on purpose*?"

"Yup. A kid. Only seventeen."

"Oh my God. Why?"

"He supposedly wanted to create a new challenge people could do and post online."

A new— The explanation is even more ludicrous than I imagined. I was lucky because, despite having lost everything in the fire, I had Josh. But what about people who have no one to come to their aid? "What was he thinking?"

"He claims—although it didn't sound like it was verified—that someone promised to give him a thousand dollars if he could do it. The security footage the cops got shows the kid starting the fire, but nothing of this supposed other person." She shrugs. "He probably made it up when he got caught. Trying to shift the blame or something. Anyway, according to the kid, the fire wasn't supposed to spread. It was just supposed to burn a little, and then he was going to put it out, but his fire extinguisher malfunctioned." Zoe rolls her eyes.

"His lawyer should've advised him to shut up." Josh would have.

"Probably. But some people just think they're too clever for the police."

"What a fool." The kid's life is basically ruined, and all over a stupid internet challenge.

We gossip some more until Zoe gets a call and has to go to handle some kind of personal emergency. I wave her goodbye, then head back home. The traffic's sort of crappy. Although it was sunny in the morning, dark clouds are slowly forming in the sky. I check the weather app at a red light—rain is expected in the afternoon.

Crap. Better get back before the roads get slick. I love watching rain, but hate driving in it. The roads get too slippery, visibility drops and people in Southern California drive like idiots. And if there's an accident, the traffic becomes impossible.

The clouds have spread over almost the entire sky by the time I drive through Josh's gates about an hour later. For some reason, my heartbeat starts to accelerate.

I clench and unclench my hands around the steering wheel as I kill the engine in the garage. Leaning my head against the headrest, I breathe at a steady pace, willing my heart to settle. Instead, it only beats faster, almost like I'm having a mild panic attack.

Did the update about the fire upset me more than I expected? Hard to believe—my reaction seems too over the top.

Calm down, Ailee. Think of something soothing. Like an ocean.

Instead, my mind conjures Josh's intense, dark eyes. Those beautiful lips that make me weak in the knees. His scent, which drives me crazy. His specially formulated bath products that turn me on every time I shower because they remind me of him. And how much I wish I could bury my nose in his neck and inhale.

My breathing shallows. *Am I actually* panting? Sweat mists over my skin, and I put a hand over my chest. If heart conditions ran in the family, I might assume I'm having a heart attack or something.

I open the door and stumble out of the car. The air in the garage feels colder than it should. Am I having some kind of reaction? But all I had was that Americano. I'm definitely *not* allergic to coffee, and I'd better stay that way!

My hands shake. I open my purse for an EpiPen, then stop. I'm not having trouble breathing. I'm panting, but getting the air in just fine. Still, something's not right. My skin is too tight and tingly. The air enters my lungs cold, then leaves overheated. My knees tremble.

I stagger toward the door to the house. My nipples ache inside my bra, and my thong chafes my inner thighs. I bite my lip to contain a groan as the friction sends tiny, tingling shocks through me.

What the hell? How can I get horny from underwear chafing? It should be uncomfortable, not arousing.

But the flesh between my legs slickens, the heat becoming unbearable.

I reach under my skirt and yank the thong off before it turns me into some kind of deviant. Clutching it in my fist, and praying that a cold shower will take care of these weird sensations, I start toward my room...

...and come to an immediate, abrupt halt when I catch sight of Josh dozing on the sofa. He's topless. One arm is thrown over his forehead, and it's as though a kind of halo surrounds him. His muscles should be softer and less defined in relaxation. But they remain hard and ridged, from the broad shoulders to the thick chest and tight abs. My eyes roam over his body shamelessly, etching the masculine perfection into my brain.

The gray sweatpants drape over his crotch, creating an even more obvious outline of his cock. From the position of the shadows, he's sporting an erection. It's thicker and longer. Hot sparks run through me, and I bite my lip to contain a low moan welling in my throat.

My mouth waters as delicious shivers run through me. I want to suck the cockhead into my mouth and see how it feels. I want the taste of him on my tongue.

What's *wrong* with me? I don't understand where this urge is coming from, but I feel like I'll die if I don't have him in my mouth. I crave it like air. The ache between my legs intensifies, and my fingers twitch with the need to touch him.

I tiptoe toward him, my legs trembling. Anticipation and need course through me. His chest rises and falls, his mouth relaxed and malleable. *He called me beautiful, but he's the beauty.*

I want to wake him up with my mouth. But not with something as clichéd as a kiss. I want to pull his cock into my mouth, then run my tongue over the head. And when he opens his eyes, I want to have my way with him. Ease the painful ache building inside me.

I put a hand on the back of the sofa and lean over Josh. This position makes me feel powerful and naughty. He looks so innocent in sleep, his impossibly long and thick lashes lying demurely just above those high cheekbones. My fingers long to trace every line on his body, from the strong column of his neck to the collarbones and pecs and the defined section of his abs.

Biting my lip, I lower my trembling hand until it hovers over his waistband. His body generates *so much heat.* I slide a single finger under and pull it down with a slow, delicate touch. *He isn't wearing underwear.*

His cock springs up, as though relieved it's been liberated from confinement. The sight is even more impressive than I imagined. Thick veins line an impossibly thick and long shaft. The head is perfectly plum-shaped, and dark purple from so much blood pooling there. The tip drips with precum.

I grip him, and it's so thick there's a good inch of space remaining between my fingertips and my thumb. The veins pulse against my palm, and I feel it all the way to my slick flesh.

Josh's eyes open to narrow slits. "Klein?" he rasps, his voice rough with sleep. "What—"

"Shh…" I put a finger over his mouth.

He shuts up. To reward him, I pump him slowly, earning a deep, throaty groan that makes my toes curl. I grin. I love it that I can affect him like this. I love it that the musky scent of him is growing stronger with excitement.

My hair falls over my shoulders. He tunnels his large hand into my curls to keep them out of my face. Heat flares in his eyes, now fully open, as he looks up at me, then licks the finger I have on his mouth. The touch sends shivers racing down my back and ending in my clit. A moan wells in my chest. I lean down and wrap my lips around his cock to contain the sound.

"Fuck. Klein…"

His voice is raw with desire. Every muscle in his body tenses, then begins to shake. The tip of my tongue flicks over his opening. Salt and something uniquely Josh flood my mouth. I hum softly, enjoying the flavor, then bob my head shallowly. He's so big, my mouth is stretched to its limit. It's tough to move much without scraping him with my teeth.

But he rewards my effort with pants and groans. His pelvis jerks whenever he can't stop himself from moving and seeks more of what I can give him. I feel powerful and sexy—something I've *never* felt before. I wrap both of my hands around him, but there's still more left. I pump while sucking him like he's my favorite lollipop. Although my jaw starts to ache a little, I could do this forever as long as he moans my name like I'm the only woman for him, like now.

"Klein, oh shit, baby—"

I pull him in deeper, and he lets out a strangled sound. His hips come off the sofa, and his cock spasms. Hot cum coats my mouth like warm caramel. I swallow, feeling dirty and sexy. *This is the first orgasm I've given him.* A dark flush colors his gorgeous face as it twists with pleasure. His teeth dig into his lip. He clenches his hands into fists, and every muscle in his body bulges. His chest doesn't rise or fall anymore—as though he's holding his breath and trying to prolong the moment.

I flick my tongue under his cockhead, then smile when he trembles in response. My heart flutters at seeing him lost in pleasure I just gave him, and emotions I can't identify swell.

"Klein, am I dreaming?" he murmurs, his eyes dazed.

I laugh softly. "No. You're not. And now that I've woken you up, Sleeping Beauty, I'm about to have my way with you again." Then I swing around, swing astride and fit my pussy right over his cock.

31

JOSH

SWEET JESUS.

AT THE FEEL of her slick, molten core over me, my dick springs to instant hardness again. I don't think I've ever recovered this fast, but Klein is like cock magic.

She said this wasn't a dream, but it has to be. I've been fantasizing about her for days and I'm too exhausted from sleep deprivation to be awake. She's too sweet, too eager. At the same time, the feel of her hot mouth around me felt very, *very* real.

But she's too shy to behave this boldly—

Whatever. I'm going with it.

She rocks against my length and my scalp prickles as electric pleasure sparks along my spine. She looks down at me like a goddess, her chin raised with feminine power. Her pouty lips beckon me for a hard kiss. I start to reach for her when she grabs the hem of her shirt.

"My breasts hurt."

She raises the garment over her head and tosses it aside. Then she undoes the clasp of her bra and lets it fall.

Holy shit. Her breasts are even more ravishing than I imagined. I always knew she had lovely, generous curves, but this is perfection. Her rosy nipples are pointed, making me want to take them into my mouth.

As she moves along my cock, her breasts swell and ebb, commanding all my attention.

"They still hurt." Her raw eyes beg me to do something about it.

I cup both of them in my hands, their hard tips in the center of my palms. They feel incredible, soft and heavy and warm. My own blood is so hot, I'm amazed steam isn't hissing out of my ears.

"Klein, baby…" I knead the soft flesh, loving the way it molds to my large, calloused hands. I pinch the nipples between my fingers and tug.

She arches into my hands. "Please."

My control starts to fray. I bring her down, flicking my tongue against a nipple, then quickly suck it into my mouth. Her fingers dig into my chest as she grinds against me. Her uninhibited reaction is so erotic, it stokes my desire further. If this is a dream, it's the best one I've ever had.

I move with her, increasing the suction. I love every little gasp and moan, the low purring sounds she makes as she loses herself in the sensation.

She's so drenched over me, her juices trickle down between my legs. I let go of her nipple with a pop. "Were you this wet while you were sucking my dick?"

"Yes. I wanted to suck you off so bad."

My cock swells bigger underneath her slick flesh.

She continues, "I saw you and couldn't resist. Did you like it?"

"Couldn't you tell? I fucking loved it. When you had me in your mouth, it felt like you owned me—and you were mine." That mutual possession filled me with a monstrous lust that refuses to be satisfied.

She flushes. "You *are* mine. And I'm yours."

Heat blazes through me at her shy admission. The words seem to carry more weight than my ring on her finger.

I switch nipples and grind my pelvis against her. She hangs on to me, a thin film of sweat glinting on her gorgeous skin. I don't understand how a woman can taste this good—sheer cream and sugar and everything that makes her feminine and beautiful. I push a finger between our bodies and slowly rub it against her swollen clit.

She lets out a soft cry. "Oh my God, that feels so good."

But it isn't enough to satisfy me. I need to taste her all over, and I'm not having her for the first time on a sofa.

I kick off my sweatpants, then cup her ass and stand up. She yelps in surprise, wrapping her legs tightly around my waist, looping her arms around my neck. The position has her nipples rubbing against my chest with each step, and I shift so that every time I take a stride, my dick bumps against her clit. Her muscles tighten with tension, and she bites her lip.

I lean in and kiss her as I walk up the stairs. She pulls my tongue into her mouth just like she did with my cock. My blood pressure skyrockets. Klein is going to be the death of me, but it's going to be the sweetest death anyone could ever imagine, and a better one than I deserve.

I take her to my room and lay her on the bed. She's divine on the sheets, and I pull the skirt off her and throw it on the floor.

Her dark eyes on mine, she spreads her legs. "Please," she says. I brace myself over her, one hand on each side of her head. Then I kiss her, tasting a hint of coffee and that honeyed flavor I associate uniquely with her. Her eager tongue tangles with mine, her hands roaming all over my body.

I grab her wrists and pin them by her head. "Behave," I warn. "Don't push me too hard." Although I came only a few minutes ago, my body is already ready for another orgasm.

"I just want to feel you," she says, licking her lips. "I want to feel all of—"

I kiss her hard to steal her breath and shut her up before she can say more. She moans softly against my mouth, and I rain delicate kisses all along her sensitive neck.

I move down to her stunning breasts, lingering over her nipples, flicking my tongue over them and teasing them until they're impossibly hard. She moves her legs restlessly, tilting her hips, trying to press her slick folds against my shaft to relieve the pressure building inside her.

I move lower, brushing my mouth along the gentle slope of her belly. I adore that she's so soft and feminine.

I throw her legs over my shoulders, but she puts the soles of her feet on my back and spreads her knees, presenting herself like an exquisite feast for me to enjoy.

My tongue glides along her flesh, lapping up the abundant juices on her hot pink core. She tastes like honey and nectar. The flavor goes straight to my head, and my cock is now painfully hard.

I use my tongue and lips on her, licking and sucking. She rocks against my face. I revel in her surprising lack of inhibition. This is what *I'm* doing to her. My Klein, my beautiful little Klein.

Her breathing begins to hitch. I push my tongue into her pussy, and she twists and rocks even harder against my face. Tension coils inside her, her belly jerking. I suck her clit hard, and hum to create vibration.

"Oh my God, *holy*—!" she screams, her back bowed in climax. She goes rigid and then begins to shake as she rides it out.

Watching an orgasm breaking over her is such a gift. Male satisfaction fills my heart. This is *always* how she should be: glowing and sated. I lick her again for a final taste, then let go of her wrists to wipe my mouth.

"That was incredible," she whispers, her eyes glazed. "But—"

"What do you want, baby? Tell me."

"I want you to absolutely wreck me," she says. "I want to feel your cock inside me, Josh. I want to feel it filling my pussy."

I clench my jaw as I fight for control. This woman instinctively knows how to push all the right buttons. I thank my lucky stars that I got the vasectomy a while ago so I'll never procreate, and I also pat myself on the back for always using condoms. I'd never go bare with Klein if I wasn't one hundred percent certain that I was clean.

"In the interests of full disclosure, I'm clean," I tell her.

"I know," she says, her eyes shining. "I trust you. You're too meticulous to be sloppy about your health or protecting your partner."

Her trust shakes my remaining control. I'm humbled to receive it and grateful that she believes I'm worthy of it.

I take her mouth hard, my tongue invading as I put two fingers into her pussy to ready her. No matter how much urgency I feel, I don't want to thrust into her like a horny teenager and risk hurting her. The only thing she'll feel in my bed is pleasure.

Her inner muscles tighten on my fingers. *Damn.* I move them in and out, spreading them slightly to stretch her. A shaky breath pulls out of her, her face flushed with anticipation and need. She moves to the gentle rhythm I set, her breathing jerky.

I push a third inside. The grip becomes even tighter. I curl them, rubbing softly, and her body spasms like she's being shocked. She stares at me, mouth parting slightly.

What the hell? Nobody ever touched her G-spot before?

Her exes were idiots. But, better for me. I thrust my fingers until I'm soaked to the wrist, then pull my hand away and slowly sink into her slick depths.

Holy God. Being inside Klein is like being allowed into heaven. She's so hot, so tight. Her wetness soaks me instantly, and my balls start to tighten.

Beads of sweat pop along my hairline as I hold back. Her eyes flutter closed, her expression sublime. I slowly withdraw and push into her again, setting a good, steady tempo to help her get used to my size. She moves with me, just as greedy for me as I am for her.

Her fingers trace the taut muscles on the back of my neck, then tunnel into my hair.

"How does it feel?" she asks. "Do you like it?"

I look down at her questioning face and nod. I've never been with a woman this generous with her body. "Amazing. How about you?"

"I love it. I love everything we're doing together, Josh."

I can't hold back anymore. I push her hard, and she shivers, then lets out one moan after another. An orgasm builds inside me, ready to unleash, but I rein myself back, using every ounce of self-control I possess. I'm not coming until she does.

Her back arches, and she screams as she comes. That's a pretty powerful orgasm, but I know she can hit a higher height. So I push her harder and higher. The only sound in the room is our flesh slapping together and our uneven breathing and moans. Lust and need roar in my veins.

"Please, Josh, yes, yes, *yes!*" she screams as she convulses again...and then again. My grip on my control is tenuous, but I manage to hang on. I want her to experience another one, even better than the ones she's had before.

The bed creaks as I drive into her relentlessly. She throws her head back, the beautiful curls spreading on the sheets like platinum clouds. Her eyebrows pinch. Her entire torso comes off the bed as she screams until she's hoarse. She spasms around my cock, and her juices drip down to my balls.

I can't hold on anymore. I let go, filling her with my cum.

32

AILEE

CONSCIOUSNESS SLOWLY EMERGES from a restorative and relaxing sleep. Something warm and supple lies underneath my hand. I flex my fingers against it. *Hmm, that feels nice.*

Another something is massaging my lower back. I swear I don't have anything this nice in my room. *Did Josh replace the mattress in my room with a self-massaging type—*

Wait! I'm naked. And that's not some built-in mattress massager, it's long, strong fingers digging into my knotted muscles!

My mind races as I try to remember what happened. Josh flashed his scrumptious torso and the outline of his enormous cock by putting on a pair of gray sweatpants. After getting an eyeful of masculine perfection, I went out...then came back home...saw Josh sleeping...

The rest of the memory is a little hazy. But I'm certain I made the first move because I remember vividly what it felt like to take his *dick into my mouth.*

And then... Then...

I straddled him like a horny hussy and took off my shirt and bra, telling him my breasts hurt, like I wanted *him* to do something about it.

My heart drops to my stomach. He even got to put his dick inside me without a condom. He said he'd had a vasectomy and was clean—he was quite emphatic about it, and I trust him. But I've never done it bare like that to avoid any unwanted consequences.

In rubber, we trust.

But everything was just *crazy*. Normally, I'm not like that *at all*. It had to have been a really, really dirty dream because I saw Josh topless and my brain *immediately* went into X-rated territory like some kind of movieland Jezebel.

But if it was a dream, why is my face buried in Josh's chest, and my leg wrapped around him? And why is he just as naked as I am? Even with my eyes closed, I can tell who it is. The gorgeous, lean body? It's like my fingers can read Josh Braille. That scent that never fails to turn me on?

Oh yes, I can tell. Even now, I'm getting a little wet. My cheeks turn hot so fast, I'm shocked I don't just combust.

It's okay, I tell myself. This isn't the end of the world. I can sneak out and regroup. If I can just elegantly pull back one of my legs, which is thrown over his taut waist, my thigh so close to his penis...

I try to move, then give up. My muscles are like Jell-O. If I try to move, I might brush against his private parts, and then it'll look like I'm trying to seduce him. Again.

Awkward. And embarrassing.

My emotions are all over the place. Josh famously never sleeps with the same woman twice. So we aren't doing this again. It's a crime that I used up my one time with Josh and can't recall it with crystal clarity to replay later.

Disappointment bursts in my chest. *Is he already tired of me?* Despite my fuzzy memory, I know the sex we had was amazing. I can tell from the way I'm sore—in a *very* good way. Another kind of body Braille.

I've never felt this relaxed, safe and happy after sleeping with a guy. Normally I wake up slightly dissatisfied, like I've been denied the final bite I needed to be fully sated.

I really hope it was as good for him as it was for me, but given his history—

"What are you thinking about?" Josh asks. "You're so tense."

"I'm just...awake," I squeak. "Not thinking."

He snorts, but the sound is affectionate. "You've been awake for a while. So. What's up?"

"Well…"

"Tell me."

"I just, um, want you to know that I am *not* usually like that." I wave my hand, unsure how to pick the right words. I'm not the lawyer here.

"Define 'that.'" *And, of course, Josh is.*

"Uh…" I clear my throat, trying to gather my courage. I hope I never get cross-examined by him in court. "Like…doing things to you while you were asleep. That was so wrong. I should know better. I don't know *what* came over me." I cringe inwardly. It isn't easy to lay out the humiliating thoughts, but I don't want to lie to him after taking advantage of him.

He tenses. His dark eyebrows pinch together as displeasure clouds his eyes.

Oh crap. He's upset. The silence suffocates me, and I start to talk to make him understand: "It really isn't like me to be so forward, and I'm not that sexy or hot or anything like that and—"

"Are we speaking the same language?" he demands.

I hesitate, unsure where this is going and not wanting to upset him more. "Yes…?"

"Oh?" He couldn't sound more doubtful. "Because I don't think we're operating from the same definition of 'hot.' Or 'sexy.' I almost died from wanting you, and I won't allow you to put yourself down."

"But—"

He puts his hand over my mouth. "No buts. I mean it. You're a damn sexy woman, and you'll never disparage yourself again. If you do"—he pauses, his brow furrowing—"you'll be punished."

My mouth dries. I recall his earlier warning that if I ever call him "boss" again, he'll kiss me until I remember who he is. Like, that kind of punishment? Or maybe a…spanking…? "How?" I ask, a little bit breathless.

"Something will present itself." The dark glitter in his eyes promises that he will push my body to the limit to teach me a lesson.

I lick my lips. Whatever he does will test me, but he'll never really hurt me. I always feel safe around him.

"Um." I glance at our bodies entwined on the tangled sheets. "So does this mean I'm sleeping in your bed from now on?" I ask, just to be certain.

"Yes."

"And we're going to...do it again?"

"Do *you* want to do it again?" His fingertips slide along the curve of my shoulder. A hot jolt pounds through me, and I wish I didn't have a leg over him because I'd love to clench them together the ease the ache.

My heart beats faster. I lift my gaze to meet his. "I think so. And hopefully this time I'll remember every detail."

His eyes widen. "You *don't remember*?"

"Sorry, but it's a little hazy." I bite my lip. "Actually, I wasn't feeling all that great when I came home."

All the delightful, teasing tone in his voice vanishes. "Okay, wait. What happened?"

"Nothing really. I went to look at some books, then ran into a neighbor from my old building, so we had some coffee, and then I came back. But once I got home, I started to feel *really* weird."

His intense eyes focus on me. "Weird how?"

"Just sort of hot and itchy all over, like I was having an allergic reaction. But I was breathing fine, and no bumps or hives. So I figured it must have been from the stress of the fire and everything. My renter's insurance hasn't paid me a penny yet." I shrug, not wanting to worry Josh unnecessarily.

But he stares at me, a hint of horror rippling over his face. "This neighbor—male or female?"

"Female—"

"Do you know her well?"

"Sort of. I haven't known her that long, but if it weren't for her, I might've died in the fire. She knocked on my door to get me out. I didn't even know anything was wrong until she woke me up."

"Did she try to save anyone else?"

I think about it. "I'm not sure. I don't remember seeing other people with us, though."

He stiffens. "Can you describe her?"

His reaction is a little unnerving, but I trust he has a good reason.

"She has gorgeous, dark hair and stunning blue eyes. She seems to exercise a lot. Has the body for it. And her name is Zoe. She used to live in Vegas until she moved to Los Angeles for a job. She—" I stop because Josh is paler than the sheet. Even his lips are white. "What's wrong? Are you okay?"

It takes a moment before he can speak. "Yes." He shakes his head. "Uh, not really. No."

He gets up and leaves the room, his long strides eating up the distance between the bed and the door. I stare at the door, suddenly breathless and feeling like I've done something wrong. I've never seen him this upset. *But what did I say?*

He returns soon with his phone. He leans over me, bracing himself on a hand next to my hip, and flips the phone around. "Is this her?"

I blink at a photo of Zoe on the screen. "Yes. How do you know her?"

"You need to stay away from her," he says tautly.

"What? Why?"

"She's my mother."

My jaw slackens. *His mother? Whaaaat?*

"My mother." The muscles in his jaw twitch. "The woman who gave birth to me. And she's a fucking sociopath."

33

JOSH

Klein's eyes go round. She stares at me like she can't understand what I'm trying to tell her. Regret and self-loathing squeeze around my neck like deadly vines. I should've known something was up when Mom stayed this quiet, this long, especially after Bryce told me she hit him—because that's escalation. But I thought she might be lying low after trying to mess with Bryce and failing so spectacularly. Should've expected her to try something.

It was only a matter of time until she tried something with me—and it's finally happened.

Klein continues to look at me like she's waiting for an explanation. Normally, I don't explain myself—or my past. I'm always scared of what I might discover if I talk about myself. The therapist said it'd be good for me to open up, but he would never understand the terror of realizing that you might end up like your amoral mother.

But Klein isn't just anyone—she's my fiancée. The woman I want to come home to every night. The woman I want to build a life with.

The woman *I'd die to protect*. The weight of the recognition sinks into me. I finally understand that this is what it means to be a true Huxley. It's more than just a family motto. It's about being inspired to live a life of loyalty and unity—to put the interests of others before my own without hesitation.

I flex my hands, not wanting to reveal my relationship with someone as unhinged as my mother. At the same time, Klein has to know. Keeping this about myself out of shame would put her in danger.

"This is going to be an ugly story," I say. "So...get comfortable."

Klein looks into my eyes for a moment, then wraps her arms around me, as though sensing that I need the comfort of her touch.

I relax into the embrace, even though my heart is in turmoil. As long as she's holding me, the situation doesn't seem as dark and foul. "My birth mother is from a mafia family in some country called Nesovia. Her father, Vincent, is the head of its largest family. Nesovia's sexist customs and attitudes mean that Mom would never normally control that crime family, but she badly wants to be in charge.

"When they wanted to expand into America, she saw an opportunity to make an impression on her father. My family was on his radar as potential legal support to help ease his family's way into America, except the Huxleys don't represent any type of organized crime. But she wanted to present her father with the best, so she did what was necessary—which was seduce my father and marry him. And have his children."

Klein gasps.

"When Dad found out the truth, he was furious. It didn't matter that his wife was a mafia princess. The Huxleys would never get involved. He felt deceived and betrayed, and didn't believe the marriage could go on. He tried to divorce her as amicably as possible, but that wasn't what she wanted. By then she had become obsessed with Dad for real. So to prevent him from divorcing her, she decided to kidnap Ares, Bryce and me. Bryce and I were eight at the time. Ares was a little older, and fought against her enough that Bryce and I were able to escape. But it left all of us scarred in our own ways."

I take a deep breath before proceeding. "She left Ares in a forest fire to die."

Klein covers her mouth with a hand. "Oh my *God*, I'm so sorry. I can't imagine..." Tears of sympathy glisten in her beautiful violet eyes. "Why isn't she in jail?"

Bitterness drips into my tone. "Grandpa didn't want to see his baby girl rot in jail, so somebody took the fall for her. And there was nothing we could do about it. No hard evidence to throw her in jail, except for the testimony of a highly traumatized and injured boy and his younger brothers. So Dad got what he could—a quick divorce and full custody of us kids."

As Klein processes, a thought flickers over her face.

"What is it?" No matter how tiny the detail, I can't overlook it if it's about Mom.

"That thing about somebody else taking the fall for her... She said a seventeen-year-old kid set the apartment on fire because he was trying to start a new challenge to post on social media. Apparently, he was told that he'd be paid if he was successful. I'm just wondering if *she* was the one who instigated the kid."

"It wouldn't surprise me. That's her standard MO. You not feeling well..." I hesitate for a second, wishing I could spare Klein the detail. But the more she knows about Mom, the better prepared she'll be. "She probably drugged you."

"*What?*"

I nod. "When you had coffee with her."

"But she didn't make the coffee. We were at a café. You don't think she owns the place, right?"

"Did you take anything from her? Go to the bathroom while she sat at the table with your drink?"

Klein thinks for a moment. "She handed me some syrup for my coffee."

"There you go. She probably tampered with it."

Klein's jaw slackens with shock.

"She's very quick. And using drugs on people is actually pretty popular on that side of the family. Her brother Harvey is the same way, tried it with Ares. You *have* to stay away from her. Please." I clench my hands as the urge to rush out and find Mom and make her pay pounds into my head. Except that wouldn't solve everything. The law doesn't like it when we take matters into our own hands.

"I will." Klein reaches out and holds my hand. Then thoughts flicker across her face. "You also told me to stay away from Kenna. Is she somehow related to all this?"

"Yes," I say, laying everything on the table. "She's working for one of my uncles on that side of the family and feeding information to Mom at the same time. None of them can be trusted."

Klein nods, her eyes solemn as she gazes up at me. "I understand. I won't give either of them a chance to hurt me—hurt us. I promise."

BY THE TIME we head to the kitchen to grab something to eat, it's already after eight in the evening. We make some simple sandwiches and clean up.

I hate it that a moment that should have been happy and intimate was ruined because of what Mom did to Klein. Mom can come after me —but she isn't allowed near Klein.

Klein goes to take a shower, so I walk up to my office and pour myself a glass of Hibiki. *Why didn't Mom make contact with me directly?* What does she think she can get by going to—or through—Klein? She moved in to Klein's building before the Peking Town video went viral. Did she sense my attraction to Klein even before I made it public?

It's possible she heard something from Kenna. And the only thing Mom would need to do to ingratiate herself with Klein would be showing a bit of kindness. Klein's so unused to it and so generous by nature that if you give her a drop of consideration, she'll return it tenfold.

Mom has to take bigger risks now to get what she wants. Harvey isn't the only one in her way. She's probably freaked out about Roland. Has Vincent made contact with Roland—or vice versa? Does she think she can manipulate me through Klein? And...then what? Use me to get through to my brothers...or destroy her brothers? Or both?

You're the most like me.

Yeah, she might think I'd see things her way if she gave me sufficient motivation.

I never wanted to get involved with the Dunkels. I would love it if somebody dropped a bomb on them. But neutrality is no longer an option, especially when Klein's safety is at stake.

I open the bottom drawer on my desk and pull out a black business card with an international number written on it in gold ink. It arrived in my office on my thirtieth birthday in a #10 envelope. No return address, nothing to indicate what it was about. I called the number out of curiosity.

"Hello, grandson," came Vincent's voice. The velvety texture made my skin crawl.

Nausea welled in my gut, I hung up, then went to Bryce's office. Amélie, his assistant, didn't try to stop me because she knows I sometimes like to wait for my twin in his office. An identical envelope to the one I got was in the stack of mail on his desk. I grabbed it and shoved it into my pocket before leaving. Bryce didn't need the bullshit.

Then I stopped by Ares's office. He had a court appearance, and I managed to grab the envelope off his desk as well. He especially doesn't need to hear Vincent's nasty voice or justifications. That fucker made it clear who mattered the most in his world—his daughter, not us.

I don't know why I never threw out the card. I should've. But I tossed it in the bottom drawer of my home office desk and never looked at it again—until now.

It's almost like my gut knew I might need a way to contact Vincent one of these days. I purposely relax my jaw, then call the number.

As soon as it connects, I say, "I want to see you."

Vincent chuckles with satisfaction. The sound is surprisingly irritating. I press my lips together to contain any sarcastic remarks.

"Of course. I always knew patience would pay off." He sobers. "I'm always available to see my beloved grandson. Let me have my assistant send you my address."

34

JOSH

LET me have my assistant send you my address. Spoken as though he were some kind of legit businessman, not a mafia boss with blood on his hands.

Vincent isn't in Nesovia like I expected. He's actually enjoying himself in La Jolla. I hate it that he's here, in the same state, although it does make it easier to go see him. I resent that I have to go at all, when I could've spent a lazy Sunday with Klein, naked in bed. Instead, I'm in La Jolla in one of my best power suits and a wine-colored tie. Silver cuff links in the shape of the Huxley wolf glint at my wrists. They remind me that no matter what, I'm a Huxley, not a Dunkel. I'm Prescott Huxley's son, and nothing of Zoe Dunkel can affect me.

I climb out of the rental car and squint at the beautiful beachfront property, built of blindingly white stones and with an immaculate garden. Doesn't surprise me. Mafiosos like to spend money on nice things. Besides, being in SoCal gives him the best position to watch his children fight to the death for control of the family empire.

He claims he disapproves of family hurting each other. But I don't buy it. Vincent should've selected an heir already—he's far from young at this point—but he's been keeping it to himself, letting Mom and Harvey battle it out, with me and my brothers as pawns to be moved around, even sacrificed, as necessary. Harvey mentioned to Bryce that Roland—the youngest—is Vincent's favorite. It's possible he already knew about the truth behind Roland's death and wanted to exact some sort of revenge on Mom and punish Harvey for failing to protect his baby brother. What better way to torment them than silently taunting them: *Neither of you is good enough, so fight it out for my amusement.*

Still, I wonder... Am I doing the right thing by being here? I plan to propose a solution to ensure his misbegotten asshole children don't involve us in their war. I'm sick of it. With Mom's escalation—going after Klein directly, undoubtedly to use her to try to manipulate me—it could get deadly. The Dunkels can rip each other apart all they want, but they aren't allowed to hurt us Huxleys. I don't want Mom trying to drag Klein into the fight, either. My focus is on building a stronger relationship with her, without the Dunkels' civil war hanging over us.

I hit the big wooden door hard with the bronze knocker. A few minutes later, the entrance cracks open. A nondescript man in a crisp black suit comes out. A butler? A fake bodyguard? Hard to tell. The man's thin, but wiry. His looks are as average as you can get: medium brown hair and eyes in an unimpressive face that's seen just enough sun to avoid being pale. A great companion to keep around if you don't want to be noticed.

"Mr. Huxley?" he says in precise English.

"Yes. Who are you?"

"My name is Mick. This way, please." He steps aside and gestures me in.

The interior of the mansion is cool. Thick curtains keep much of the sun out, giving it an odd, gloomy feel. At night, this would be a perfect spot to film a vampire movie. It takes talent to turn a La Jolla property this dreary.

Mick leads me through the dimly lit hall until we reach double doors at the end. He pushes them open to a grand suite with a balcony that would overlook the Pacific if someone would just part the blackout curtains. A shiny Steinway baby grand stands to my left. Doubt it's for Vincent, since he's only used his hands to kill, not create anything beautiful. Certainly not his monstrous children.

I scan the room, pausing when my eyes land on an elderly man in a plush leather armchair in the shadowy sitting section. I almost don't recognize him—he's so...small. And thin. My memory of him is from when I was seven. Back then, he towered over me like an unshakable oak.

The years haven't been kind to him. Thin skin hangs off his bony face and slim shoulders, mottled with liver spots. If he hadn't spent decades solidifying his position, somebody probably would have eliminated him a while ago.

"Josh." His voice is slightly reedy, but there's still some steel underneath that says, *Don't fuck with me.*

"Hello," I respond, hiding my surprise with a cool façade.

"Come closer." He gestures. "Let me see you."

The decades-old resentment bubbles up, but I paste on a smile, the kind I wear when I'm about to face opposing counsel. "Yes, Grandfather."

When I stop two feet away from him, he looks me up and down, then stares into my unblinking eyes. I arch an eyebrow and meet his gaze. I won't let an old, dying lion of a man intimidate me.

A moment later, a corner of his mouth tips upward. "As I expected. Sharp. Ruthless. A true Dunkel." He practically purrs with pride.

My stomach churns. *Fuck you, asshole. I'm a Huxley.* I swallow the words—they won't help me get what I want—but can't stop my mouth from twisting into a sarcastic line.

Either Vincent doesn't notice or doesn't care. "It's good to see you again, Josh. I missed you."

"I hope you understand that I can't say the same."

He chuckles, then gestures at me to take the armchair to his left. "Something to drink?"

I sit back and cross my legs. "No thanks." If I could, I wouldn't even breathe the air in this house.

"Suit yourself." He pours himself some Yamazaki 55. I'd love a glass, but then, it's Vincent Dunkel, and who knows what he might add to the whiskey. I bet he's doing this on purpose, which makes me even more irritated and determined to turn down anything edible he offers. "You're still in a snit because I didn't toss her in jail."

A snit? "Don't minimize my life experience. Jail is the least she deserves."

"She's your mother, Josh. Her blood—the family's blood—flows in your veins."

"I'm not a Dunkel."

"You keep telling yourself that. Just because you bear your father's name doesn't mean you're really a Huxley deep down. There's a great potential for ruthless violence in you." He puts the bottle back. "I like that."

I clench my teeth. It's almost like he and Mom had a conference and conspired to call me a monster. "We can agree to disagree."

He takes a sip of the Yamazaki. "I'm surprised you haven't killed Zoe yet. I thought you were going to. You absolutely despised her."

I narrow my eyes slightly. How much does he know about my past indiscretion?

"Even now I can see the murderous intent in your eyes. It's too bad your father got custody of you. I could've honed you into a weapon, unrestrained by anything as cumbersome as the law or morality."

"The law *is* my weapon, morality my guiding principle," I say flatly.

"See?" Vincent lifts his glass toward me and sighs. *Your father ruined you.* "Although...I do wonder why you decided to give *yourself* a weakness."

"Weakness?"

"Your fiancée."

A muscle near my eyebrow twitches. The urge to leap over and strangle him explodes in my mind, but I pull myself together.

"A very nice girl. Too sweet, though. As fluffy as cotton candy. Tug at her a little, and she rips apart." He *tsks*. "You like her, don't you?"

I pin him with an icy stare.

He smirks. "I'm not the only one who's noticed."

"If you are such an observant man, why don't you stop your children from fighting and creating so much collateral damage?"

"Can't stop the rule of nature—survival of the fittest. I will not let someone weak control the empire. Speaking of which..." A hint of true affection warms his smile. "There's a person I want you to meet."

A man steps out of the shadows behind Vincent. He stands tall, like a century-old oak—very much reminiscent of Vincent in his prime. A jagged white scar by his left eye mars his otherwise flawless, tanned face. Other than that, he's a carbon copy of Vincent.

The man smiles. "Hello, nephew."

"Hello, Roland."

He cocks an eyebrow. "You know me?"

"You're pretty famous."

He smiles, then perches on the armrest on Vincent's seat and places his hand on the back of the chair like a knight guarding his king from danger. The old man pats Roland's hand, the favoritism obvious. "You're such a good child. I can't believe I almost lost you."

"You'll never lose me, Father."

Vincent pats Roland's hand again, then rises to his feet. "I'll leave you two alone so you can speak freely."

Vincent tries to place his hand on my forearm, but I shift away. A flash of hurt cuts through his otherwise self-satisfied mask, but almost immediately, his expression smooths back to impassivity. "Enjoy, children." Mick trails behind him.

Roland takes the seat Vincent occupied just moments ago, and the symbolism isn't lost on me. "You sure you don't want anything?" He knocks back the whiskey Vincent left as well.

"No."

"I don't drug people, Joshua."

"Of course not." I flash him a blank smile.

"I'm nothing like your mother or Harvey."

"Maybe not. But I don't know enough about you to make that judgment."

"Yet here we are." He pours more whiskey. "If you were going to side with your mother, you wouldn't be here."

"She inserted herself into a situation where she shouldn't have. You wouldn't forgive her if she messed with Kenna, would you?"

Roland's gaze sharpens. "No, I wouldn't. But you should know I have no plans to hurt your girl. I've been keeping an eye on her to keep her safe from Zoe." He reaches up and scratches the back of his head, elaborately casual. His suit sleeve bulges. "You received the photos and text when her apartment burned down, didn't you? Zoe's handiwork, by the way."

That was him? "Should I thank you? You didn't stop Mom."

"My men's instructions were to keep your girl safe, not 'stop Mom.'" He gives me a nice-guy smile.

If he thinks this puts me in his debt, he's sorely mistaken. "I don't care about this war between the three of you, but I don't want the Huxleys, or my fiancée and me, to be dragged into it. I want my family to be left alone, no matter who takes over the organization."

"That's going to be me—count on it."

"Out of the three, you're the least objectionable. At least you didn't try to drug us, kidnap us or leave us to die. And you haven't tried to get to our women. Things like that matter."

He laughs. Hope he doesn't think I was being complimentary. That's setting the bar pretty low. "You take your family motto too seriously."

"Because only people who are worthy of loyalty and unity get to be part of the family. But then, you wouldn't understand. The Dunkels never made the cut."

"Like we want to be bound by something as ridiculous as your motto," Roland sneers. "Zoe was an idiot to marry Prescott, and even a bigger idiot to fall for him and you boys." His eyes flick in my direction. "No offense, but you and I both know she can't play by the rules, especially something as rigid as *pietas et unitas.*"

"None taken." I share his opinion about Mom's feelings. I steeple my fingers. "Anyway, you aren't stupid. Harvey's no match." I believe that. Even without Vincent putting his weight behind him, Roland is capable enough. Near-death experiences can change a man, and he didn't return to play nice.

"So. What would you give me in return?" he asks.

I'm not foolish enough to make the first offer. "What are you thinking?"

His eyes brighten. "I have a proposal." He leans forward. "Zoe loves her children very much." He sees my look. "Oh, but it's true."

"Uh-huh." If kidnapping and drugging is love, I don't want to know what Roland considers hate.

"I want to see her get backstabbed by the child she's most partial to." His eyes meet and hold mine.

Every instinct in my body screams that it's a lie. She doesn't care for me at all.

He shakes his head, reading me perfectly. "It's not a lie. She's also the most proud of you. Every time she speaks of you, she glows. It's a bit sickening, actually. Doesn't mean she lacks feelings for Ares and Bryce, but you hold a special place in her heart. And I don't care how you do it, but I want to see you betray her. I want her to know what it's like to be backstabbed by someone she admired and trusted." His words end on a bitter note.

"Sounds personal."

Roland's mouth twists. "I worshipped Zoe. I thought she was like a goddess because she was always so capable and strong, and she never let anything get in the way of her goal. I just didn't realize that to her, *I* was one of those obstacles. What she doesn't know is that if she'd just *asked*, I would've sided with her to take Harvey out. Unlike her, I don't backstab people who do me favors." His eyes swing back to me. "I want to see her *suffer*. If you can deliver that for me, I'll leave you and your family alone."

I hold his stare. "Define 'leaving us alone.'"

"Nobody bearing the Dunkel name or belonging to the family empire will go near anybody bearing the Huxley name or contact you. We will disavow any connection between your family and ours. It'll be as though we're strangers." He doesn't break eye contact the entire speech. Then he adds: "Forever. You have my word."

35

AILEE

I HEAD to Max's and my favorite mom-and-pop café in downtown. She's finally back, and of course, we have to hang out

Fluffy Haven is a small café with the best chocolate scones in the city. The elderly couple that owns it must make most of their money from the scone—not the coffee, because they have some of the cheapest brew in town. But everyone who drops by to grab a cup also gets a scone or two.

Max waves from the booth in the back with the most privacy. I take my tray, laden with a sugary coffee and chocolate scone, and head over. "You look *amazing!*" she squeals, and jumps up to hug me as soon as I place the tray on the table.

I squeeze her back, enjoying the tight embrace. She's a great hugger.

"So do you," I say. Although her hair is in a messy bun and she's wearing a sweatshirt and tights, she screams confidence.

She smiles. "And you're *really* dressed up." Her eyes move up and down, taking in my high ponytail, fitted green dress and pointy sandals. "Got a date with Josh after this?" She waggles her eyebrows.

I laugh and sit down opposite her. "No. But I'm meeting his mother later."

"Wow! Already at that phase?"

I shrug, then take a sip of the hot coffee. "She wants to talk." But I don't know what she wants to talk *about*. Akiko was nice to me at the dinner, but maybe secretly she doesn't approve?

Obviously, I wouldn't say anything in front of the others to save your pride, but really, Ailee, you should know better. I sigh. Good old Mom's voice, right on cue.

But I'm not going to let myself think negatively. Akiko seems sweet and kind, and I'll take her at face value until I have a real reason not to.

"So where are you staying?" I ask. Max's mom passed away last year, and as far as I know, she doesn't have a father. At least, *I've* never seen the man, even though we were neighbors. And she and her boyfriend don't seem to be at the stage where she'd feel comfortable sharing a living space. "Sorry we haven't gotten to talk about getting a new place. I didn't think you'd be back until next week."

"Neither did I, but there was a change of plans." Max rolls her eyes, then munches on her scone. "So typical of him. I'm staying at a hotel right now. It's comfortable enough. And I drove by our old apartment on the way here." She shakes her head. "There's nothing left of the building except some blackened I-beams."

I nod. "Yeah, it's pretty crummy." We sit and think about that for a moment. "So, you want to get a new place together? We can look this week."

"Sure, but..." She frowns. "Aren't you with Josh now?"

"Yeah, but I can still pay half the rent. I don't mind."

"Don't be ridiculous."

"Plus"—I lower my voice—"the thing between me and Josh...it isn't really real."

"What do you mean?"

I explain the six-month commitment Josh made to spare my pride. As I speak, I realize that we have less than five months left. The idea makes my shoulders sag. Although Josh and I slept together yesterday, we still haven't discussed what's going to happen to our engagement. I should talk to him about it, but then he left early this morning. And a cowardly little bit of me was secretly relieved that I didn't have to broach the subject.

"Ailee, he wouldn't have agreed to do that if he didn't care about you," Max says. "You guys are doing a really slow burn, but it'll turn into something more."

I shake my head and let out a wobbly laugh, abruptly realizing that, once again, I went for my default response: *Good things don't happen to me. And if they do, they don't last for long.*

Max gives me a skeptical look and takes another bite of her scone. "You sleep with him yet?"

My cheeks warm before I can say a word.

"Ah-*hah*! That blush says everything!" She leans closer. "He was good, right? I got something to make it even better." She pulls out a box out from her big tote bag. "Tada! I got you a surprise subscription to the Year of Coming First. I didn't know your new address, so I had them deliver the first box to my office. But I'll change it as soon as you send it to me."

I cover my mouth in shock. But at least the box is discreet. "Purple and pink? It's like some kind of baby product," I say, looking at the packaging.

"The activity *does* occasionally lead to procreation, so..." She shrugs with a mischievous spark in her eyes. "Check it out."

Looking around to make sure that nobody's paying attention, I open the box and rummage through the crinkling tissue papers. The first thing is... A pair of silver nipple clamps. *Seriously?* The instructions say they vibrate, but they seem a little too heavy. "I don't think these are really for me," I say with a small giggle.

"Don't know that until you try." Max makes a rolling gesture. "Keep digging."

"There's more?" Shoving them to the side, I pull out a very nice-looking pair of panties in a gorgeous, satiny red. The shade is super sexy, but not something you always see in stores. Somehow Silicone Dream got the color just right. Having an extra pair wouldn't be so bad, since I still haven't found the ones I lost, and there hasn't been a chance to replace them yet. Underneath the underwear is an instruction booklet for the panties. "Instructions to put on underwear? Especially when you're old enough to buy sex toys?"

Max starts laughing, then nearly chokes on her coffee.

I hand her a napkin, and she dabs her mouth and chin while giving me a small, anticipatory smirk. I glance at the cover of the manual, my opinion on humankind sinking lower. But...oh, wait. The *panties vibrate, too?* And come with a remote control? I upend the box, and a sleek black cylinder rolls out, chic and discreet.

"Look at that. You can use an app if you download it to your phone. Then connect your device to the Bluetooth on your phone and control it, whichever is more convenient. How high tech," I murmur as I glance at the manual.

"Sex toys have come a long way. But all the advancement has been for a good cause," Max says, then picks up the remote control. Her index finger runs over a little dial on the side that looks like a mouse wheel, then she taps the end of the stick.

Abruptly, the panties start to dance. The crotch part clatters loudly on the table. *Oh crap.* I slap my hand over it. "Turn it off!" I whisper, praying nobody notices.

Max taps the tip of the remote again, and the panties quiet down.

I look around. Everyone's either busy enjoying their coffee and scones or has their nose to their phone, thank God. "What the hell? This underwear *rattles*!" I say, doing my best to keep my voice down.

Max takes a sip of her drink. "Because you aren't wearing them. But at least you know they work."

"I can't wear something that *rattles*, Max! With my luck, I'll go viral as Rattle Pussy."

She laughs until tears fall from her eyes. "It won't if it's flush against your private parts, so don't worry. It also has a crotch hole, in case you want your partner to do something about your horniness. The size I ordered should be snug enough for you, so you don't miss out on the motor action. I have a sense for these things."

My jaw slackens at how smug she sounds. "How do you know all this?"

"Because I also have a pair, and they work great."

"Isn't it better to just use a regular vibrator?" I'm not certain the tiny motor in the panties would be enough to push anybody over. I know I need more.

"In public?"

"*What?* Why would you want to masturbate in public?"

"For the thrill? Because you're being bad? I don't know. Whatever gets you off. Why does anybody masturbate?" She shrugs, but there's a glint in her eyes. "Maybe the men in my life are unreliable."

I pull my lips in. I'm learning more about my best friend's sexual preferences—and possibly her relationship history—than I ever wanted to.

"*You* can wear it to work, if you know what I mean." She raises an eyebrow suggestively.

"*No.*"

"Josh won't mind."

"Have *you* worn them to work?"

This time Max chokes for real—and very badly. A mouthful of coffee ends up on her sweatshirt. "Oh shit. Fuck," she mutters. "No. *Hell* no. I'd rather die a virgin."

I laugh at her scrunched face. "A little late for that."

"Okay, fine. I'd rather give up sex for the rest of my life." But even as she says it, a strange redness suffuses her face. Not like a flush of interest, but not quite from humiliation, either. I can't put my finger on it, which makes me want to probe, in case she needs to get something off her chest.

"Did something happen between you and Jeffrey?" I say, bringing up her boyfriend.

Her eyes narrow. "Yeah. He's been cheating on me. Caught him red-handed."

I blink. It takes a moment for me to process. "What the... I'm so sorry." Max didn't say a word, and I feel like a horrible friend for staying ignorant. Was she consoling me about Chad when she was grappling with Jeffrey's betrayal? "When? What happened?"

"I ran into him and his side chick. In *Tokyo*! He had his tongue down her throat so far, I'm surprised she didn't die. But then, his tongue is even shorter than his dick."

I nod in shock. Jeffrey seemed like a great guy. Guess you can't judge someone by their smile, no matter how friendly.

"Do you know that asshole told me he didn't have *time* to go on a long vacation with me? Then he had the gall to tell me we'd always had an open relationship—which was news to me—and I was the stupid one for 'not taking advantage.'" She bares her teeth in a rictus of a smile. "It was just fucking fantastic because my *dad* was there too and sided with *him*."

"Your dad?" My tone says, *You have a dad?*

"Yeah. That cheating scumbag. I hate him. He's been dead to me since he turned his back on me and Mom when I was a kid. He can go to the ninth circle of hell for all I care." The fire raging in her eyes says if he doesn't get there himself, *she'll* send him there. "But that wasn't even the worst part."

I blink. "There's *more?*"

"Oh, yeah. Of course there is! Rhys saw the whole thing."

That would be the cherry on top of the crap cake. She isn't fond of her boss.

I cover my mouth. "I'm so sorry," I say again. "You deserve better."

"Goddamn right I do. And I want to sue that hotel in Tokyo for saying there was only one room available during our stay."

"Want me to check?" I offer. "I'm sure Huxley & Webber has at least one lawyer who specializes in that sort of thing."

"No." Max sighs, shoulders sagging. "I'm sure there was a liability clause somewhere in the thick stack of papers Rhys had to sign to check in."

"You didn't have to share a room with him...right?"

Max sniffs, then takes another bite of her scone. "I'm just unlucky in relationships. I need to find myself someone like Josh. Honorable. Smart. *Hot.* But not my boss. Never the boss."

"Definitely not." I nod, wondering if Max was forced to share a room with her boss. That'd really suck, given how much she dislikes the man.

She swirls her coffee morosely. "Too bad his twin's taken. What was his name...?"

"Bryce. And he *is* taken. But so what? The firm has plenty of great associates. I'm sure I can play matchmaker for you and some hottie lawyer. Trust me."

36

AILEE

After offering to find Max a new man and chatting with her about finding a new place—which we aren't going to yet—I head to a cute little Japanese style parfaiteria of Akiko's choosing. Himeko opened a couple of months ago, and there's a line wrapping around the block.

–Me: Are you already here?

–Akiko: Yes. And I have a table. Come join me inside.

I peer through the window and see somebody waving. Feeling very self-conscious, I walk up the line and step inside. A sweet melody is playing on the sound system, and the décor is all cute Japanese dolls in gorgeous kimonos arranged along the high shelves. An overwhelming aroma of chocolate, cream and sugar hits me. Maybe the place sells more than just parfaits.

A bright smile lights Akiko's face as I approach her table. Her eyes curve into crescents, which I find sweet. She's in an elegant ivory top and navy skirt, and I'm glad I dressed up.

"Hello, sweetheart, so good to see you," she says, and pulls me into an embrace.

I hug her back. I always thought I was small, especially compared to my runway model sister, but Akiko is even more petite than I am. "Same. Did you wait for long?" I glance at the line as we sit down.

"Oh, no." She seems to find the notion amusing. "I'm one of the four investors, so there's always a table for me." She winks.

"Really?"

"Mm-hmm. I always wanted to bring Japanese-style desserts to America, and it just seemed to make sense. But before we order, are you allergic to anything else?"

"Other than seafood? No." I think for a moment. "Please don't tell me this place serves a pufferfish parfait."

"Ah, no. That'd be a little too exotic for my taste." Akiko laughs as she picks up the menu. "I've had their Imperial Strawberry parfait before. It was quite good. But their Deutsche parfait is pretty good, too."

I study the options. The Deutsche features *twenty-seven* layers of chocolate in various forms—cream, shaving, brownie, meringue, syrup... "I'll go for the Deutsche," I say, then almost swallow my tongue at the price. *Is that a typo?*

"I'll get the cherry one. It looks really good, doesn't it?" Akiko says it with so much enthusiasm, I can't do anything but nod. I'm sure that asking if there's a typo on the menu isn't the right way to go.

The server comes over and takes our order. Akiko orders caramel apple tea for us, saying it's a treat I have to experience.

The waiter returns with our drink. Inside our cups are thin apple slices shaped to look like rosebuds. The server pours hot tea. As the fragrant liquid fills our cups, the apple slices unfurl like a blooming rose.

"Wow, that's gorgeous," I say breathlessly. I've never seen anything like it.

Akiko merely smiles. "Perfect for teatime, isn't it?"

I nod. Her casual happiness reinforces that we're from two very different worlds. My idea of "fancy" is a porcelain cup with a saucer, but for Akiko, it's apple slices blooming like flowers in a teacup so elegant it probably cost more than my entire month's pay.

The waiter returns with two stunning parfaits, each one big enough to be a meal in its own right. And the chocolate is way too pretty, with gold flakes glinting on top.

"This is...*art*," I say, actually kind of awestruck.

"Delicious, too." Akiko takes a bite of her cherry parfait.

I scoop up the top layer, along with the gold flakes, then moan softly. The most intense chocolate flavor coats my tongue, without being overly sweet or bitter. It's perfectly balanced—the best chocolate I've ever had.

Given how small of a portion she served at dinner, I thought Akiko wouldn't want to polish off all this dessert, but the bright smile on her face says she plans to indulge thoroughly. My mother would never allow me to devour this many calories in one sitting without saying something about my paunch and how I need to lose some weight. "Not asking for the moon here," Mom told me often. "Only about twenty pounds or so."

"I wish I had the patience to create something like this." Akiko sighs.

"I'm sure you could. Your food was amazing."

She laughs. "It's just a little hobby."

"Practical, though. I'd love to be able to cook like you."

"Why?"

"To feed Josh? He loved the yakisoba I made. Lareina and Fiona forwarded me your recipe." I shrug helplessly. "I just want to be a better fiancée."

She tilts her head curiously. "Most women say they want to be good wives."

Oops. I didn't say "wife" because I couldn't. I'm not going to make it to the wedding stage. I clear my throat. "Well... You have to be a fiancée before you can be a wife."

"True. But seriously, Josh doesn't need anything as complicated as what I make. And you have a busy career."

The earnest way she speaks shocks me. *Me? Have a busy career?* My work keeps me occupied, sure, but most people don't speak about my job like this. My parents have always thought I'm wasting my life at Huxley & Webber, and Katt pities me for not doing better. But Akiko, a woman who looks like she was born to money and has lived in wealth and luxury all her life, speaks like my job's critical and deserves to be respected.

"I'm just an assistant," I say with an embarrassed smile.

Her expression doesn't change. "Yes, I know. But how is that not busy or important?" She reaches out and squeezes my hand. "Always treat yourself with respect and kindness, my dear. If you don't, nobody else will."

Am I being unkind to myself? It isn't something I've ever thought about.

Akiko goes on. "Women are told to be sweet, considerate and kind to others, but not to themselves. Quite often, we actually put ourselves last. Don't do that."

"But...wouldn't that make me selfish?"

"No. You can't expect others to love you if you don't love yourself. You're a beautiful person, Ailee. You deserve good things, but you have to believe it and say it out loud."

I cock my head. "Say it. Out loud."

"That's right. If you don't take that step, it stays as a fuzzy concept in your head. The spoken word has an amazing power to help clarify one's thoughts and desires."

I take a moment to process. I've never been encouraged to put myself first, or say what I want out loud. Suddenly, I realize that my family basically turned me into somebody who thought occupying the same space as them was a great honor.

Akiko smiles as though she can see the thoughts crossing my mind. "Your personal time is valuable. So you shouldn't have to slave away in a kitchen to make things that take hours. Besides, Josh likes simple food. Tacos. Hamburgers. Roast chicken. Rosemary garlic roast chicken is a favorite. I made it every week when he was in high school, and he bolted it down like he was starving, although he quit eating like that once his growth spurt ended. He's especially happy if it's paired with roasted red-skin potatoes. If you want the recipes, I can send them to you. They're so easy to make. Only takes ten minutes to prep, and an hour in the oven."

"Thank you. Yes, I'd like that very much."

We chat some more over the tea and parfaits. Akiko's hilarious, and I find myself laughing a lot. When my belly's full of chocolatey goodness, Akiko pulls out a discreet matte-finish paper bag in creamy peach. "This is for you."

"Oh..." *Shit! Were we supposed to bring gifts?* "I didn't bring anything." I try not to squirm.

"Oh, don't worry, you weren't supposed to."

This woman may be the effortlessly gracious person I've ever met. "What is it?"

"You can open it."

I pull a box out and open the lid. Inside is a set of absolutely gorgeous pearls. They have an extraordinary lavender luster with little diamond accents to add glitter. "I've never seen this color before."

"Do you like them? They're from my family in Japan. We do love our pearls." She smiles. "There's an ethereal glow about these that reminds me of you. And I want you to have them."

I gape at the necklace, bracelet and earrings, then raise my eyes to stare at her. "Thank you, but I couldn't possibly—"

She pats my hand. "You're Josh's fiancée and soon-to-be wife, which makes you my daughter."

My arguments die in my throat. *But this isn't a real engagement!* I need to tell her the truth, but the possibility that the warmth in her face might cool freezes my tongue. "I...don't know what to do with these," I manage awkwardly.

"There's nothing to *do*, really. Just wear them on special occasions. I think they'll go very well with your pretty violet eyes."

I flush at her sincerity. "You don't think that Josh is too good for me?" I almost slap my own mouth shut. *She told you to be kind to yourself!* But old habits die hard.

She sits back and blinks. "Goodness, no! Why would I think such a horrible thought? I trust Josh's judgment. He's always been a smart and capable boy. He can be a bit aloof and inexpressive, but that's to be expected."

"Because of what happened to him when he was a child," I murmur.

Surprise flickers in her dark eyes. "Yes. Did he tell you?"

I nod.

She gives me a long, curious stare. "Well. If he told you about that, then he trusts you. And you are most definitely worthy of him."

"But..." I don't finish the thought. I used to think nothing of repeating what my parents or Katt said about me—that I wasn't worthy, that I was lazy, that I wasn't even trying. But after spending time with Akiko, I don't want to believe that anymore. "I feel like this is a dream, and I'm afraid to wake up."

"Why would you believe something good must be a dream? Live in the present—it's the manifestation of the way you've lived your life. You and Josh have been around each other for three years. You can tell a lot about a person over such a long time. I suspect you liked him."

I nod.

"He must've loved what he saw in you." She squeezes my shoulder, a surprising gesture from a woman who seems so physically reserved. "Do you think Josh is foolish? Or impulsive? A man who doesn't understand what's important?"

"No, of course not. He's the most brilliant man I know."

She gives me an angelic smile. "Then perhaps you should trust his judgment."

37

JOSH

"You know whatever Roland can give you, I can too."

I stop on my way to board the jet back home. *Harvey.* Did he follow me all the way from L.A.?

I tilt my head and look at the man who used to slip candy bars into my hands when I was little. I liked him—until the truth about Mom's background blew up in our faces. Afterward, I couldn't trust him or his motives, especially after learning that he and my mom had been engaged in a lifelong battle for supremacy and control over the family empire and they didn't care whose blood they needed to spill along the way.

He isn't an exact copy of Vincent, not the way Roland is, but he's a solid man with broad shoulders, hard muscle encased in a bespoke suit. His hands have thick fingers and big, bony knuckles that say he doesn't need a gun or a knife to fuck you up.

I give him an icy stare. "Adding stalking to your repertoire now?"

His smile is friendly and overly white. "I was in the neighborhood."

I grunt and resume walking toward the tarmac. "Here? At the airport?"

"Why not? It's a nice area—great weather, by the way. And the air is so much cleaner. Less traffic."

"Is Vincent refusing to see you?"

The muscle in Harvey's cheek twitches, but a practiced smile soon replaces it. "Dad's a very busy man. You know how it is. And Roland's all talk. Nothing to back it up. Too young, and he hasn't had time to establish himself within the industry, if you know what I mean."

"Be that as it may, he seems pretty close to Vincent."

Harvey makes a big deal out of appearing to contemplate that, then finally lets out a sigh. "My father is sentimental. He's just thrilled to have his youngest child back from the dead, you know? Back in his life. But how long will it last once he realizes that I'm the better choice? The one with the experience and all?"

A wistfulness fleets over Harvey's face, but I don't buy it. The fucker's incapable of feeling something as human as familial disappointment.

"The needs of the business will change his mind. After all, he made it clear only the strongest shall inherit the earth."

"That was the meek, not the strongest."

Harvey laughs like I just made a joke. "Can't be meek in this business. Not if you want to be on top."

"I'll keep that in mind. That's my ride." I tilt my chin at the waiting jet.

The humor vanishes from his face. "I'll tell you something as a gesture of goodwill."

Goodwill? "What, you want me indebted to you now?"

"This one's a freebie. Because I want you to think about my abilities and be all impressed and shit." He looks around theatrically, then puts a hand over his mouth. "Kenna Miller works for Zoe."

Hmm. So Harvey isn't entirely clueless. On the other hand, he doesn't seem to know that she's actually a double agent for Roland, which might've impressed me. Or maybe Harvey's keeping that close to his chest.

"Zoe has something on Kenna, something that could land her in jail."

"Like what?"

Harvey leans forward and lowers his voice. "Like murder." He flashes his teeth in a sharklike grin. "Didn't know that, did you?"

"Wouldn't have made a difference in her role for your family, would it?"

"No. She was going to have Kenna pretend to be the girl Ares supposedly saw in the fire—but who knew that other girl was actually real?" He spreads his hands.

I clench my jaw. Mom's the cause of Ares's long-term pain, but instead of making it up to him, she's been trying to exploit it. But then, if she reacted with compassion, she wouldn't be our mother.

Harvey takes a toothpick out of his pocket and puts it into his mouth. "Kenna hasn't been very useful since lately, and you know what Zoe does to pawns who no longer have any value. But maybe you can return the favor—and use her against my sister. I'm sure you'll think of something with that brilliant mind of yours."

The suggestion is tempting. After all, if Mom can be ruthless and efficient, so can I. But that would make me no different from her. I don't indulge in heartless exploitation, unlike Mom and her family. I'm not like them. Will *never* be like them.

"If you ever need more information or help, you know where to find me. Don't forget, the enemy of your enemy and all that. This beef you think you have with us—it's really only with your mom. The rest of the family is just...family." He tries to clasp my shoulder, but I shift out of the way.

"Don't hold your breath, Harvey."

38

JOSH

THE ENTIRE DRIVE home from LAX, anger, resentment, and fear take turns hijacking my body. Negative energy seems to crackle along my skin. It's like seeing the Dunkels has left a thick coat of filth all over me.

Impulses—none of them legal—flow through me, whispering all the ways I could get rid of Mom...and Vincent, and Roland, and Harvey. All the ways I could hide the bodies. If the Dunkels are gone, things will become more peaceful.

I park my car and breathe, my hand braced on the steering wheel. I don't want to go in like this, not when I'm full of darkness. I'm afraid of giving in—and tainting everyone, especially Klein.

What are you afraid of? What do you think you'll do to her? Dad's voice asks.

Not sure what I might do, but I'm scared anyway. Mom probably didn't mean to leave one of us to die in a fire. It just happened because she's who she is. Roland's words ring in my head. The way his gaze bored into me like an ice pick piercing my skull. Harvey's velvety tone, the Dunkels'—and my own—conviction that I'll be like my mother...

I give myself a slow five count to steady my nerves, then consciously relax my shoulders, paste on a smile and walk inside.

The place smells amazing—like roast chicken and potatoes and...

home. The lingering miasma from seeing the Dunkels starts to slip away, and my smile feels less forced.

"Baby, I'm home." The words roll out naturally, like I've said them thousands of times before. It feels *good* to say them—*to Klein.*

She pokes her head out of the kitchen and smiles. "Welcome back."

She's so beautiful. She shines like the brightest star—the only light that's clean and pure in my life. Suddenly, the urge to hold her swells. If I can just get close enough, my world will be right again.

I push my finger into the knot of my tie and pull it down. The smooth red silk drops to the floor. Her eyes follow it, then take in my face. *What does she see?* I wonder, a fist closing around my heart. Hopefully nothing dark or sinister, because I don't know what I'll do if she pulls away.

But she widens her smile and spreads her arms.

I stride across the kitchen, then claim her mouth and devour her. She kisses me back, as though she's channeling her bright energy into me. The sense of helplessness and anger subsides. I have Klein in my arms—my precious North Star that never leads me astray.

She loops her arms around my neck, rubbing her little tongue against mine like an eager kitten. The heat in my blood burns away the clammy darkness. Gratitude and an achy need for her feel like something physical is filling me up. My hands trace the beautiful curves of her shoulders and breasts and cup the soft mounds and squeeze, earning a soft sigh. She isn't wearing a bra. *Good girl.*

I swipe the pads of my thumbs over the hard nipples again and again. She shivers against me, her breathing shallowing.

"Oh my God," she says, pulling back to drag in air. "You're driving me crazy."

"Like you aren't doing the same to me." I hoist her up on the marble kitchen island, positioning her so her hips are just off the counter's edge. I drop to my knees, moving between her soft thighs. I crave her like the last drop of water in a desert. Only her on my tongue can quench the searing heat burning in my veins.

My hand braces the spot next to her hips. I reach underneath the pink skirt and rip the string at the side of the thong. The thin scrap of fabric slides down her thighs with a soft whisper.

"Josh." Her hands dig into my hair, but instead of pulling me toward her, they keep me away.

I move my eyes to look up at her. "What's wrong?"

She tries to close her legs as well, and I shrug them onto my shoulders, keeping them spread with a gentle stroke of my palm over her thigh.

Her face is flushed, but not just with heat. Embarrassment casts uncertainty over her face. "This is really awkward." She clears her throat, her eyes darting away.

I blink slowly. "You don't have to do anything except enjoy it."

Her face is redder than a ripe cherry. "What if you, um, don't like it?" Vulnerability shakes through her, and I hear the unspoken question: *What if you decide you don't like me afterward?* Her fingers in my hair clench hard enough to make me wince, but instead, I laugh darkly.

"Baby, you have no idea how long I've wanted to do this. You smell incredible—like a woman, like my Klein. Like the person I want to devour and wake up next to every morning."

She exhales...but doesn't let go. A multitude of emotions cross her face as they war within her. What past asshole of a boyfriend hurt her? I want to go back in time and pound the guy's face.

"I don't like it when you think or talk badly about the woman I care about, Klein," I confess, barely refraining from telling her I've loved her for a long time because I'm afraid I might scare her away. She's more skittish than a startled bunny.

Her eyelashes flutter as she takes a stunned moment to process, then she meets my eyes. "You care about me...?"

I look up at the vulnerable hope pooling in the deep violet of her gaze. My heart throbs. "Ailee Klein, I wouldn't be on my knees in front of you if I didn't."

She bites her lip again. Her brow furrows as she looks down at me, although the pressure in her hands remains the same. "Are you going to punish me?" Her voice is shaky with trepidation and anticipation.

"Yes. I'll punish you every time you say something negative about yourself, no matter the place or time."

Her throat works, but she slowly relaxes her hands. I push the skirt out of the way and breathe in her scent, biting back a groan. She's hot all over, and I'll stay on my knees forever as long as I get to be between her legs.

I part her folds and use my tongue to tease the soft pink flesh. She lets out a soft sigh. I can't believe she was going to deny us this gratification. I pull her clit into my mouth and gently suck, flicking the tip of my tongue over the swollen nub. Her thighs tremble. Her hands dig into my hair, pulling me close now.

Yes, my beautiful girl, ride my face and make yourself feel good.

As if she hears my thoughts, she gently rocks against my face. I love that she's getting greedy for the pleasure I'm giving her. She cranes her neck, her glorious hair cascading around her shaking shoulders and breasts.

"Oh my God, oh my God," she whimpers.

I lap her up, drinking in her honeyed juices. Every whimper and moan raises my temperature. My cock strains against the confines of my clothes as need throbs in my veins.

"Josh, that feels amazing. Yes, right there," she says, moving against me to show exactly what she means.

I push two fingers into her tight pussy and pump. The hot juices drip down all the way to the heel of my hand. Her response is so erotic, it's such a turn-on. She grinds herself against my mouth. I add another finger while I suck and lick her stunningly responsive clit.

She screams, then grinds as she rides the wave. My movements grow more frenzied. I'm determined to push her to another height with my mouth. I want her to remember how much I crave her—all of her.

She comes again. Her shriek fills the kitchen until suddenly, the sound turns hoarse as though she's losing her voice. Her knees tremble as her legs fold.

I pull her close and carry her to the huge dining table, then spin her around. She slaps her palms on the cool glass to brace herself. I press my hand on her back, push her down until she's bent over the table. Her beautiful ass sticks out. I rub my palms over each cheek, enjoying the taut curvature.

"Jesus, you're so perfect." Impatient, I rip away at my belt and slacks and pull out my throbbing cock. The veins on my dick jerk. "I can't wait." I position myself and push in.

"Yes, oh *yessss*..." She pants as the slick muscles tighten around my cock. She's searing hot, and my control snaps.

I drive into her hard, desperately trying to erase all that's happened since I walked out the door this morning. She moves with me, intensifying our pleasure. I love it that I can make her go crazy with lust. I love it that I can satisfy her and give her everything she needs. But I haven't forgotten the promise of punishment. I smack one cheek hard enough to leave a palm print. She gasps.

"For your punishment." I rub the red spot and smack her again. Her pussy spasms around my cock. I bite my lip to contain a groan. "Count, baby," I tell her. "Five more."

"Yes," she moans.

I give her a smack; she flinches. "One." I rub the spot, which is quite red. I give her another on the same cheek. "Two." She groans against the table, the muscles of her butt quivering. I stroke tenderly, then smack the other cheek.

"Three." A moan.

I smack it again. "Four." And again. "Five." With each spank, her pussy pulses and overflows with slickness.

"My pretty girl, don't forget—I love everything about you. Nobody says shit about you and gets away with it, not even *you*." I pound into her ruthlessly.

"Yes, yes, yes," she screams.

The beginning of an orgasm winds inside her. The muscles in her back contract more starkly. I dip a finger between our bodies to get it wet, then push into the tight opening above her pussy. Her back arches. She screams my name as a climax overtakes her.

My name on her lips is the only thing I need. *Klein, my Klein, mine*. I groan harshly as I empty everything inside her.

39

AILEE

After three powerful orgasms, my muscles are like soggy noodles. I can only manage to sprawl on one of the dining chairs. It's still unbelievable how loud and demanding I was, moving with him like that. I'm usually restrained during sex because I'm worried that I might be too loud or clingy, but with Josh, the anxiety to be perfect isn't in the driver's seat anymore. It's hot as hell that he loves it when I'm honest and vocal.

At least I don't look lewd with my shirt still on and skirt demurely covering me, even though he tossed my underwear to goodness knows where. Hopefully it didn't land in the dinner I made for him. But thank the lord Akiko shared his favorite meal with me. It looks like he could use some comfort food.

Josh takes off his jacket and vest and throws them over the back of a dining chair. His shirt is untucked—but I like the messy look. Makes him appear more human and approachable, something only I get to see.

He carves up the roast chicken I pulled out of the oven just as he arrived.

"This looks amazing," he says. "Rosemary and garlic, my favorite. And the potatoes, too!" They were cooked in the chicken dripping and juices.

I smile. "I had a feeling this meal would be a hit."

"Are you becoming psychic in addition to all your other charms?"

"Maaaybe. Plus I had tea and a parfait with Akiko this afternoon."

"Ah. You two go to that dessert place she invested in?"

"Yeah. It was amazing." I sigh at the memory of the delicious parfait. "I don't think I've ever eaten so much chocolate in my life."

His lips curve. "If you want, we can go sometime. I haven't tried it yet, although I had to pop in for the opening to support Akiko."

I nod, trying not to read too much into his suggestion, which sort of makes it sound like we'll stay together for longer than the agreed-upon six months. Although he said he cared for me, that was in the throes of desire. People say things they don't really mean when emotions are high. And even though Josh is one of the most deliberate people I know, that doesn't mean he's untouched by feelings.

Trust him. Trust yourself. Let things play out without forcing expectations.

"Did you get the pearls?" he asks as he places two plates of chicken and potatoes on the table and pours us a couple of glasses of the white zinfandel I pulled out of his wine cooler.

"How did you know?" I accept the wine with murmured thanks and sip. It's surprisingly crisp and goes well with the chicken.

He takes the seat next to me. "She gave sets to Ares and Bryce's wives, too. They're from her family in Japan. They're the *real* family heirlooms." He gives me a meaningful look before biting into the poultry.

Oh, wow. No wonder Akiko reacted so strongly to Josh's claim of my previous ring being an heirloom. Now I feel more awkward about receiving the pearls without telling her the truth. I should keep them safe in my closet. That way when Josh finds the love of his life, Akiko can give them to her.

"You should wear them to the opera next month," he says.

"The *opera*?" I squeak, glad my mouth is empty.

"Uh-huh. Elizabeth invited us. It's for a good cause."

"You mean Elizabeth Pryce-King?" I ask. She's the only one in his circle I know of who connects everything to some charitable clause.

He nods.

"But I don't know anything about operas. Besides, it sounds so… fancy."

He snorts. "Not that fancy. You dress nice, mingle, pretend to enjoy people singing at the top of their lungs in a language you don't understand, and talk about how marvelous all the arias were." He waves his fork, then spears more chicken and potatoes, and washes them down with the wine.

I giggle. "You honestly don't understand what they're singing on the stage? You seem like the type to speak multiple languages."

"I speak English—obviously—and Spanish and some French and Japanese. That's it. This opera is German. *Fidelio* by Beethoven." He shrugs. "I might understand 'hello!' in German, if somebody says it. If they sing it, forget it."

I laugh harder.

"But I don't mind. The point is raising money for some charity."

"I can see how it'd be worth the time." I savor my final bite. I'm not super hungry after all the chocolate.

"Yes, but it's also an opportunity for us to be seen together as a couple. With the pearls from Akiko."

The image he creates makes my heart flutter, but caution holds me back. "But they're too precious."

His eyebrow rises in a warning. "Nothing is too precious for you."

"But you said they're heirlooms."

"Exactly. Which is why they should be worn. So everyone knows that you're with a Huxley."

I fidget with the wine glass, running my finger up and down the stem. Although I'm trying to live in the moment, my mind can't help racing to the future. "Josh…what we have—it's only for six months. And we don't even have *five* months left now. What if—"

"Klein."

I stop and wait for him to continue. Nothing happens. So I prompt him: "Yes?"

He hesitates. Anxiety, fear and grim determination pass over his face in rapid succession. *Why is he reacting like I asked for a kidney?*

"Klein." He says my name again like it's some kind of magic word. "We initially agreed to six months, but that doesn't mean we have to stick to the timeline." He takes a moment, as though searching for the right words. "An agreement can be modified if both parties are amenable."

"Riiight." I nod slowly, unsure where we're going with this.

"We don't have to force ourselves to end it at six months just because that's what we initially said. To be honest, we didn't even decide on that deadline ourselves. It was just that ridiculous challenge Chad threw at you. Right? So we can find our own fulfillment by ourselves, as a couple, without any artificial deadline, by taking it one day at a time."

I blink a couple of times. Taking our situation one day at a time was an option I'd been considering, but I didn't realize Josh thought the same. The knowledge is surprisingly comforting and reassuring. Just not having a deadline makes our relationship feel more solid—after all, every journey starts with a first step. Josh and I can stay together for as long as we want.

He gazes at me steadily. "The truth of the matter is I've liked you for a very long time. When I said I cared about you, it wasn't just about getting into your panties."

My heart stops just before my brain short-circuits.

"I just never wanted to admit it. I didn't think I was good enough."

I shake my head. That doesn't make sense. Why is he saying what *I* should be saying? "That's ridiculous," I blurt out.

Self-deprecation cuts through his face. "But it's true. Remember what I told you about my mother?"

"But that's her, not you."

"What do you think about her?"

"Zoe?" I purse my lips. From the intense look in his eyes, my answer is going to be important, and I don't want to say the first thing that comes to mind—*She's a horrible person for trying to kidnap and hurt her own children.* "She was nice to me, but knowing what I know now... I think she's highly manipulative and doesn't mind who she hurts for expediency. I'm so sorry that all those awful things that happened to you. You don't deserve any of them."

He lowers his eyes for a moment, like a man bracing for a certain defeat, and sympathy wells inside me. The Josh Huxley I know is confident and proud. When he raises them again, his expression is blank. "I never wanted to find love. I never wanted to care for anyone other than my family because you can't escape blood ties. My mom used to tell me that she was most proud of me out of all her three boys because I was the most like her."

His mask splinters, showing bleakness underneath. My heart shatters for him.

He continues: "And because I was such a fool, I was elated when she told me that. I loved her and I wanted to make her proud. I was overjoyed that I was like her, until I realized that she wasn't anything like what I believed. She's amoral and out of control. She doesn't care about collateral damage as long as she gets what she wants." His voice cracks. "Sometimes I'm terrified of the possibility that I really am like her. There are times I feel the urge to do something I shouldn't so I can hurt her the way she hurt me." He shakes his head. "And that can't be normal, can it?" It isn't a question but a desperate plea to be free of the heavy burden he carries. He's afraid to answer the question because he doesn't trust himself.

"Why not?" I say gently. "Wanting to get back at someone who hurt you doesn't make you a sociopath. That's just being human."

He gazes at me, half hopeful, half scared, and suddenly I hate Zoe. Josh is the kind of man who shines no matter where he is, radiating power and self-assurance, and she's sown him with self-doubt.

I hesitate, then make up my mind. He revealed his private, guarded self. Sharing something I've always felt ashamed of is the least I can do to help him see that he isn't as bad as he fears. "I'm sure you saw that my parents aren't the nicest people—at least not to me. I don't know why, but they're always really good to Katt, but never to me. They always called me a failure, said they were embarrassed that I didn't do better. They think I should be more like Katt because we're twins. Fraternal, so we aren't identical, but to them that's not the point. We have the same genetic material, we came out of the same womb at the same time, so why is she so successful, and I'm just a nobody?"

Old bitterness shakes my voice. But Josh leans over and places a tender kiss on my forehead, communicating everything I need to pull myself together.

I exhale. "There are times when I'm just angry and frustrated. I want to tell them that they're wrong and that they're being intentionally cruel to me. I want to shake them until they see *me*. Their daughter, who needs their kindness just as much as their favored child. Sometimes I want to show them that I'm happy without their approval, even though there are times when, you know, I crave their acceptance.

"But just because I occasionally want to be mean to them doesn't mean I'm a bad person. It's more like making sure those who hurt us understand our pain. Just a natural reaction. The important question is, do you give in to those negative urges purely for self-gratification? If not, then I think you're okay. It breaks my heart to realize that you thought you might be a bad person." I thread my fingers through his and tighten them until our palms are pressed together. "You're one of the nicest, sweetest people I know. You're my Prince Charming, or maybe the brave knight who came to slay the dragon and save the princess. Doesn't matter which—you're perfect in my eyes."

40

JOSH

KLEIN'S WORDS settle over me. Her eyes shine as she gazes at me with a soft smile. Several heartbeats pass, but somehow the moment doesn't feel real.

All my life, people have called me capable, smart, cold, intellectual and calculating. But nobody ever said that I was *okay*, that my struggles were human and natural. Klein's eyes glow with sincerity, her smile slightly tremulous as she awaits my reaction.

I've been too much of a chickenshit to make myself truly vulnerable to her until now. How counterproductive I've been. The breaths I take seem easier because she sees who I am as a person. I told her I liked her, but I realize that's not the right word. This tight, achy, hot, painful feeling in my heart can't possibly be something as mundane as mere *liking*. It's more like...love—the kind of love that fills your soul rather than steals it as a prideful keepsake. The kind that makes you feel whole and motivates you to be a better person so you can be worthy.

The knot that started in my throat when she began talking thickens, and I can't get the words out to tell her how I feel. My heart throbs at the sweet acceptance and affection in her eyes. So I do the only thing I can.

I cradle her beautiful face and kiss her. She moans against my mouth, her fingers digging into my shoulders.

She tastes sweeter than any nectar, and I delve deeper into her—reveling in her light and sharing my soul with her. Our breaths mingle. She pulls me closer, like she can't bear to let go. My head spins. I fist her overflowing, cloudlike curls, amazed at the impossible softness.

I wrap my arms around her. She immediately puts hers around my neck, her legs around my pelvis. Our mouths fused in hunger, I carry her up the stairs to the bedroom, then carefully place her on the soft mattress. I prop myself on my hands and study the soft lines of her face, the brilliant light of her violet eyes. Her fingertips trace my cheeks and jaw.

Her eyes on mine, she undoes the buttons on my shirt, pushes it out of the way—and it feels like she's baring my soul. Vulnerability wraps around me, until she smiles like I'm the most amazing thing in her world.

All the walls around my heart crumble. She makes me feel weak and powerful at the same time. Shaking, I shrug out of my clothes, letting the custom-tailored garments fall in a heap on the floor. Her trembling desire overheats my blood.

I push her shirt up and pull it over her head. The sight of her already pointed nipples fuels my lust. I lift my eyes to hers, wanting her to see the raw desire in their depths.

Her smile grows playful and confident, like a woman who knows she's special to the man sharing the bed with her. "Like what you see?"

"Yes," I manage before placing a soft kiss on each of her eyelids, then pulling her nipple deep into my mouth.

She rewards me with a throaty moan as she arches her back, pushing her nipple closer. I adore her greed for what I can give her. She's wanton with only the skirt around her hips, slickness pooling between her legs as though she didn't come three times less than an hour ago.

But the moment feels different. Before, I wanted to lose myself in her and feel whole again in her presence. This time I want to be one with her to show her how much I love her. I long to show her gratitude for seeing me in ways that I never did, for understanding me in a way I never thought possible.

She runs her warm hand along my shaft, lets out a hum of appreciation, then looks up at me. "I want it."

"It's all yours." I glide my cock between her folds. Hot liquid drenches me.

My heart pounds in my head, screaming, *I love this woman, I love this woman, I love this woman.* She grinds against me. The movements are designed to torment me and make her feel good.

She grips my cock. I grow harder and bigger, anticipating the pumping motion of her hand. But instead, she holds my cock tight and moves her hips, rubbing the opening of her pussy along the cockhead teasingly. I watch satisfaction and lust play on her pretty face, then bite back a curse. The sensation of her dripping pussy is too much. She is going to be the death of me.

"Now," she says, "it's *my* turn to punish *you* for carrying around such terrible thoughts about yourself. I don't ever want you to think that you aren't worthy of love—or of all the amazing, beautiful things you have in your life."

"You don't think you're punishing me right now?"

She laughs. "Not even close."

Her hands slap against my shoulders, and I let her push me onto my back. She gets rid of the skirt, then straddles me. She looks powerful as she gazes down, her eyes narrowed to glittering violet slits.

She takes my cock again, this time gently moving her hand along my shaft. The slow pace winds me up as anticipation pounds in my veins.

Her leg muscles flex as she raises her hips and positions herself over my tip, then slowly lowers herself. I watch, mesmerized as she takes me agonizing inch by agonizing inch. A little more, a little more, a little more...

She stops, biting her lip. Her brow furrows, then she raises herself. Although she's dripping wet, taking me in all the way in one motion might be too much.

I reach out to run my hands over her thighs. She shakes her head. "No."

"Don't you want to feel good?" I reach for her again. "Let me help."

"No," she says again. "You'll just take it. I know what you're trying to do."

"What am I trying to do?" I ask, desperate to have her move faster, to take more inside.

"You just want to get me hot and bothered so you can avoid the punishment." She cups my face and gives me a beautiful smile. "You're perfect the way you are. Nothing can change that."

Despite the sexual frustration building inside, I have to smile. "Yes, ma'am."

"That's better." She moves over me slowly and leisurely, taking her time. Her breasts bob up and down with every bounce, one nipple still glistening with saliva. I'm dying to pull the other one into my mouth.

"Let me suck your other nipple and make you feel good."

There's a spark of interest, but she shakes her head. "I don't know if you deserve it." She cocks a teasing eyebrow. "That seems more like a reward for you."

"I've learned my lesson now." I try to sound humble. From her throaty laugh, I don't think I succeed.

She leans over me, her curls falling over us in a cascade, creating an intimate cocoon. She dips her head, her feathery breath grazing the side of my neck. It's all I can do to not push my hips upward, thrust myself into her slippery warmth.

There's a sudden pain on my neck. Her teeth close over my skin, but not hard enough to break it. The sting makes me expel a rough breath. She sucks the spot long and hard, then licks as though healing it.

"That should do it," she says with a satisfied smile. Then she frowns. "Is it going to upset you if there's a mark on your neck? I should've thought about that before..."

I run my fingers through her curls. "It's fine if it's *your* mark." Lust and affection rush over me, wresting control out of my already tenuous grip. "Let everyone know I'm taken every time they look at me."

Then I grip her hips and brace my feet and start to move both of us, bouncing her and thrusting forward, driving deeper inside her. She's so hot, so perfect.

She throws her head back. "Yes!" Her chest shudders with each shallow breath.

"You're *mine*," I grind out, unable to stop myself.

"And...and..." she pants, but then loses herself in rising orgasm.

It doesn't matter. I know what she wanted to say—and I've been hers all along without realizing it. I wrap my arms around her, taking her mouth, and explode into the sweetest oblivion I have ever experienced in my life.

41

JOSH

I STOP at the deli that's a block away from the firm and grab a quick turkey-and-ham sandwich. Nothing but mayo and mustard on top because, for some reason, the lettuce they use tastes like dirt. Something about it just makes the sandwich taste wrong.

"Anything else?" the cashier asks, flashing a smile and blushing at the same time.

I shake my head and swipe my card. "Thank you."

"Bye," she says with a sigh, but I've already turned and started toward the exit. When Klein's hickey was on my neck, women didn't give me that unnecessarily lingering look. Sadly, it faded too fast. I should get her to do it again later. I purse my lips with displeasure—women can wear rings to show they're taken, but it isn't as easy for men. Our only real option is a wedding band.

I walk briskly to the office, slightly behind on a contract review that Sandra wanted. Apparently, the angelfish's death inspired her to be more creative and socially conscious because she lost sight of her true self in the pursuit of fame and fortune. This somehow translated into *get me out of my existing contracts.*

I advised her that it was unlikely that she'd be able to terminate them early without paying heavy penalties—I don't remember every detail of all her deals—but she wants me to try. So here we are. I shake my head inwardly. Who discovers her true self and purpose in life because of a dead angelfish except in Hollywood?

The upshot is that it's going to involve working overtime. Which is irritating, because I have a more important project to work on.

At least I'm satisfied with the design for a custom ring, and the jeweler is working on turning the design into reality. I plan to propose to Klein—again, and for real this time—in a grand romantic setting. That embarrassing video shouldn't count. In fact, it needs to be forgotten. She deserves better.

Hopefully, my effort will show her that my feelings for her are sincere, and that I'm making a real commitment—not this six-month bullshit. Because just telling her I want to change the agreement wasn't enough. She needs to see that I care about her through my actions.

"Josh."

That voice. My jaw clenches and relaxes, but I keep on walking.

"Josh." A hand grazes my forearm.

I spin around, jerking my arm out of her grasp and raising a fist.

Mom stands with her hands at her sides. A tragic smile graces her beautiful face, tears glistening in her blue eyes. A hell of an act, but not something I'm buying.

A couple of people glance our way. I lower my fist and paste on a smile, aware of the optics. If this is how she wants to do it, we both can play the game.

"What are you doing here?"

"I wanted to see you."

"For what? You going into acting? Need a representative so you can make the most out of that talent for lying?"

Her lips tremble. "You don't have to be so cruel."

"Cruel?" Rage churns in my head. How dare she come to me? My voice shakes with barely suppressed contempt and fury. "Cruel is drugging your children. Cruel is trying to kidnap them and leaving one to die in a forest fire. Cruel is you showing up again, acting like a fucking victim."

Her face crumples. "I understand you're upset."

"*Upset*? Is that really the word?" I lean in. "Stop minimizing what you've done."

"Can't you see that I had no choice? I wanted to keep our family together. I still love your father."

"I don't believe you. The gossip rags from your country showed you dancing and partying with all those hot shots. You've been living the high life of a mafia princess. Don't tell me you've been repenting for all the things you've done."

Frustration flashes in her eyes. "Akiko has poisoned you against me."

"She hasn't done shit. That woman was an angel for marrying a single dad with three fucked-up kids, who were fucked up because of *you*. She could've married anyone, but she married Dad because she loved him. She never planned to use him or the family. She always supported me and my brothers. She's the mom I *wish* I'd had." I point my finger at Mom, who's gazing at me like my words are shredding her. "It disgusts me that your blood flows in my veins. I'll never be like you."

A single tear wells and then falls from her right eye. "No. You say that because you *are* like me. I don't take kindly to people who hurt me, either. But there is a difference between us. I'm capable of realizing when something has been done for my sake, whether I wanted it or not. And I know how to appreciate that." She draws herself up. "Later, perhaps, when you're older, you'll understand what I've done for you."

How can she say so much bullshit with such sincerity? It's sickening. "Is that why you went after Klein and burned down her apartment building?"

"Klein? You mean Ailee?" She frowns. "You know why I did that."

"No. I don't."

Mom shoots me pitying look. "I could tell you were in love with her. But for some reason, you kept resisting. I just wanted to give you a little push. It wasn't that difficult."

"Most people would just set up a date."

Mom blinks. "A *date*? But that's so...plebian. How about I take care of that obnoxious dentist for you instead? Would that prove my sincerity?"

"Please, don't. I don't need your brand of 'help.' And stop interfering in my life."

She sighs, as though she can't fathom what she's supposed to do with a singularly stubborn child. "You're just upset because you *think* I used Kenna to spy on you."

"Didn't you?" I say. "You weren't supposed to approach us until we turned thirty, but you sent her to us way before that. Just like with my girlfriend back in high school."

"It isn't my fault your girl wasn't seasoned enough to be subtle," Mom says, like I'm unfairly accusing her.

"You broke the spirit of the divorce agreement."

"Oh, come on. If I'd wanted to break the damn agreement, I would have. I wouldn't have bothered with an emissary."

"You shouldn't have bothered with anything. Just lain low and played dead."

"Like my baby brother Roland?" She smirks. "I know you met with him. And I'm pretty sure he gave you a sob story—that he was just a *wittle victim*," she sneers. "Did he cry, protesting that all he's guilty of is being the baby of the family?" A snort. "But that's bullshit. He's a fucking liar. A usurper. Why else would he have played dead for so long?" She seethes with hatred. "Whatever he promised, he won't honor it. You think I'm bad—he's far worse."

"At least he hasn't tried to kill us or sicced spies on us," I say coolly, even as she stirs up doubts. "People like Roland and you don't understand friendship or loyalty, just self-interest. He doesn't benefit from messing with me and the family, but you do. That fact alone makes him far palatable than you."

Something flickers in Mom's eyes, but then vanishes. She gives me a pitying look. "He isn't as innocent as you think. Do you think Kenna works for me? She works for Roland. She's smitten, and so is he, even though he tries to hide it. But I can tell. He treats her differently."

"Guess he has a heart, unlike certain people." I give Mom a disdainful look.

"Think what you will, but you'll know I'm the only one you can depend on. You say I only care about self-interest, but mine aligns with yours—I want to keep you and your brothers safe. I'm even giving you something that'll make Roland behave." She pulls a memory stick out of her purse and places it in my breast pocket. "You and I share the same blood—I love you and your brothers very much. I want the best for all of you, for our family of five." She lowers her voice. "When I get rid of the assholes in my way, we'll be together. Until then, just remember I'm always proud of you."

∼

MY GUT KNOTTED TIGHT, I return to my office and close the door. I reach into the bottom drawer and pull out a separate laptop without anything on it except an Internet connection, a browser and the standard apps that come with the operating system. I have no idea what's on the memory stick, and I'm not using my work laptop for it. Who knows what kind of virus or Trojan is on it? Wouldn't surprise me if Mom tried to hijack the firm's entire system.

At the same time, I'm curious to see what she thinks can control Roland. The man didn't give off an easy-to-bend vibe.

Two files. One video and one text. So far, everything looks innocent. I click on the text file first. A random string of numbers occupies the top line. Right underneath it reads: *A drum with the parts and the bat, caught in an abandoned fishing net and ropes.*

What does that mean?

I play the video next. No sound. A grainy but decent enough resolution to be able to recognize the players.

A younger version of Kenna Miller is standing near a dumpster under a street light. She grabs something that looks like a baseball bat and hits a man who looks to be at least twenty years older than her in the temple. The man raises his arms to protect himself, but too late. He drops. She continues to beat him over and over again. She doesn't stop even after the man quits moving. A dark pool of blood slowly expands on the pavement around his head, but she keeps going.

The entire clip is a little over two minutes with nothing but her smashing his face. A lot of fury. Very personal. No wonder Mom's been able to use it to control Kenna. The man in the video isn't exactly small—a few inches taller than her. The area seems a bit seedy, and it's nighttime, so it's possible he made some kind of threat or tried to assault her. But there's nothing else in the clip, so the motive would be unprovable. What *can* be proven is that she killed a man in a frenzy.

I go back to the text file. If the drum's "accidentally discovered," it'll provide the body and the weapon. Cops and the DA can assign the worst possible motive, claiming her secretly disposing of the victim and the bat means she knew what she did was indefensible.

I copy and paste the string of digits into a Google map. It shows a location on the Pacific coast, near the Bay Area. Kenna was probably too frazzled to be methodical about disposing of the body and weapon. I tap my fingers on the space next to the mousepad. *What was the story after the video?* Either Roland or Mom helped her hide the evidence. He might've fallen for Kenna's pretty face, but Mom would've tried to use her.

I close the laptop and put it back in the bottom drawer. Mom's been plotting for a long, long time to come to this point. For what? Just to take over Vincent's crime family?

My gut says it's not that simple. A woman this devious, patient and thorough wouldn't have waited this long. She might've known for a while that Roland wasn't dead as well.

The fact that Mom's motivation might not be what my brothers and I have been assuming sends chills down my spine. I don't believe for a second that our meeting outside the deli was a coincidence. She wants something from me.

But what? Maybe threaten Roland and make him back off?

If Mom's correct, she should've used the evidence to control him because he might do whatever's necessary to keep Kenna out of jail. Or maybe Mom wants to throw me a bone. A show of goodwill. She might believe I might soften my attitude toward her.

Another scenario is that she wants me and Roland to turn on each other. Wouldn't it please her to know Roland and I had become enemies over Kenna?

A couple of knocks on the door yank me out of my darkly spiraling thoughts. "Come in."

The door opens and Klein sticks her head in. "You haven't gone to lunch yet?"

I point to the bag from the deli. "About to start." *If I have enough appetite for a sandwich after my encounter with Mom.*

The smile on Klein's face is as sunny as the bouquet of violet Thai orchids in her hand. "I saw these on the way back to the office, and decided to grab them for you. These other guys aren't looking so great anymore." She pulls the pink carnations and yellow tulips from the vase. The tulips' petals are starting to discolor at the edges. She replaces the water and sticks the fresh orchids in the vase.

As she busies herself brightening my office, the clammy darkness over my mind recedes. It's amazing what her mere presence can do.

She finishes arranging the vase and retreats a step, casting a critical eye over her work. Then, instead of heading back to her workstation, she clasps her hands and studies me.

"Is there something else?" I ask.

A silent battle plays out on her expressive face before her chin firms. She walks around my desk and places a quick peck on my cheek.

Her sweet scent fills me head, and the touch of her lips is fleeting but achingly sweet. Surprise then pleasure unfurls in my heart, and I smile.

"That's better," she says with satisfaction. "No more gloominess."

She noticed. I thought I was subtler than that.

I start to reach for her, but she takes a quick step back, wagging a finger at me, and makes her exit.

I sigh and put my fingers over the spot on my cheek. There's a tingling warmth that commands my attention and leaves no room for the earlier apprehension.

Mom said that I'm the most like her. *She's wrong. I am a fucking Huxley, and I'm nothing like her.*

42

AILEE

I NEVER QUITE UNDERSTOOD WHY people spent so much money on private jets until now. Josh's plane is incredible. It has a separate bedroom, a shower, plus a vanity and a small closet where you can hang your clothes. The shower has the same set of toiletries as the ones at home, only in mini bottles.

Earlier, I might've fretted that we were from two separate worlds, but now I shove away the thought. After all, we've tentatively agreed to let our relationship run its natural course. Regardless of where we actually end up, I don't want to stew in doubt and have regrets in the future.

Enjoy the moment. Trust in yourself—and Josh, too. Trust that things will work out.

The flight from Los Angeles to San Diego is too short for a nap, but the seats are wide and plush, the leather buttery soft under my skin. I look around once again at the sparkling ivory interior with dark sage accents, taking it all in. Josh slips a fat grape between my lips. I chew automatically, savoring the sweetness bursting in my mouth.

"I've never traveled this fancy before in my life," I say.

He looks at me indulgently. "Get used to it. This is how you travel now."

I smile, then stretch my legs in front of me. "Love it that the tips of my toes touch nothing."

He laughs.

"I'm ready for tonight. Packed a couple of dresses and makeup."

"For what?" he asks in genuine confusion.

"So I look pretty. I'm going to need to freshen up." He gives me an odd look, but before he can say anything, I add, "I even listened to some famous arias and overtures from *Fidelio*."

He smiles. "There's no pop quiz at the end of the concert."

"It was for my own edification," I say primly. "Are Ares and Lareina coming?"

"No. She's too busy prepping for her next art exhibition, so he's skipping this one. To make up for it, she promised to donate a piece to the Pryce Family Foundation for their next charity auction," Josh explains. "And Fiona and Bryce won't be joining us, for obvious reasons."

"She's still nauseated." I sigh in sympathy. "At least she's okay in the morning."

She whined through a group text: *Why is morning sickness called morning sickness, even though I only want to throw up in the afternoon and evening now?*

Lareina had the most lawyer's-spouse-like response: *You can start calling it non-morning sickness. It's not like the name is legally protected with a trademark or anything.*

"Once we land, a team Lareina organized will come and help you get ready for this evening's performance. Something about hair and a facial and...stuff." Josh makes a vague gesture.

I gaze at him with a hint of hesitation. Ever since she started modeling, Katt has spent hours and hours to get ready for fancy events. One time I asked Mom about getting my hair done with Katt's stylist for the senior prom, and she laughed in disbelief. "Why bother? You'll never look that pretty even if you invest twice the energy and time."

That stung—probably more than it should have, given that I was just a teenager. I never asked again and managed to do what I could for myself. The idea of having a team of professionals to make me beautiful for the evening is exciting, but part of me is also afraid of being disappointed.

Don't let her ruin it for you, I tell myself, refusing to let my doubts destroy the joy of being dolled up. I want to be beautiful on his arm, and like magic, Josh has arranged to make it happen with Lareina.

When we land, a sparkling white limo is waiting on the tarmac. *Holy moly.* I've never been inside a limo before, not even for my prom. Katt couldn't go because of a photoshoot in Budapest, and my parents didn't want to pay for such a "wasteful extravagance," although what they really objected to was spending money on *me.*

My default mode clicks on: *Don't let people spend money on me that they don't have to.* It's one I acquired from the old, familiar guilt about the medical costs of saving my life after I developed my seafood allergy.

Then I shake my head. Why *shouldn't* money be spent on me? Why *shouldn't* Josh splurge to make us happy? It isn't a wasteful extravagance if it's something he can afford and we both enjoy it. *I'm worthy of the good things in life, too, dammit!*

I take Josh's hand. He gives me a curious look.

"Thank you." I smile. "You planned everything perfectly."

He smiles back, then presses a soft kiss on my forehead. "My pleasure."

A uniformed chauffeur opens the door, and we climb in. Josh pulls out a bottle of Dom from a silver ice bucket.

"Did you ever work as a bartender?" I ask, admiring the expert way he pops the cork and pours two flutes.

He laughs. "No. Why?"

"You're so good at opening the bottle, but at the same time I can't picture you working part-time in school."

He snorts with amusement. "I didn't grow up as spoiled as you think. Granted, the family's well off, but I was expected to do chores and get a part-time job in high school. Akiko said it'd be good for me to learn the value of honest work."

"I always knew I liked her."

"My boss was heartbroken when I quit. Apparently their sales plunged after I left."

"Where did you work?"

"Starbucks."

I chuckle softly. I can picture girls coming by to order drinks, hoping to chat with the handsome barista. Maybe even create their own meet-cute moment.

"To the most beautiful woman I know," he says.

My face warms with pleasure. "To the most wonderful man *I* know."

We clink glasses. I start to take a sip, then stop. The bubbly wine's scent stings my nose like vinegar. But it's Dom. How can that be? I try again, but—just can't. I put the glass down, but Josh has already taken a sip of his.

"What's wrong?" he asks.

"It just smells a little off to me."

He raises the glass to his nose and sniffs. "Seems okay."

I frown. "Weird. But it might just be my nerves."

"Still nervous?"

"A little. I keep thinking I'm ready for tonight, but then feel a little scared when I think about what Lareina has planned for me. I just have no idea what's going to be involved."

He squeezes my hand comfortingly. "It'll be something good. She swears you'll get my money's worth."

My lips twitch. That's something she'd say.

"And you'd better, because I want to spoil you rotten. You've been working hard, and I feel a little guilty that you go home and cook most days." He frowns a little, and I run my fingertips along the furrowed spot soothingly.

"But I enjoy feeding you. You're such an appreciative eater." I'm valued at work, but the efforts I've made in my personal life have either gone unnoticed or been belittled by my family. He probably doesn't understand what his genuine recognition and thanks do to me, but I simply adore the way his eyes light up with delight or how hot he is when he's in the kitchen with his sleeves rolled to help clean up.

I brush my lips over his cheek, then smile when the tips of his ears redden. "So what are you going to do? Join me?" As soon as the question is asked, I realize how ridiculous it sounds. He already looks perfect. His hair is slicked back, revealing his smooth forehead. His skin is absolutely flawless. If I didn't know better, I'd swear he's wearing concealer—there isn't a single blemish on his face.

"No." He heaves a sigh like it's the greatest tragedy ever. "I'll be working."

"On what?" As far as I know, his work calendar is clear for the weekend.

"Sandra has a lot of contracts, and she's still very"—he shakes his head—"determined."

"I feel bad for her agent." The man sounded like he was in tears when he called the office.

"He'll get his cut, just not as much as he would've liked. The rumor is that he was counting on the earnings and already splurged on a new boat he can't really afford."

I wince. "Ouch." But the story isn't really surprising. Ever since I started working at Huxley & Webber, I've seen one too many celebs and "their people" make bad financial decisions. I used to think that there was no way someone who made millions a year could struggle to pay their bills, but it happens all the time.

The limo stops in front of a stunningly beautiful building with golden fairy lights glowing along the walls. One side of the structure is made entirely of polarized glass. So. This is where the fairy godmother production happens to make me beautiful for the fancy event. My belly flutters. Thinking of all the gorgeous women who used to grace Josh's arms, I pray they make me at least that pretty, and that I won't embarrass him at the opera.

"Enjoy." He kisses me on the mouth, just as the driver opens the door for me.

I kiss him back. "See you soon."

43

AILEE

Josh wasn't kidding when he said he wanted to pamper me.

"Your shoulders are way too tight," Leslie says, then puts me through a Thai massage, hot stone massage and scalp massage, although I'm not sure how my scalp is related to shoulder tightness.

She kneads me like I'm some sort of intransigent dough that refuses to become soft and malleable. I can't complain because it feels amazing to have my muscles turned into warm goo. *Does Katt do this every time she needs to get ready for an event?* If so, it's no wonder she looks radiant. I could definitely get used to this.

Another person, whose name I didn't catch in my gooey stupor, clucks her tongue at the state of my skin and has me bathe in squishy mud, while a thick layer of seaweed sits on my face. Leslie comes back for an oil massage to work fragrant lavender oil into my skin and work out whatever kinks she might've missed the first time around. I sigh with appreciation. Josh really *is* a man worth spoiling if this is how he repays me for my little efforts.

The loveliest pink lacquer goes on my nails. Then comes my hair. I press my lips together at how unruly it is. It looks like a mushroom cloud of atomic devastation. "Really curly, huh?" I say with a small smile.

273

"Yeah, but it looks good. Your hair's fantastic. Thick and glossy," Monica the hairstylist states with a twinkle in her dark eyes. "Lots to work with. No need for extensions to give it volume." She takes my hair, dries it, sprays in some products, then braids it into sections and twists them into a complex updo that I never thought was possible with hair like mine. She sticks several freshly cut purple orchids into the thick mass. "Perfect. Look at you. You look like a princess." Monica grins.

"Oh my God, you're a *genius*!" I say, unable to tear my eyes from the mirror. "I didn't know my hair could look like...like..." For maybe the first time in my life, words fail me.

She laughs. "I got the magic hands," she says, wriggling her fingers.

"Magic isn't enough to describe this. I think you've destroyed the laws of physics. Thank you!"

"Like I said, great hair. Made my job easier." She puts some very light makeup on my face, focusing on bringing out my eyes and lips. "You look like a little fairy. I love it."

I simply can't believe how amazing my reflection looks. Confidence and joy soar in my heart. I'm dying to get into my dress for the evening —the one I carefully packed for the event.

Finally, I shrug out of the robe and put on the gorgeous off-the-shoulder royal-purple gown that clings to my curves and accentuates all my assets the right way—as Max might put it—then slip on a pair of gorgeous silver stilettos with faux-diamond accents around the ankle straps. I stand and stare myself in the mirror. My eyes sparkle, and my cheeks are flushed with excitement. I feel like Cinderella, ready to attend the ball with my Prince Charming.

Just then, Josh steps inside.

My breath catches. He's strikingly handsome in a black-and-white tuxedo. It fits his broad shoulders perfectly, then molds to his chest and slim waist. The man radiates a cool authority and power that warns people to keep their distance. But when he looks at me, warmth enters his eyes, and it makes me special, like I'm the only woman in his world.

His eyes roam over me, head to toe and back up to my face. He steps forward, then grasps my shoulders, his palms warm and tender on my bare skin, and places a careful kiss on my lips to avoid smudging the scarlet tint.

"You look so beautiful. Can't believe you're mine."

I look up at him with all the love and trust welling in my heart. "Thank you. You look *very* handsome yourself."

Smiling, he flicks a petal on one of the orchids in my hair. "The flowers look so good on you. We should plant these in our garden."

"Really?"

He nods. "These are just so *you*. Pretty, fragrant. Delightful."

He extends a hand to one of the staff. She brings over two boxes—one with the Sebastian Jewelry logo and the other containing the pearls that I received from Akiko. The woman opens the lid on the first one, revealing a gorgeous diamond-and-platinum tiara. It's just big enough to make a statement without being pretentious. The gorgeous, glittering stones and chic design are fit for a princess.

"Wow," I breathe.

"A tiara for my princess." He smiles, then places it carefully on the crown of my head. Monica comes over to secure it with bobby pins.

Once Monica's finished and retreats, I study my reflection. The tiara sparkles like a crown on my head. And I *do* feel like a princess.

Josh reaches for the pearls next. He places the dangling earrings on my earlobes. Then the bracelet circles my wrist with a soft click of the clasp. Finally, he steps behind me and loops the stunning necklace around my neck, his fingertips brushing against my bare skin, sending shivers down my back. He lowers his head until he can whisper into my ear, his breath tickling my sensitive earlobe. "I love the way you smell. What did they do?"

"A massage with scented oil. It was really nice, but I like the way your shower gel smells on me better."

His eyes flare, and his arm around my waist tightens. I turn in his embrace and press my forehead to his, inhaling the shared air between us.

"There's something I need to confess to you," I say, my eyes on his Adam's apple. A mixture of anxiety and anticipation spark along my nerves. When he doesn't respond for a few moments, I look up at him.

The humor slips from his face at my serious expression. "What is it?"

"Privately," I murmur.

He gestures at the staff to leave us. When everyone is gone and the door closes, I exhale slowly.

"I did something bad," I say.

"How bad?"

"I had some negative thoughts about myself earlier, before the event, even though I didn't mean to." I try to look penitent. "I shouldn't have done that."

He stands like a statue, but the tip of his eyebrow twitches. "No, you shouldn't have."

"So I should probably be...punished."

His warm palms stroke my ass, then squeeze. "And how do you propose I should do that?"

"With, um...this?" I reach into the clutch and hand him the sleek cylinder.

He takes it and studies it, half curious, half turned on. "A remote control? To what?"

"My friend gave me an annual subscription to the Year of Coming First. A pair of crotchless vibrating panties came inside the first box. And this is the remote control," I explain. My cheeks burn, but I don't want to chicken out. Sexual excitement isn't the only thing driving me. It's trust that he'll safeguard me—and my heart.

Heat erupts in his eyes. He taps the button at the end.

A soft vibration pulses against my clit. I let out a shaky sigh, my eyes fluttering.

"How does it feel?" His low voice washes over me, making me shiver.

"Good, but not enough."

"Enough to keep you simmering?"

"Yes."

He chuckles wickedly, then rolls his thumb over the wheel. The intensity shoots up. I gasp. My knees buckle. I grip his forearm so my butt doesn't hit the floor.

"This is perfect," he purrs, then returns the intensity back to the lowest setting.

I look up at his satisfied expression. In this position, my face is at his crotch, and I can see his thickness straining against the pants. I run my fingertips over his length, keeping my touch feathery. "You're so hard." And ready to be pulled into my mouth or into my pussy. Anywhere where we can make each other feel amazing.

"Watching you breathe makes me hard." He pulls me up and holds me tight.

My eyes slide to the closed door behind him. "Do you think that has a lock?"

"No. Doesn't look like it," he says.

"Mmm. Too bad." I graze the backs of my fingers along the thick girth of his shaft. "I could've sucked you off before we head out."

He presses his lips together as though containing a groan. "You're going to be the death of me."

"Blame yourself." I smile at him. "You make me feel safe and confident. I've never felt this secure with anyone before. I feel like you won't judge me, no matter how outrageous my demands might be." My cheeks are so hot I feel like my face will burst into flames.

His breathing roughens. "Jesus. Klein, baby, you can't say stuff like that to a man when he can't do anything about it."

I press my body closer and rub him gently through the clothes. "Later. I'll let you do anything you want with me."

"Anything?" Desire glitters in his fathomless eyes. I can't look away.

"Yes. It will satisfy you, and it'll make me feel good. But most importantly, it will also teach me a lesson. That I'm worthy and beautiful. And that I shouldn't doubt your judgment."

44

JOSH

Klein's fingers flex on my forearm as we walk inside the opera house. It's a modern structure with bronze mirrored walls and chic contemporary chandeliers hanging from the cathedral ceiling. A thick burgundy carpet muffles our footsteps, and empty wine glasses and round coasters dot several tall tables.

I had the driver take the scenic route along the Pacific so that she could enjoy the gorgeous blue ocean and take her mind off what's to come. I love the way her eyes sparkle, how she flushes with pleasure at the scenery and her sheer confidence after being pampered and fussed over. Lareina and Fiona were right to suggest that I treat Klein to a team of experts who can make any woman feel special and beautiful. Not that Klein ever needs anybody to make her shine. She's like the moon in the sky. She already glows, just because she's who she is.

Other than to repay Elizabeth's favor, I harbor a selfish reason for bringing Klein here. I want to show her off to everyone. To announce that she's my woman—and that they'd better treat her with respect.

Also, the events Elizabeth hosts have tight security. Assholes like my mom and her brothers won't be able to enter to cause trouble.

Klein lets out a soft breath. I place a hand on the back of her neck and stroke the taut skin to soothe her.

"What's wrong?"

"Just a little nervous. I've never been to anything like this before. Katt never took me to anything fancy."

"Relax," I say. "Nobody here bites. They prefer to munch on beef tartare canapés."

She giggles, then eyes a tray on a waiter's hand as he passes by. "They look delicious."

"We'll grab some later."

I scan the audience, looking for someone kind to introduce her to. I spot Elizabeth chatting with Barron Sterling ahead of us. She's dressed elegantly as always—in a magenta-and-white gown that hugs her lean figure. Barron's gray hair glints under the chandelier. A bespoke tuxedo fits his frame well—he wouldn't wear it otherwise. He's built like a tank, with thick bones and still a decent amount of muscle on him, although he's gotten softer recently. The man's older than dirt, with great-grandchildren, and he probably just doesn't give that much of a damn anymore.

"Let's go over and say hello to those two," I say to Klein.

She squints at Elizabeth and Barron. "Who are they?"

"Family friends," I say, keeping things simple. "You'll like them."

She straightens her spine as though readying herself for battle. I slip a hand into my pocket and quietly raise the intensity of the vibrator. Gasping, she swivels her head in my direction. I give her a look.

"What was that about?" she whispers, her face reddening and her eyes glazing with pleasure.

"Relax. Or I'll give you a *reason* to relax."

Her face flames. "You wouldn't...!"

"I totally would. I brought you here to meet some people and have a good time."

"I thought you believed in the charity the concert is for?"

"You having fun is the cause. The charity is secondary. I already donate tons of money to various organizations. Didn't have to come here just for that."

She licks her lips, then squirms. "Fine. But can you please l-lower it? It's too distracting, which means I really *won't* be able to relax."

The glimmer of her getting turned on makes my dick eager. But I can't go around with a hard-on already.

I kill the unit. She lets out a soft sigh, eyes closing briefly and shoulders sagging. "Thank you."

"My pleasure." She laughs like I intended. "Now, be good or get punished."

I lead her toward the two.

"Hello, Josh." Elizabeth smiles, then glances at Klein, her smile still warm and welcoming. "And this must be your fiancée."

"Yes. Ailee Klein. Klein, meet Elizabeth Pryce-King and Barron Sterling."

"Hello. Nice to meet you." Klein and Elizabeth shake hands. "I used to wonder what woman would nab his heart, and you're exactly what I expected. *Love* your hair, by the way. It's so pretty."

Klein flushes, too shy and pleased. "Thank you. You're stunning, too."

She turns to Barron, who takes her hand and kisses the fingertips. She starts slightly, but he lets go like a gentleman without commenting on her reaction.

"I can't put my finger on it, but you look familiar," he says.

"She's Katt Klein's sister," Elizabeth says.

He stares at her blankly.

"The model," Elizabeth says.

"A fraternal twin," Klein adds with a forced smile, likely bracing for some negative comparison.

Barron frowns impressively. "Hmm. Doesn't seem likely."

Klein stiffens. I scowl at the old man, ready to rip into him if he says anything hurtful.

"You have the bone structure of a model, but you look like a more relaxed sort of girl. The type who'd love to sit down and share some of my favorite sugar cookies and some Earl Grey tea. Justin and Nate—my grandnephews—dated a few models, and those girls all acted like I was trying to commit murder if I offered them a nice, tasty cookie." He rolls his eyes. "Models."

I lean over to Klein. "He's really fond of his sugar cookies."

"Thanks, I...got that." She smiles. "I'd love to have cookies with you.

If you want, I can even bake some for us. I have the best double chocolate chip cookie recipe. They taste like soft fudge."

Barron turns to me. "You seem to have chosen well, young man."

Beside me, I can practically sense Klein relaxing, growing open and warm.

I smile. "Thank you. I think so. And how is Stella?"

"Oh, capital! Keeps me on my toes, I can tell you that." He turns back to Klein. "Also makes a mean batch of cookies." He winks.

"Unless it's a secret, I'd love to get that recipe from you," Elizabeth says. "My son is obsessed with baking after watching *The Greatest British Bake Off*. Since I have to at least try whatever comes out of the oven, I prefer that it's something good. The tart he made last time was... To borrow my cousin's chef's phrasing, 'Only fit for pigs that you find particularly displeasing.'" She sniffs daintily.

Klein laughs. "Of course."

"By the way, you're coming to the art auction that I'm planning in L.A., right?" Elizabeth says.

Klein glances up at me. I make a go-ahead gesture with my hand. "You can go if you want. She's inviting you."

Klein relaxes and smiles. "Sure. I'd love that."

"Excellent. I'll be there too. You should come as well," Barron says to me. "I'll bring Stella, if I can convince her to get on the jet." He turns to Klein. "She didn't want to make the trip tonight. Too enamored with her new grandbaby to leave."

"Perfect. It'll be awesome," Elizabeth says, her eyes bright. "I'll add you to the invite list."

"Where's Tolyan?" Barron says, looking around. "Isn't that *his* job?"

It's true, her "assistant" is missing. The rumor is that her husband, Dominic King, insists Tolyan be present, especially when Dominic can't accompany her himself. That Russian is most definitely a bodyguard, even if Barron doesn't seem to realize that.

"He's helping with the security because the team the organizers hired flaked out and sent only half the number of people contracted for." Elizabeth scowls. "I swear, if anything happens, I'm going to hire Prescott to sue." She takes security as seriously as anyone I've ever met —myself included. But her concern is understandable. Some psycho breaking into your home and trying to kill you and your husband tends to make you paranoid. "Anyway, I'll remember to add you, don't worry." She smiles at Klein.

It's nice to see the way Elizabeth and Barron warmly take Klein into their fold. Not that I really had any doubts.

A new wave of guests comes over to say hello to Elizabeth, and an art collector starts talking to Barron about some new artists he met. Since Klein wanted the beef tartare canapés earlier, I grab a couple of tiny plates from a passing waiter and hand one to her.

"Oh wow, look what the cat dragged in."

Klein's body tightens, her hand flinching and almost dropping the canapé. I can feel my face twist at the smug, annoying voice. I turn around to see Katt standing with a hand on her cocked hip and a superior sneer, like she owns the entire opera house.

45

———

AILEE

Every muscle in my body stiffens. *Katt?*

My sister looks as glamorous as ever, outfitted in a red dress with a plunging neckline that reaches her navel. Her hair lies sleekly around her expertly made-up face, and a fortune in diamonds glitters from her ears and neck. She glares at me, her mouth twisted into an ugly line.

Coco appears as well, coming to stop next to her like a backup. She's in a mermaid dress that's an unfortunate shade of yellow and makes her look like a jaundiced tuna. She's also wearing the exact same sneer as Katt.

I press my lips to avoid laughing, because that'd only upset Katt. But it's almost comical, like those two rehearsed the sneer together so that they would look identical. They look more like sisters than Katt and I do.

Her eyes rake me up and down, and the tips of her mouth curve downward. Irritation and jealousy flash in her eyes. What does she find annoying *now*? It can't possibly be that I'm too embarrassing for her. I know I look awesome tonight. Maybe she's envious that I'm here with Josh. After all, she had the audacity to claim that she was engaged to him.

Her expression turns soft, her eyes shimmery with sugary affection as she looks at Josh before it becomes sullen as she glowers at me again.

Not sure why she's upset. It isn't like I stole Josh from her—they were never in a relationship in the first place. She gazes at my hair critically for a bit, then her frown deepens. Finally, she eyes the plate of canapé in my hand, then at my belly, then smirks. She doesn't have to say it: *You sure you can afford to eat that? With* your *belly?*

Embarrassment and shame surge. It's a reflex. I start to lower the plate, looking around for a place to deposit the food, then catch myself. *Why am I reacting this way?* Why allow her to destroy my good mood? I look down at the plate. I've been *wanting* to eat this since I got here, and Josh got it for me. It still looks delicious, and I deserve to enjoy good things.

Josh steps forward, his jaw tight, but I put a hand on his rigid forearm. As much as I appreciate his protectiveness, I need to do this on my own. I want to show Katt that she can't put me down like she used to anymore.

Holding her eyes, I lift the plate, pick up the canapé and bite into it. An intense beef flavor mixed with savory mustard and shallots explodes in my mouth. The crunchy crust adds to the texture. *Yum.* Can't believe I almost gave it up to please Katt. I start chewing deliberately.

"Have some dignity," Katt says between clenched teeth, unable to bear it anymore. "You eat like a pig."

"A very *happy* pig," I say with a smile, then inhale. "You should try this. It's *really* tasty. Might improve your disposition. And you should quit frowning so much. You aren't as young as you used to be, and you don't want to develop any more wrinkles."

Katt turns crimson. My heart pounds with rebellious exhilaration. I've never spoken back to her like this, but it feels amazingly good to assert myself, rather than letting her walk all over me like before.

"How *dare* you talk to me like that?" she spits.

"Easy." I take another bite and make sure to chew ostentatiously. "I'm your sister, not your doormat."

Coco takes a half step forward, as though she's just tag-teamed off Katt. "You might be a happy pig, but I guess you aren't hot enough for Josh to fuck yet." She glances at the way Josh stands close to me and sneers. "So why are you still hanging on?"

I blink. She said some nasty things in her email, but I never expected her to say anything like that to my face. But at least she's consistent.

"Who the hell are you to talk to my fiancée that way?" Josh demands. "And how would you even know?"

Coco flinches at his cold tone. "You're still with her. And you don't sleep with the same woman twice."

Katt nods, like a trusty yes-woman.

"Oh," Josh says. "I understand now. Well, allow me to set you straight, since you seem to be speaking from your own general experience. See, men don't go for a second helping when the first was subpar. Barely even mediocre. Why waste the time and energy and effort—and money—on something so unsatisfactory?"

Coco looks like she's about to faint.

He continues, "Now, apparently, we dated once? I really don't remember. But you really should quit before you humiliate yourself any further. I never slept with you. I'm never going to sleep with you. I think we might've had a dinner together—and that's all there's ever going to be between us."

She turns deathly pale. Katt glares at me like this public evisceration is all my fault.

"Look, Coco," I begin, keeping my voice gentle. I actually feel a little bit sorry for her, even though she was nasty. "You don't have to waste your energy cutting me down, hoping that it'll make Josh choose you. He's a human being with his own feelings and agency, and if he wanted to be with you, he would've committed already. There are other men out there. And some are for you, the kind of men who will cherish you and love you just the way you are."

Coco's face crumples. Her eyes flash with something like fury and hurt, but she doesn't lash out. Katt is positively seething, monumentally angry that I'm not folding like she expected me to.

"And for my part…" I tighten my arm around his waist. "I have no desire to let this man go without a fight. No matter what anyone might say, as long as we both want each other, he's mine, and I'm keeping him."

46

AILEE

As soon as I finish speaking, chimes ring in the lobby, and the lights flicker slowly a couple of times. The crowd starts to move toward the auditorium. Katt and Coco take advantage of the moment and slink away.

I let them, watching them dwindle with their tails tucked while my spine is straight and head held high. Power and strength seem to sizzle in my veins. I've never talked like that before, but it feels *so good* to just say what's on my mind without worrying about someone else's judgment or my place in life. Accepting that I'm entitled to want what I want is liberating. And powerful.

Josh loops his arm around me. "Jesus, that was hot," he whispers into my ear.

My heart pounds harder, for reasons that have nothing to do with telling off Katt and Coco. "Did you like it?"

"Loved it. I'm hoping somebody recorded and uploaded it online so I can watch it over and over again." He pulls me close and presses his cheek against mine, the gesture intimate and sweet. "In the interests of full disclosure, I'll never stop wanting you."

"Good. I was planning to chase you with a stick if you did." The joke slips out easily, but instead of my usual worries pouring into my head, I just feel good. In control.

He laughs, then kisses me. The lights flicker again, three times now.

"Isn't that a signal to get to our seats?" I ask.

He nods. "Alas, yes."

He links our hands and leads me along until we reach a huge box. It's luxuriously appointed with a cushy dark burgundy leather couch big enough for three. A few decorative pillows in white and gold are laid artistically, and a couple of armchairs sit on either side.

I rush inside and look around. From up here, I can see everything clearly, from the orchestra pit to the stage. A couple of gorgeous silver boxes on the small side table catch my eye. "What are those?"

"Opera glasses."

"Nice! I read about them, but wasn't sure about getting some."

"Why not?"

"Well...we may not see any more operas."

"So? You might have more fun with them." He hands me a box. I open it and find a stunningly beautiful pair of silver-and-gold binoculars on a thin, elegant chain.

He sprawls in the middle of the couch, then grasps my arm and pulls me down with him. I fall onto his lap with a gasp. Something long, hard and thick prods at my butt. *Oh, hello.*

I turn to look at him better. His eyes glitter, reflecting the lights from the auditorium and the stage. Sweet pulsing starts against my clit, and I gasp, pleasure simmering in my blood.

"Am I being punished?" I murmur.

He lowers his head until his lips are so close to mine that they're grazing my mouth. "No. I'm rewarding you for being confident and awesome. I'm going to tease you and make you come. Then when you're shaking from head to toe, I'm going to fuck you silly."

Heat sears through me. My body's already ready for whatever he has in mind. But—

"What if people see?" I keep my voice low, like I'm afraid somebody might overhear us. It feels really illicit.

"Nobody's going to notice anything. Everyone's too busy watching the opera."

"But there are lots of people with opera glasses. What if they decide to watch *us*?"

"Then they'll get an eyeful of how I pleasure my woman."

My mouth dries. He's looking at me. If I tell him no, he won't push. My head says I should be scandalized and ask him to wait until we're alone. But...

The lights over the audience section dim gradually until we're plunged into darkness. Josh and I maintain eye contact in the shadowy booth. The crowd claps, then quiets down. I can barely make out his outline. The vibration between my legs feels too good, and my breathing shallows.

We're up fairly high, and the chances of somebody looking up in our direction when the stage is below us is miniscule. Besides, the balcony won't let people see what we're doing below chest height anyway.

The vibrator pulses harder. I don't want to wait hours to have this man, whose eyes burn with a hunger that sends hot shivers down my back and makes my toes curl. I want the reward *now*—and to feel him moving inside me as the orchestra and singers fill the auditorium with music.

I grasp the back of his neck, then slowly move my hand up, tunneling my fingers into his hair. His breathing roughens. I run my other hand down his chest...to his perfect abs, hidden underneath the tuxedo. The vibrator works more vigorously. Electric shocks streak through me, and my clit throbs, my flesh growing drenched.

I flick my tongue over his mouth. He parts it, and I slip inside. His fingers flex against the small of my back. The pulsation between my legs heats my blood, but he's deliberately holding back, teasing me, trying to draw the moment out.

I pull his tongue into my mouth and suck it. My hand travels lower until I can palm his throbbing cock through the clothes. He groans—a sound only I can hear over the high notes from the soprano. The knowledge makes me feel naughty and superior at the same time.

He slips his large, calloused hand underneath my dress, running it over my skin. Everywhere he touches tingles. If my body could talk, it'd sigh and whimper, begging for more. The emptiness between my thighs aches badly. I shift, straddling his thick, hard thigh, and grind against it, while I busy myself with discreetly freeing his cock.

Instead of helping, he rolls his forefinger over the wheel on the remote control, until stronger shock waves pulse through me. I sigh with bliss, then shiver when he strokes his thumb along the crease of my crotch, making me lose focus for a moment. I fumble until I pull out his cock through the open fly. It's hot, precum slippery along the shaft. I grip it, then swipe my thumb over the cockhead.

He bites his lip, but I can still hear the low groan. It rumbles in his chest, pressed against me. My nipples bead in the bra. I whimper, and he slips his finger between the slit on the bottom of the vibrating underwear and teases the opening of my pussy.

"Yes," I hiss, then pump him hard.

He half laughs, half groans softly. "Patience." He doesn't push his fingers all the way. Maybe only an inch or two. It drives me crazy, and my inner muscles tighten, trying to keep him from retreating.

"Please. You said you wanted to reward me. So reward me. Make me come."

He shudders, then pushes two thick fingers into me until they bump against my G-spot. I swear I see stars, but then the vibrator suddenly buzzes at the maximum level.

I crash my mouth against his to contain a scream. He cradles the back of my skull, kissing me and shoving his tongue into me like he's fucking me with it. I grind against him shamelessly. His fingers invade again, then spread inside me, stretching and readying me for his size. Even though we've been sleeping together for a while, I can't seem to get used to his girth.

He pulls his hand out and licks the juices off. "Tasty." He puts one of the pairs of opera glasses around my neck and dips his head until his breath feathers my ear. "Now, take some pillows and kneel on them. Then lean over until you can brace a hand against the balcony rail and hold the glasses like you're enjoying the show."

My heart pounds. "Seriously? But...won't that make it...too obvious?"

"That depends on you."

I should say no, but the delicious heat is still coursing through me, and the vibrator, whose intensity Josh lowered, continues to pulse hard against my clit. Not only that, I feel too empty. I want his cock stretching and filling me *right now.*

Wordlessly, I do as he says. Then I realize I'm positioned so that it looks like I'm leaning over with excitement from my seat.

Well, I'm certainly excited. Hot wetness trickles down my inner thighs, and the vibration is killing me.

"Spread your legs."

I part them.

"A little more. Come on. Show me how much you want to be rewarded."

I widen them as much as I can.

"There we go." Josh moves behind me and pushes my dress up until it's gathered at my waist. "You enjoying the show?"

"Too much," I say breathlessly. Although I have the opera glasses raised, I have no idea what I'm seeing; my entire attention is focused behind me.

He chuckles. "Good girl."

I can hear little movements behind but I'm totally clueless about where he is or what he's doing. He isn't touching me, so... *Is he getting undressed? Is he—*

I almost scream when I feel his mouth closing over me. *Oh my God.* I start to lower my glasses, but he smacks my ass, reminding me I'm supposed to be watching the stage.

Some singer is crying, "Nein, nein, nein!" but I hardly appreciate it. Josh's tongue feels amazing, licking my flesh while the vibrator torments my swollen clit. Then he pushes it into my pussy and laps me up. I shiver, biting my lip. My eyes close as I enjoy the sensation. He knows exactly what I like—what I need. My toes curl, and I resist the urge to move my hips against his face. I'm supposed to look unaffected, although I'm not sure how well I'm pulling off. My breathing is too erratic, my heartbeats too loud. Surely somebody can hear them over the music.

He pushes the vibrator hard against my clit while he devours me. I clench my teeth to contain a scream as I climax. I shudder against his face over and over again.

He kisses my thighs, licking the slick liquid dripping down there. Then his mouth is gone. I lick my lips, anticipation winding in my belly. What's he going to do next?

His hands grip my pelvis. My pussy clenches. His cockhead rubs against the opening, teasing. I can't control myself. I rock back a little, demanding he hurry up.

He lets out a dark laugh, then his cock pushes into me. My whole body seems to stretch, and I have to inhale to deal with it. Then he slowly pulls back...and slams into me.

My body shakes with the force. My braced arm trembles. But it feels *so* damn good, especially with the vibrator still going strong.

"Don't move," he says just loud enough for me to hear.

Then he drives into me, the rhythm diabolically fast and hot. Heat burns every cell in my body. The need to move with him is overwhelming, but I tense myself to keep still. "Fuck. You're so tight," he groans.

"You're—just—too—big," I manage to say, then arch my back, as another powerful wave of orgasm starts to crest over me. It breaks with enough force to leave me dazed. He slams into me again and again, his movements becoming frenzied. My vision almost shorts out. If I weren't braced against the railing and he weren't holding my hips, I'd fall into a heap on the floor.

The soprano hits a high note as the orchestra crescendos.

"Fuuuuck." Josh lets out a moan as he abruptly stops thrusting and shudders. Hot fluid fills me, and I groan with satisfaction.

The crowd erupts into applause with cries of *bravo*!

47

AILEE

THE NEXT LITTLE while is a haze. I try to recover while feigning composure.

"Can you turn off the vibrator?" I whisper. "It's making me too... needy."

"So? I like keeping you simmering." Josh's eyes are dark as he looks into my gaze. "Do you have any idea how hot you are?"

I flush. "What I am is *messy*." Thank God it's hidden underneath the clothes, but I'm drenched between my legs. My pussy feels unusually hot and tingly, probably from having his cum inside. It isn't our first time, but we've never done it in public. All my senses are hyperaware and overly sensitive. I sigh softly. "I need to go to the bathroom, and I don't want the underwear to buzz."

He cocks an eyebrow. "Buzz?"

"Yes. If it's not flush against me, it makes noise. I'd rather not have someone in the bathroom hear it."

He flips it off. "Can't have that. It's our secret."

"Thanks. See you soon."

"Take your time," he says, annoyingly composed. "The second act won't start for half an hour."

I nod and head out, trying not to stumble.

Languidness leaves my muscles relaxed as I look for the bathroom. Sex with Josh always does that to me. It's better than any drug and far more addictive.

I spot the bathroom, then grimace at the line. It's worse than an airport on the Sunday after Thanksgiving. Am I going to be able to pee before the intermission ends?

After several minutes, the line has barely moved. I pull out my phone from the clutch to check the time. I have twelve minutes. Guess I'll have to miss part of the second act. There's no way I'll be able to get through another hour and fifteen minutes without using the bathroom.

"Pretty crowded, huh? You'd think they'd open another bathroom for us ladies."

The voice is friendly and warm. Normally it'd make me smile and respond in kind. However, all the effervescent bliss drains away, replaced by bone-chilling shock.

I turn slowly, willing it to be anybody but...

"Zoe?" I whisper.

She smiles. "Hello. Big opera fan?"

48

JOSH

I STRETCH my neck in the box, very aware of the satisfied grin on my face. Bringing Klein here was a great decision. I'm so proud of the way she handled herself against Katt and Coco.

She has the kind of gentle soul that everyone strives for. It's what makes her rare and precious, even if she doesn't realize it. But she's come a long way since our video went viral, and the surge in her confidence is amazing.

Her staking her claim in front of these women set my blood on fire. If it hadn't been for the fact that the performance was about to start and we needed to take our seats, I might've dragged her back to the limo and fucked her right then.

But it was actually better in the box. So in a way, I got what I wanted. We both did, based on the desperate way her pussy milked my cock.

I head out to grab a bottle of white wine for Klein in case she's thirsty. The lights in the lobby flicker twice, to alert everyone that intermission is about to end. Unfortunately, Klein is nowhere to be found. Just how bad is the line at the bathroom? I spot Elizabeth coming from the direction of the ladies' room and approach her.

"Have you seen Klein?" Then I remember that she might not know who I'm talking about. "Ailee. My fiancée."

She shakes her head. "No. Why?"

"She went to the bathroom, but hasn't come back."

"That's strange. I was one of the last ones in there."

Unease settles over me.

"Did you try calling her?"

I pull out my phone and call Klein's number. It rings a few times, then goes to voicemail. I shake my head.

"That's odd. Maybe she got talking to someone and lost track of time?"

"Yeah. Maybe." Even as I say it, I know Klein isn't gossiping with anybody. Other than Elizabeth, Barron, Coco and her shitty sister, she doesn't really seem to know anybody here. Not only that, charity operas aren't her scene.

Apprehension rears its ugly head, but I shove it aside. Needless panic won't do any good. I text Klein.

—Me: Where are you? Are you okay?

I wait a few moments. Nothing.

Dammit. I head back to our box, in case her phone battery died and she's already there. I really hope it's something as benign as that.

My phone buzzes against my chest. I pull it out, then exhale with relief when I see a text from Klein. She sent a photo. I tap to open it.

My blood turns to ice. It's not a cute selfie or something pretty she saw and wanted to share with me. It's her strapped to a chair with her hands behind her back and ankles tied to the legs. Her mouth is stuffed with a ball, and a long strip of cloth around her head keeps it in, effectively gagging her. Her eyes are wide and glazed with terror.

Tremors run through me. *Fuck.* The setup is quintessential Mom. Another text.

—Klein: Pretty, isn't she? Things didn't have to get this ugly if she hadn't resisted the family reunion. Not sure why, since I was so nice to her. Regardless, it won't do for her to be so rude to her future mother-in-law.

—Me: Where the fuck are you?

—Klein: On a boat. Find me. Alone. Let's have a proper reunion. It's long overdue.

I rush out, cursing that I didn't rent a car. The limo is too cumbersome, and I don't have time to wait for the chauffeur.

I burst out of the main entrance and run down the steps as quickly as I can. I almost crash into Tolyan, who has his face in his phone.

"Got a car I can borrow?" I ask.

Only his eyes move as he looks at me. "Don't you have a limo?" His voice is gravelly, as though he hasn't spoken in days.

"Yeah, but this is urgent. Can't wait for my driver. Can you help—"

"Your name isn't Elizabeth King." Tolyan taps the phone screen, jerking his chin at the opera house. "They're starting."

Impatience wells, but I stomp on it. "They got my money. It's important."

Still glaring at the phone, he reaches into his pants pocket and tosses me a fob. "Take this." He points to a black Mercedes coupe parked three yards from us.

"If you ever need to fuck somebody up in court, call me," I call out as I run to the car.

He laughs. "The day I need to fuck somebody up in court is the day I retire."

I jump into the car, start the engine, then floor it, trying to work out the logistics of what Mom has done.

Klein's been gone for less than half an hour, so she couldn't have gotten very far. Mom said she was on a boat, but given her personality and preference, it won't actually be a *boat*. It'll be some grand yacht where she can show off. Because this reunion isn't about convincing me, but forcing me into accepting the outcome she wants.

As I drive, I call Dad using the hands-free function on the car.

"Hello?" He sounds confused. "Aren't you at—"

"Mom took Klein," I cut in. "She claims to be on a boat. We're in San Diego, but no cops or sirens. She specifically asked me to come alone. I'll share my location as soon as I find her."

"Got it." He hangs up.

I drive along the coastline...and soon hit the nearest marina. Mom didn't have much time to work with, so Klein is stashed somewhere close. I start location sharing with The Fogeys and my brothers, then look around. Countless boats...and of course *five* yachts.

Fuck.

I'm not going over to all five. Klein may not have much time. Mom's capricious and has a terrible temper. She actually hit Bryce—hurting Klein wouldn't even be an afterthought.

The first yacht doesn't seem like it. Too much in the way of generic rich-dude vibes. My gut shivers at the name on the second yacht—the *Archidamia*. The ancient Spartan queen who rallied women to defend their homeland. It would appeal to Mom's long-held bitterness that Vincent never gave her a fair shot because she's a woman.

A dinghy is waiting for me. No sailor manning it, but I know Mom sent it.

I hop on and go over to the *Archidamia*. Nobody on the deck. *Weird.* I thought she'd come in person to "welcome" me.

It's an effort to think past the adrenaline. *How much time do I have before Mom decides she's tired of keeping Klein alive?*

I pull my phone back out and take a good look at the photo she sent. Not the deck. More like a room. I make my way to the cabins, and open the door to the first one.

What the fuck?

I almost take a step back. The cabin is an exact replica of Dad's home office. Dad's sitting at his desk, reviewing a thick stack of papers. He's in one of his favorite navy suits, one Akiko had custom-made in Japan. What's he doing—

The illusion is so good that it takes a moment before I realize I'm looking at a wax figurine.

I do a quick check of the room, making sure there's no one under the desk, then leave and go to the next room. It's a copy of Ares's office at Huxley & Webber. A wax Ares leans against the edge of the desk, smiling at a wax Lareina. It's so realistic—like Mom's taken a slice of life from Ares and Lareina's marriage—that chills skitter along my back.

The next room is Bryce's bedroom. I've never seen it, but I'm sure it's a precise duplicate. A Bryce figurine has his arms wrapped around a Fiona figurine with a barely there baby bump. Their fingers are linked, and the genuine love in their eyes seems very real. The chills now turn to sheer dread.

I rush into another room—hoping it's where Klein is. But instead, it's a copy of Akiko's kitchen—except it's a total horror show. A figurine stands at the counter, its head missing. Its height and the elaborate kimono indicate it's supposed to be Akiko. A knife is stuck to the chest, and on the wall is spray-painted *DIE, YOU FUCKING BITCH!* in a bright blood red. I swallow, nausea roiling in my belly. Is Mom going to hurt Akiko too?

I spin around and dash to the last room. I blink, unable to process what I'm seeing. Mom has recreated the meditation room from my home, including the tatami mats and the stone garden. Even the individual rocks are the same. A small copper pot is on an old-style stove—also something I have in my home.

Where's Klein?

I swivel my head, my heart in my throat. She has to be here!

Shit. Has Mom already done something awful? Tossed Klein overboard, maybe? My skin turns clammy with panic. I'm going to jump in the water and search until I find her. I'm not going anywhere until—

In my peripheral vision is a blonde tied to a chair in the farthest, dimmest corner of the room. *Klein!* Her eyes are open, but she can't make any sound. I start toward her, but Mom steps out from a hidden exit behind Klein and puts a gun to her head. "Hello, Josh."

Horror and loathing pound at me. "Put the gun down!" I grind out, desperately fighting the terror rapidly swelling in my heart.

She chuckles. "Or what?"

I clench my hands. I have no weapons. Trying to jump her would be stupid. If I get shot, who's going to save Klein? Dad's probably arranging for some backup, but it won't be instant. I need to do whatever I can to buy some time. "Is this how you greet your son?"

"You didn't even offer me tea." She shrugs. "I hear you're good at making matcha."

Impatience shoots through me, but I feign a smile. "If you wanted some green tea, all you had to do was ask." With more willpower than I've ever mustered, I force myself to walk over to the tatami mats and start the tea. Mom follows, the gun still in her hand. She sits across from me on the mat.

"You don't have to look at me like I'm a monster."

I shake my head. "Just a kidnapper." I wait for the water to heat. "Did you drug her?" My voice shakes with barely suppressed fury as I glance at Klein, who still hasn't tried to say anything, not even through the gag.

"Nooo… Contrary to rumor, I'm not a complete psycho. I have my code."

Coulda fooled me.

She sighs. "I just want us to be together. Be happy."

"Hell of a way to go about it." I check the water temperature. Have to make sure it doesn't boil. Although I don't really give a shit about feeding her properly prepared matcha, I don't want her to find fault and lose control.

"Regardless of what you might think, I do still love Prescott. You hate my father because he didn't put me in jail. I hate him for not having the guts to confront me. Instead, he took what I love the most from me. He doesn't understand what it's like. His stupid sons don't know anything, either."

Finally, the temperature is right. I carefully pour the water into a cup, add the appropriate amount of powdered green tea and start whisking.

"Because of him that I lost the love of my life to that cunt. I lost you to *her*!" Mom raises her voice shrilly. "She poisoned you against me!"

"You did that all on your own," I mutter under my breath. I hand Mom the tea, then make myself a cup.

She holds the cup in both hands and stares at the frothy surface. "He told me a year ago that he took my family away because I took away his. He blames me for Roland, you see. But is it my fault that Roland is weak and pathetic? He thinks he can be somebody, but he's nothing. Same for Harvey. They think they're so clever, just because they were born with penises." She laughs, like it's a particularly funny joke. "But even now they're drinking the poison I formulated specifically for them. Actually, there might be enough accumulated in their bodies that it might be kicking in."

"And Vincent? Are you going to murder your own father?"

"Sweetheart, in our family it's not murder. It's clearing the path. We all must do what we must. He held me back, so I'm repaying his interference tenfold. He should thank me, really. Now he can go join that slut who bore him Roland." Mom sneers, then soon smiles.

I hold my cup, warming my hands without drinking. She might've tampered with the matcha powder. Or just this cup.

"I killed her, too, by the way," she adds, looking at me expectantly.

"Because she was in the way?" I say finally.

"No." There's a small scoff in her tone. "Because she annoyed me just by existing. She took far too much of Father's time and attention." A hint of jealousy seethes underneath her cold words. She can't stand it that she had to share.

"Does Vincent know?"

"Maybe. But it doesn't matter. He only cares about Roland, not some bimbo he banged a few decades ago." She sips the tea. "Ugh, bitter. Why do you drink this dreck?" Despite the complaints, she sips some more.

Still, I don't drink mine. She could've taken something earlier to make her immune to whatever she might've added to the matcha.

Her phone beeps shrilly four times. She checks the screen. A slow smile splits her face, revealing rows of bone-white teeth. "Oh, look. They all died of massive heart attacks."

What?

"And then veins burst in their brains. How sad." She faux-pouts. "Now I'm just a poor orphan. Even my unborn nephew is dead."

I frown. "Unborn nephew?"

Mom blinks innocently. "Didn't you know? Kenna was pregnant with Roland's son. She thought no one knew because she wasn't really showing, but..." A shrug. "I might've let her live if I could be certain that she wasn't pregnant with a boy. It's so...*complicating.*" Mom smiles again. "But no, I'm alone. Except for you, your brothers and your father. I just need to get that bitch Akiko out of the way."

Madness dances in her eyes. The icy chill spreads until not even the tea can warm my hands. She lives in her own world, believing only her version of reality. She would never accept that none of us agrees with her. She might even harm Klein and my sisters-in-law if her twisted logic decides they're the threat to her idea of a "happy family."

I'll be damned if I'll let her. Even if it costs my life, I'm going to keep my family safe. "What if I stop you?"

"Stop me from what?"

"Doing this. Hurting the family."

She snorts. "Didn't anybody teach you to love your mother?"

"They did. And I do love Akiko."

She explodes to her feet. "*She's not your mother! I am!*"

I jump to my feet as well. The water I left in the pot is now boiling. "She's been a true mother to me, unlike you!"

"You stupid, ungrateful...!" She swings the gun up.

I go low and lunge at her. A loud gunshot, followed by a thud as Mom slams into the mat on her back and loses her grip on the gun. A metallic clatter, and she screams. The water in the kettle spreads all over the mat.

Yes!

I lunge for the gun, but she kicks it out of reach, then comes at me with surprising speed and power. A sharp sting on my arm. A gash forms on my arm and drips blood, dotting the floor crimson.

Surprised, I glance at her. She's holding a small knife. "I always have a backup."

I grab the copper pot and swing it as a makeshift weapon. It's awkward, but better than getting sliced up. Her blue eyes glow as she lashes at me over and over again, each strike vicious. From the way her pupils are dilated, she must've taken something to improve her strength and speed.

"Close your eyes, Klein!" I call. This is going to get ugly and brutal.

Adrenaline pumping, I kick at Mom's knee as she takes a swipe. The tip of the knife cuts through my forearm like butter. But my foot connects with her knee and something crunches.

Screaming, she loses her balance. I don't bother to go for the gun. I launch myself at her, aiming my knee at her ribcage. She rolls out of the way and plunges the knife into my thigh. Out of reflex, I pull it out and stick it into the closest part of her I can reach.

She hollers. More blood than I ever imagined a human being can hold gushes out. I blink, dazed. I might've severed an artery.

Her complexion turns ashen. She opens and closes her mouth as though in disbelief. I shake as nausea roils in my gut. I can't move or process. It doesn't seem real.

Within a few minutes, the light in her eyes fades.

I stare at her for a moment, inhaling the metallic smell. I keep thinking she's going to get back up, like some kind of horrible bleeding Terminator. She's the kind of monster that never dies.

But she stays inert. My heart thuds, and I look down at the wound on my leg. Thankfully she doesn't seem to have hit anything critical, despite the burning sensation. Part of me just wants to sit and breathe, but I shove it aside, standing and wincing when the pain radiates sharply. I limp over to Klein, who's watching me.

"Why didn't you close your eyes?" I undo the gag.

As soon as the ball's out of her mouth, she starts wheezing and coughing. "Careful," she rasps. "Zoe hid a razor in the gag."

I shiver at Mom's depravity. No wonder Klein couldn't say anything. I run a soothing hand along her back, then quickly untie her hands and feet.

She says, "And I kept my eyes open because I wanted to see it. We'll share this moment—I'm not letting you carry the burden on your own."

My hands begin to shake, and soon the rest of me follows suit. "Klein," I say. I don't know why, but hot tears drip from my eyes. My chest feels off. An inexplicable sorrow wells even as relief that it's all over settles in my heart.

She wraps her arms around me. "I know. I'm here." She places a kiss on my forehead. "I'm not going anywhere."

I hold her close and weep until the backup finally arrives.

49

JOSH

EVERYTHING THAT HAPPENS after the authorities confirm Mom's death feels unreal. My head is foggy. I wondered what it would be like when my brothers and I were finally free of Mom's presence. Now that she's gone...

I'm not sorry, but watching the life pour out of her was hard. Much more harrowing than anything I could've imagined. Still, if I had to do it all over again, I wouldn't hesitate.

Aunt Jeremiah sends Barry to represent me during the police questioning. Another sign the family's got my back. My dad and aunt are too close to the matter to be objective. Despite his laid-back playboy image, Barry is an attack dog, heavily favored by Aunt Jeremiah. He knows exactly what to do.

The firm puts me on a month-long leave, paid. The Fogeys, the elders of the family, do it because they believe I won't take time off otherwise.

They shouldn't have worried. I spend most of my days with Klein. Her silent presence and strength are better than all the therapists I've worked with put together. I don't really want to talk. I just want to be supported. And with her, I don't have to say anything to be understood.

The Fogeys also offer to give Klein therapy and whatever else she needs. She tells them she just needs to spend some time with me. "We won't push. But if you change your mind or think of something you need, just let us know," Grandma says.

Klein's friend Max stops by. She checks her thoroughly to make sure she's unharmed, then hugs me tightly. "Thank you for saving my bestie. If you ever need anything from me, just ask."

Then they go off to the living room to chat. Max looks like she really needs some reassurance. The news made everything sound even more sensational, but then, they need the clicks.

Suddenly, Klein raises her voice. "You're *pregnant*? Not with Jeffrey's baby, right?"

Max hisses something, and they put their heads together. I let them be—it's probably good for Klein to think about something other than what Mom did to her.

Mom wasn't bragging about how devious she was. Vincent, Harvey, Roland and Kenna are all dead of heart attacks and brain hemorrhages. I shudder at the elegant lethality, then contact Akiko and urge her to get a comprehensive medical checkup, with a special panel done for slow-acting poisons. Mom burned with hatred for Akiko. When she finally tells me everything's fine, I relax a little.

Dad was right. Until I decided to get engaged to Klein, I wasn't acting like a true Huxley. A true Huxley wouldn't entangle himself with a woman who wasn't worth dying for, who doesn't inspire you to act from the bottom of your heart. A Huxley doesn't just recite *pietas et unitas* over and over again. When the shit hits the fan, you jump into the fray, no matter the potential cost.

I hold Klein's hand in mine and kiss her fingertips, filled with gratitude and love. She nuzzles me softly, the tender show of affection soothing my soul.

The day before my leave is supposed to end, the new ring from Sebastian Jewelry finally arrives.

And Klein bursts into tears and asks, "Are you dumping me?"

50

AILEE

WE NEED TO TALK. In your office. Is today at 10 okay for you?

When I get the text from Chad's wife, Autumn, I stare at it for a while. What does she want? The anniversary ring? Crap, Josh threw it away, and I totally forgot about it.

Basically, I've already won the bet with Chad, so he should just replace it with his own money, but at the same time I feel like I owe Autumn something. Although I had no idea he was married, I inadvertently hurt her.

Since I have a doctor's appointment at eleven thirty, I figure I can get everything done back to back. When I reach the office, she's sitting in front of my desk, her belly hugely swollen. Instead of glowing with the joy of upcoming motherhood, she's haggard, with dark circles under her eyes and limp hair. Her mint-green maternity dress hangs off her drooping shoulders, and the tip of her nose is red, as though she's been crying a lot.

"Hi. You wanted to see me?" I say softly, taking my seat.

"Hello." She sniffs. "Ugh. I don't even know how to begin."

"It's fine. I know this is going to be...awkward." I try to smile for her.

She exhales shakily. "Chad..." She presses her lips together. "He's been cheating on me."

I sigh. "I'm so sorry." I can't think of anything else to say. How do you comfort a pregnant woman who's realized her husband is an unreliable, cheating scumbag?

"It isn't your fault. He, uh, has other women. Yeah. Plural. They all thought he was single...and he promised to *marry* them"—her voice cracks—"just...*stringing them along*." Tears drip from her eyes, and she angrily wipes them away. "I thought he was just busy, you know? Trying to build a better life for us and...and our baby." She snorts a laugh. "Stupid, huh?"

I pluck a few Kleenex and hand them to her. "No. Not even a little. There's no shame in trusting your husband. *He's* the one who betrayed *you*."

She shakes her head, still deep in self-recrimination. "I had to dig around—I thought what happened at the restaurant was just some misunderstanding or, or *something*...except nothing added up." Her chin wobbles, then firms. "I want to divorce that son of a bitch. And I want to make it *hurt*. You know all the lawyers here, right? Who's the nastiest? Like, the most *vicious*? I'll pay with blowjobs if I have to. I want to leave that bastard with *nothing*. *Less* than nothing. I want to take what's left of his *hair*."

Sweet Jesus. "I know just the man. Let me introduce you—personally—to Bryce Huxley. He'll clean Chad out."

Autumn flashes a small but genuine smile. "Great. Can't wait." She shifts. "By the way, I'm starting a Let's Fuck Chad Up club and inviting all the women he lied to. The idea is to find various ways to disrupt his life and screw him the way he did us. You're welcome to join anytime. It'll be fun."

～

You're pregnant.

I keep rolling the two words around in my head. It seems like a joke, but the doctor was serious. Not only that, she even did a vaginal ultrasound to prove it, although how I'm supposed to know if those grainy dots were babies or not is beyond me.

And not just one baby. Twins!

I kill the engine in the garage and cover my mouth with a hand. How did this happen? Josh said he had a vasectomy. So how did these babies come about? They're most definitely not Chad's. They're too young, which sounds sort of funny, given that they're barely eight weeks old.

I would've never thought I was pregnant, but when food started to taste a bit off, I began feeling exhausted and my period didn't come, I had to go in, just to be sure. And the doc wanted to check for pregnancy because vasectomies can fail.

"You heard about that famous case, right? The Hollywood producer? Seven kids with seven different women because his vasectomy failed— all in four months! If a Hollywood hotshot with all his money can get a bad vasectomy, why not your man?"

If the doc thought that would make me feel better, she was sorely mistaken.

I start to get out of the car, but there's a call from an unknown number. Maybe from the police about Zoe's death? They ruled it self-defense, but they needed to interview multiple times to make sure they had every detail for their records.

"Hello?"

"My gosh! It's taken *forever* to reach you!"

My stomach knots. "Mom?"

"Yeah! I missed you."

I say nothing because I can't say the same.

"So. When's the wedding? Your father and I should be there. After all, you're marrying into the Huxleys."

"What happened to being a bad daughter and stealing your precious Katt's *fiancé?*" I ask bitterly.

Mom laughs. "Are you holding on to a grudge? It's unbecoming, dear. Unkind, even."

"Do you get the news?"

"Of course."

"Do you know that I was kidnapped and almost died?"

"Yes, we did hear something about that. But you're all right!"

I bury my face in my hand, suddenly too exhausted. "Were you sad because you couldn't claim the life insurance?"

"Oh, honey, we weren't worried about the insurance! It was a moot point, after all. I mean, since we were going to be invited to Josh Huxley's wedding. Is it true he's close to Elizabeth Pryce-King and Barron Sterling? We saw photos. They're really *rich*, Ailee!" Mom's practically panting with excitement.

"Why do you want to come to my wedding? Can you tell me at least three reasons without mentioning Josh or his family and friends?"

Mom hesitates. "Well. We're your family, of course. And...we raised you with love. Hmmm... Also, I don't want to be crass, but—you owe us."

"No." It's so weird that I'm not even disappointed anymore. It's like I've lost all expectations. "You're not invited. None of you. I owe you nothing. We're done. If you want it more formally, I'm sure something can be arranged through one of the lawyers at the firm."

"Ailee—"

"Please don't call me again." I hang up and block the number. *It feels good to set boundaries.* Inhaling, trying to shift gears, I go into the house. How should I break the news? Will Josh be surprised or upset or...?

Hopefully, surprised and happy. I place a hand over my belly. I want my babies to be born in love and joy.

Josh is sitting on one of the living room couches. He pulls out a velvet box from a luxurious, glossy blue-and-white bag and opens the lid. The size of the highly saturated blue gemstone in the center makes it impossible for me to breathe. The band is simple but chic. The design of the ring clearly indicates it's for...*an engagement.*

"Are you dumping me?" I blurt out. Then, before he can answer, tears start to flow. My heart hurts at the idea. Actually, I'm outraged too! I'm pregnant with his babies, damn it!

"What? No!" He jumps to his feet. "Klein, don't cry! I'm not dumping you!" He wipes away at my tears, but they continue to drip down my face.

"But why do you have that ring? It's an engagement ring, isn't it?"

"Yes, but—"

"You already bought me one." I thrust my left hand at him.

He shoves his hand into his hair. "Right." He blinks, eyebrows pinching hard. "Can you please stop crying?"

"You can't even come up with a good excuse."

"No, that's not it. It's just..." He inhales. "I wanted to ask you properly."

"About what?"

"I really wanted to do it romantically, too."

"I don't understand." My voice cracks through the tears.

Helpless, he drops to a knee and pops open the lid. "Ailee Klein, will you marry me?"

I stare at him. I'm the one who just found out she's pregnant, so why is *he* acting like he's lost his sanity? "But we're already engaged!"

"But I never asked you properly. It was forced on you by the circumstances. I felt that it wasn't right." He shakes his head. "I want you to have a grand proposal."

I laugh through the tears at his forlorn and slightly disappointed expression. "Okay." I take his face in my hands. "The answer is yes. It's always been yes." I wrap my arms around him. "Now, I'm going to tell you a secret."

"Okay. Good. I'm good at keeping secrets." He looks at me earnestly.

"First, I love you. I think I was in love with you way, way, waaay before that whole restaurant scene."

His eyes light up. A brilliant smile breaks over his face. "I love you too, Klein. I think I fell in love with you a long, long time ago, too."

I press my forehead on his, maintaining eye contact. "And second, whoever did your vasectomy did a pretty shitty job. Because I'm pregnant. With twins."

51

JOSH

"REALLY?" I croak.

I'm sure that it kind of sounds like I'm disappointed. But nothing could be further from the truth. It's a blessing. I only got the vasectomy to avoid procreating. I was terrified I'd create mini-Zoes because I might be just like her deep inside.

But being with Klein has shown me that that isn't the case at all. I'm my own person—and a Huxley.

"Uh-huh," she says, peering intently at me.

I place a reverent hand over her belly. "Our babies."

"Yeah. Two of 'em."

I run a hand over my mouth. "I'm going to be a father."

"Twice over." She smiles.

I embrace her. "Thank you."

She relaxes in my arms. "My pleasure. I'm glad. I was worried that you might not be excited."

"Are you *kidding*? We're creating a couple of mini-yous. I can't wait."

She laughs. "They might end up more like you."

"Doesn't matter. Our babies will be beautiful, just like their mother." I kiss her. "Ai-chan."

She blinks up at me. "Hmm?"

"Ai-chan—my sweet little love. I finally feel like I've earned the right to call you that."

Her shining eyes soften. "You always had the right to call me that, Joshua Huxley."

TITLES BY NADIA LEE

Standalone Titles

Beauty and the Assassin

Oops, I Married a Rock Star

The Billionaire and the Runaway Bride

Flirting with the Rock Star Next Door

Mister Fake Fiancé

Marrying My Billionaire Hookup

Faking It with the Frenemy

Marrying My Billionaire Boss

Stealing the Bride

∾

The Huxley's

The Accidental Marriage

Her Wicked Husband

His Temporary Fiancée

∾

The Lasker Brothers

Baby for the Bosshole

My Grumpy Billionaire

The Ex I'd Love to Hate

Contractually Yours

Finally Forever

Still Mine

The Unwanted Bride

The Pryce Family

The Billionaire's Counterfeit Girlfriend

The Billionaire's Inconvenient Obsession

The Billionaire's Secret Wife

The Billionaire's Forgotten Fiancée

The Billionaire's Forbidden Desire

The Billionaire's Holiday Bride

~

Seduced by the Billionaire

Taken by Her Unforgiving Billionaire Boss

Pursued by Her Billionaire Hook-Up

Pregnant with Her Billionaire Ex's Baby

Romanced by Her Illicit Millionaire Crush

Wanted by Her Scandalous Billionaire

Loving Her Best Friend's Billionaire Brother

ABOUT NADIA LEE

New York Times and *USA Today* bestselling author Nadia Lee writes sexy contemporary romance. Born with a love for excellent food, travel and adventure, she has lived in four different countries, kissed stingrays, been bitten by a shark, fed an elephant and petted tigers.

Currently, she shares a condo overlooking a small river and sakura trees in Japan with her husband and son. When she's not writing, she can be found reading books by her favorite authors or planning another trip.

To learn more about Nadia and her projects, please visit http://www.nadialee.net. To receive updates about upcoming works, sneak peeks and bonus epilogues featuring some of your favorite couples from Nadia, please visit http://www.nadialee.net/vip to join her VIP List.